C000176503

A CUT
ABOVE

A CUT ABOVE

Colette
CADDLE

POOLBEG

Published 2001
by Poolbeg Press Ltd
123 Grange Hill, Baldoyle
Dublin 13, Ireland
E-mail: poolbeg@poolbeg.com
www.poolbeg.com

© Colette Caddle 2001

Typesetting, layout, design © Poolbeg Group Services Ltd.

The moral right of the author has been asserted.

3 5 7 9 10 8 6 4 2

A catalogue record for this book is available from the British Library.

ISBN 1 84223 080 8

All rights reserved. No part of this publication may be reproduced or
transmitted in any form or by any means, electronic or mechanical,
including photography, recording, or any information storage or
retrieval system, without permission in writing from the publisher.
The book is sold subject to the condition that it shall not, by way of
trade or otherwise, be lent, resold or otherwise circulated without the
publisher's prior consent in any form of binding or cover other than
that in which it is published and without a similar condition,
including this condition, being imposed on the subsequent purchaser.

Cover Design by Slatter-Anderson

Typeset by Patricia Hope in AGaramond 11/13.5

Printed and bound by
Omnia Books Ltd, Glasgow

About the Author

Colette Caddle lives with her husband and son in County Dublin.

For Tony & Peter
with all my love

Prologue

Monday morning, 21st August, 2000

Toni threw the notebook down on the table in front of her and flopped back in her chair. The conservatory was her favourite room in the house and with the early morning sunshine streaming in, it was even lovelier than usual. But it was useless trying to work. She just couldn't concentrate. Though, God knows, there were plenty of issues at the Blessington Clinic that she should be addressing. Staff problems, a fall in business, ethical issues – life in cosmetic surgery was never dull.

Alice Scully put her head around the door. 'Would you like a coffee, Toni?'

'I've just made a fresh pot, Alice. Sit down and I'll pour you a cup.'

The housekeeper shook her head. 'I won't, thanks. It's such a lovely morning I thought I'd get the bedclothes washed and out on the line.'

Toni sighed as Alice hurried off. The woman was supposed to be taking it easy but there was no slowing her down.

Chloe stuck her head around the door. 'Oh, what are you doing here?'

Toni brightened at the sight of her stepdaughter. 'I thought you could use some company.'

Chloe sighed. 'There's still no sign of the postman. How come he's always early with bills and junk mail and late with the important stuff?' She paced the room nervously.

Toni laughed. 'It's ten o'clock. He should be here soon.' Chloe had been a bundle of nerves all weekend knowing that the first round of offers of college places would be posted today. 'Tell me, are you nervous in case you don't get a place, or do?'

Chloe sank down into a chair and sighed. 'It would be kind of nice if I got UCD and not Trinity. That would solve all of my problems.'

'And if you get both?'

Chloe made a face. 'I suppose I'll have to try and persuade Dad to let me go to UCD.'

Toni frowned. 'I hope you've given this enough thought, Chloe. Deciding on a college on the basis that that's where your boyfriend is going is not a very good reason. You're going to be studying medicine for a long time. Don't dismiss Trinity on a whim.'

'Dad's asked you to try and get around me, hasn't he?' Chloe scowled.

Toni shook her head. Theo and she were way beyond having a reasonable discussion about Chloe's future. 'No, I just want to make sure you realise what you're doing.'

'I'm going to call Mark and Ollie to see if they've got any news yet.'

Toni sighed as Chloe flounced out of the room. She

2

hadn't intended to say anything to Chloe about college. It was enough that it was the main topic of conversation – or more accurately argument – between her father and her. But Toni was afraid that Chloe had now reached the point where she would turn down Trinity purely to spite him. This was a difficult time for the girl and it wasn't going to get any better. Not when Toni finally worked up the courage to talk to her. She kept finding reasons to put off the conversation but it would have to happen soon.

A thump in the hall as the post hit the floor interrupted Toni's thoughts. She got up, went outside and scooped up the letters. She smiled as she saw the two official letters for her stepdaughter. 'Chloe,' she called. 'Chloe, the post's here.'

Chloe appeared at the top of the stairs with the phone still in her hand. 'Oh, Ollie, it's here! Look, I'll call you back in five minutes. Wish me luck.' She flew down the stairs and took the envelopes Toni was holding out to her with a small nervous smile. 'This is it, then.'

Toni grinned. 'Looks good. Well, go on, open them!'

Chloe tore open the first envelope and squealed. 'Yes! Medicine at UCD.'

'Congratulations, love.'

'Thanks.' Chloe opened the second envelope. 'It's Trinity.'

And despite her earlier comments Toni noticed a distinct note of pride in her voice. 'Now you are in a position to make a decision,' Toni said gently. 'Think long and hard, love, and don't let anyone influence you one way or the other.'

Chloe gave her a quick hug. 'I'd better phone Mark,' she said and charged upstairs.

'You'd better phone your father, too,' Toni reminded her. 'He should be at the hospital by now.' She went back into the conservatory and sat down. Okay, it was time. Once Chloe had decided which college she was going to accept, Toni would tell her. And she'd make sure that Theo was there when she did. They had to do this together.

Moments later Chloe was back again, her face miserable. 'Mark didn't get an offer.'

'Oh, the poor boy. Is he devastated?'

Chloe nodded. 'I've told him he's sure to get an offer in the second round.'

'And is he?'

Chloe nodded. 'Yeah, I'd say so. I suppose Dad will be thrilled.' Theo French had never approved of Chloe's boyfriend.

'Of course he won't,' Toni said with more conviction than she felt.

'What has he got against Mark? Is it just because he's Daniel's son?'

Mark was the son of Daniel Wheeler, the chairman and managing director of the clinic where Toni was director of administration and Theo was a non-executive director. The two men had some very different views on cosmetic surgery and their relationship was polite but distant.

'No, I think he's just being a possessive Dad who realises his only daughter is growing up.'

Chloe smiled reluctantly. 'He can be a terrible old fuddy-duddy. Why on earth did you marry him, Toni?'

'Chloe! What a question!' Toni smiled at the typical teenage bluntness.

The girl shrugged. 'Well, it can't have been his looks, so what *was* the attraction?'

Toni stared out into the garden. Chloe was right. Theo could never be described as handsome. The nose was too hooked and his face too narrow. But there was something arresting about his features nevertheless. She remembered the awed silence that would descend on the administration department on the rare occasions that he'd drop in. She had been a lowly secretary in those days and he'd never even noticed her. But she noticed him. He was hard to miss, striding around arrogantly as if he owned the place. He practically did. Theodore French was the top surgeon and Sylvester's was the largest general hospital in Dublin. He had a reputation for being very tough with his staff but was forgiven it because he was such a brilliant surgeon. She remembered how the nurses used to joke about The French God. There was one suggestion that he probably walked on water in his spare time and could turn a fish supper into a feast for thousands.

To Toni he was someone she admired from afar. But it was a completely different story the day he first walked into the clinic.

She'd been standing in reception, flicking through the appointment book when he'd approached. Sandra had just nipped out to the ladies' and there was no one at the desk.

'Excuse me, do you work here? I've an appointment with Mr Wheeler.'

She looked up into piercing blue eyes and all her normal polite and witty repartee went out the window. She stared at him blankly, lost for words.

'The name is Theodore French. I've an appointment with Mr Wheeler? Mr Daniel Wheeler?'

Toni realised he was looking at her as if she was a moron and quickly pulled herself together. 'Of course, Mr French. Please, follow me.' She led the way to the meeting room, conscious of his gaze on her slim figure in her business suit. Flustered, she introduced the two men and took her seat at the conference table.

Daniel saw Theo's questioning look. 'Mr French, this is my colleague Toni Jordan. She's in charge of administration.'

Theo turned the intensity of his gaze on Toni once more. 'Really? How interesting.'

Daniel had watched, amazed, as his normally gutsy outspoken manager flushed like a schoolgirl.

'He was so different from any man I'd ever met,' Toni finally answered Chloe's question. Her answer sounded lame even to her.

Chloe heaved a dramatic sigh. 'So it wasn't his sexy body then?'

Toni laughed, and Chloe thought how pretty she was despite her boring clothes. Her stepmother lived in plain, functional business suits and she never wore make-up to work – not that she needed any. With natural dark colouring, high cheekbones and large hazel eyes she always looked good. On the rare occasion that she left her wavy hair loose around her shoulders, Chloe joked that she could pass for her big sister. The only time Toni made anything of her appearance was when she went out in the evening and then she could look quite stunning. As she watched her stepmother now, Chloe wondered for the hundredth time what had brought Toni and her dad together. They had nothing in common and there was nearly twenty-four years between them. In fact, Toni was closer in age to Chloe!

'He was very attractive in his own way,' Toni was saying. 'But it was more his presence and power that did it for me. I was incredibly attracted to him.' *Like a moth to the flame.* 'I couldn't believe it when he asked me out.'

Chloe nodded sagely. 'You were flattered.'

'I suppose I was.'

'Not a great reason for getting hitched.'

Toni looked up sharply, but Chloe was plaiting her fringe absently. 'There was a bit more to it than that,' she protested lightly.

'Whatever. I'm just glad you did marry him. Before you moved in this house was like a damn mortuary. Sometimes I felt like we'd all died with Mummy. But when Dad married you it was like we'd been given a second chance.'

Toni took her hand and held it tightly.

Chloe was startled to see tears in her eyes. 'Toni! What's wrong? I'm sorry, I didn't mean to upset you!'

Toni gave a shaky laugh. 'You didn't. I'm just remembering how sweet you were when we met.'

Chloe arched an eyebrow. 'Fooled ya, didn't I? Look at the monster I turned out to be.'

Toni laughed. 'The honey monster, maybe.'

'You must have been the only couple ever to take a kid on your honeymoon!'

'We couldn't possibly have left you behind.'

'It was a wonderful holiday,' Chloe said wistfully. 'I'm definitely going back to California someday.'

7

Toni blew her nose and smiled. 'Yes, it was nice.'

'Nice? It was the best! I never thought I'd see Dad on the back of a horse. And once he was up there he thought he was John Wayne!'

'He was sore for days,' Toni remembered.

Chloe snuggled up against her like a child and breathed in her musky perfume. 'Maybe if we took him back there he'd lighten up a bit.'

Toni stroked her hair absently. 'He's under a lot of pressure.'

Chloe snorted. 'Yeah, work, work, work –'

The sound of the phone ringing in the hall interrupted them.

Chloe jumped up. 'That will be Ollie. Oh, I hope she got a place in DCU. She'll be crushed if she didn't.'

Toni stared miserably into the garden. How weird that Chloe should start questioning her about her marriage now. Just when it was about to end.

Chloe came back into the room, breaking in on Toni's thoughts. 'It's Dad's secretary. She wants to talk to you.'

'To what do I owe the honour?' Toni said drily, going out into the hall. Emma Dunphy rarely called Toni unless she had to. And if Toni called Theo, Emma treated her with cool disdain as if she had a nerve disturbing The Master.

'Yes, Emma?'

'Toni. Sorry for bothering you,' – Emma sounded anything but sorry – 'but do you know where Mr French is?'

'He was in Oxford for the weekend,' Toni said, 'but he was due back on the first flight this morning.'

8

'Yes, I *do* know that. I made the booking,' Emma said shortly. 'But he hasn't arrived yet. I thought he might have gone home first.'

'I'm afraid not. The flight must have been delayed. Have you tried his mobile?'

'It's switched off.'

'Of course it isn't,' Toni said dismissively. Theo never turned off his mobile. 'He must be out of range.'

'Then I'll just have to keep trying. Thank you, Toni. Sorry for disturbing you.'

After Emma had banged down the phone, Toni hung up and walked back into the conservatory.

'I thought Dad would have been on the phone by now,' Chloe said, standing up.

'It looks like his flight has been delayed.'

'Well, I'm going to call Ollie to see what the news is.'

'And I'd better go to work. Congratulations again, love.'

' Thanks, Toni. Seeya tonight.'

An hour later Toni parked in the small car park outside the Blessington Clinic and ran up the steps. 'Hi, Sandra. Everything okay?' she asked as she crossed reception to her office.

'Eh, not really,' the receptionist whispered uneasily, hurrying after her. 'Mrs Phillips is early but she won't sit in the waiting-room.'

Toni stopped in her tracks. 'Why not?'

'Little Mindy Norton and her mother are in there,' Sandra mumbled.

'The old bitch!' Toni exploded. A rabid dog had

9

ravaged Mindy Norton and her right eye was the only recognisable part left on her face. 'Where did you put her?'

'In your office. Sorry, Toni, there was nowhere else. I didn't know what to do —'

'That's okay, Sandra. You did the right thing. Now, why don't you make Mrs Norton a nice cup of tea and give Mindy a lollipop? I'll see to Mrs Phillips.'

Sandra heaved a sigh of relief. 'All right then. Oh, before I forget, Mr French's secretary called. She says he hasn't turned up yet.'

Toni frowned. Where on earth had Theo got to? 'Okay. Thanks, Sandra.' She threw open the door of her office and looked with distaste at the woman sitting on the small sofa. Well over sixty, Cora Phillips was dressed in a skirt that was shorter and tighter than the one Chloe wore when she was out to upset her father. Toni wondered which bit of her was getting tucked or nipped this time. She pasted a professional smile on her face. 'Good afternoon, Mrs Phillips. I'm afraid I'll have to ask you to wait outside for Mr Perkins.'

The woman put down her magazine and levelled a cold glare at Toni. 'I'm staying right here. You people charge enough. The least you can do is provide a decent waiting-room.'

Toni resisted the urge to grab the woman by the scruff of her expensive suede jacket and throw her out on her ear. 'We do, Mrs Phillips. It's right over there.'

'Well, there should be a separate one for Mr Perkins's patients. It's just not . . . right!'

The stiff smile faded from Toni's face. Dealing with

10

miserable old bitches like this was the worst part of her job. 'Now you look here –'

'Mrs Phillips! How lovely to see you!' Robert Perkins strode into the room past Toni, his arms outstretched. 'Why don't you come with me? Did someone get you a coffee? No? See to it, would you, Toni?' He shepherded the woman outside.

'No sugar,' Mrs Phillips barked over her shoulder.

Toni banged the door after them and buzzed reception. 'Sandra? Would you get Mrs Phillips a coffee? That's with three sugars.' She sat down behind her desk and hurled a biro at the door. What a great day this was turning out to be. Bitches like Cora really pissed her off. How on earth could she look at someone like Mindy and feel anything other than pity? And how could her co-director, Robert Perkins, tolerate it? But then she already knew the answer to that. Money. Daniel Wheeler had been right in his reservations. He should have kept the practice small and not allowed the likes of Perkins to muscle in. Since he'd joined the Blessington it seemed more like a beauty salon than a clinic. But if it wasn't for the money the cosmetic end of the business brought in, they probably would have gone under years ago. Daniel was too easy-going when it came to chasing up patients who hadn't paid their bills. Often he had taken on cases knowing that he wouldn't be paid – but he couldn't turn bad cases away, especially if they were children.

And so she had thought that it was a good move to expand. But then it had been Theo's idea and in those days she had thought all of his ideas were brilliant.

Thinking of Theo reminded her of Emma's message.

11

Where the hell *was* the man? It was so unlike him not to get in touch. He was a stickler for punctuality and if he was going to be late for an appointment, he always called. She rang his mobile number.

'The customer you are calling may be out of range . . .'

Toni hung up on the automated voice. She called the hospital. 'Emma? It's Toni. Has Mr French turned up yet?'

'I'm afraid not.' Emma sounded agitated. 'And I've checked with the airport. His plane did land on time.'

'Then he must have missed it. Did you call his hotel?'

'Yes.' Emma hesitated.

'And?' Toni prompted. It wasn't like Emma to be reticent.

'It's a bit odd, actually. He never checked in.'

'Sorry?'

'He didn't stay at the hotel, Toni. Does he have friends in Oxford? Someone he could have spent the night with?'

Toni ignored the implication. 'He has some colleagues, of course, but none that he'd stay with. Could you ring around, Emma? Maybe call the conference organisers, some of the delegates –'

'I already have, Toni. But the thing is he never attended the conference either.'

'This is ridiculous, Emma. He can't have just disappeared off the face of the earth!'

There was a short silence at the other end of the phone. Then Emma's voice, hesitant and unconvincing: 'No, no of course not. I'm sure there's a reasonable explanation.'

Chapter One

Toni zipped up her shorts, pulled on an old white T-shirt and dragged her hair under a battered baseball cap. It was a beautiful day and she'd decided it would be good for body and soul to do a bit of gardening. Well, it might clear her head if nothing else. She wandered downstairs and was just filling the kettle when Theo arrived in with the Sunday papers.

'Morning.' He sat down at the table and began to scan the headlines.

Toni yawned widely. 'Hi.'

'You got home very late.'

Theo's voice was even and he didn't even raise his eyes from the paper in front of him but Toni could smell an argument in the air. She groaned inwardly. *Not today, Theo*. She was too hung over for this. She usually only had a couple of drinks when she went out with Jade, but last night she'd felt like another. And then another.

Toni sighed. Sometimes her nights out with Jade were all that kept her going.

13

'Sorry if I woke you,' she said now to Theo, her tone conciliatory.

'Where did you go?' .

'Just to the Chinese. Jade likes it there,' she added lamely. *Why are you apologising? Normal people eat Chinese food. Normal people think it's okay to eat after nine at night. Normal people have a life!*

Theo snorted. 'I'm surprised the woman eats at all. She's ridiculously thin.'

'She has a high rate of metabolism and she works out,' Toni replied calmly as she made a large pot of tea. 'Shall I make you an omelette?'

'You'd only burn it. I'll just have toast and orange juice.'

Toni made a face at him, put bread in the toaster and went to the fridge for the juice. After setting the table she rummaged in the press for some painkillers.

Theo watched as she swallowed them down with a mouthful of tea. She met his gaze steadily, daring him to comment.

'I think the toast is ready,' he said instead and she turned in time to see smoke rising from the toaster.

'Shit!' She extracted the blackened bread gingerly and threw it in the bin. 'I'll make some more.'

'Don't bother. I'll have brunch at the golf club. Where's Chloe?'

Toni abandoned the toaster and sat down. 'She's gone to a study group in Ollie's house.'

Theo's brow wrinkled in annoyance. 'That's an excuse if ever I heard one!'

'That's not fair, Theo. Chloe's been studying very hard.'

'Maybe, but these so-called study groups are just an excuse to get together and discuss boys or pop groups. There won't be a tap of work done.'

Toni smiled. She must remember to ask her stepdaughter who her favourite 'pop group' was. 'I'm not sure I agree. I think brainstorming sessions can be quite useful.'

'You would.' Theo's voice was dismissive.

Toni rolled her eyes and sighed. The man could be so bloody archaic at times. He didn't have a clue how to talk to Chloe, always rubbing her up the wrong way. But why did that surprise her? He couldn't communicate with a thirty-three year old so what hope did he have with a teenager?

Theo's eyes flashed at her obvious irritation. He drained his glass and stood up abruptly. 'I'll leave you to recover from your hangover.'

'Don't hurry back,' Toni murmured as the front door slammed. She sipped her tea and began to relax. A day alone in the sunshine and fresh air would do her good. It would revive her and prepare her for the week ahead. And it might even help her to forget how unhappy she was.

She thought back to a time when Sunday mornings had been special, full of laughter and love. That was when she was with Ian. Usually after much arguing and tickling, he would clamber out of bed and go and make breakfast. He would arrive back, grumbling that she just used him as her sex slave and gofer and they'd sit side by side munching toast and chatting companionably. Sometimes after they'd finished eating, they'd make love among the crumbs, dress lazily and then stroll down to the local pub just in time for opening.

She laughed wryly as she thought of how different things were with Theo. In her six years of marriage, she couldn't remember them ever staying in bed all morning. In fact, on the few occasions that Theo spent the entire night with her, he was usually gone seconds after the alarm went off. As for cosy, boozy afternoons in the pub – her husband would be positively shocked at wasting his time in such a way. And as for drinking –

Toni jumped as the dog next door yapped irritably, snapping her out of her reverie. She put her mug in the sink and went out to the shed to get her gloves and trowel. Kneeling down beside the flowerbed, she started to weed. It was only ten o'clock but already the sun was intense on her back. She threw herself into her work and, after completing the weeding, clipped the hedge and mowed the lawn. She was red-faced and sweating by the time she'd finished but she was also relaxed. After putting all her tools away, she took a beer from the fridge, brought it outside and flopped down on the grass.

'It's well for some,' Chloe remarked when she emerged from the house to find Toni stretched out on the lawn, the empty bottle beside her.

Toni shaded her eyes and looked sleepily at her stepdaughter. 'What are you doing home? What time is it?'

'It's just gone one. I came home early. It was a complete waste of time. The gang was more interested in sunbathing than studying. Bloody weather!'

Toni smiled proudly. And this was the girl that Theo thought he had to keep tabs on. 'Why don't I make us some lunch and then you can study in the conservatory? It will be nice and cool in there.'

Chloe stretched out and closed her eyes. 'Sounds good. Call me when it's ready.'

'Yes, my lady! Of course, my lady!' Toni stood up and went inside to prepare a salad. Even she could manage that. Once the cooker wasn't involved, her food could be quite edible. Of course it helped that Alice always left the fridge well stocked with cold meats and fish.

As she worked she thought about Chloe, the one part of her marriage that was a success. Chloe had added to her life enormously. And despite Theo's comments otherwise, she felt she'd been a welcome addition to Chloe's life too. Toni had always tried to be open and honest with the girl, answering all her questions, however embarrassing the topic. But Chloe had become a lot more secretive in the last few months and Toni was sure there was a boy on the scene. About time too, she thought privately. Thanks to Theo, Chloe's life seemed to revolve around school and success. She needed to have some fun. Toni felt a little hurt that Chloe hadn't confided in her about her love life. But then she was probably terrified that her father would find out and put a stop to it. No, she was right to play this one close to her chest. Good luck to her! She poured sparkling water into two glasses and went to call her stepdaughter. It would be nice to have a relaxing lunch, just the two of them. And afterwards. . . well, afterwards she'd find something else to take her mind off her problems. She must be one of the few people in the world who looked forward to Mondays!

* * *

Monday, 8th May, 2000

'Now if you select that column there,' Jade said patiently, 'and press the "sum" icon, it will automatically total the figures and put the sum in the next field.'

Sandra Tomkins, receptionist at the Blessington Clinic, looked blank.

Jade sighed. Why was she doing this? She was a nurse, for God's sake, not a teacher. And Sandra could be a particularly difficult pupil. 'Here, let me show you again.'

As she started to type in some figures the phone rang and Sandra rushed gratefully to answer it.

'Good morning, Blessington Clinic, can I help you? Oh, hello, Mr French. No, no he's not in yet – yes, I'll get him to call you as soon as he gets in. Of course – thank you. Goodbye, Mr French.' Sandra hurriedly wrote down the message and trotted off to Robert Perkins's office with it.

'You could have just as easily handed him the message when he came in,' Jade pointed out when she returned.

'No, I might have forgotten. And Mr French would be very annoyed.' Sandra shuddered at the thought of facing the angry consultant.

'He's only a man like any other, Sandra,' Jade said, irritated.

'Well, he scares the hell out of me. I don't know how Toni could have married him.'

I won't argue with you there, Jade thought, but said nothing.

'Maybe it was because he was her boss,' Sandra mused aloud. 'Some girls are into that.'

'But he's never *been* her boss, Sandra.'

Sandra sighed with exaggerated patience. 'Well, not as

18

such, no. But he brought her into the clinic, didn't he? It's the same thing.'

'But he didn't. In fact, if anything, it's down to Toni that Theo got involved with the Blessington in the first place.' *But we won't hold that against her.* 'You've got to remember, Sandra, that originally this was just a consulting room. Daniel Wheeler inherited the building from an uncle and transferred his private rooms here from Sylvester's. He brought Toni with him as his PA. She had been working in the admin area at the hospital for, oh, it must have been five years. After a year or so Daniel hired me when he started to carry out surgery here and needed a full-time nurse.'

Sandra nodded. 'Oh, I see.'

'Theo only joined as a non-executive director when Daniel needed extra investment.'

'Gosh, I thought Theo had started the Blessington.'

'I'm not surprised, the way he throws his weight around.' Jade laughed. 'But no, this is and always has been Daniel Wheeler's clinic. And then Robert Perkins came on board when Daniel expanded the clinic to encompass cosmetic surgery. Robert, God bless him, was the one who hired dear Vicky.'

Sandra made a face at the mention of Vicky Harrison. 'I don't know what I ever did to that girl but she's always really bitchy to me. And what about those boobs? They can't be real!'

Jade laughed. The other nurse was rather well endowed. 'I suppose it makes her a walking, talking advertisement.'

'I like Daniel the best of all the directors,' Sandra confided.

'And what about Toni?'

'Oh, she's great. I never think of her as a director. She's my boss.'

'I think that's sexist or something,' Jade said drily.

'Oh, I don't mean it to be.' Sandra looked worried. 'The place would fall apart if it wasn't for Toni.'

'Daniel is a bit scatterbrained,' Jade acknowledged.

'But he's so nice and all his patients adore him. I'm surprised he ever went into business with Mr French and Mr Perkins. They're very different.'

Jade smiled. Sometimes Sandra hit the nail on the head without even realising it. Daniel would never have chosen either Theo or Robert as partners. They were a necessary evil. The price of having rooms in such an old house that needed money sunk into it on a regular basis. Money that Daniel didn't have and Theo French did. Then Theo brought in his old buddy Robert who specialised in 'bums and boobs' because that was the kind of surgery that brought in real money.

Jade had taken an instant dislike to Perky and had considered leaving. Working with Daniel was great but working for someone as patronising as Robert didn't appeal to her one bit.

'Please, Jade,' Daniel had entreated. 'I'd be lost without you. We'll be hiring another nurse soon and she can work for Robert if you dislike him that much. But I'm sure you're too professional to let personal feelings get in the way.'

Jade had bristled at the taunt and responded exactly as Daniel had expected. She stayed.

'And I don't know how Toni could marry the man,' Sandra's persistent prattle broke in on her reminiscences.

Jade shrugged and concentrated on the screen. Sandra

was too fond of gossip for her liking and she wasn't going to encourage it.

Sandra wasn't put off by Jade's silence. 'I mean, he's so much older than her what could they have in common?'

'I really don't know, Sandra.'

Sandra's eyes widened. 'Was your husband older than you, Jade?' she asked hesitantly.

'Three years,' Jade said shortly.

'Oh, that's the perfect age gap,' Sandra said relieved. 'My mam always says –'

Jade stood up abruptly. 'Sorry, Sandra, lesson over for today. I've got to get to work. See you later.'

'Oh, right, thanks,' Sandra said to Jade's receding back. Lord, but the woman was as tight as a clam! All this time working together and Sandra still knew next to nothing about Jade Peters's personal life.

Jade made her way up to the little office she shared with Vicky, stopping to get a coffee on the way. There would have been plenty of time to show Sandra a few more functions of Excel, but she couldn't face the girl's rather obvious attempts to extract information about her personal life. It was hard enough trying to fend off her interrogation about Toni. And at the moment Jade felt very protective towards her friend. Toni had seemed particularly glum on Saturday night, drinking a lot more than usual. It was surprising that she had suggested going out at all. They usually never met at the weekends which were strictly reserved for family in the French household. Though that didn't seem to be the case lately. Chloe was studying for her Leaving Certificate and Toni didn't seem to spend much time alone with Theo. Jade sipped her coffee thoughtfully. She hated to admit it but she completely agreed with Sandra. What *had* Toni Jordan seen in Theodore French? And how could she have let someone as gorgeous and funny as Ian Chase slip through her fingers?

Jade had had plenty to say on the subject at the time, but once Theo's ring was on Toni's finger, she hadn't uttered another word.

But she missed Ian. He was a nice guy and great company and they'd had some great nights out as a foursome. Her husband had taken to the man immediately, much to Jade's relief. Usually Aidan had hated being dragged along to the hospital do's because he didn't know who they were gossiping about half the time and didn't much care either. But Ian made him laugh with his impressions of the hospital hierarchy – although Aidan didn't believe they could possibly be as mad or bad as Ian made out.

'They are,' Jade had assured him. 'Complete nutters, most of them!'

'But Ian's one of them,' Aidan argued.

'I suppose he is.' Jade had looked surprised. Ian had been consultant anaesthetist in Sylvester's for quite some time now. 'But he's not like the others.'

Aidan had laughed. 'You can say that again. The man's almost normal!'

Jade sighed sadly as she thought about those happier times. If only it were possible to turn the clock back. She often wondered if Toni would like that too but it was a question that she couldn't and wouldn't ask.

Chapter Two

Tuesday, 9th May, 2000

'There was a bit of a mix-up in the appointments so there are only three operations tomorrow.'

Toni sighed. Vicky was always having a go at Sandra but it didn't help when the receptionist made cock-ups like this.

'The ear surgery at eight,' Vicky was saying, 'the birthmark at ten and then the nose job at twelve.'

'Rhinoplasty,' Daniel corrected automatically.

Vicky yawned and flicked her blonde hair over her shoulder. 'Whatever.'

'Morning, everyone.' Robert breezed in ten minutes late and took his place opposite Daniel.

Since the day Robert had joined the Blessington he had been late for meetings. Jade maintained it was his way of demonstrating how important he was. Daniel might be the boss, but Robert Perkins was an eminent surgeon and should be shown the appropriate respect.

'So where are we at?' he asked as he ran an eye down the agenda in front of him.

'Good morning, Robert,' Daniel said equably. 'We were just going through my list for tomorrow.'

'Oh, yes. Did I mention I've had to bump your ear surgery? I have an urgent eyebrow lift.'

'There's no such thing as an urgent eyebrow lift,' Daniel said drily.

'Oh, but there is! She's flying out to the south of France the next day.'

Daniel laughed at the serious expression on his colleague's face. 'Well, I'm terribly sorry for upsetting the lady's plans, but I've got a kid whose parents have been saving for months so that he could have this surgery.'

'You must reconsider, Daniel . . .'

Daniel didn't even lift his head from the agenda. 'No, Robert, I must not. The paediatric anaesthetist is booked and I have no intention of cancelling him. Now, Vicky, would you like to continue?'

Robert gave an angry snort and helped himself to coffee.

Vicky flashed him a sympathetic smile before continuing. 'You have six consultations this afternoon and surgery tomorrow morning in Sylvester's. Then that afternoon you have ward rounds. Thursday you have a clinic here for return visits and five operations that afternoon in Sylvester's starting at two. Then on Friday you are operating here all morning and the afternoon is given over to first consultations.'

'Where's my list?' Robert interrupted. 'I thought *I* had the theatre on Friday.'

'No, Robert,' Jade interrupted smoothly, 'you definitely asked me to switch you to Thursday.' She caught Toni's eye and winked.

Toni buried her head in her notes. Robert had switched

days to avoid working with Jade. Or, to be more accurate, to ensure he'd be working with Vicky. Though 'work' probably wasn't the correct word, Toni thought, remembering the day she had walked in on them in the kitchen. Robert had Vicky pressed up against the fridge, his tongue halfway down her throat and Vicky's left leg had been practically around his waist! Toni had considered giving a discreet cough but decided that in the interests of a relaxed working environment it would be more diplomatic to withdraw quietly.

'That's nothing,' Jade had scoffed when Toni had told her. 'I caught them at it in the recovery room one night.'

Toni shuddered. 'Oh don't! Even the thought of it makes my stomach churn! How can she?'

'She's mesmerised by the colour of his money' had been Jade's caustic reply.

Toni smiled now at the memory.

'Oh, did I? Yes, right, of course,' Robert was muttering now. 'Are, eh, you on duty that day, Jade?'

She flashed him a brilliant smile. 'Afraid not. Vicky will have to look after your needs.'

Robert eyed her suspiciously over the rim of his glasses but Jade gazed back innocently.

'Let's move on.' Toni broke in on the loaded atmosphere. She turned the page and the others followed suit. She nodded to Vicky who quickly ran through Robert's list without further interruption.

'Anything else?' Daniel asked Toni.

'Just one more item. Our costs are up five per cent on last month.'

Daniel stroked his beard thoughtfully. 'That's quite a lot, isn't it? Do we know why?'

25

'No idea,' Toni replied lightly, 'but Jade is going to do a stocktake this afternoon so we'll know more after that.'

'Couldn't Sandra do the stocktake? It's ridiculous that a nurse has to do it,' Daniel complained.

Toni shook her head. 'Sandra can take care of general office stuff but I'd prefer someone who knows what they're doing to deal with the medical supplies.'

'We're very busy today,' Robert said quickly. 'Why not let Vicky check the stock tomorrow?'

Jade and Toni exchanged glances.

'That makes more sense,' Daniel agreed. 'Well, if that's everything?'

Toni nodded and everyone stood up.

'Robert, have you got a minute?' Daniel asked as the others filed out of the room. He watched the older man settle back in his chair and sighed. He'd rather face a lengthy and difficult surgery any day than deal with Robert Perkins. Normally he managed to avoid the man, leaving Toni to deal with his various foibles, but he couldn't this time. He had kept his head buried in the sand for far too long. But things had been brought to a head when Toni had come to see him a couple of weeks ago. . .

'Daniel, I don't want to worry you, but I'm a bit concerned about some of Robert's cases,' she'd said, her beautiful face grave.

The absent-minded smile had faded from Daniel's face to be replaced by a worried frown. 'What is it, Toni?'

'I don't have all the details,' she'd started carefully.

'Just tell me, Toni,' Daniel had said flatly. They'd

known each other too long for this kind of pussyfooting around. And if Toni was worried enough to bring it to him, then Daniel knew he had a problem.

Toni had taken a deep breath before replying. 'Some of the operations he's carried out lately weren't, in my opinion, really necessary and there were a couple that weren't – wise.'

'Are you saying he put patients at risk?'

Toni shrugged unhappily. 'I'm not qualified to answer that. But from an administrative point of view, I *can* say that our legal position wouldn't be strong.'

'Jesus! What the hell has he done?'

And then he had sat getting paler and angrier as Toni read details of seven cases from her notebook. Amongst them a liposuction case on a forty-three-year-old woman who was a heavy smoker and extremely overweight and a young mother suffering from postnatal depression who wanted – and got – a breast reduction. Daniel winced. He was against plastic surgery for vanity's sake but understood that usually there were more serious reasons why people were prepared to undergo such an ordeal. It was the surgeon's job – no, his duty – to ensure that the patient was doing it for the right reasons *and* had thought it through. The whole situation made Daniel feel sick and he knew he must take action.

Now, Daniel's eyes flickered over the man in front of him with barely concealed distaste. He noted the greased-back hair, dyed a ridiculous blue-black like a raven's wing, the shiny, manicured nails and flamboyant paisley bow tie. Daniel couldn't abide or understand such vanity in a man.

Robert smiled back confidently. 'Can't stay long, old man. I've a patient in twenty minutes.'

'I'll be brief,' Daniel said curtly.

'Is it about my advertising proposal? Have you reconsidered?'

'No, I haven't.'

Robert frowned in annoyance. 'I must say, Daniel, you're being terribly old-fashioned about this. Advertising in magazines like *Cosmopolitan* and *Tatler* would bring in a lot more custom. I had eight patients from the UK last month alone. Eight!'

'And you know what my feelings are on that,' Daniel retorted bitterly. 'It's bloody ridiculous. These patients are treating our clinic like a holiday resort. "Will I go to Greece this year? No, maybe Turkey would be nicer. Oh, no, I'll go to Ireland instead and get the fat sucked out of my stomach!"'

Robert shrugged. 'That's the world we live in, old man. Everyone wants to look perfect and it's much cheaper for them to come here, what with the exchange rate. And then there's the added bonus of telling their friends that they were only in the Emerald Isle for a little holiday.'

'But it's wrong, Robert.' Daniel stood up and started to pace, pulling at his beard with agitated fingers. 'They aren't taking the proper amount of time to consider the seriousness of the surgery. They're jumping right in and, I have to say, I don't think you're doing much to discourage them.'

'If they want to spend their money who am I to stop them? Anyway, if I turn them away they'll just go to

28

someone else. And that's their prerogative, Daniel. They're adults, for God's sake.'

'Not always.' Daniel's expression darkened. 'What about that eighteen-year-old girl from Manchester who I found sobbing in the waiting-room a few weeks ago? She'd had her consultation and breast enhancement within two weeks, for God's sake! She didn't know what she was doing and she ended up even more self-conscious than she had been when she was flat-chested.'

'That operation was a complete success,' Robert argued. 'And we shouldn't have to reverse an operation just because a patient changes her mind.'

Daniel took several deep breaths in an effort to calm himself. 'Robert, you have carried out liposuction on three patients in the last month who should have been refused the operation.'

Robert's eyes narrowed. 'That's not true.'

Daniel looked at him, his gaze candid. 'Yes, it is, and your quarterly report showed an increase of twenty-five per cent in these operations. How do you account for such an alarming increase?'

Robert laughed. 'It's spring. The women want to get rid of the flab before they don their bikinis.'

Daniel clenched his fists tightly. It was exactly this sort of flippant comment that made him regret ever agreeing to Robert's appointment in the first place. 'But these women in particular were not suitable candidates,' he pointed out, struggling to keep his voice calm. 'Two were very overweight and one suffered from diabetes.'

Robert looked at him coldly. 'A very mild form I assure you. I don't take risks, Daniel, and I resent your implication that I do. These women are looking for a miracle cure and I try to give it to them. Of course, if they're obese, I send them away.'

'They don't have to be obese to be at risk,' Daniel persisted despite Robert's rising colour and the angry glint in his eye.

'Not one of my patients has had problems after surgery because of a weight problem.'

'Not yet,' Daniel flung at him. 'You've been bloody lucky!'

'Lucky! How dare you?'

Daniel ignored Robert's outraged expression. 'I dare because the patients of this clinic come first. Now, I've decided to bring in a new rule to reduce the risk of unnecessary operations taking place. From now on, the first consultation must take place at least three weeks before the operation and the second within ten days of the procedure.'

'But that's ridiculous! We'll lose all our UK customers if we do that!'

Daniel shrugged. 'If we do, we do.'

Robert stood up and glowered down at him. 'You are overreacting, Daniel, as usual. You know you can't bring this in without putting it before the board first!'

Daniel's eyes were cold and determined. 'Then that's what I'll do.'

Robert snorted, muttered something under his breath and flung out of the room, slamming the door behind him.

Daniel sank back in his chair and massaged his temples. He was fairly sure he would win this one. The board consisted of Toni Jordan, Theo French, Robert and himself. He would have Toni's backing for sure – anything to keep Robert's 'cosmetic drive thru' under control. And he believed he could count on Theodore French's support too. Not necessarily because the other surgeon would agree with him but because Theo was terrified of the clinic being sued for malpractice. Yes, his new system would get board approval and that would slow Perkins down. For a while anyway.

'Something's going on,' Jade said without preamble when they were in the privacy of Toni's office, with two mugs of coffee.

'But what?' Toni replied. She was a little distracted realising that Daniel was probably confronting Robert at this very moment. 'What could Vicky possibly be up to? What's in it for her?'

'Dunno, but Perky is either involved or protecting her.'

Toni nodded thoughtfully. 'His behaviour was a bit odd.'

'Though Daniel didn't seem to think so,' Jade added.

'For goodness sake, Daniel wouldn't notice if there were neon-flashing signs all around him saying, "Warning, something fishy's going on here!"'

Jade laughed and they sipped their coffee in silence for a moment. Then Toni set down her mug and looked at Jade with a twinkle in her eye. 'How do you feel about a bit of detective work, Ms Peters?'

A smile spread slowly across Jade's face. 'Tell me more, Holmes!'

'Okay, here's the plan. We'll let Vicky go ahead and check the stock tomorrow.'

'And?'

'Then *we'll* do it again.'

Jade nodded enthusiastically. 'Let's do it.'

'I'm afraid it will mean working late.'

'No problem.'

Toni smiled gratefully. 'It will be safer if we do it after hours. It would ruin everything if Vicky realised what we were up to.'

Jade's perfectly plucked eyebrows went up an inch. 'Don't worry about that. Her three brain cells will be worn out after a real day's work.'

Toni laughed. 'You're so cruel.'

Jade grinned. 'So if we find any discrepancies, we confront Vicky on Thursday?'

Toni shook her head. 'No, I don't think so. I think we should just keep an eye on her for a while. Try and figure out what's going on and if Robert is involved. We can't go making wild accusations.'

'I suppose you're right.' Jade agreed reluctantly, disappointed that she wouldn't get the chance to pin the other nurse up against a wall and shine a bright light in her eyes.

'Of course I am. Okay then. We'll meet here tomorrow night, say about seven?'

'Okay, boss. I'll wear my mac, trilby and dark glasses. What's the secret password?'

Toni laughed. 'You do know you're certifiable, don't you?'

* * *

Later that evening, Toni stood in her kitchen and studied the contents of the fridge. She was eating alone tonight as

Chloe was playing basketball and Theo was eating out – she couldn't remember where. The fridge was packed with food but nothing took her fancy. It was all too damn healthy! All the things that Theo liked, thanks to his devoted housekeeper. She shut the door and went out into the garden. To hell with it! She'd order in later *and* open a bottle of wine. It was a beautiful evening and the sounds of summer filled the air. Toni sighed as she listened to laughter and glasses clinking in a neighbouring garden and smelled the unmistakable aroma of barbecuing steak. She had foreseen such evenings in the French household but casual wasn't Theo's thing. Place mats and linen napkins were more his style. No paper plates, cold beer and children munching on burgers with tomato sauce dripping from their chins. She wandered around the flowerbeds checking her plants and then settled in a large garden chair to enjoy the last of the sun. She tried to relax but her mind was working overtime. She was dying to know how the meeting with Perky had gone but Daniel had been tied up all day and there hadn't been an opportunity to ask. Maybe she'd call him at home – it would certainly be easier to talk. She went in search of the phone – which was the problem with these cordless jobs. You left them down and forgot where. She finally discovered it in the sitting-room under Chloe's history book but by that time she'd decided it wouldn't be fair to disturb Daniel at home. She'd leave it till morning. Instead she dialled for a curry, opened a bottle of wine and carried her glass back out to the garden, remembering to bring the phone with her. She sank back into her chair and closed her eyes. It was nice to have the place to herself, though she'd been looking forward to telling Theo about Perky's latest behaviour. She knew her husband would not be impressed – finally, an issue that they could agree on. Now wouldn't that make a pleasant change!

She sipped her wine and thought about the other issue of the day. The mystery about the rise in the clinic's costs and Robert rather enthusiastically volunteering Vicky to do the stock take. Very strange. Daniel would be really cheesed off if Robert were involved in anything remotely dodgy but she wasn't going to mention it until she and Jade got to the bottom of it. Thank goodness for good old reliable Jade, always happy to turn her hand to anything. Unlike Vicky who was very particular that she carried out her duties as a nurse and nothing more. Jade was particularly adept on the computer and Sandra had benefited greatly from her tuition, her skills improving daily. Which was just as well because Perky and Vicky were always looking for excuses to complain about the girl. They would like nothing better than to see Sandra fired. But Toni and Jade would do everything they could to make sure that it didn't come to that. Sandra needed this job.

She was an only child whose father had died several years ago. Her mother – now only sixty-three – had contracted MS shortly afterwards. The symptoms had been quite mild for the first few years, but in recent months Valerie Tomkins had degenerated quite rapidly and sometimes had to use a wheelchair. Toni, realising the extra burden on Sandra, had offered to put her on a three-day week, but the girl had been horrified.

'This job is the only thing that keeps me going, Toni,'

she had said, her eyes filling with tears. 'And, and we need the money.'

Toni had been shocked that she hadn't seen the signs earlier. She'd just taken Sandra's cheeriness at face value. She had told Jade about the conversation and they'd agreed to keep a closer eye on their receptionist in future.

Toni had assured Sandra then that her job was completely safe and that she could work whatever hours suited her best. If Perky knew he'd be disgusted but it looked like Sandra was going to be with them for the long haul. Toni smiled sadly. Sandra belonged at the Blessington with the rest of the misfits. The two anaesthetists they usually used weren't based at the Blessington and were never in the building longer than they had to be. Toni doubted they even knew the names of her staff. The company that came in to clean was made up of middle-aged women who seemed to spend most of their time giggling and whispering about the clinic's patients and the funny operations that went on in the place. Vicky Harrison, the voluptuous, backbiting nurse was determined to get a rich man – and if he was under eighty it would be a bonus. Slippery Robert Perkins was obsessed with money and younger, well-endowed women. And Jade Peters, while attractive and funny, was almost obsessively secretive about her private life. As for herself, Toni laughed aloud. Her problems and idiosyncrasies were too numerous to mention. In fact, Daniel Wheeler was probably the only normal person in the clinic. Just as well the patients didn't know that!

Chapter Three

Wednesday, 10th May, 2000

Jade closed the door as quietly as its age would allow, collected her post and crept up the stairs.

'Mrs Peters? Is that you? Yoo-hoo.'

Jade slumped resignedly against the bannisters. 'Yes, Mrs Stewart, it's me.'

A wizened little woman in black leggings and sequinned top, with a cigarette hanging out of her mouth, tottered into the hallway. 'Come on down, love. I'll make a cup of tea and we can have a nice little chat. I've hardly seen you all week.'

'Sorry, I've been busy.' It wasn't a lie and doing the stocktake after a long and difficult shift had exhausted her.

'You got a letter. I think it's from the bank.'

'Really?' Jade said through gritted teeth. A downside of living here was that her landlady always had a good nose through the post. 'Look, I'll pass on that tea, Mrs Stewart, if you don't mind. I just want go to bed. I've a bit of a headache. Night.' She hurried on up the stairs.

'Please yourself,' Patsy Stewart muttered, went back

into her sitting-room and poured herself a straight gin.

Jade hurried up to her room, kicked the door shut after her and flung her bag and the letter on the bed. After plugging in the kettle carefully – the flex was frayed and the plug loose – she spooned two teaspoons of coffee into a large cracked mug and went over to the tiny fridge to inspect the contents.

Four yoghurts, two days past their sell-by date; a carton of milk; half a carton of cream cheese and an egg. Nothing appealed. There were two chocolate biscuits left in the press. What the hell, she'd push the boat out and eat both of them! She took out the milk – damn, there was only a drain left – and made her coffee.

She carried her 'dinner' over to the one threadbare armchair in the cold, damp room and turned on the tiny portable TV. She flicked through the stations until she found BBC's *Changing Rooms*. Her favourite. She often thought about writing to them. Now this room would be a *real* challenge!

She thought wistfully of the beautiful house she'd left behind. A corner house sitting in a leafy cul-de-sac just off Collins Avenue, it was the house that she'd thought she would end her days in. The huge garden where her grandchildren would play – *no! Stop it!* She tried to concentrate on the shelves Handy Andy was erecting but her heart wasn't in it. Her eyes flickered to the letter on the bed. It would be a polite reminder of the debt remaining and an offer to renegotiate her payment plan. The civility of the whole thing irritated her. She didn't want letters or phone calls or cosy chats with one of the bank's advisors. She just wanted to pay them the damn money and be done with it. Another couple of months would do it and then she'd be able to breathe again. She could have asked Toni for an advance on her salary in order to clear the debt. She had no doubt that Toni would have agreed. But then she would have had to tell her the whole sorry story.

Of course Toni knew that when she and Aidan had separated they had sold their house in Glasnevin. 'Too many memories,' Jade had explained lightly when Toni asked why she was giving up her home. Now her friend was under the impression that she lived in a plush new apartment and Jade did nothing to disillusion her. It was bad enough having to live in this hellhole with a pathetic old drunk for a landlady, without the whole world knowing about it.

The shrill sound of the doorbell startled her. After a few moments, the determined caller rapped the knocker long and hard.

'Hey! Stop that,' Patsy Stewart shouted as she made her way down the passage. 'I'm coming, I'm coming.'

Jade held her breath as Ma Stewart opened the door, straining to hear the conversation. After some discussion, the front door was shut again and she could hear Patsy's step on the creaking staircase.

There was a rap on the door. 'Mrs Peters? Mrs Peters? There's a man wants to talk to you.'

Jade opened the door a couple of inches. 'Tell him I'm not in, will you?' she pleaded.

Patsy eyed her warily. 'Are you in some kind of trouble? 'Cos I don't need that in this house. I don't want all sorts of shady characters coming knocking on my door –'

'It's my husband,' Jade cut through her tirade. 'And I assure you, despite his appearance, he's . . . a decent man.'

Patsy's pencilled eyebrows went up an inch. 'I see. You two separated then?'

'That's right.' Jade resented every word. She hadn't told her best friend the details of her separation so she was damned if she was going to tell this old crone.

Patsy nodded sympathetically. 'Fair enough, love, but you're going to have to talk to him. I don't want him coming back at all hours and banging the door down. So you put him straight, there's a good girl.'

Jade sighed. 'Well, okay then, but not up here.'

'You can use my front room,' Patsy said graciously.

And you'll be in the next room with a glass against the wall, no doubt, Jade thought grimly. 'Thanks, Mrs Stewart.'

Patsy led the way downstairs and stood watching as Jade opened the front door. 'Come on in, Aidan.' She led the way into Patsy's shabby sitting-room and closed the door firmly in Patsy's face.

'Hiya, love. How are you?' Aidan smiled nervously.

Jade sat down on a hard-backed chair. 'I asked you to stay away from me,' she said dejectedly. She'd already moved twice in an effort to get away from her husband.

He looked sheepish. 'I just wanted to see you.'

Jade looked sadly at his bent shoulders, shabby jacket and battered trainers. It was hard to believe that this was the smart, handsome architect that she'd married nearly twenty years ago.

'How's work going?' he asked.

Jade nodded again. 'Fine.' *Why do we have to go through this every time, Aidan? Why bother with the small talk? We both know why you're here.*

He rubbed his tobacco-stained hands together

nervously and Jade noticed that his nails were bitten. 'What do you want?' she asked finally. The sooner he left the better. It broke her heart every time she saw him.

'If you could just lend me a few quid,' Aidan said, his faded eyes pleading. 'Whatever you can spare.'

'I can't spare anything,' she told him bitterly. 'I'm still paying off your debts, remember?'

He looked away, his eyes full of pain. 'I know, love. I'm sorry. I've let you down terribly. Not a day goes by that I don't think about it. I failed you. I was a lousy husband.'

'Not always,' Jade reminded him. She couldn't stand it when he started down the road of self-pity.

'No. Not always,' he repeated quietly.

'Are you still going to the meetings?' Jade asked.

He looked away. 'When I can.'

Jade laughed bitterly. 'Ah, yes. It must be hard to fit them in between all the jobs you've got on.'

Aidan flinched. 'Ah, don't, love.'

Jade watched him angrily. 'I'm not giving you more money.'

'Just fifty quid, even twenty.'

Jade saw the desperation in his eyes and weakened as she always did. 'Wait here.' She ran upstairs for her purse. She knew without checking that there was only thirty pounds in it. She took twenty and went back down to him. 'It's all I can afford.'

'Thanks, love. Thanks.' He stuffed it into his pocket and turned to leave.

'Aidan?'

He paused, his hand on the door handle.

'I don't want you to come here again.'

41

'But, Jade –'

'I mean it, Aidan,' she said, her voice quiet but determined. 'I don't want to see you again. You're going to have to stand on your own two feet from now on. I can't continue to support you.'

He nodded sadly. 'I understand. Thanks for this. Take care of yourself, love.'

Jade shut the door quickly. She couldn't bear to watch him walk away. Her sweet, kind, charismatic husband. Where had he gone?

She hurried back upstairs before her landlady realised that he'd gone. She knew that if Patsy Stewart questioned her about him she was likely to lose her temper and tell her where to go, and however much she hated living here she couldn't afford to move. In the privacy of her room she curled up on the bed and let the tears come. It might be two years since she'd thrown Aidan out, but it still hurt as if it were only yesterday.

She remembered the day well. She had been enjoying a day off from the clinic, catching up on all the things she'd been putting off. One was to write to her sister, Anita, in Australia. When she'd finished she'd gone into Aidan's study in search of a stamp. He was out working on a large new property in Delgany at the time. She'd paused to admire the drawings spread out on his desk. He was such a great architect and she was so proud of him. She resumed her search and after a fruitless rummage through the drawers, she decided to try his filing cabinet. Maybe he was more organised than she thought and filed them under 'S'. The smile had died on her lips as she came across the stack of crumpled-up envelopes wedged at the bottom of the drawer. It was the Telecom logo that first set off alarm bells in her head. That and the stark red line across the top of the page. It was a final notice and it had arrived two weeks ago.

'Oh, dear God.' Jade had sunk into a chair and started to go through the other letters with trembling hands. The electricity bill, their joint credit cards and – dear Jesus! – a brief note from their insurance company saying that their motor and household policies had lapsed. 'Oh, Aidan, what the hell's going on?' she'd groaned.

Picking up the phone, she'd dialled his mobile. 'Aidan? It's me. You have to come home.'

'What's wrong, love? Are you sick?'

'No, nothing like that.'

'Then what is it? I'm really very busy –'

'I don't care how bloody busy you are! Get your ass back here now!' She'd hung up the phone and gone out to the kitchen to get a drink.

When Aidan had arrived home, she had been sitting at the kitchen table with a large vodka and the pile of bills in front of her. His face fell. 'I can explain.'

'You can try,' she'd said grimly.

'It's just a cash-flow problem. I didn't tell you because I didn't want to worry you.'

'You'd prefer me to get arrested for driving without insurance,' she had retorted scathingly.

'Don't be silly, of course you're insured. I took care of that last week.'

'How kind.'

Aidan ignored her sarcastic tone. 'Look, Jade, this has

43

been a very difficult time for me. Browns haven't paid their bill yet and Seamus Phelan is about to declare bankruptcy. I'll be lucky if I get a tenth of what he owes me.' He had sat down at the table and put his head in his hands.

Against all her instincts, Jade chose to believe him and they had talked long into the night about what needed to be done. Aidan would go to the bank manager the next morning to discuss a temporary loan and Jade would call the ESB, Telecom and the credit card companies and agree a payment plan.

'But you mustn't keep problems like this to yourself in future, Aidan,' she had warned.

He'd looked suitably chastened. 'I know, love. I'm sorry.'

And that was the end of that – or so Jade had thought. They were on the breadline for a while. There were no Saturday nights down the pub, no eating out and certainly no foreign holidays. But they'd coped and life had carried on as usual. Until the day that Jade had bumped into Seamus Phelan on O'Connell street.

They had made awkward, mundane conversation for a few minutes until Jade could stand it no longer. 'I was very sorry to hear about the business, Seamus,' she had blurted out.

Seamus had given her an odd look. 'I beg your pardon?'

'Aidan told me you had to declare bankruptcy,' she had explained gently.

Seamus had laughed. 'Then he's having you on, Jade. Unless of course he knows something that I don't!'

Jade had laughed too although it hadn't been easy. 'I must have got it wrong. Sorry.'

'Don't worry about it. Listen, I'd better be going. Take care of yourself, Jade, and tell Aidan I'll be in touch about the new apartment complex in Swords.'

'I will. Bye, Seamus.' Jade had walked back to work in a daze. Aidan had lied to her. There was no way he could have made a mistake. Seamus Phelan was responsible for more than fifty per cent of his business. So why had he lied? Seamus had paid him and he'd spent the money. But on what? What could be so expensive that he hadn't paid any of their bills?

She'd confronted Aidan again that night, but this time she was ready for him. She'd spent a quiet half-hour at the clinic making phone calls and her worst fears had been confirmed. Aidan was also behind on his repayments for his car and – the most shattering piece of news so far – the mortgage. The building society was threatening to repossess her beautiful home.

She had prayed that Aidan would have a reasonable explanation. That he'd persuade her it was a temporary glitch and there was nothing to worry about. But her hopes were in vain and no one was listening to her prayers that night.

Jade got up and went over to the tiny sink in the corner and doused her face in cold water. Then she took a small bottle of vodka and a glass from her kitchen press. Her emergency supply. She'd never liked the idea of becoming a solitary drinker – it would make her as weak and pathetic as Aidan – but sometimes even she had to break the rules. She sat down on the narrow bed, stacked the pillows behind her head and sipped her drink. Maybe she should find somewhere else to live. She wasn't sure she could trust Aidan to stay away. But the thought of notifying the clinic of yet another change of address was not appealing and it was unlikely she'd find somewhere as cheap. No, if Aidan came back again she'd just have to be more forceful. Maybe if she threatened to tell his mother the truth about their separation that would do the trick. But she wasn't sure she could do that. Because at the end of the day, Aidan Peters was the love of her life and doing anything to hurt him went against every fibre of her being. She stared blankly at the TV and drank the vodka diluted by her tears.

Chapter Four

Monday, 22nd May, 2000

'So we're agreed?' Daniel Wheeler looked at the other three directors.

Theo gave a curt nod.

'Absolutely.' Toni smiled.

'Bloody ridiculous,' Robert muttered.

'Robert,' Theo warned through gritted teeth. He looked at his watch. 'If there's nothing else?'

Daniel shook his head and managed to smile at the only non-executive director. 'No, Theo. Thank you for your time. It was good of you to come at such short notice.'

Theo glanced briefly at Robert. 'Not at all. We don't often have emergency general meetings.'

'Thank goodness,' Toni said under her breath. Two weeks had passed since Daniel had tackled Robert and the atmosphere in the clinic ever since had been electric.

'Come along, Toni. I've booked Chapter One for lunch.'

Toni looked crestfallen. 'Oh, sorry, Theo, eh, I can't.'

'Nonsense,' Daniel said jovially. 'You go and have a

nice lunch. Treat her to a glass of wine too, Theo. She's been working very hard lately.'

'I've noticed,' Theo said drily, holding the door for his wife.

Toni smiled wanly at Daniel and preceded her husband out of the meeting room. 'I really can't afford to take a long lunch, Theo,' she tried again.

'Oh, for God's sake, Toni. You're not indispensable. Anyway, I have a consultation at three. You'll be back behind your desk by two-thirty at the latest.' He strode across reception and held the front door open for her.

'Well, okay then,' Toni agreed reluctantly. She hadn't expected this. It had been a long time since Theo had suggested lunch. In the early days they had always gone out to lunch or dinner after a board meeting. It had been one of the things Toni had really enjoyed. Sitting over a good bottle of wine, discussing the clinic. Toni had felt that Theo respected her opinion then.

She glanced now at the grim set of his jaw as they got into his large Mercedes. This was going to be fun. Not.

'Chapter One,' she said brightly as she strapped herself in. 'It's ages since we've been there.'

'You were supposed to be there three weeks ago,' Theo reminded her, 'but you were otherwise engaged.'

Toni nodded silently, remembering the row when she'd refused to cancel a night out with Jade.

Theo had been furious. 'You see that woman every bloody day and Nigel is only in Dublin for one night.'

'And you knew that your cousin was coming but neglected to mention it,' she retorted.

'I've been busy.'

48

'Well, maybe you should get your secretary to check with me in future,' she'd snapped back and gone to meet Jade.

'The meeting went well,' she said now, determined to make an effort. Surely they could manage a couple of hours without arguing?

'I'm not sure Robert would agree.'

'No.' Toni smiled. 'We've certainly upset his gravy train.'

'You're being a bit unfair, Toni. You wouldn't see anything wrong with someone in another profession trying to make some money.'

Toni looked incredulous. ''Some! The man is loaded! And you're right, I think this profession *is* different. He is capitalising on people's feelings of inadequacy and lack of confidence.'

'Are you saying cosmetic surgery should be outlawed?' he countered.

Toni shook her head vehemently. 'Of course not but there should be tighter controls. You must agree?'

Theo inclined his head in acknowledgement. 'There is room for improvement and there are definitely some very questionable practitioners out there, but,' he shook his finger at Toni, 'Robert isn't one of them.'

'I know that, Theo,' she relented, 'but he could be a bit more . . .'

'Humble?' Theo suggested with a wry smile.

Toni laughed. 'That would be a start.'

'He has his faults but he is a good surgeon.'

Toni said nothing. She didn't want to spoil the almost pleasant atmosphere that had developed. Maybe lunch wouldn't be such a trial after all.

'You do know that these new rules of Daniel's will seriously affect the Blessington?'

Toni nodded, with a worried frown. 'Certainly our number of UK clients will fall.' Daniel had seemed unconcerned when she'd warned him of this. Sometimes she found his scatterbrained approach to finance a bit trying.

Theo pulled into a parking spot on Parnell Square. 'Your Irish patients may be affected as well. A lot of new clinics have popped up in the last eighteen months and not all of them are run by people with Daniel's morals.'

Toni sighed. Theo was always having a go at Daniel. Mind you, Daniel wasn't much better. They tolerated each other but no more than that. It wasn't always easy being in the middle. Especially so because she usually agreed with Daniel.

They were quickly seated in a quiet corner of the restaurant and Theo ordered – without consulting her – a bottle of Sancerre. Toni picked up the conversation again. 'It seems we're caught between a rock and a hard place. Daniel's new system will save people unnecessary pain and money, but it will piss them off too. They won't agree to wait that long for an operation if the clinic down the road will do it in half the time.'

They paused as the waiter poured their wine and took their order – steak and salad for Theo and duck in a rich sauce for Toni. She ignored his look of disbelief as she ordered a portion of fries on the side.

'So you don't actually agree with the new system,' he said.

'Oh, I do! But with my administrator's hat on, I can see it might cause some financial problems.'

Theo smiled sympathetically and stood up. 'It's not easy balancing money and conscience, is it? Excuse me a moment. I just need to check in with Emma.'

Toni watched him thoughtfully as he went outside to call his secretary. She had forgotten what it was like to conduct a normal conversation with Theo. At times like this she caught a glimpse of the man she'd fallen in love with. Still authoritative and opinionated, but at the same time incisive and wise. She'd respected him so much in the early days of their marriage, even excusing his patronising ways. It was only natural that such a well-educated man would find fault with her simple reasoning.

Theo returned to the table and sat down, placing the white napkin carefully in his lap. 'You know, Daniel should get out of private practice and stick to the hospital,' he said, immediately dispelling any warm feelings she'd developed towards him in the last twenty minutes.

She paused while their food was being served before replying. 'Why on earth would he do that?'

Theo sliced a minute piece of fat from his steak. 'It's not a business for the faint-hearted, Toni. And make no mistake, it *is* a business.'

Toni watched him eat with concentrated precision and tried to imagine him digging greedily into a bag of chips. She failed. 'Daniel isn't in it for the money.'

Theo looked amused. 'Very admirable.'

Toni flushed angrily. 'Yes, it is very admirable, Theo. To me and to all the people he's helped.'

Theo nodded with mock enthusiasm. 'The man should be canonised without a doubt.'

51

Toni looked at him curiously, her face slowly breaking into a smile. 'You're jealous.'

Theo gave her a withering look. 'I don't think so.'

'You are!' Toni laughed delightedly.

Theo put down his knife and fork and pushed his plate away. 'Don't be so bloody juvenile, Toni.'

Toni bit into a chip, enjoying his discomfort. 'It's because his patients love him, that's it, isn't it? Your patients admire and respect you but they don't love you. They're too scared of you to love you.'

'Ridiculous.'

Toni shook her head emphatically. 'No it isn't. They're *all* scared of you. The patients, the doctors, the nurses and that's the way you like it. But occasionally,' she continued, almost talking to herself now, 'you would like to be on the receiving end of a look of pure trust and love from a sick child, a grateful parent or –'

Theo threw down his napkin and stood up. 'Spare me the amateur psychology, please!'

Toni smiled as he stormed off to the gents'. She'd obviously struck a chord. Interesting that the invincible Theodore French was capable of vulnerability on occasion. At least in his professional life. There was no sign of any such weakness at home. Theo saw himself as the head of the family and expected his wife and daughter to accept his pronouncements without question. Over the years Toni had learned to handle it – following her friend Dotty's excellent advice – by just ignoring him. Chloe sometimes got her way through wheedling, cajoling or just plain begging. But as she got older she was becoming rebellious and Theo's draconian attitude didn't help. These days he seemed to do nothing but harangue Chloe about her studies and question her suspiciously about her social life. But it was his constant instruction as to how her future should develop that would eventually drive Chloe away. Marianna had left her a small trust fund that she would receive on her eighteenth birthday and Toni wouldn't be at all surprised if the girl used it to buy a flat.

'Would you like some tea?' Theo asked stiffly, resuming his seat.

'Cappuccino,' Toni replied. *I never drink tea after a meal. You'd think he'd have noticed after all these years.*

Theo beckoned the waiter and ordered coffee for her and tea for himself. 'And could you bring the bill, please?'

'To get back to these new procedures, Theo. Why did you agree to them if they're going to be bad for business?'

'I agree that some steps should be taken to safeguard the patient and it makes sense from a legal standpoint.'

Toni rolled her eyes.

'You may mock, Toni, but a nasty court case could put the Blessington Clinic out of business for good. Anyway, as I was saying, I believe Daniel's idea is a good one but he will probably have to compromise on the time scales. We can see how it goes and then reassess the situation in a few weeks.'

Toni looked at him suspiciously. 'Did you say that to Robert?'

Theo gave a small, smug smile. 'I did suggest that he might be as well to sit back and let the problem sort itself out.'

Toni shook her head in disgust. 'I just don't believe you! You're as bad as he is!'

Theo's smile disappeared. 'Look, Daniel has got exactly what he wanted and I'm sure if it proves to be a non-starter, he will be the first to admit it.'

'And everything will go back to the way it was,' Toni added.

Theo shrugged. 'If it's what your customers want.'

'Patients, they're patients!'

Theo leaned across the table and took her hands in a firm grip. 'No, Toni, they're customers. They're not sick. They don't need surgery. They are doing it out of choice. Paying to get their bodies carved up in the name of vanity!'

Toni stared at him, incredulous. 'You don't approve?'

'Of course I don't approve!'

'I never realised. Robert's your friend. And you were the one who wanted the clinic to branch into cosmetic surgery.'

Theo sighed impatiently. 'Because it is a business. A very lucrative one.'

Toni looked at him, bewildered. 'But how can you reconcile that in your mind? You don't approve of something but you give it your backing in order to make some money?'

Theo gave her a pitying look. 'You are so incredibly naïve, darling.'

'Maybe I am. But at least I have a clear conscience. I have nothing against cosmetic surgery where it will clearly benefit the patient psychologically. What I object to is Robert – and surgeons like him – operating on anyone who comes through the door with cheque book in hand. It's not medicine and it's not business. It's exploitation and it's dangerous.' Toni picked up her bag and stood up. 'And now I'd like to go.'

'Certainly, my dear.' Theo gave her a grim smile and followed her out of the restaurant.

Toni paused beside the car, taking deep breaths to calm herself. 'I'll walk back.'

'Oh, don't be ridiculous. Get in the car.'

Toni shook her head. 'No, I need the air. See you tonight.'

Chapter Five

Friday, 26th May, 2000

Mark kissed Chloe tenderly and then propped himself up on one arm so he could see her properly. He never got tired of looking at her. She was so beautiful with her silky dark mane, startling blue eyes that looked into his very soul, and a body that had the most incredible effect on him. 'Had you any problems getting out?' He stroked her cheek gently.

'No. Dad was working late and I told Toni I was staying over in Ollie's.'

'I don't see why we have to do all this creeping around,' he complained.

Chloe sighed. 'It might be easier if your surname wasn't Wheeler.'

'For God's sake, we're not Romeo and Juliet!'

'It will be okay once the exams are over,' Chloe promised. 'Dad doesn't believe in me doing anything other than studying, eating and sleeping at the moment.'

'But you have to take a break sometimes,' Mark protested.

Chloe giggled as she ran her hand over his smooth chest. 'I'm not sure this is the sort of break he'd approve of!'

Mark grinned and pulled her closer so that he could feel her bare skin along the length of his body. 'Maybe not,' he murmured and bent his head to kiss her again.

'I should be going,' she said half-heartedly.

He kissed her throat. 'What's the rush? They're not expecting you home.'

'I'm not staying *here* all night! It's freezing.' She shifted slightly to avoid the spring that kept digging into her back. They were in the back of his mother's car, which was parked in the garage beside his house. 'Anyway, what if someone comes out?'

'It's after midnight, Chloe. Mam and Dad will be in dreamland by now. Just stay for another little while,' he pleaded. 'I'll keep you warm.'

Chloe grinned. 'How are you going to do that then?'

'I'm sure I'll think of something!'

Mark smoked a cigarette and watched as Chloe buttoned her shirt and pulled up her jeans.

'I wish you wouldn't watch,' Chloe complained.

'I like watching.'

'Tough!' She pushed him out of the car and fiddled with her zip. Getting dressed in the back of a car was really sordid and Mark watching made it even worse. She combed her fingers through her hair, jumped out of the car and kissed Mark lightly on the lips. 'I've got to go.'

Mark followed and pulled her back for one more kiss before quietly opening the garage door.

58

Chloe peered anxiously over his shoulder. 'Are you sure there's no one around?'

Mark patted her hand reassuringly. 'Will you relax? No one is going to see us.'

But as they stepped out into the driveway, the garage door slammed behind them and Chloe jumped as a high-pitched alarm went off and lights started to flash.

'Shit!' Mark looked anxiously up at the house. 'Dad's put the bloody alarm on! Quick, hide in the garden! And for God's sake, be quiet.'

'It's a bit late for that.' Daniel was at the front door, tightening the belt of his dressing-gown. 'I think you two had better come inside.'

Chloe stared at Mark, her eyes wide in panic. 'What are we going to say?' she hissed as they followed Daniel into the house. 'Dad will kill me *and* you if he finds out about this.'

'Don't worry. It's cool,' he said with more confidence than he felt. 'Dad won't tell him.'

'What is it, Daniel?' Meg Wheeler called down.

'Don't worry, love. Just a cat. Go back to sleep. I'll be up in a minute.'

Mark smiled gratefully. 'Thanks, Dad, sorry about that. I'll just take Chloe home . . .'

Daniel glared at him. 'Not so fast, young man. You have some explaining to do.'

'We haven't done anything wrong,' Mark protested.

'Really? And I suppose you're going to tell me that Chloe here has a passion for cars – particularly 1994 Micras and couldn't wait until daylight to get a look at your mother's?'

Chloe went as red as a beetroot and prayed for the ground to open up and swallow her.

'Dad! You're embarrassing her! Look, we just wanted a little privacy. It's not like there's any in *this* house!'

Daniel looked at him thoughtfully. 'Privacy, eh? And, Chloe, does your father know where you are?'

Chloe shook her head mutely.

'I see. So where does he *think* you are?'

'At my friend Ollie's. That's where I'm going now, I just stopped by to say hello . . .'

Daniel looked at his watch with raised eyebrows. 'Really?'

'Oh, Dad, come on! You were young once, remember?' Mark protested angrily.

'I hope I showed my lady-friends a bit more respect. If I remember rightly, we used to go to the cinema or to a dance.'

Chloe bent her head, letting her hair fall across her face to hide her burning cheeks.

'Dad!' Mark was pleading now.

Daniel sighed. There was no point in prolonging the poor girl's agony. 'I'll say no more about this now but don't ever put me in this position again. Apart from anything else, Chloe, I have no intention of deceiving Toni and your father.'

'Oh, please don't tell them!' Chloe begged. 'I promise, Mr Wheeler. We won't do it again.'

'Then we'll leave it at that. Now, Mark, ring for a cab. Goodnight, Chloe.'

'Goodnight, Mr Wheeler. Sorry.'

'Night, Dad.'

'Is everything all right, love?' Meg asked sleepily as Daniel climbed back into bed beside her.

'Fine, pet. You go to sleep.' He turned over on his side and wondered if he needed to have strong words with his eldest son. He was a responsible lad – well most of the time he was – but messing around with Theo French's daughter, of all people! Daniel sighed heavily. He hoped Mark had remembered to use a condom. The possible consequences if he hadn't didn't bear thinking about. At least not tonight. He had laser surgery at eight. It was time to get some sleep.

* * *

Ollie stood at the corner of her road shivering. She wished she'd listened to her mother and worn a jacket, but it would have looked naff over her gorgeous new red hipsters and clingy black cropped top. Goose pimples stood out in droves on her bare white midriff, and her feet in their skyscraper platform sandals were like blocks of ice. She hopped anxiously from foot to foot. Chloe should have been here ages ago. She craned her neck eagerly as she saw a taxi approach and heaved a sigh of relief when it pulled in beside her and Chloe jumped out.

'Jeez, Chlo! Where the hell have you been? I was worried and Mum's going to be wondering where we are. I swore we'd be home before two.'

Chloe grinned as they walked hurriedly down the road. 'Oh, stop fussing, Ollie! We're only ten minutes late.'

Ollie snorted. 'You can talk! Your dad would go spare if he knew you were out at all!'

Chloe sighed. 'I know. It's a real pain. I can only get

him to agree to me going to Old Wesley if your mum is picking us up.'

Ollie frowned. 'But Mum never picks us up.'

'*He* doesn't know that.'

Ollie shook her head. 'Weird.'

'What are we going to tell your mum?' Chloe asked as the turned into the Coyles's driveway.

'Oh, that the first taxi-driver looked shifty and we waited for another one. She'll love that. Think we've been real responsible.'

Chloe looked at her in admiration. 'You're good. You're really good.'

Ollie gave a small bow before putting her key in the lock. 'Learn at the feet of the master!'

Mary Coyle heard the front door close and the whispering and giggling in the hallway. She turned over to look at the clock. They were a bit late, but nothing to get excited about. She always worried when her wild, headstrong daughter was out partying but it gave her some comfort if Chloe French was with her. She was a good steadying influence. Mary hated it when Ollie talked about leaving home and getting a flat. But she'd have some peace of mind if Ollie moved in with Chloe. She heard steps on the stairs and then Ollie's door closing softly. She closed her eyes contentedly. Now she'd be able to sleep.

'So, tell me?' Ollie looked expectantly at her friend curled up in the opposite bed.

'Tell you what?' Chloe asked, sleepily.

'You know what! Come on, Chloe,' she wheedled. 'I'd tell you.'

Chloe laughed softly. 'Sure! So what happened with Alan Pearson, then?'

'He's history! I wouldn't have done it with him if we were the only two people on a desert island!'

Chloe laughed softly. 'It didn't look that way last week. You were all over each other like a rash!'

Ollie shrugged nonchalantly. 'That was last week. It's important to experiment. It adds to your wealth of experience.'

'Or your reputation as a tart,' Chloe replied, only half joking. She was a bit worried that Ollie was getting a name for herself. She seemed to have dated half the boys in Wesley.

She yelped as Ollie tumbled into the bed beside her.

'Stop avoiding the issue,' her friend ordered. 'You're not going to sleep until you tell me everything.'

Chloe sighed. She'd have to come up with something to satisfy Ollie. Otherwise she'd never get any sleep tonight. 'We didn't do it,' she muttered finally.

'Get out of here! You were in the back of his mum's car in a garage, all alone, in the dark and you're telling me you didn't *do* anything!'

Chloe was glad it was dark and Ollie couldn't see her face turn crimson. She didn't want to talk about Mark. He was special. 'We did *do* things,' she admitted finally. 'We just didn't go all the way.'

Ollie's eyes narrowed. 'Are you sure?'

'Of course I'm bloody sure!'

'Did he use a condom?'

Chloe felt her cheeks get even hotter. 'He didn't have to!'

'Maybe,' Ollie said mysteriously. 'Did he put it in and tell you that he got it out in time?'

'Olivia Coyle!' Chloe turned away angrily and stared at the wall.

'Oh, okay. There's no need to sulk!' Ollie went back to her own bed.

'Sorry. 'Night.'

''Night.'

Chloe pulled the duvet up to her chin and closed her eyes. No doubt Ollie would begin the whole discussion again tomorrow morning. Deep down, she figured her friend was jealous. She'd never gone out with a guy for more than a few weeks and Chloe and Mark had been together for almost a year. He was the only boyfriend she'd ever had. They'd actually known each other for years, often bumping into each other at the clinic. Chloe had always secretly fancied him. He had the same dark-red hair as his dad but he was much taller and had an amazing smile that showed off almost perfect white teeth. And those beautiful blue eyes – she sighed, hugged the duvet to her and remembered the warmth of his body against hers. She hadn't lied to Ollie. They hadn't actually 'done it', though she'd been tempted. With the tight rein her dad kept on her, it was the best opportunity they'd had yet. But at the last moment, Mark had paused and looked deep into her eyes.

'Are you sure this is what you want?' he'd asked softly.

And Chloe, though disappointed, realised that he must really love her because it was fairly obvious how excited he was. But, he was willing to wait. God, she loved him! And she was glad they hadn't 'done it'. When it did happen it should be something special, not a quick, furtive romp in his mum's car. No, Chloe dreamed, it should happen somewhere beautiful and special. Because their love was special and she knew she would never love anyone the way she loved Mark.

Ollie lay staring into the darkness, her mind still too active for sleep. She thought of the dreamy look on Chloe's face when she talked about Mark. The girl had it bad and she didn't even know if he was any good in bed yet! Ollie thought Chloe was nuts tying herself down to one guy when they hadn't even finished school yet.

'We've got so much living to do!' she'd say. 'There's so many guys out there just waiting to be jilted by us!'

To Ollie's eternal exasperation, Chloe would just laugh. That knowing laugh that meant 'you don't know what it's like to be in love'. Well, Ollie didn't want to know! She was too young to limit herself to one guy. Chloe was a bit straight-laced like that. She was good fun after a few drinks but she just laughed at any of the guys who came on to her.

'You're putting them off,' Ollie would say crossly. 'They think you're a tease.'

'That's their problem,' Chloe would say carelessly. 'I'm just being friendly.'

Ollie would make a face. Didn't the girl realise that when she smiled at a bloke, he thought all his birthdays had come together? She didn't seem to have a clue how gorgeous she was. She was one of those sickening girls that would look good in a sack. Some nights she'd turn up in jeans and a sweatshirt while Ollie had spent hours tarting herself up and donning the skimpiest clothes her mother would let her out of the house in. But Chloe didn't even have to comb her hair to attract the guys. They were like moths to a flame. It would totally piss Ollie off if wasn't for the fact that Chloe was her best friend in the world. She snuggled down under the covers and wondered, sleepily, if the guy she'd snogged tonight would call her tomorrow like he'd promised. 'Probably,' she murmured with a smug smile and closed her eyes.

Chapter Six

Friday, 2nd June, 2000

'Theo, we have to talk.' Toni rehearsed the words, keeping her voice level. It was important that she remain calm. She got upset too easily and Theo loved it when she did. He would give her that cold, pitying smile and tell her they would discuss the matter calmly when she had gotten over her little tantrum. It drove Toni nuts. But it wasn't going to happen tonight.

She'd been waiting three hours to talk to him. He had told her he'd be late but she'd stayed up anyway. She'd made up her mind to talk to him and she wasn't going to put it off any longer. Things had deteriorated speedily and Toni wondered if Chloe had noticed that when the three of them were together, Theo directed all his conversation at her. When there was only the two of them conversation was clipped and confined to the banal. The rest of the time, Theo ignored her.

She was dying for a drink but was afraid that if she started she wouldn't stop. She paced up and down the large dining-room, its gloominess reflecting her mood.

Theo always insisted on dining in here. When he was out, Toni and Chloe ate in the kitchen. Or on a nice day, they'd take their meal out on to the patio or into the conservatory. But for Theo, dinner had to be served in the dining-room. It wouldn't be so bad if he'd allow her to re-decorate it in brighter colours. But he'd vetoed that immediately.

'You have a rather individual style, dear,' he'd said drily. 'Don't inflict it on the rest of us.'

At the time, Toni had thought he was reluctant to change things because of Marianna and that he was worried it would upset Chloe. She didn't mention it again realising that Theo and Chloe probably needed time to get used to a new woman in their home.

Toni laughed now at her own stupidity. Theo hadn't been remotely sensitive about his first wife. And he didn't show much consideration for his daughter either. There was no doubt he loved her, but in a very detached sort of way. And, Toni realised, it was the same with her. She was no more than a possession to him, one that had turned out to be a disappointment.

She jumped when she heard the front door slam and the unmistakable sound of his steps in the hall. He went straight out to the kitchen and she could imagine him removing his covered plate from the fridge and pouring himself a large glass of water. Moments later he appeared in the doorway, tray in hand. 'What are you doing up?'

For a brief moment, Toni thought she saw a flicker of pleasure in his eyes, but then the impassive mask was back in place. She felt a wave of sadness engulf her. She watched him settle himself at the table and pour half a glass of the burgundy she'd opened. He hadn't even bothered to say hello.

'We need to talk,' she said taking the seat at the opposite end of the table. It still didn't sound right despite her rehearsal.

'What about?' Theo ate the chicken salad that Alice had prepared lovingly before she went home. It was always salad when Theo was late. He wouldn't eat anything heavier after nine o'clock. Toni had teased him about it when they were newly-weds and often tried to tempt him with Chinese takeaway or fish and chips. But even then he would give her a tight-lipped, tolerant smile and refuse.

Toni sat watching him now, her hands clasped tightly in her lap. When her family and friends had tried to persuade her not to marry this man, she'd told them that age didn't matter. But it did. Theo treated her like a child. One to be occasionally indulged spoiled and punished when she disappointed. But from that first day in the clinic's reception, she'd behaved like a star-struck teenager, totally in awe of this great man. And he had never deserved the pedestal she'd put him on.

She realised he was waiting for an answer, a bored look on his face.

'This isn't working out, Theo,' she said clearly.

He continued to fork salad delicately into his mouth. 'What isn't?'

She watched him sadly. 'Our marriage. And I think it's time we admitted it.'

'Well, don't let me stop you.' He shot her an amused glance.

'Theo! I'm serious!'

He put down his fork and lifted his glass to his lips before replying. 'I realise that, Toni. What do you propose we do?'

Toni stared at him. It was as if she'd just suggested they buy a new car. 'I want a divorce.'

Theo threw back his head and laughed.

Toni looked up, startled. She'd prepared herself for a number of reactions but she hadn't expected this. 'You think this funny?'

Theo wiped the corners of his mouth on his napkin. 'Well, yes, I do actually.'

'May I ask why?'

'I just can't believe you've even asked!' His expression darkened and his eyes were cold and hard. 'I won't give you a divorce, Toni. Not now, not ever.'

'Theo, please. We must talk.'

'I've nothing to say. If you want to leave, then leave. You *do* realise we'd have to be separated for years before you actually *got* your little piece of paper, don't you?'

She met and held the cold blue gaze. 'There's no rush and I don't want to do anything until Chloe has finished her Leaving Cert.'

'How very noble of you,' he sneered. 'You know she's going to hate you for this?'

Toni dug her nails into her palms. 'She's an intelligent girl. I'm sure she's sensed that there's something wrong. She'll understand.'

'You think so, do you?' Theo stared oddly at her. 'It was hard when she lost her mother. But she was young enough to get over it. But you came into her life when she was at a very vulnerable age. And now it's "Thank you

70

very much. It's been nice – but I've had enough of being a stepmother."'

'That's not fair! I love Chloe, I'd never desert her –'

'No, just me,' he flung back angrily.

She said nothing. It would be easy to reel off all the reasons why he'd driven her to this, but it would get her nowhere.

'Hell, you just don't give a damn how much you hurt me, do you?'

Toni looked at him in astonishment. If she were an innocent bystander, she'd be feeling sorry for Theo right now, convinced that he was the injured party. The man should be on the stage. 'This wasn't an easy decision, Theo. I didn't make it lightly. Now, can we just sort things out between us? Decide what has to be done? I don't want lawyers turning this into a sordid mess.'

He turned around to look at her. 'You've already talked to one, haven't you?'

'I just made a few enquiries.'

He moved closer, his face just inches away from hers, his eyes hard and angry. 'You scheming little bitch! I suppose the two of you were trying to figure out how much you could squeeze out of me! Playing "let's stitch up the surgeon!"'

Toni forced herself to stand her ground. 'No, of course not. I'm not interested in your money!'

Theo smiled down at her and placed a gentle kiss just under her earlobe. 'That's good to hear, darling, because you won't get a penny out of me.'

Toni jumped as he strode from the room slamming the door hard behind him. Well, at least he hadn't hit her.

Mind you, it might be easier if she had some bruises to show people. But Theodore French was much too controlled for that. And why use your fists if you could do a much better job with your tongue?

She carried her glass and the wine bottle out to the conservatory. It was nearly eleven and she had an early start tomorrow but she knew that a night's sleep was unlikely. She'd just ended her marriage, for God's sake. She'd actually told Theo it was over. After all the years of living with his sarcastic comments and jibes, she had finally ended it.

She still had a vivid memory of the first time he'd humiliated her in public. They were having dinner with Francis and Dorothy Price. Francis was a heart surgeon at Sylvester's and one of the few people Theo looked up to. Conversation, as usual, had centred on the hospital and Toni had been phasing in and out of it when out of the blue Theo asked Dorothy what she thought of his wife's outfit. Toni had been wearing a simple white shift dress with shoestring straps. Before she could answer, he'd continued, 'Bit young for you, my darling. You should get Dorothy to bring you shopping.'

Toni had stared at him. She wasn't thin-skinned but his comment had hurt.

Dorothy, who'd been listening to Theo's barbs all evening and was heartily sick of them, gave him a cool look before smiling kindly at Toni. 'Actually I think she looks beautiful. If I had a body like that, I'd show it off too.'

Toni had been surprised at this unexpected ally and smiled gratefully at the older woman. Then had begun the only real friendship Toni was to develop with any of Theo's set. Dorothy Price – 'call me Dotty' – was quick-witted, charming and funny and Toni was always playing around with table arrangements so they could sit together at the many boring functions they had to attend. Francis Price was actually quite a nice man. Probably because he was nearly a decade older than the others, above their political wrangles and close to retirement.

'He used to be just as driven as Theo,' Dorothy had confided. 'With an ego the size of a small planet! But he's mellowed with the years, bless him. I quite enjoy his company now. We can actually talk about things other than that damned hospital!'

Toni had only been married to Theo a year when Dorothy had imparted this snippet of information and it had made her feel slightly sick. Probably because Dorothy's description of her marriage sounded so horribly familiar.

Dorothy had smiled brightly when she saw the look on Toni's face. 'It will be different for you, dear. You're young and clever. You'll keep him young too. Just don't let him turn you into something you're not.'

Toni gazed up at the stars as she remembered Dorothy's words and wondered if Theo had succeeded in doing exactly that. She was only thirty-three but apart from her nights out with Jade she lived the life of a nun. And that reminded her of the other problem with her marriage. Their love life, or lack of it rather. On the rare occasions they did make love there was none of the closeness that Toni craved. Theo didn't believe in snuggling up together or indulging in pillow talk.

Foreplay was predictable and mechanical and Theo's technique often left Toni feeling as if she'd been attacked by the lord of the manner rather than made love to by her husband.

Leaving the empty glass and bottle in the kitchen she went upstairs. She moved silently past Chloe's room, glanced briefly across at Theo's door and carried on into her own little sanctuary. She hadn't been in Theo's room in months, though thankfully Chloe probably wouldn't realise that.

They had always had separate bedrooms. Toni had been completely shocked at first but Theo pointed out that it made more sense given the size of the house and the odd hours he worked. After a while, Toni got to quite like it. It was quite exciting each time her door would open softly and Theo would slip into bed beside her. It was almost like he was a forbidden lover – very Mills & Boon! It took a while for her to realise that he was always the one in control. He decided if and when they made love while she would just lie there wondering and waiting like an expectant and hopeful mistress.

Maybe that was the point, she mused as she undressed. Maybe he considered himself still married to Marianna and she had always been The Other Woman. It was a pity that wasn't the case. Then she would be able to just walk away and not have to worry about separation or divorce. She laughed bitterly to herself as she thought of Theo's conviction that there was another man involved. If she managed to get herself out of this mess, she just might go and join a convent! Life would be a lot simpler.

Chapter Seven

Tuesday, 6th June, 2000

Jade sat in the restaurant, a glass of water in front of her, and waited for Toni. She'd suggested they meet here rather than the pub because Toni was often late and it wasn't easy to sit in a bar for long without buying a drink. But in The China World restaurant she could sit reading the menu undisturbed until her friend eventually turned up. Then dinner and a bottle of house red would cost the grand total of sixteen quid each and Jade would save money by walking home – it only took twenty minutes. Toni thought she did it for the exercise. That was a laugh! She'd always hated any form of exercise but thankfully Toni didn't seem to remember that.

It amazed her that Toni never asked her why she always wanted to eat in the same restaurant – set dinner menu, £9.95 – but then being married to Theo, she was probably just glad to get the opportunity to eat some ethnic food. Mustard on his steak was about as adventurous as Theo got. The waitress passed the table again and flashed her a friendly smile. We're probably their best customers, Jade thought, chuckling to herself. Over thirty quid a week – sometimes nearer to forty when Toni insisted on buying an after-dinner drink. Jade double-checked her purse. Twenty-three pounds and some loose change. She'd have about eight quid to see her through the rest of the week if she was careful. It would mean she'd be walking everywhere but she was used to that. And living in Cabra she was near to the Clinic and to town. There was no doubt life would be a lot easier financially if she didn't meet Toni so often. But if she gave their dinners up she knew she'd completely lose the plot. Sitting alone in that bed-sit night after night was heavy going. There was nothing to do but go over her past and wonder if she should have handled things differently. If she had, would she be still living in her nice house? If they'd had a child, would Aidan have been more resilient?

'Jade! Sorry I'm late – or are you early?'

'You're late as usual,' Jade laughed.

Toni settled herself in the seat opposite. 'Well, you looked like you were deep in thought. Who were you mentally assassinating?'

'Perky of course,' Jade said smoothly.

Toni smiled her thanks as the waitress handed her the menu. She didn't really need to read it. She knew it off by heart. 'But Robert hasn't done anything – lately.'

'Pity,' Jade murmured. 'I was so sure he and Vicky were on the fiddle.'

'Me too, but we were both wrong.'

When Toni and Jade had carried out the second stocktake their results were exactly the same as Vicky's. Even worse, when Toni had gone back to check her figures again it transpired that Sandra had made a typing error. Vicky had got a lot of mileage out of that one. Sandra had been miserable for days.

'I still don't trust either of them,' Jade was saying now. 'But let's not talk about them. They'll only put me off my food.'

Toni closed the menu. 'The usual?'

'Why not?'

The waitress approached and Toni gave the order. 'Two spring rolls, one chicken curry, one kung po prawn, both with fried rice and a bottle of the house red. And this is on me,' Toni added when the waitress had left.

'No, Toni –'

'Yes, it is,' Toni insisted. 'I've had you working some ridiculous hours lately and doing all sorts of things that are way beyond your job spec. I owe you one.'

Jade smiled broadly. 'Okay, then, thanks.' This would mean that she'd be sixteen quid richer this week. She'd be able to treat herself to a takeaway some evening, maybe even buy another bottle of vodka . . .

'No problem.'

'So how are things?'

'You don't want to know.'

Jade frowned at the dark shadows under Toni's eyes. 'Try me.'

Toni waited for the waitress to pour their wine and took a drink before replying. 'Last Friday I told Theo that I wanted a divorce.'

Jade's eyes widened. 'I didn't know that things were that bad.'

'They're not, really. He doesn't beat me or anything

77

like that.' She gave a small, nervous laugh. 'And he's not seeing anyone else. It's just –'

'There's nothing there any more?' Jade suggested.

'There hasn't been for a long time,' Toni admitted. 'I tried to ignore it – I mean no marriage is perfect – but it's just wearing me out. There used to be good times and a few bad times. Now it seems that it's all bad times. I can't remember the last time we made love.'

'You're not sleeping together?'

Toni laughed. 'Oh, we've never done that!'

'Sorry?' Jade looked puzzled.

'Slept together,' Toni explained. 'We've always had separate bedrooms.'

'Weird.'

'I can see that now. But when Theo suggested it I thought he was being very thoughtful. He has a lot of early starts and if he is feeling stressed he goes out driving at night.'

Jade looked at her in disbelief. 'Driving?'

Toni shrugged. 'He says it relaxes him. Usually it's the night before a particularly difficult operation.'

'Well, I suppose we all have our own ways of dealing with stress but separate bedrooms?'

'I thought – when we first got married – that it was for Chloe's sake. She was only eleven after all and seeing another woman in her mother's bedroom might have freaked her out.'

'But you don't believe that now?'

Toni laughed bitterly. 'Theo isn't that thoughtful or sensitive.'

'So has he agreed? To the divorce, I mean.'

'No chance.'

Jade patted her hand. 'That's probably just a knee-jerk reaction. He'll come round.'

'I'm not so sure. But I don't understand why he'd want to stay with me. We haven't been happy for a long time and now that he knows that I want to go, why would he want me to stay?'

'Maybe he doesn't think it's that bad,' Jade suggested.

'But we can barely exchange two words without it turning into an argument.'

Jade laughed bitterly. 'Isn't that what marriage is all about?'

'God, I bloody hope not! What a depressing thought. No, you're wrong. Look at Daniel. He's got a very happy marriage.'

'True,' Jade acknowledged. 'Anyone else?'

Toni made a face.

'So how did you leave it?'

'He said he would never agree to a divorce, that I could leave if I wanted to but he would never give me a penny. I can't believe he thinks that I'm just after his money.'

Their starters arrived and Jade tucked in hungrily. 'You should just leave. The sooner you separate the better.'

Toni shook her head miserably. 'I can't do that to Chloe. Not while she's doing her exams. When they're over, then I'll go.'

'How do you think she'll take the news?'

'Theo says she'll hate me but I don't believe that. It might take a bit of time but I hope she'll get used to the idea.'

'Well, I'm sorry it's come to this, but I think you're doing the right thing.'

'I always believed in the 'till death us do part' bit,' Toni said with a sad smile. 'But I was never the kind of wife Theo wanted and if I'm honest I just married an image.'

Jade cringed at the brutal honesty.

Toni shrugged. 'You warned me I was making a mistake. I just wish I'd listened.'

'I get no satisfaction in being right, I can assure you,' Jade retorted. 'All sorts of strange couples make it work. I was hoping you would be one of them.'

'Why did you and Aidan break up, Jade?' Toni asked suddenly. 'You seemed the perfect couple.'

'Just like you and Ian,' Jade shot back.

'Sorry?' Toni stared at her, a mixture of hurt and surprise in her eyes. Jade hadn't mentioned Ian's name in years. Why bring him up now?

Jade sighed. 'I'm sorry, Toni. That was below the belt. I don't know why I brought it up.'

'That's okay,' Toni said faintly and pushed her food around her plate.

'So what are you going to do now?'

'I wish I knew. Theo's acting as if nothing has happened. No, that's not really true. He's barely talking to me. I just hope Chloe doesn't notice.'

'Have you talked to a solicitor?'

Toni shrugged vaguely. 'I just made some enquiries.'

Jade rummaged in her bag for a pen. 'Here, ring this guy.' She scribbled a name on a napkin and handed it to Toni. 'He looked after my sister's divorce. He was good and not too pricey either.'

Toni looked at it doubtfully. 'I don't know.'

'You need to know your rights. Trust me, Toni. I've seen what Karen went through.'

'How come you haven't divorced Aidan?' Toni asked suddenly.

'I . . . we . . . never got round to it,' she finished lamely.

'Maybe you'll get back together.'

'No, that's not going to happen.'

Toni looked at the closed expression on Jade's face. 'What did he do that was so bad?'

'Look, I don't want to talk about it, okay?' Jade's voice was cold and hostile.

'But I'm telling you *my* problems –'

'You volunteered the information,' Jade pointed out in her usual direct manner.

Toni nodded. 'Yes, you're right. Sorry.'

Jade's smile was impersonal. 'No problem. Where the hell are those main courses? I'm starving.'

Chapter Eight

Thursday, 8th June, 2000

'Okay, Mam. I've fed the dogs and watered the plants. Is there anything else you want me to do?'

'No, Sandra. You sit down and eat your dinner. You must be tired after your day's work.' Valerie was glad she was going into the MS Care Centre in a couple of weeks. It would give Sandra a much-needed break.

Sandra dropped a kiss on her mother's hair. 'I'm fine, Mam. You concentrate on getting over this attack.'

'I'm not sure I will this time,' Valerie Tomkins said in a rare moment of disillusionment.

'You will. You always do.'

Valerie watched her daughter worriedly as she served up their food. Sandra always refused to talk about the possibility of her not recovering from an attack. So Valerie would have to do her best to get better. Follow the bloody diet, take her starflower oil capsules – she had been taking evening primrose oil, but apparently these were even better. Not that Valerie could see any evidence of this.

'Now, eat up.' Sandra set the poached chicken and steamed vegetables in front of her.

Valerie stared at her plate dejectedly. 'I'd prefer steak and chips.'

'Now, Mam,' Sandra said. She poured two glasses of water and they started to eat.

'Will you be all right while I'm in the care centre?' Valerie asked, as she picked clumsily at her food.

'Of course I will. Do you want me to cut that up for you?'

Valerie shook her head stubbornly and continued to hack at the pieces of chicken.

Sandra pretended not to notice when a pea flew off the table followed closely by a carrot.

'Bugger!' her mother muttered angrily.

'Here. Let me,' Sandra said gently. She cut the chicken into even smaller pieces and mashed the vegetables together. 'There, how's that?'

'It looks like baby food,' Valerie said miserably but obediently took the spoon Sandra offered her. 'Thanks, love.'

'Have you written me a list of what you want in the shops?'

'Yes, if you can read it. There's nothing much.'

'Still,' Sandra rolled her eyes, 'you know what my memory's like!'

Valerie smiled. 'You'd forget your head if it weren't screwed on. But you'd better remember to look after my plants while I'm away.'

'I will, I will,' Sandra promised. Her mother's greenhouse was her pride and joy. Sandra knew she'd have to leave home if she forgot to water the plants and check the temperature every day. She couldn't see the attraction herself. If her mother had grown a few roses or lilies or something, well, that would be different. But no, that was too boring for Valerie Tomkins. She went for the more unusual, tropical plants. Sandra couldn't begin to remember their names.

'And don't you come visiting me every day,' Valerie warned. 'Your Aunty Barbara will be dropping in and no doubt Mrs Byrne will come in to see me. She's very kind and she makes the nicest scones I've ever tasted.'

'You shouldn't be eating scones,' Sandra said mildly. She wasn't sure her mother's diet made a blind bit of difference but she would never say so.

Her mother smiled her wide, beautiful smile. 'A little of what you fancy does you good!'

Sandra started clearing away the plates. 'True.'

'I'll do those.' Valerie pulled her walking frame towards her and stood up slowly.

'You look steadier today,' Sandra remarked.

'Do I, love?'

Sandra washed and Valerie dried and they spoke of the garden, the neighbours, what was on television later and the latest gossip from the clinic.

'Have you got the hang of that computer yet?' Valerie asked.

Sandra made a face. She'd always been terrified of computers. But she was even more nervous of the damn thing since she'd made that mistake on the stock control. She was so thick. Everyone else could use the system no problem. Even that cow, Vicky. But Sandra just couldn't figure it out. And as for that bloody printer! 'I'm getting there,' she said brightly.

'That's good. You've done so well in this job. Much better than in that auctioneer's office.'

'Yes,' Sandra agreed lamely. She'd been let go from her last job after she'd managed to delete the payroll file and, to add fuel to the fire, it turned out she hadn't run the backup program correctly the night before.

'I just don't understand it,' her manager had said, scratching his head. 'No one has ever managed to do that before. It's a secured file.'

Sandra was lucky that he'd been so desperate to be rid of her he'd given her a reference.

'You are happy in the clinic, aren't you?' Valerie asked anxiously.

'Oh, yes, Mam! It's great. Mr Wheeler is lovely and Toni is really nice. And Jade is great. But Vicky – she's an awful bitch.'

'There's always one. What about that surgeon who used to give you a hard time? The one with the head dyed off him?'

Sandra giggled at her mother's description of Robert Perkins. 'I try and keep out of his way. I don't think he likes me. But when he's with the patients – especially the women – he's as nice as pie.'

'There's a surprise,' Valerie said drily.

'And he gets on well with Vicky too,' Sandra added thoughtfully. Strange that. No one else got on that well with Vicky. Mind you, no one liked Mr Perkins much either.

'Well, keep on the right side of him, love,' her mother

advised. 'Don't answer back or give him any reason to fault you.'

'I won't,' Sandra said obediently. 'Now, why don't you go inside and put on the telly? *Emmerdale* will be starting soon. I'll bring in the tea.'

'Thanks, love.' Valerie shuffled slowly into the living-room and settled herself on the sofa. She lifted her legs up and fixed pillows under them and behind her back. It took a long time to get comfortable these days. More than it used to. She'd have a cup of her special tea before she went to bed. That would relax her and dull the pain.

Sandra carried in a tray and put it down on the table next to her mother. 'Here we go. I brought you a Jaffa cake.'

Valerie grinned. 'Oh, is it my birthday?'

'No, but, like you say, a little of what you fancy . . .'

'Speaking of which, why don't you arrange a couple of nights out when I'm away?'

Sandra shrugged, her eyes on the TV screen. 'I'm not bothered.'

Valerie shook her worriedly. 'It's not right. A girl of your age should be out several nights a week, not stuck in with her mother.'

'I'm just as happy here.'

'Seriously, love. You need to have more company your own age. Why don't you give Caroline or Susan a call?'

'We've sort of lost touch,' Sandra mumbled. The last time she'd gone out with her friends, it had been a total disaster.

Caroline, hellbent on getting drunk, had chatted up every guy in the pub and then had wanted to go clubbing. And Susan had sat staring morosely into her drink and confided in Sandra that she was sure her husband was having an affair.

'You're better off single,' Caroline had told Sandra bitterly. 'Just look at me and Suz. Old before our time, we are. Dealing with screaming kids all day and cranky tired husbands at night. If I could live my life over again I'd never get married!'

Susan had sniffled into her drink. 'I would. I love Dave. I'd do anything for him. But he doesn't find me attractive any more. I know he doesn't.'

Sandra had looked helplessly from one friend to the other. This was not the image of marriage she had cultivated in her little dream world. When – if – Mr Right came along, he would love her and cherish her always. He would remember her birthday and their anniversary and be kind to her mother. He would be attractive, not handsome – Sandra believed in being realistic, even in her dream world – and have a good, sensible job.

'Well, I think that's a mistake,' her mother was saying. 'It's important to hang on to your friends. You never know when you might need them.' She blew her nose and gave her eyes a surreptitious wipe.

Sandra patted her hand. 'Don't worry, Mam. I'll be fine.'

'I'll always worry about you. Aren't you my daughter?' She eased her hand out from under her daughter's with a slight wince.

'Oh, sorry Mam, did I hurt you?'

Valerie smiled. 'No, love. I'm grand.'

Chapter Nine

Tuesday, 13th June, 2000

'Chloe? Chloe? Come on, you'll be late.' Toni walked back into the kitchen and sat down.

'What is it today?' Theo asked without looking up from his newspaper.

'Biology.' Toni buttered a slice of toast.

'She'll sail through it.' Theo's voice was smug.

Toni sighed irritably. It was exactly this kind of comment that had poor Chloe's nerves in shreds.

'Dad thinks I'm going to get straight A's in everything!' she'd said tearfully only the previous night. 'And I'll be lucky if I scrape a pass in geography!'

Toni had slipped a comforting arm around the teenager's shoulders. 'You've worked hard, Chloe. Your dad knows that. He's just trying to encourage you.'

'Well, I wish he wouldn't. Why can't he be like Ollie's parents? They just tell her to do her best. *They* don't expect her to get the highest marks in the class!'

Toni had silently applauded Olivia Coyle's parents.

She didn't agree with all this pressure over examinations and points.

Moments later, Chloe shuffled into the kitchen and sat down and Toni jumped to her feet. 'Will I make you some toast? Or would you prefer cereal?'

'Just coffee.'

Theo lowered the paper and gave her a disapproving look. 'Coffee isn't going to keep you going for three hours. Have some cereal.'

'I don't want any bloody cereal, okay?' Chloe jumped up and ran out of the kitchen.

Theo shrugged and went back to his newspaper. 'Nerves are good.'

Toni glared at him and went after her. Chloe was sitting on the stairs, her head in her hands. 'Are you okay?'

Chloe blew her nose loudly. 'Yeah, fine. I'm just dreading this paper. Is Dad furious?'

Toni shook her head and smiled. 'No, he says nerves are good.'

'They don't feel it,' Chloe muttered. 'I think I'm going to throw up.'

'Come on. Have some toast. It will make you feel better.'

'No, if I go back in there he'll start preaching again.'

'Then I'll bring it up. You go and look over your notes.'

'Thanks, Toni.' Chloe dragged herself upstairs and Toni went back into the kitchen.

Theo threw her a scathing look. 'There's no need to mollycoddle the girl. She's going to have to get used to taking exams. The Leaving Certificate is a piece of cake.

Wait till she starts medicine.' He stood up, drained his coffee cup and tucked the newspaper under his arm. After collecting his keys, he ran up to see Chloe.

'Good luck, darling. You'll do fine.'

'Thanks, Dad.' She smiled shakily at him.

He blew her a kiss, ignored Toni, who had just walked in behind him with a tray, and was gone.

Toni, hoping Chloe hadn't noticed the snub, grinned at her stepdaughter. 'There, you see? He never even mentioned an A!'

'Let's see if he's as light-hearted when the results come in,' Chloe said darkly.

'You're not really worried, are you?'

'No. I know I'll probably do okay. I just don't know if I can live up to his expectations.'

Toni sat down on the bed and took Chloe's hands in hers. 'Now you listen to me. Your dad will be proud of you no matter what your results are like. He might nag you a bit, but it's for your own good. He just wants the world for you. Every dad does.' Toni hoped she sounded convincing. The truth was that she was sure Theo would take it as a personal affront if Chloe didn't get enough points to get into medicine. In fact he'd probably be quite upset if his daughter wasn't in the top 5% of her class!

Chloe's face relaxed. 'Yeah, you're right, Toni. Sorry. I'm a bit hyper this morning.'

Toni patted Chloe's hand and stood up. 'I'd better get my act together or I'll be late.' She went into the bathroom and turned on the shower. She felt guilty about the lies that had just tripped off her tongue, but what else could she say? Chloe needed reassurance.

She showered quickly, hurried into her bedroom and was buttoning her white shirt when Chloe tapped on the door.

'I'm off.'

Toni hugged her. 'Best of luck, love. Drop in when you've finished and let me know how it went. I'll treat you to lunch.'

'I'll probably be too upset to eat,' Chloe moaned.

'Then I'll eat yours too,' Toni said cheerfully. 'Now scoot! You'll be late.'

'Bye.' Chloe ran down the stairs and out the front door.

Toni put on her shoes and tied her damp hair back in a tight ponytail. She grinned at her reflection in the mirror. Theo hated it when she wore her hair like this. The smile faded from her face. There really was nothing to laugh about. She could hardly bear to look at her husband these days and if they brushed against each other in a doorway or their fingers touched across the dinner table, Toni had to stop herself from flinching. It was obvious that Theo wasn't any happier than she was so why didn't he want a divorce? She hadn't turned into a clone of his first wife, which is what he'd really wanted, though Toni knew that she and Marianna were complete opposites.

Marianna had been a primary school teacher but she'd given up work as soon as they'd married. When Theo had pointed out to Toni that there was no need for her to work either, she had told him that the clinic was very important to her. He'd accepted that. At least she'd thought he had.

Marianna had been the perfect mother, housewife and

hostess for Theo. She cooked, baked *and* taught Chloe how to play the piano at the tender age of three.

In fact, Toni reflected, the only area where she outperformed Marianna was in the garden. Her cooking was mediocre, she was bored silly by all of Theo's pompous colleagues and their stuffy wives and she was tone deaf. But in the garden she was in her element. It had been an overgrown mess when she'd first married Theo. But in the evenings and at weekends she'd weeded and dug till her hands were callused. Then she'd planted flowers, herbs and some vegetables. Even Alice had been impressed. Theo thought that pruning the odd rose tree or flower arranging would have been more suitable hobbies for a surgeon's wife but when he'd ventured this opinion, Toni had just laughed and kept digging.

In the early days, when Theo had tentatively asked her how she felt about children, she'd assured him that she was content to be stepmother to such a lovely child. This had pleased him. But then again, had it? Toni could never be sure *how* Theo felt about the possibility of being a father again. Any time she'd tried to get him to open up on the subject he'd made light of it, joking that he was probably better qualified to be a grandfather than a father. She was happy enough to leave it at that – possibly even relieved. She just couldn't imagine having a baby. *Or not Theo's baby*, a little voice said. She jumped up, grabbed her bag and ran down the stairs. There was no point in going down that road.

Alice was letting herself in the back door just as Toni was putting on her jacket.

'Oh, good morning, Toni. I thought you'd be gone by now.' The tone was disapproving.

'Yes, I am running a bit late. I was talking to Chloe. She's worried about her exam this morning.' Toni wondered why she was explaining herself to this woman who barely talked to her the rest of the time.

'She'll do fine,' Alice said firmly. 'She has her father's brains and I lit a candle for her on my way in.'

'Oh well, that should do it, then.' Toni grinned.

Alice looked up sharply.

'Got to go. See you later,' Toni smiled back innocently and escaped out the back door. Over an hour later, she swung into the car park just as Daniel was carrying a stack of files up the steps. After locking the car, she ran to hold the door open for him. 'Morning, Daniel. How are you?'

'Thanks, Toni. I'm grand. Lovely morning, isn't it?'

Toni smiled. 'It always is when the exams are on. Poor kids.'

'Biology this morning. Mark's a nervous wreck.' Daniel's eldest was hoping to get enough points to do computer science.

'Chloe's the same.'

'The best days of their lives, eh? Cobblers!' He laughed loudly and strode down the corridor, whistling.

Toni smiled as she went into her own little office. It was a pity Theo wasn't as laid back about the exams as Daniel.

'Morning, Toni.' Sandra came into the room carrying a mug of tea.

'Hi, Sandra. Thanks.' Toni eyed the tea dubiously. As always it would be too strong and too milky. That's the way Sandra liked it, so that's the way she made it for everyone else. Unless Toni managed to sneak into the kitchen without Sandra noticing, she'd be forced to drink the tepid mixture. Either that or the busy Lizzie in the corner would be the unfortunate recipient. Again!

'It's a busy day today. Mr Perkins has eight operations this morning,' Sandra told her.

'Has the first patient arrived yet?'

'Yes, she's in the waiting-room and looks as if she just stepped off the cover of *Cosmo*.'

'Why do they do it?' Toni murmured.

'Asked me for camomile tea, she did,' Sandra continued. 'I ask you! I think some of them think they're in the Mayo Clinic, the airs and graces of them!'

'Has Daniel got a nine o'clock?'

'Yes. It's that little boy with the gammy hand.'

'Jamie Michaels?'

'That's the one, poor little fella.'

Toni had to agree. Jamie was only three but had been a regular visitor since he was six months old when his hand had been crushed in a car accident. This would be his fourth operation but hopefully his last. 'Is he here yet?'

'Daniel just called him.'

Toni looked at her watch and smiled. It was only eight-forty but then Daniel didn't believe in hanging about. 'And is Perky –' she stopped short. Damn Jade for coming up with that bloody nickname! '– is Mr Perkins in?'

'Yes. I just brought him in coffee and the newspapers.'

And that, Toni thought wryly, summed up perfectly the difference between the two men.

Toni's phone rang. 'Hello? Toni Jordan. Jade, hi. Yes, come on up.'

Sandra went to the door. 'I'll leave you to it. Now, you drink your tea before it gets cold.'

Toni was still grinning when Jade Peters knocked on the door and walked in.

'Hi, Jade. I didn't think you were on duty today.'

Jade perched her slim frame on the arm of a chair and rolled her large, green eyes dramatically. 'I wasn't supposed to be. But Ms Harrison has one of her headaches.'

Toni grimaced. Vicky Harrison had more sick days than she had hot dinners. 'I'm beginning to think that girl should be a patient not a nurse.'

'Lord, imagine having to nurse that silly cow? Now, let's have a look at the work roster for next week. I want to make Vicky pay for sticking me with Perky today!'

Sandra finished the letter she was typing, pressed the save button, then the print button and looked expectantly at the printer. It remained stubbornly silent.

'Hi, Sandra, how's it going?' Chloe bend down to look over the receptionist's shoulder. 'You forgot to press "okay".' She hit the button and the printer sprang into action.

Sandra smiled gratefully. 'Thanks, love. I'm so useless. I can never get the silly thing to work.'

'You're not useless,' Chloe told her, irritably. Then she added more kindly. 'Some people are just more technically minded than others.'

'Well, never mind about me. How did you get on in your exam?'

Chloe shrugged. 'Okay, I think.'

'I'm sure you'll pass with flying colours. You're bound to with such a clever father.'

Chloe scowled angrily. 'What the hell has that got to do with anything?'

96

Sandra's cheeks reddened. 'Well, it's just that . . . all I meant was . . .'

'Is Toni free?' Chloe cut her off impatiently.

'Yes, love. You go on in. Do you want me to get you some tea or coffee? Or what about a nice cool drink . . .'

Chloe looked shamefaced. Fighting with Sandra was like pulling the wings off a fly. 'No, thanks, Sandra. I'm sorry for biting your head off. I'm a bit stressed at the moment.'

'Of course you are. Isn't it natural? I always hated doing exams. A nervous wreck I was.'

Chloe moved quickly in the direction of her stepmother's office. 'Thanks, Sandra. I'll go on in then. Seeya later.'

Toni was just finishing a call when Chloe walked in. She looked at her watch in astonishment. 'Lord, I'd no idea it was so late! So come on. Tell me. How did it go?'

Chloe's face lit up. 'Brilliant, Toni, but if you tell Dad that, I'll deny everything!'

Toni smiled. *No chance of that.* 'Oh, I am glad.'

Chloe paced up and down the tiny room too excited to sit down. 'It was incredible. Everything I revised in the last couple of weeks seemed to be on the paper. It was a miracle!'

'Well, Alice *did* light a candle for you,' Toni informed her.

'Did she? The old pet! So where are we going for lunch? I'm starving!'

Toni picked up her bag and stood up. 'How about the Indian restaurant. I fancy some chicken tikka masala.'

'Yum!'

The two walked across reception, said goodbye to

Sandra and emerged into brilliant sunshine. Toni paused to put on her sunglasses.

Chloe laughed. 'Now you look like one of your patients! Did you ever see anything like that waiting-room? There are three women in there wearing shades *and* coats! In this weather!'

'People are very self-conscious about plastic surgery,' Toni said in her professional voice. 'Now, will we drive or walk?'

'Oh, let's walk. I've been stuck in a dark hall all morning – I could do with some air.'

'I'm not sure you'll get any here,' Toni said drily as they reached the road and the fumes of a passing bus overpowered them. They walked quickly and within ten minutes a smiling waiter had opened the door for them and led them to a table by the window.

Chloe sat down and opened her menu. 'How about a drinky to celebrate?' she said hopefully.

'Nice try, kiddo, but I'm working and you have to go home and study for tomorrow's exam.'

Chloe groaned. 'You're no fun.'

'I know. But I promise I'll make it up to you when the exams are over. We'll do something really special.'

'Who's we?' Chloe asked quietly.

Toni looked up in surprise. 'You, me and your dad of course.'

'Then I think I'll take a rain check.'

Toni put down her menu and stared at her. 'Chloe! Why?'

Chloe fidgeted with a strand of hair. 'Oh, come on, Toni. It would hardly be a fun night out, now would it?'

Toni looked steadily at her stepdaughter. 'I don't know why you say that. I'm sure we'd have a great time.'

'Please, Toni! Don't lie to me. I know there's something wrong between you and Dad.'

Toni's heart skipped a beat. It would be a disaster to let the girl know how bad things actually were. She had to keep up a front until the exams were over. She smiled apologetically at Chloe. 'It's nothing for you to worry about.'

'Stop treating me like a kid, Toni. Tell me.' Her eyes were dark with worry.

Toni hesitated for only a second. 'There's nothing to tell, Chloe. We had a silly argument. A storm in a teacup that's all forgotten.'

'What was it about?'

Toni looked at her with raised eyebrows. 'Mind your own business! You don't tell me about your love life, do you?'

Chloe grinned. 'So it was a lovers' tiff?'

Toni rolled her eyes. 'You could say that. Now, let's order. Then we can discuss where we'll have this big celebration.'

Chloe's face relaxed visibly.

'Well, if you're sure.'

'I'm sure.'

'Okay, then. Can Ollie come? It would be really nice. She's my best friend and . . .'

Toni nodded and smiled as Chloe chattered on excitedly, and wondered how and when she was going to explain to the girl that she was divorcing her father.

Chapter Ten

Thursday, 15th June, 2000

'You can't be serious?' Toni stared at her husband, immaculate in his black dress suit.

'Of course I am. You must come tonight, Toni. I'm speaking at this dinner.'

'Tell them I'm sick,' Toni said dismissively and went back to her book. She had no intention of spending the evening pretending to be a loving and devoted wife in front of Theo's yes-men.

'Don't be such a bitch, Toni. This was arranged months ago. You're expected.'

She put down her book and stood up to face him. 'Tough.'

Theo held her gaze, his eyes cruel. 'If you don't come, I'll tell Chloe, right now, that you're walking out on us.'

Toni's eyes flickered hesitantly between him and the door. Chloe had geography tomorrow – her worst subject – and had been closeted in her room since she'd got in from school. She was pale, exhausted and looked totally miserable. 'You wouldn't . . .'

'Oh but I would, my darling,' he said silkily.

Toni looked into his eyes and knew he wasn't bluffing. She pushed past him and went upstairs to dress.

'Do hurry, *darling*,' Theo called after. 'We don't want to be late.'

Chloe wandered in as Toni was applying her makeup. 'You going out?' She flopped onto the bed and watched.

'Unfortunately.'

Chloe laughed. 'Let me guess. A spectacular night out of fine wines, good food and lively conversation with Dublin's finest?'

Toni grinned. 'They're not quite the words I'd have used.'

'Will Dotty Price be there?' Chloe had met the woman a number of times and liked her just as much as Toni did. Dotty was unimpressed with status and rank and more interested in people. There weren't many of the hospital bunch you could say that about!

Toni was frowning worriedly. 'I'm not sure. She was due to go in for some tests.'

'To Sylvester's?'

Toni laughed. 'Lord, no! Dotty wouldn't let that lot anywhere near her! She was going into the Mater Private.' She sighed guiltily. 'I really should have visited her or at least called.'

'I'm sure she's fine. If she's not there tonight someone is bound to know how she's doing.'

'Yes.' Toni stood up and slipped her dress over her head.

Chloe's eyes widened and she let out a low whistle. 'You're wearing that?'

102

'What's wrong with it?' Toni said defensively.

'Nothing . . . if you're going to the Oscars!'

Toni studied herself in the mirror. The dress *was* quite dramatic. She'd bought it for the Sylvester's Christmas dinner dance and then chickened out of wearing it at the last minute. But it seemed perfect for tonight's performance. Flame red, it shimmered with her every move, the material clinging seductively to her body. The high cowl neck looked demure, until she turned to reveal the deep plunge at the back. That would show Theo not to blackmail her!

'The men are going to get cricks in their necks trying to see your bum!' Chloe giggled.

Toni's nerve started to waver. 'Maybe I should change –'

'No way!' Chloe protested. 'It might liven things up a bit. Go on, Toni. Live dangerously!'

Toni met her stepdaughter's mischievous gaze in the mirror and smiled. 'You're right. Now, get me my coat, the long black one.'

'Aren't you going to show Dad your outfit first?' Chloe asked, fetching the coat from the wardrobe.

Toni concentrated on putting in her earrings. 'Eh, no. I think I'll surprise him.'

Theo went to take her arm as they climbed the steps to the Shelbourne ballroom but Toni pulled away, her eyes cold. 'Don't push your luck. I'm only here for Chloe's sake.'

Theo glared back. 'What have I ever done to deserve the way you treat me, Toni? Your behaviour is disgraceful.'

'Well, blackmailing me into accompanying you tonight is a good example,' she retorted as they made their way to the cloakroom.

'You do exaggerate so. I don't know – My God! What the hell are you wearing?'

Toni had taken off her coat and handed it to the girl behind the counter. She looked at him calmly. 'I bought it with your card in Brown Thomas. Don't you like it?'

She started to walk away before he had time to reply, affording him an excellent view of her naked back.

Theo practically threw his coat at the girl and went after her. 'Now, you've gone too far –'

'Dotty!' Toni's voice and expression softened when she saw her friend. The two women embraced warmly, while their husbands shook hands.

'Toni, you look beautiful! Doesn't she look lovely, Francis?'

Francis Price's eyes twinkled appreciatively. 'Charming, my dear. You're a lucky old dog, French.'

Theo grunted. 'Drinks?'

'White wine would be lovely, Theo,' Dotty replied.

'A large Scotch, old boy.' Francis pulled out a cigar and fumbled in his pockets for matches.

'I'll have the same.' Toni turned to talk to her friend.

'A white wine?' Theo asked, his voice steely.

Toni barely glanced at him. 'No, *dear*, a large Scotch. Straight.'

'I'm so glad to see you, Toni,' Dotty said as Theo gave the waiter their order. 'I've already been in to rearrange the place-names.'

'Good woman. Now tell me. How are you? You look well,' Toni lied. She had been quite shocked at how thin and gaunt her friend had become.

'Don't bullshit me, dear, I look terrible,' Dotty said calmly. 'The damn cancer is back.'

Toni instinctively reached out her hand. 'Oh, Dotty, I had no idea! I'm so sorry.'

'I'm going in for some treatment. Apparently they're optimistic.' She gave a small, cynical laugh and turned to accept the wine glass from Theo. 'Thank you, my dear.'

Theo shoved a whisky into his wife's hand and turned to talk to Francis.

Toni hardly noticed, all her attention now focussed on Dotty. 'How long is it since you were first diagnosed?'

'Oh, it must be more than ten years ago now.'

'Treatment has come on in leaps and bounds since then,' Toni said inadequately.

Dotty smiled kindly. 'Of course it has. I'm sure I'll be fine. But let's talk about something more cheerful. How is that lovely stepdaughter of yours?'

Toni happily changed the subject. She had no words of comfort for Dotty. It was clear from the woman's attitude and her changed appearance that the situation was more serious than she was letting on. But Toni knew from experience that you couldn't push someone into talking about it. She made up her mind to invite Dotty out for a quiet lunch.

'Another drink?' Francis hovered over them, waving his empty glass around.

Toni drained her glass. She'd felt like getting drunk before, but she really wanted to now. 'Yes, please.'

'We should go in.' Theo's voice was tight with disapproval, his glass full.

'There's plenty of time! Same again, girls?'

Dotty beamed at her husband. 'Lovely!'

Francis squeezed her arm affectionately and went to

the bar, leaving Theo to fume as the women continued the conversation.

'The exams seem to be going really well for Chloe,' Toni was saying, 'although the poor girl is exhausted.'

'You must throw her a huge party when it's all over,' Dotty told her.

'Time enough for parties when the results come out,' Theo said grimly.

Toni ignored him. 'I thought we'd go out to dinner and bring along some of her friends.'

'Has she a boyfriend?'

Toni's gaze flickered briefly towards Theo before answering. 'I'm not sure,' she replied, her eyes twinkling.

Dotty's eyebrows shot up in mock surprise. 'A good-looking girl like that! She must have!'

'She's not interested in boys,' Theo said coldly.

Dotty slapped his hand playfully and laughed. 'Silly man!'

Toni laughed at the outraged expression on Theo's face. It wasn't often his opinion was questioned and even rarer that anyone had the audacity to call him a 'silly man'! She told Dotty so when they went out to the ladies' to freshen up before dinner.

'Well, he'd be a much nicer person if someone put him in his place more often,' Dotty replied in her usual forthright manner. 'I'm sorry, my dear. But he does behave as if he has a rather large poker stuck up his arse!'

Toni threw back her head and laughed. 'Oh, Dotty, you're a terrible woman!'

Dotty eyed her shrewdly. 'Well, at least I can make you laugh. You don't seem to do as much of that as you used to.'

'I'm fine.' Toni concentrated on applying her lipstick. She would love to be able to confide in Dotty, but now wasn't the time or the place.

'You must fill me in sometime,'

'On what?' Toni asked innocently.

'On why you're dressed purely to shock your husband would be a good starting point.'

The smile faded from Toni's face as she met Dotty's candid gaze in the mirror. 'It's stupid, isn't it?'

'I have no idea, Toni. You tell me.'

Toni opened her mouth to reply, but Dotty put a finger to her lips and nodded towards the stalls. 'But maybe not now. We must have that lunch *very* soon.' She put her arm through Toni's and led her back to the function room.

Toni felt the high her two whiskies had given her ebb away as she and Dotty threaded their way through the room in search of their table. Not a difficult task, she noted miserably when she spied Francis and Theo sitting in front of the small dais at the top of the room.

'Hello, Toni.'

She whirled around to see the owner of that melodious, familiar voice. 'Hello, Ian, how are you?'

'Fine. That's a nice dress you're almost wearing.'

Toni felt her cheeks flame as his eyes roamed over her body.

Ian saw the hurt expression in her eyes. 'I'm sorry, Toni. I didn't mean –'

'Aren't you going to introduce me?' A tiny dark-haired woman appeared at his side and slipped an arm possessively through his.

'Oh, Carla. This is Toni Jordan. Toni, Carla Doyle.'

The two women nodded coolly. Toni had seen Carla with Ian before but they'd never actually come face-to-face before.

'Toni is married to the great Theodore French,' Ian explained in a bitter voice.

Toni smiled tightly. 'And when I'm not working on my needlepoint, I run a clinic.'

Carla's eyes narrowed speculatively. 'You're married to Theo French? I'd love to meet him.'

Toni nodded wearily. Everyone always wanted to meet her esteemed husband. 'Maybe later. I should go. I believe we're under starter's orders. Nice to meet you, Carla. Goodbye, Ian,' she said coolly and walked away with her head held high.

Theo stood up to hold her chair as she approached. She ignored his questioning look and sat down, conscious of the envious glances from the other women at the table. Silly cows! How could they be fooled by his phoney act? *You were,* she reminded herself.

He sat down beside her and she was grateful that he wasn't opposite and she wouldn't have to avoid eye contact all night. Dotty had managed to secure the place to her right and Francis had ordered her another whisky. She toasted him gratefully.

Theo pursed his lips in disapproval. 'Slow down, for Christ's sake,' he said through gritted teeth.

Toni ignored him and drained her glass.

'Good woman,' Francis said delightedly. 'I love a lady who knows how to drink!'

Dotty chuckled at the look on Theo's face. 'He looks as if he's swallowed a wasp!' she whispered in Toni's ear.

Toni giggled. 'I'd better behave myself or I'll be sent to my room when we get home.'

Theo turned his back on them and bestowed a charming smile on the woman to his left.

'Tina, isn't it?' he asked, staring intently into her eyes.

'Tracy,' the girl breathed, 'I'm with Alan Mackey.'

'Of course. Alan's a lucky man.'

Tracy giggled and Toni and Dotty exchanged amused looks.

Tracy's partner turned a shrewd gaze on his boss. 'Evening, Mr French.'

'Alan,' Theo acknowledged him briefly.

'We were just talking about the new laser equipment The Blackrock Clinic have installed,' Alan told him. 'They say it will knock at least an hour off most operations.'

Theo gave him a mocking smile. 'Really, Dr Mackey? And who are *they*?'

Alan flushed. 'Well, the reports in the newspaper . . .'

'Ah, the *newspaper*. Then it must be true!'

Toni frowned as a couple of the women tittered at his put-down but thankfully Tony Chapman, another of Theo's staff came valiantly to Alan's rescue. 'Actually I know a guy working over there and he told me that they're fitting in at least four extra operations a week.'

Theo buttered a slice of brown bread carefully before replying. 'Speed doesn't necessarily spell success, wouldn't you agree, Mr Price?'

Francis let out a booming laugh. 'Ha! True enough, Theo! Too many bloody surgeons are letting the machines take over. It will all end in tears, mark my words.'

The conversation carried on in this vein throughout

the meal and Toni and Dotty talked quietly to each other. Then came the speeches, each one longer than the last.

Toni looked surreptitiously at her watch and wondered how much longer it would be before they could leave. Theo had been droning on for ages and the combination of whisky and wine was catching up on her. She could barely keep her eyes open. The only amusement afforded to her and Dotty was the redhead across the table who kept chattering all the way through Theo's speech in a very loud whisper.

'Who *is* she?' Dotty whispered to Toni.

'Tony Chapman's latest – I can't remember her name. Somehow I don't think she's going to last long.' Toni watched delightedly as Theo's eyes kept flickering down to the woman, his hands clenching the side of the lectern in barely suppressed fury.

He had just finished and was resuming his seat to polite applause when the redhead said quite clearly. 'Isn't Toni the image of Catherine Zeta Jones with her hair done like that? You know the one who's married that old guy? What's his name, Douglas?'

There was a stunned silence at the table and her partner looked nervously at his boss. Dotty hooted with laughter. 'You know, you're right. I never noticed it before! Isn't that funny? And they've got so much in common too.'

Toni smiled sweetly and kicked Dotty's ankle under the table. She glanced at Theo from under her lashes, curious as to how he was taking all of this, but Theo was looking at his watch.

'Catherine who?' he asked and a collective sigh of relief went around the table.

110

Chapter Eleven

Friday, 23rd June, 2000

'Can I help you?' Sandra looked curiously at the man wandering around reception. He was quite attractive in a serious, reserved sort of way, although he was very thin and his clothes had seen better days. He definitely didn't look like a client of Mr. Perkins.

Maybe he was an odd-job man looking for work.

He approached the desk hesitantly. 'Good morning. Is Jade Peters about?'

Sandra was surprised at the cultured, gentle voice.

'I'll just check. Your name please, sir?'

'Just say it's a friend.' He looked around nervously.

Sandra watched him from under her lashes as she dialled Jade's extension. Toni picked up. 'Oh, Toni, did I dial the wrong number? I was looking for Jade.'

'No, Sandra, you got the right number, I was just passing. I think Jade's in theatre.'

'Oh, right, okay. Thanks, Toni.' Sandra hung up and smiled apologetically at the man.

'I'm afraid she's not available –'

'Please, I have to see her. It's really important. I'll wait all day if I have to.'

Sandra was alarmed at the urgency and determination in his voice. She glanced nervously at the phone and wondered, if she rang for help, would it get there before the man got around the desk. 'I'm sorry, sir, but Jade is in theatre.'

Aidan leaned across the desk and stared intently into Sandra's face.

'Now look, Miss. I don't want to cause any trouble. I just want to talk to my wife.'

Sandra's eyes widened in astonishment. This dishevelled, broken man was Jade Peters's husband?

'Tell her I won't take up much of her time but I'm not leaving until I see her.'

Sandra hurried around the desk and put a calming hand on his arm. 'Come with me,' she said quietly and led him into the kitchen. 'If you'll just wait in here I'll see what I can do. But, if she's in surgery, Mr Peters, I can't interrupt her. You'll have to come back.'

'I told you, I'll wait.' Aidan sat down at the table, his face stubborn.

Sandra sighed and backed out of the kitchen, closing the door firmly behind her. It was unlikely that anyone would stumble upon him in there. Daniel would be in theatre, Mr Perkins and Vicky weren't in today and Mary, the new nursing assistant, hadn't come on duty yet. She hurried upstairs and peered in the door of Recovery. Jade was just wheeling the patient in. Sandra tapped urgently at the door.

Jade stripped off her gloves and mask, dumped them

in the basket and came over to the door. 'What is it, Sandra?'

'You have a visitor, Jade,' Sandra whispered.

Jade frowned. 'A visitor?'

'Yes. I've put him in the kitchen.'

Jade looked up sharply. 'Him?'

Sandra nodded dumbly.

Jade looked over her shoulder at the patient. 'Can you stay here for a few minutes, Sandra? Mary should be in soon but if you've any problems come and get me.'

Sandra watched her leave and wondered why she hadn't told Jade that the visitor was her husband. She looked nervously at the woman on the trolley. 'Please come in soon, Mary, please,' she prayed.

Jade ran down the stairs, along the corridor and stopped short outside the kitchen. It had to be Aidan. She pushed the door open.

'Hiya, love.'

Jade ignored his greeting, came into the room and shut the door. 'What are you doing here, Aidan?'

'I needed to see you.'

'Well, you've seen me. Now go.'

'Jade, don't be like that.' Aidan looked like a dog that had been kicked by his beloved master.

Jade sighed. 'What is it, Aidan? More money?'

He looked even more hurt. 'No, nothing like that. I have some news.'

'Oh?' Jade said tiredly and wondered what trouble he was in now.

'It's my mother.'

'Is she sick?' Jade was immediately concerned. She'd

113

always got on very well with Barbara Peters and had agreed readily when Aidan asked her to hide the real reason they had separated. It would have broken her heart.

Aidan leaned forward on the table and put his head in his hands. 'She's dead, Jade. She died this morning.'

'Oh, God, I'm so sorry, love!' Jade dropped to her knees and pulled him into her arms.

Aidan held her tightly and silent sobs racked his body.

When he eventually relaxed his hold, she sat back on her heels and handed him a tissue. She watched sadly as he dabbed at his red-rimmed eyes. 'What are the arrangements?'

He shrugged. 'I'm not sure. I've left it all to Ann.'

Jade nodded. Aidan's younger sister was more than capable of organising everything. And she'd probably prefer it that way. She checked her watch. 'Look, I'm off duty soon. Why don't you go over to the café on the corner and I'll meet you there?'

Aidan brightened slightly. 'Really?'

'Of course.' She escorted him back down the corridor and out into reception. 'Now, you go on and get yourself a strong cup of tea. I'll be as quick as I can.'

Aidan smiled gratefully and left. Jade took a deep breath and hurried back up to the recovery room. 'Sorry about that, Sandra,' she said briskly.

'No problem,' Sandra smiled, happy to be relieved of her duty. 'Is everything okay?'

'Fine,' Jade said shortly without looking at her.

'Good, see you later then.'

Jade watched the door close behind the receptionist. Strange, she was sure Sandra would be dying of curiosity about her mysterious visitor. It wasn't like her to be discreet. Jade's thoughts were interrupted by a low moan coming from her patient.

'You're okay, Pamela. It's all over now.' She checked the woman's blood pressure, updated the chart and buzzed Mary who wheeled the patient off to a private room for the night. Then she went to her office, checked her messages, grabbed her bag and ran downstairs. On her way she put her head into Toni's office.

'I'm heading off, Toni. Everything okay?' Her voice was light but her eyes were sharp. Sandra had probably been spreading the word by now.

Toni looked up absently from her work. 'Yeah, fine. See you tomorrow.'

Jade relaxed. Toni obviously knew nothing. 'Okay. I'm on the bleep if Mary needs me, but I think it will be a quiet evening.'

'Don't worry. Daniel's working late anyway. Are you going out?'

'No!' Jade knew she'd overreacted. Toni was only making conversation. She smiled apologetically. 'No. Just looking forward to a quiet night in front of the telly.'

'Sounds good. Seeya.'

'Bye, Toni.' Jade crossed reception to the main door – there was no sign of Sandra – and hurried across to the tiny café.

'Cup of tea, love?' Aidan stood as she walked in.

'No, coffee please.' She nodded at the waitress who was smiling curiously at her. God, maybe this hadn't been the best venue to choose. Tongues would wag. Everyone from the clinic popped in here at some time or another. Well, except Perky. He wouldn't be seen dead in a place like this!

Stop bloody worrying, she chided herself. Sandra will have told everyone by tomorrow anyway. She concentrated her attention on her husband and ignored the curious waitress hovering nearby. 'Tell me what happened.'

'She went up to bed at nine. Ann brought her a cup of tea and toast this morning.' He shrugged. 'And she was dead.'

'Oh, poor Ann. What a terrible shock! How is she?'

Aidan looked down at his cup. 'I don't really know.'

Jade stared at him. 'You mean you haven't been over there yet?'

He shook his head.

'Oh, Aidan, you have to! You're her brother!'

'Exactly!' he hissed back. 'And look at me? Hardly a credit to the family now, am I?'

Jade stared silently at him, taking in the frayed cuffs of his shirt, the stains on his jumper and the unshaven face. 'Come on. We're going to get you cleaned up and then we're going over there.'

'We?'

'Of course,' she said briskly. 'I want to pay my respects too. Come on.' She swallowed the last of her coffee and stood up. 'We'll go to Henry Street first and get you some clothes.'

'But I can't afford –'

'Don't worry. I'll pay for them.'

Aidan followed her obediently to the door. Jade glanced nervously up at the clinic windows as they walked past. What would Toni think if she saw them together? But that was the least of her problems at the moment. Her priority was to make Aidan look presentable as cheaply as possible.

Within minutes they were in Dunnes Stores and after leading Aidan to the menswear department she stood back and watched as he wandered through the racks of clothes. Finally, when she realised that a) he didn't know where to begin and b) he didn't care, she took over. 'Here, let me have a look.' She breezed up and down the aisles examining the merchandise with a practised eye. Within minutes she'd selected a pair of black chinos, a white shirt, a black tie and some black shoes. 'I'm afraid I can't run to a jacket,' she said apologetically.

'Don't worry. I still have my leather jacket. That will do fine.'

'You always loved that jacket.'

Aidan grinned suddenly. 'Well, you spent enough on it. Why wouldn't I?'

Jade felt herself responding to the tenderness in his eyes. *No, no, no. There's no going back, Jade. Nothing's changed. You're just feeling sorry for him.* She turned her back on him and went off to pay for his new wardrobe. Twenty minutes later and a lot poorer than she had expected they made their way up north King Street towards Jade's flat. 'I'm afraid you'll have to make do with me trimming your hair,' she told him as they turned into her street.

'That would be great, Jade. Thanks.'

As they climbed the steps of number 67, Jade prayed that Patsy Stewart would be sleeping it off in front of the TV, though the way her luck was going today, that was unlikely.

'Just be as quiet as you can and if the old trout appears leave the talking to me,' she instructed. She put her key in the door. Aidan followed her silently into the dark, narrow hall.

'I hope you're not thinking of moving him in here.' Patsy appeared beside them before they'd even got the door shut. 'That room's only a single, you know.' She looked suspiciously at the bags Aidan was carrying.

'Tell me about it,' Jade muttered before turning to smile politely at her landlady. 'He's just visiting, Mrs Stewart. He'll be gone in half an hour.'

'Oh, now you know me, love. Very broadminded, I am. Always willing to bend the rules. Especially for my friends. It's just that another body would add to me costs –'

'Like I say, Mrs Stewart. He's not stopping.'

'If you say so.' Patsy shuffled off back down the hall.

'Pleasant woman,' Aidan said drily when they were in the safety of Jade's room.

She laughed. 'Oh, yeah, salt of the earth. Okay, here's a towel, soap and shampoo. The bathroom is the last door at the end of the hall.'

Aidan threw the towel over his shoulder and opened the door. 'Listen, Jade, thanks for all this.'

'Forget it. Just hurry up before the old biddy realises that you're using the facilities.'

Aidan nodded and shut the door quietly behind him, giving Jade a moment to sit down and think. Not necessarily a good idea at the moment. What had she got herself into? On the other hand, what else could she have done? He was *still* her husband and his mother *had* just died. She was the only one he could turn to. At least now he would look reasonably presentable at the funeral – damn, they'd need to get flowers! Jade thought miserably about her dwindling cash.

Aidan arrived back ten minutes later wearing her towel wrapped around his waist. The hairs on his chest glistened with drops of water. Jade quickly averted her eyes. It had been a long time since she'd seen her husband without any clothes on and it didn't help that this room was so tiny and claustrophobic. 'I'll go down and phone a florist while you get dressed.' She took care to slip past him without touching.

'Flowers. I'd forgotten.' Aidan looked crestfallen.

'Don't worry. I hadn't.' She smiled kindly and escaped into the hall. Taking a deep breath and putting her husband's naked body firmly out of her mind, Jade ran down to the public phone by the door and picked up the Golden Pages. She thought of the two hundred pounds in her post office account – all her savings. A decent wreath would set her back at least forty quid. And Aidan would need some money to get him through the next few days – 'One thing at a time,' she muttered as she dialled the number of the nearest florist.

Two hours later, Ann Peters opened the door and threw her arms around her big brother. 'Oh, Aidan, thank God you're here! I'm so glad to see you.'

Jade stood in the porch and watched as Aidan rocked his sister in his arms. She hoped fervently that he didn't intend to disappear out of Ann's life again. Nine years younger than her brother, Ann had been a surprise baby – but a very welcome one. Mother, father and son had all doted on the little girl and when Leo Peters died suddenly eleven years later, Aidan had become even more important in Ann's life. But from what Jade had been able to piece

119

together from this afternoon's conversations, Aidan hadn't been near Ann or his mother in over a year.

Aidan finally pulled back from his sister, concerned eyes searching her face. 'Are you okay?'

Ann nodded bravely. 'I am now you're here. And you, Jade?' She turned to hug her sister-in-law.

'Hello, Ann. I'm so very sorry about your mum.'

'Thanks. She was very fond of you, you know. She was really upset when you and Aidan split up.'

Jade nodded dumbly. *What the hell could she say to that?*

'Let's go inside. I'll get us all a drink. I'd offer you tea but the stuff is coming out my ears.'

'I'd prefer a drink,' Aidan assured her.

'Me too,' Jade said fervently, following them inside. She never thought she'd set foot in this house again but it looked as if her life had caught up on her. She'd been a fool to ever think she could just walk away.

Chapter Twelve

Saturday, 24th June, 2000

'To Chloe and Olivia.' Theo lifted his glass and smiled proudly at his daughter.

Toni raised her glass of champagne. 'Chloe and Olivia.'

Chloe grinned back at them. 'Thanks Dad, thanks Toni. And thank you so much for this.' She fingered the silver ring on the third finger of her right hand.

Toni looked pointedly at Theo who ignored her. It had been her idea to buy Chloe a present.

'Shouldn't we wait for the results first?' he had said drily when Toni suggested a night out to celebrate the end of Chloe's exams.

'This isn't about grades and points, Theo,' Toni said reproachfully. 'It's to congratulate her on getting through a difficult time and to wish her success in her new life.'

'Right.' Theo hadn't been impressed. But now he smiled and nodded benignly at his daughter as if it had all been his idea.

Toni quelled the irritation that was always near the

surface these days. 'So what now?' she asked the two girls.

Ollie drank her wine greedily. 'Now we relax, laze and have a good summer.'

'That doesn't sound very productive,' Theo remarked as he looked around impatiently for a waiter. They'd been here almost fifteen minutes and no one had come to take their order.

Ollie snorted in disgust. 'Won't we spend the rest of our lives being productive?'

Toni grinned. 'You're quite right, Ollie. You enjoy yourself while you're young.'

Theo scowled at her before addressing his daughter. 'What do you think about that, Chloe?'

Chloe took a deep breath before replying. 'I'd like to work this summer.'

Theo's face lit up with approval. 'Excellent idea! What did you have in mind? I could probably get you a job in the hospital. Maybe as a nurse's assistant. That would be good work experience.'

Chloe glanced nervously at Toni. 'I thought grape-picking.'

Theo's smile disappeared. 'Over my dead body.'

'Dad!'

'Theo!' Toni glared at him.

Theo ignored his wife and looked coldly at his daughter. 'I haven't forked out a fortune on your education so you can gad about the French countryside picking grapes!'

'We were thinking of Tuscany actually,' Chloe said casually.

'Worse again. Bloody Italians can't keep their hands to

themselves. Anyway, who exactly is "we?" Are you going, Ollie?'

'No way! That's too much like hard work for me.'

Theo waved away the waiter who'd finally approached to take their order. 'So who are these friends, Chloe?'

'No one you know, Dad,' Chloe lied.

'Look, let's discuss this later,' Toni intervened when she saw the nervous expression on Chloe's face. Why did she get the feeling there was a boy at the bottom of all this? 'This is supposed to be a celebration and I'm starving.'

Chloe shot her a grateful look. 'Me too.'

'There's nothing to discuss, Chloe. You're not going.' Theo beckoned the confused waiter. 'What's the fish of the day?' he asked, ignoring Chloe's mutinous look.

Toni smiled reassuringly across the table. A smile that said: 'Leave it for now. I'll help if I can.'

Chloe sighed but nodded her acknowledgement and buried her head in the menu.

Ollie ordered crab claws to start and fillet steak to follow. 'Do you have any chips?'

The waiter eyed her disdainfully. 'No, but we have new potatoes and a selection of vegetables.'

'I'd prefer chips,' Ollie said obstinately.

Toni laughed. 'I quite fancy a few chips myself.'

'Me too,' Chloe agreed.

'Maybe you could do something for us?' Toni gave the morose waiter her most charming smile.

He sighed heavily as if she'd asked him to serve the chips in newspaper. 'I'll see what Chef says.'

'And a large bottle of sparkling water, please,' Theo asked.

'And some more of this,' Chloe held up her glass. 'It's lovely'.

'Two glasses of champagne are more than enough at your age, young lady,' Theo said, his voice loaded with disapproval.

Ollie giggled. 'You should see her after a few lagers.'

Chloe laughed weakly and kicked her friend under the table. 'She's just kidding, Dad.'

'I certainly hope so.'

'Are you planning on going away this summer, Ollie?' Toni changed the subject.

'Oh, I'll probably head off on one of these cheap last-minute deals down to Ibiza or Majorca.'

'You could get a job in a bar and stay for the whole summer,' Chloe suggested.

'Cool! I never thought of that.'

'I thought you weren't interested in work,' Theo said drily.

'Oh, well now that wouldn't be *real* work, Mr French.' Ollie's eyes twinkled mischievously. 'Think of all the men I'd meet if I was working in a bar.'

'I doubt your parents would approve.' Theo's face was even grimmer than his voice.

'Ollie's winding you up, Dad,' Chloe said with a beseeching look at her outspoken friend.

Ollie winked back.

Toni bit her lip. Maybe bringing Ollie with them tonight hadn't been the best idea in the world. Theo would probably forbid Chloe to ever see her again for fear Ollie would lead his little girl astray.

'Still,' Ollie carried on as their starters arrived, 'I might

124

come to Tuscany with you after all, Chloe. Think about all the free wine we'd get!'

Toni smothered a laugh, Chloe buried her head in her starter and Theo glowered at Ollie.

'Great food, Mr French. Thanks for inviting me.'

'You're welcome.' He bit viciously into a chunk of melon.

'How are the chicken wings?' Toni asked her stepdaughter.

'Fine,' Chloe mumbled.

Toni sighed. Poor Chloe. *And poor me.* For this was yet another row that Chloe would want to involve her in. But that wasn't going to happen. It was time to tell her the truth. And time to move out. She had put a deposit on an apartment in Clontarf. It was a bit pricey because it had two bedrooms, but Toni wanted to have a place where Chloe could stay over. That's of course if she wanted to *and* if she was still talking to Toni following the separation.

'Is there something wrong with your food?' Theo's enquiry was stiffly polite as he looked at her untouched smoked salmon in front of her.

'No, it's fine, thank you,' Toni said equally politely and started to eat. *Thank God this is nearly over. I can't handle this charade any more. I can't continue to live like this. I have to get away. I'm sorry, Chloe, I'm so sorry. But you'll fly the nest soon. And I'll always be here for you if you need me. Always.* She took a gulp of wine and swallowed her tears with it. But no one had noticed. Theo had gone back to ignoring her. Chloe was deep in her own thoughts. And Ollie was eating heartily, apparently oblivious of any undercurrents.

Chloe chewed her food mechanically and planned all sorts of horrible deaths for her friend. Her dad was annoyed enough about the Tuscany trip without Ollie winding him up. And he didn't even know *whom* she was going with yet! She wished she were with Mark right now. In some cheap café eating tasteless pizza rather than sitting in this stiff, fancy restaurant. It was all so bloody pretentious. The kind of place where the staff looked down on customers who ordered the house wine or didn't pronounce things correctly. As for the menu! Rack of lamb *au jus*. Why didn't they just call it gravy? That's what it was! And of course, Chloe sighed resignedly, the place had brought out the demon in Ollie. She'd looked wide-eyed at the pompous waiter and asked him lots of dumb questions. Her dad had looked at her as if she had two heads. Chloe could imagine his comments later: 'Hasn't she ever *had* champagne before?' Ollie had stuck her finger in her glass and marvelled at all the bubbles. And: 'She didn't *really* think the finger bowl was soup, did she?'

Until Chloe had smacked her briskly across the knuckles, Ollie had been pulling the dish towards her and looking around for a spoon.

Chloe usually enjoyed her friend's sense of humour but it was a bit much making fun of her dad when he was the one paying.

'How's work going, Mr French?' Ollie was asking now, ignoring the warning look from her friend.

Theo looked slightly taken aback. 'Fine, Olivia, thank you.'

'Good, good. It must be very interesting.'

126

'Well, yes it is, my dear. I didn't realise you were interested in medicine.'

'Oh, I'm not. It's just the blood and gore that appeal to me,' she replied cheerfully.

The smile faded from Theo's face. 'Really?'

'Oh, yeah. I watch all those medical dramas. You know, *ER, Casualty, A&E.*'

'I can't say I've watched *any* of them.'

'Oh, you should, Mr French!' Ollie told him enthusiastically. 'They've got some really unusual cases. And lots of gunshot wounds. I don't suppose you come across many of them,' she prompted hopefully.

'Not many,' Theo said, relieved to see the main course arriving.

Ollie poked dubiously at the garnish on her steak. 'What's all this stuff?'

'Flat-leafed parsley, Miss,' the waiter said coldly.

'I didn't order that,' Ollie said haughtily, 'and where's the chips?'

'The *pommes frites* are just coming.'

Ollie opened her mouth to protest but shut it again when she saw the murderous look on Chloe's face.

'This is lovely.' Toni smiled around calmly.

Theo nodded. 'Indeed. *Bon appetit*, everyone.'

'Yeah, right,' Ollie said as a tiny dish of thin, limp French fries was placed in front of her.

She offered it to Toni.

'No, that's okay. I'll never be able to eat all of this as it is. You have them.'

'Chloe?' Ollie offered half-heartedly.

'It's okay, Ollie. They're all yours.'

'Cheers, Chlo.' Ollie beamed at her and scraped the fries on to her plate.

Chloe smiled back. She found it hard not to. Ollie was a bitch for stirring things up but she was fun all the same. Tonight would have been intolerable without her. She sneaked a look at her father. He seemed to be getting grimmer by the day and Toni wasn't exactly a bundle of laughs either.

'Have you two booked a holiday yet?' she asked suddenly.

Toni and Theo looked at each other and then both started speaking at the same time.

'It's very busy at the clinic –'

'I'm not sure I'll get the time –'

'Oh guys, that's crazy! You deserve a holiday as much as anyone.'

'And, Mr French, you'd be the first one to tell a patient the importance of relaxation,' Ollie chipped in helpfully.

'Yes, Olivia, that's true. But one doesn't have to go away in order to relax. A good long walk is just as beneficial.'

'Oh, Dad! Really! What about Toni? Don't you think she'd like to be brought somewhere nice?'

'Oh I don't mind,' Toni said quickly. 'I'm just as happy in the garden.'

'Rubbish,' Chloe scoffed. 'You love lounging by a pool with a good book just as much as I do.'

'We'll think about it,' Theo promised in an effort to put an end to the conversation.

'Great! I'll pick up some brochures for you tomorrow. What about the south of France? Or maybe somewhere more exotic.'

'Hawaii would be nice,' Ollie said dreamily.

'Yeah, Hawaii or Barbados. What do you think, Toni?'

'I think you should pick up the brochures, Chloe, and we'll have a look. Theo, could you order some wine please?' Toni begged.

'Certainly.' Theo readily agreed and signalled the waiter.

'Oh goody!' Ollie's eyes lit up.

'A bottle of the '95 Margaux.' He levelled a stern look at Ollie. 'And two cokes please.'

Ollie rolled her eyes at Chloe who just shrugged. It had been a miracle that Dad had allowed them champagne.

'We should be going soon.' Ollie looked at her watch. At least in Peg's nightclub she'd be able to have a beer.

'Yes,' Chloe nodded enthusiastically. Mark would be at the club and it would be a relief to get away from the folks. Chloe felt guilty after all the fuss they'd made over her tonight but they were proving really hard work. There was a definite atmosphere between them. She hadn't noticed it before, what with all her studying and worrying. But now, as she reflected over the last few weeks, she realised things hadn't been right for a long time. It was nothing obvious, nothing she could put her finger on. Just a coolness in the air. She thought of the day in the Indian restaurant when she'd asked Toni about the quarrel she'd overheard. Toni had dismissed it out of hand but now Chloe was beginning to wonder.

'How about some dessert?' her father was saying.

Ollie patted her flat, bare stomach. 'Have to watch the weight, Mr French.'

'I'm full,' Chloe assured him.

The drinks arrived and after a decent interval Chloe announced it was time to go.

Toni hugged her stepdaughter tightly. 'Have a good time.'

'We will. Thanks for dinner, Dad. It was great.'

'Yeah, thanks, Mr French. It was ace.'

'Don't be too late, Chloe,' Theo said gravely. 'And make sure you share a taxi home.'

'We will, Dad. Don't worry. See you. Bye.'

And they were gone and Toni and Theo were left looking at each other over the wine.

'That went well,' Toni said drily.

Theo scowled and said nothing.

Toni sighed. 'Look, Theo, it's time we talked to Chloe.'

Her husband stared moodily into his glass and didn't reply.

'It would be better coming from both of us,' Toni said gently. 'It would be easier for her.'

'Easier for you, you mean,' Theo retorted.

'I only want what's best for Chloe,' Toni said steadily.

'Then don't go.'

Toni shook her head wearily. 'I have to, Theo.'

'Why? Because of *him*?'

Toni looked puzzled. 'Who?'

'You know who. Ian bloody Chase that's who.'

'Have you lost your mind?' she hissed at him. 'I broke up with Ian seven years ago. And I left him for you, in case you'd forgotten.'

'And regretted it ever since,' he shot back.

Toni looked away. 'That's not true.'

'Isn't it? Oh, come on, Toni. I'm not stupid.'

'Yes, you are, Theo, if you think there's something going on between Ian and me. The man hates me.'

'And what about you?' Theo's voice was dangerously soft. 'Do you hate him too, Toni?'

'No, no, I don't. I feel very guilty about the way I treated him and I'm sad that I lost his friendship.'

'Friendship!'

Toni gathered up her bag and jacket. 'Yes, friendship, Theo. And now I've had enough of all this. I'm going home.'

'Oh sit down, Toni, save the melodrama. I'll get the bill.'

Toni sat down obediently and sipped her wine while Theo went up to the desk. There was no point in storming out of the restaurant like an adolescent. She needed to reason with Theo. To get him on-side. It was important – for Chloe's sake – that this separation was as amicable as possible. She wasn't going to let him turn her into the scarlet woman. She would explain things to Chloe and make it clear that there was no third party to blame or resent. Because, as she had told Theo quite honestly, the only third party she would ever care about hated her guts.

Theo came back. 'Right, let's go.'

She followed him to the door and they walked to the car in silence.

* * *

'There's something going on with those two,' Chloe said as she and Ollie hurried down the street towards the club.

'They've had a fight,' Ollie told her. 'It's obvious.'

'But it's not just tonight. They've been getting at each other for ages.'

'Maybe your dad's having a fling.'

'Now why do you say that?' Chloe asked irritably. 'Why couldn't Toni be having a fling?'

'Women don't,' Ollie said wisely. 'It's the men that go astray.'

'Dad wouldn't. Anyway, he's too . . .'

'Old?'

'Yeah.'

'He must be years older than Toni.'

'Yeah,' Chloe said again. 'All the more reason why he'd hardly be knocking around with another woman.'

'Oh, I don't know. You know the way nurses are about doctors. And he's a surgeon. The top man.'

Chloe frowned. It was true that her father was treated like a god in Sylvester's. Could Ollie be right? Could he be seeing someone else?

'Oh, let's forget about your folks,' Ollie said as they joined the queue outside the club. 'Tonight is supposed to be about celebrating, remember?'

Chloe nodded and smiled. 'Yeah, you're right. I wonder if Mark's here yet.'

Ollie sighed. 'I still think it's ridiculous that you're meeting your boyfriend. We'd have a lot more fun if it was just a girls' night out.'

'He's bringing all his mates,' Chloe reminded her.

Ollie brightened. 'Oh yeah. Does that include Justin? You know, the really dark guy? He's gorgeous and I'm sure he fancies me.'

Chloe laughed. 'Who doesn't?'

'So when are you going to tell your folks about Mark?' Ollie asked as they moved nearer the door.

'I don't know.'

'I can't believe they haven't found you out yet. But you're going to have to come clean if you want to go to Italy together. Your dad won't object now that the exams are over, will he?'

'You never know with Dad,' Chloe said gloomily. 'Maybe I'll tell Toni first. She could tell Dad.'

'That's hardly going to help if they're fighting already,' Ollie pointed out. 'He'll probably think she knew about you and Mark all along.'

Chloe sighed. 'Yeah, you're right. I suppose I'd better tell them together.'

'When?'

They reached the door and the bouncer smiled at them and stood aside.

'Soon,' Chloe said, smiling back at him and moving eagerly inside the club. 'Now forget about it for tonight, Ollie. I want to enjoy myself. Oh, look! There's Mark!'

Chapter Thirteen

Monday, 26th June, 2000

Jade looked around the room at all her mother-in-law's friends and wondered how soon she'd be able to slip away. The funeral had been a small one. Many of Mrs Peters's friends and relatives had predeceased her and Aidan's colleagues had disappeared soon after he went out of business. Only a few close friends of Ann attended. Jade sighed resignedly as she saw Aidan's maiden aunt approaching, dragging a reluctant Ann in her wake.

'Here you are, Jade! Lovely to see you, my dear.'

Jade dutifully kissed Margaret Finn's heavily powdered cheek.

'You're looking well, dear. Though much too thin.' Margaret's shrewd eyes scanned Jade's slim figure in the simple black dress, the short auburn bob and the perfectly applied make-up. She might be in her forties, but Jade was still a very attractive woman. 'I was just saying to Ann it's wonderful to see you and Aidan together again.'

'But we're not –' Jade shot an alarmed look at Ann who just shrugged. She was used to her aunt's assumptions.

'A fine man, he is – a credit to his mother,' Margaret continued. 'I never could understand why you left him.'

Jade resisted the temptation to defend herself. That's exactly what the old biddy wanted. That way she'd get the inside story as to what had *really* happened. Margaret had never accepted their story from the start.

'They don't get on any more?' she'd said incredulously to Ann and her mother. 'But they're like two peas in a pod. They'd be lost without each other.'

Jade sized the woman up. She was taller and thinner than her sister and her eyes were sharp. 'Good to see you again,' she said eventually much to Margaret's disappointment. 'Now if you'll excuse me, I think Aidan wants me.' Jade hurried across the room to her husband's side. 'Margaret's trying to grill me. Look as if we have something really important to discuss.'

Aidan, who'd been staring blankly at a family photo, turned to smile at her. 'You're more than a match for old Margaret.'

'I'm not so sure. Look, I think I'll slip away soon.'

Aidan's eyes filled with disappointment. 'Do you have to?'

'I think I should.'

Aidan nodded and patted her hand. 'If that's what you want. You've been a tower of strength. I'm very grateful.'

'Will you stay with Ann again tonight?'

Aidan shrugged. 'I may as well. It's more comfortable than Gerry's sofa.'

Jade stared at him. 'You've been staying at Gerry's?'

Aidan looked shamefaced. 'It was either that or a shelter.'

Jade thought he was being a touch dramatic but this wasn't the time to have a go at him. Gerry Carson, however, was married with three children. And his home, while comfortable, could not afford to house another adult. Especially on the sofa. 'You can't stay there indefinitely. It's not fair to Jean and the kids.'

'I know. She's been really great but I'll have to find something else.'

Jade nodded silently. 'Look I'm going now but I think we should meet up in a few days. Discuss what you're going to do.'

Aidan smiled sadly. 'It's not your problem any more though, Jade, is it?'

'I'll call you. Say goodbye to Ann for me.' She slipped quietly from the room, let herself out of the house and walked slowly down the tree-lined road. What had she let herself in for? She could have said goodbye to Aidan and left it at that. But no, she had to get involved again. 'Who do you think you are, Peters? Mother Teresa?' She turned the corner and strolled down Bulfin Road. As she neared the church she remembered that Sandra also lived in Kilmainham, quite near here, in fact. Maybe she would drop in and say hello.

Jade had been amazed when she'd walked into the clinic the day after Aidan's visit to find that no one seemed to know anything about it. Apart from a grateful smile, she hadn't had an opportunity to thank Sandra for her discretion. Jade checked her watch. It was only three o'clock but Jade knew that Sandra was off work today, preparing for her mother's return from the MS Centre. Without giving herself time to change her mind she turned into the small street where Sandra and Valerie Tomkins lived. As she walked up the path she admired the well-tended garden and wondered how Sandra managed to do a full-time job, look after her mother, do the housework *and* keep the garden looking so lovely. She rang the doorbell and within seconds a rosy-cheeked Sandra, holding a bottle of Pledge and a duster, opened the door.

'Jade! What are you doing here? Is everything okay?'

Jade laughed. 'Everything's fine, Sandra. Sorry to call out of the blue but I was in the neighbourhood, as they say.'

'Great! Come in, come in. I was just going to take a break anyway. I'm dying for a cup of tea.'

Jade followed her into the hall and looked around in admiration. The hall was deceptively large, painted a pretty eggshell green and a richly patterned rug covered the tiled floor. 'Oh, Sandra, this is so pretty!'

Sandra blushed. 'Do you think so?'

'Absolutely! It's so bright and cheery.'

'We like it,' she said modestly. 'I got the idea from an *Ideal Homes* magazine. I thought the colours would cheer the place up.' She led the way into the equally pretty little kitchen with its pine dresser and table and large comfortable armchair by the window. 'That's Mam's,' she explained. 'She loves to look out at the garden and the kitchen chairs are too hard.'

'This house is so beautiful, and tidy too!'

Sandra laughed as she put on a kettle. 'I'm doing a spring-clean because Mam's coming home tomorrow so you're seeing it at its best.'

'Is your mother very house-proud?'

'No, I'm the hygiene freak in this house. Mam's much more interested in her plants. Tea or coffee?' she asked as the kettle boiled.

'I'd love a coffee, Sandra. And would you mind terribly if I had a cigarette?'

Sandra looked at her in surprise. 'Not at all but I thought you'd given up smoking ages ago.'

Sandra made a coffee for Jade and a cup of milky tea for herself. She carried the mugs to the table and then took an ashtray from the dresser. 'If Mam was here she'd probably cadge one off you.'

Jade raised an eyebrow as she lit up and inhaled deeply. 'I didn't know she smoked.'

'Sometimes. She says it helps her relax.'

'Well, whatever works for her.'

' I don't think her neurologist would agree,' Sandra said worriedly.

They sipped their drinks in silence for a moment.

'I wanted to come and thank you,' Jade stubbed out her cigarette in the ashtray.

'Why?' Sandra looked genuinely mystified.

'For not mentioning Aidan's visit to anyone.'

'Ah, that's okay. He seemed a bit upset. Is everything okay?'

Jade sighed. 'His mother died. I've just come from the funeral.'

'Oh, I am sorry, Jade. Was it sudden?'

'Yes, she was a very healthy woman.'

'Is there any other family?'

'Just Ann, his sister. His father died a long time ago.'

139

Sandra stared sadly into her cup. 'They'll need each other now.'

Jade nodded. 'Yes. Yes, I suppose they will.'

'I don't suppose you two –' Sandra said hopefully.

'No, Sandra,' Jade said abruptly and lit another cigarette. It would have been too much to hope that Sandra had become the soul of discretion. But, when Jade looked at her crestfallen expression she immediately felt sorry. There was no badness in Sandra's nosiness. It was just her way. To her, life was one big soap opera. 'Sorry,' she relented.

Sandra smiled, relieved. She hated when Jade's face took on that closed angry look. 'That's okay. I should mind my own business. Mum's always telling me I gossip too much, but honestly, Jade, I'd never tell anyone about Aidan. Or about his mother.'

'Thanks, Sandra. So, tell me, how have you enjoyed having the house to yourself?'

Sandra shrugged. 'I've been a bit bored to be honest. I'm not really any good on my own.' She laughed. 'I have to talk to myself! No, I'll be glad to collect Mam tomorrow.'

'How is she?'

'A lot better, thank God. The rest and the company have done her the world of good. They're so nice in there. And it was wonderful timing too. She was getting a bit depressed because this attack was lasting so long.'

'It's hard to be cheerful all the time. I think she's been very brave.'

Sandra grinned. 'Me too.'

Jade finished her coffee and carried the mug to the

sink. 'My goodness,' she said looking out of the window. 'Your greenhouse is amazing! I half expect David Bellamy to appear!'

Sandra groaned. 'I know what you mean. To be honest I hate the bloody thing but it's Mam's pride and joy – oh no, I forgot to check the thermostat!' She opened the back door. 'Sorry about this, Jade. Won't be a minute.'

'Can I come?'

'Of course, if you're interested. I'm not much of a plant person myself. Now flowers I like, with lots of colour.'

'I just miss anything green,' Jade said sadly as she followed her down the path. 'I don't even have a window-box now.'

Sandra opened the door and after Jade had followed her in closed it immediately again.

Jade stared around her. 'Good lord! It's like being in the botanical gardens!'

Sandra giggled. 'It gives me the creeps. I keep expecting some huge tropical spider to come out and attack me!'

'Do you know what all of these plants are?'

Sandra shook her head. 'No. There are some herbs down that end that Mam makes tea from but apart from that I haven't a clue.' As Sandra adjusted the controls, Jade wandered down to inspect the herbs and started to chuckle as she fingered some of the leaves.

'What is it?' Sandra came up behind her.

Jade sniffed the air appreciatively. 'Your mother has interesting taste in tea.'

'What do you mean?'

Jade's eyes widened. 'Don't you know?'

'Know what?'

'These are cannabis plants, Sandra.'

'No way! Are you kidding me?' Sandra stared at the plants, her eyes like saucers.

Jade smiled. 'Nope. Your mother's manufacturing her own medicine.'

'Oh, dear. What must you think –'

'I think your mother is a woman who's trying to make life a little bit more bearable,' Jade said bluntly. 'Let her get on with it, Sandra. The less said about it the better.'

'Do you think so?' Sandra looked dubiously at the offending plants. 'Maybe I should get rid of them.'

'Don't you dare! Doesn't she deserve some respite from her symptoms?'

'She does seem to sleep much better after she's had some.'

'There you are then. Leave well enough alone.'

'You won't say anything, will you Jade?' Sandra asked as they made their way back to the house.

'Of course not.'

Sandra smiled shyly. 'Thanks. I know Mam would be mortified.'

Privately, Jade didn't think that Mrs Jenkins sounded like the type who'd care – and why should she? 'I'll never breathe a word.'

'I don't think I'll tell her that I know either,' Sandra said thoughtfully.

Jade nodded in approval. 'I think you're right.'

'How about another coffee?'

Jade looked at her watch. She wasn't due back in work until tomorrow and a long, lonely evening stretched out before her. 'I'd love one.'

Sandra smiled delightedly. 'If you're not in a hurry, I could make us some dinner and I think there's a bottle of wine in the press.'

'That's the best offer I've had in a long time,' Jade said truthfully. 'I'd love to stay. But only if you let me help.'

'Brilliant!' Sandra said delightedly. She took two chicken fillets from the freezer and set Jade to preparing some vegetables and the two women chatted easily as they worked. Jade was surprised at how relaxed she felt. She would never previously have considered having dinner with Sandra Tomkins. They had absolutely nothing in common and Sandra's incessant chatter in work got on her nerves. But she was beginning to realise that the chatter was to cover her nervousness and she wasn't remotely as feather-brained as she appeared. She also seemed much more confident in her own home. True, she was technically challenged – Jade could never see her getting the hang of the computer systems in work – but she was a damn good cook and Jade told her so when they sat down to eat.

Sandra blushed. 'Oh, it's nothing special. I quite enjoy cooking and it's been a real challenge coming up with some half-decent menus that fit in with Mam's diet.'

'Well, this is absolutely delicious. Thank you for asking me to stay.' Jade forked the roasted vegetables hungrily into her mouth. She'd been up at all hours this morning making sandwiches with Ann for the funeral reception, but she hadn't been able to eat one. She'd noticed Aidan hadn't touched anything either.

'It's nice to have the company,' Sandra was saying.

'Don't you ever have any friends around? I would have

143

thought you'd be partying while your mother was in the care centre.'

'There's no one to party with. I've lost touch with my old friends, not that I miss them. They were all married and anytime we went out they did nothing but complain about their lives. All I wanted was a bit of fun and all I got was earache.'

'That's terrible,' Jade said sympathetically. 'You'll have to come out with me and Toni one night. We usually have a laugh.'

Sandra lit up. 'Oh, I'd like that.'

Jade visualised Toni throttling her when she heard about this invitation. 'Then I'll organise it,' she said bravely. 'Though not for a while. I'm a bit strapped for cash at the moment.' Jade sipped her wine and wondered what the hell was in it that was loosening her tongue so much.

'I could give you a loan if you like,' Sandra said tentatively.

Jade looked horrified. 'Oh no! Thanks all the same, Sandra. I'm exaggerating, honestly.'

'Well, if you're sure. Now, how about dessert? I think there's some chocolate ice cream in the freezer.'

Chapter Fourteen

Tuesday, 27th June, 2000

Alice leaned across the staircase to dust the Constable that was Mr French's pride and joy. Though why he had to hang it so high up in the hall she would never understand. She could only reach it if she used the long-handled feather duster and balanced on the very tips of her toes. As she completed the job and stepped back she tripped over the can of polish and fell heavily against the wall before falling down the three steps into the hallway.

It was in this position that Toni found her almost two hours later. 'Alice! Oh my God, are you all right?'

Alice lifted her head, the effort making her wince. 'It's my leg. I tripped over the polish. Stupid to leave it on the stairs.'

'Take it easy now. Don't move.' Toni ran her hands expertly over the housekeeper's legs.

Alice gasped in pain when Toni touched her right hip.

'I'm going to call an ambulance.'

Alice looked up in alarm as Toni went to the phone. 'Surely there's no need for that?'

'Yes, ambulance, please,' Toni said into the phone and then covered the mouthpiece with her hand. 'No, Alice, we need to get you checked out. I think you may have broken a bone.'

'Oh, dear. Oh, this is terrible. I'm sorry to be so much trouble.'

Toni smiled kindly. 'Don't be silly, Alice. It was an accident.' She gave the address to the operator and hurried back to try and make Alice more comfortable. 'I'm just so glad I came home early today. How long have you been lying here?'

'I'm not sure.' Alice looked a bit dazed. 'I'd finished peeling the potatoes for dinner and I thought I'd get a bit of dusting done.'

'Never mind.' Toni looked up at the painting that Alice had been trying to clean. 'But do me a favour and leave that one to me from now on.'

Alice looked faintly shocked. 'Oh, but that's my job –'

Toni shook her head firmly. 'Your job is to look after us which you do very well. Don't worry about some old painting.'

Alice privately thought that Mr French wouldn't agree but said nothing.

'I'll go and get a blanket.' Toni patted her hand and ran upstairs. The woman was shivering – probably in shock. She must be in quite a lot of pain too. Toni was pretty sure that her right hip was broken. The best they could hope for was a clean break. But, thought Toni, as she made her way back downstairs with a blanket and pillow, Alice was definitely going to be out of action for a while.

'Do you want me to call anyone for you?' she asked once she'd made Alice more comfortable.

'There's no one to call. My sister is in Wales and there's no point in worrying her.'

'Is there no one else?' Toni felt embarrassed asking. She'd known the woman for more than six years now but knew nothing about her other than that she was a widow.

'No one,' Alice confirmed briefly.

Toni wondered wryly what crisis would have to befall Alice before she opened up and talked to her. Clearly this wasn't serious enough. 'The ambulance should be here any minute,' she said to fill the silence. 'I'll come with you to Sylvester's.'

'Oh, no, thanks all the same but there's no need for that.'

Toni sighed. 'Well, I'll call Theo and get him to meet you there.'

Alice looked horrified. 'No, no! Don't do that! I'm sure I'll be well looked after. But if you could get me my handbag from the kitchen.'

'If you want to give me your house keys I'll pick up some nightgowns and toiletries for you.' Toni volunteered.

Alice's eyes widened. 'They won't keep me in, will they?'

'I'm afraid they probably will, Alice,' Toni said gently. 'But there's nothing to worry about, I promise. I'll get your handbag.'

When she returned, Alice took the bag and rooted for her keys. 'Maybe Chloe could go round and get my things.'

'I'd be glad to –'

Alice shook her head emphatically. 'Thanks all the same but Chloe knows where everything is.'

Toni grimaced. Ungrateful old bag. 'Okay then. If that's what you'd prefer. Chloe should be home soon. I'll drive her round and we'll be up to see you before you know it.'

'There's no need for you to trouble yourself.'

Toni was happy to hear the ambulance pull up outside. 'No trouble at all.'

As the ambulance carted Alice away Toni dialled Theo's number. Of course he wasn't there and she had to deal with the unhelpful Emma. 'This is urgent,' she said tersely. 'Please page him immediately and tell him to ring home.' She hung up unceremoniously on the over-protective secretary. Moments later Theo rang.

'What is it, Toni? Is something wrong with Chloe?'

'No, no, she's fine. It's Alice. She fell down the stairs and I think she may have broken her leg. She's on her way in the ambulance now.'

'And why didn't you go with her, for God's sake?'

'She didn't want me –'

'Where's Chloe?'

'In town. She should be home soon –'

'Oh, for God's sake, Toni, I don't have time for this.'

'All you have to do is drop into Casualty, say hello and put her mind at rest,' Toni said angrily. 'It won't take more than five minutes of your time.'

'I still don't see why you couldn't take care of it.'

'She didn't *want* me, Theo.'

'Yes, well, I suppose I can understand that,' he replied caustically.

Toni ignored the insult. 'Will you call me when you know something?'

'If I've time.' Theo hung up.

Toni put down the phone and stared at the feather duster at her feet. Poor old Alice. After all her devotion and loyalty over the years, Theo saw her as no more than an inconvenience. Thankfully, Chloe would be a lot more supportive.

'Oh, poor Alice! I hope Dad is making sure she's being looked after properly,' Chloe said anxiously as Toni drove them over to Alice's little cottage.

'I'm sure he is,' Toni said with more confidence than she felt.

'She's never been in hospital before. She'll be terrified.'

Toni found it hard to believe that anything would terrify Alice. 'She'll be fine.'

Chloe shook her head worriedly. 'No, Toni, I'm not sure she will. She has almost a phobia about hospitals. She'll hate every second of it.'

Thank God Alice opens up to someone, Toni thought as she parked the car outside Alice's home. 'I'll wait here for you.' Somehow she knew that Alice wouldn't want her in her house. As Chloe hopped out and let herself in the side gate, Toni studied the pretty little cottage. Dainty lace curtains hung in each window, the woodwork and front door were freshly painted a pale shade of blue and the garden was neat and lined with a border of carnations. Toni wondered where the woman found the time to do it all and look after them as well.

Chloe emerged holding a small overnight bag and

locked the gate carefully behind her. She threw the bag into the back seat. 'I'll just nip next door and let Mrs Donnelly know what's happened.'

Toni marvelled at the girl's common sense. It would never have occurred to her to tell the neighbours, whom, it seemed, Chloe knew. Toni had no idea that Chloe had spent any time in Alice's home. She said as much when Chloe was back in the car and they were on their way to the hospital.

'Alice used to bring me over here when Mum was sick,' Chloe explained. 'She said it wasn't healthy for me to spend so much time at home. Mrs Donnelly used to have a little terrier, Sooty, and I'd play with him for hours.'

Toni gave herself a mental rap on the knuckles for all the times she'd maligned Alice Scully. The woman had obviously been there for Chloe when she needed her most.

'I always loved that little house.' A reminiscent smile played around Chloe's lips. 'It was always such a happy, homely place. There was always a smell of baking and fresh flowers – and polish, of course! Alice tried to teach me to make scones but I was useless. I made more of a mess than anything else. But she didn't seem to mind.'

Toni tried to absorb all of this as she prowled the hospital car park in search of a space. It was hard to reconcile the woman Chloe described with the Alice Scully Toni had come to know and hate. She pulled into a spot and Chloe sprang from the car anxiously. 'Do you think she's still in Casualty or will they have moved her to a ward?'

'Let's check Casualty first.'

'Maybe we should drop in on Dad and find out if he knows how bad it is.'

Toni wondered if Theo had even taken the time and trouble to find out. 'I think he's operating this afternoon,' she said vaguely. 'Let's find Alice first.'

They made their way into Casualty and moments later a nurse showed them into a small cubicle. Alice lay on a narrow trolley looking frail and ashen.

'Alice?' Chloe's voice was gentle as she took the woman's hand in hers.

Alice's eyes fluttered open and she smiled. 'Hello, Chloe love. Isn't this a fine pickle I've got myself in?'

'Poor you. Are you in a lot of pain?'

'No, they gave me an injection, but I feel very sleepy.'

'They may have given you a tranquilliser,' Toni said.

Alice looked up surprised. 'Oh, Toni. You shouldn't have come. There was no need.'

'Of course there was,' Chloe said briskly. 'Toni was worried about you. Has Dad been in?'

Alice nodded. 'When I first came in he came down to talk to the doctor. So good of him.'

Chloe smiled. 'He'll make sure they look after you, Alice. Have they told you anything yet?'

'No. They did some x-rays but I haven't heard anything since.'

Chloe looked at Toni.

'I'll go and see if I can find out anything,' Toni said, taking the hint.

As she went in search of a nurse a man hurrying in the opposite direction, his head buried in a file, crashed into her, sending her shoulder bag flying across the corridor.

'Oh, I'm terribly sorry! Toni!'

Toni looked up to find herself staring into Ian Chase's eyes.

'Hello, Ian.'

'I'm terribly sorry,' He picked up her bag. 'Did I hurt you?'

'No, no, I'm fine,' Toni assured him, more flustered by the unexpected meeting than the accident.

They stood looking at each other for a moment and then spoke together.

'I should really –'

'How are –'

They laughed awkwardly.

'You first,' Ian said with a slight bow.

'I was just asking how things are with you.'

'I'm surprised you care after the way I talked to you at the consultants' dinner.'

Toni's eyes twinkled. 'You were no worse than usual.'

Ian laughed 'I suppose I deserve that.'

'What were *you* going to say?' Toni asked curiously.

'I was going to apologise for my behaviour on said night.'

Toni arched an eyebrow. 'And you're not going to now?'

'Yes. Yes, I am. I apologise, Toni. I was both rude and insulting.'

'You were, but I understood.'

'Really?' Ian looked surprised.

Toni looked down, unable to hold his gaze. 'I've done a lot to be ashamed of myself, Ian. And I'm quite sure I owe you several apologies.'

Ian shook his head sadly. 'Oh, Toni, if only –'

'Hello, darling.'

Toni sprang away guiltily as Theo appeared behind Ian.

'Hello, Theo,' Ian said, coolly polite.

'Chase.' Theo barely acknowledged him. 'If you'll excuse us, we have some family business to discuss.'

'Goodbye, Ian,' Toni said faintly as Theo practically frogmarched her away.

'That was very cosy,' he said through gritted teeth as he steered her back towards Alice's cubicle.

'For God's sake, Theo, don't be ridiculous! We were just passing the time of day.'

'I really don't care what you were doing. Let's stick to the business at hand, if that isn't too much to ask.' He paused outside the cubicle and lowered his voice. 'They're going to have to operate on Alice and then she'll probably be laid up for some time. We need to contact a relative. Someone she can go and stay with or that can move in with her.'

'There isn't anyone. Her only sister is in Wales and she's older and not in good health.'

'Then she'll have to go into a convalescent home.'

'I'm not sure –' Toni started but Theo had already thrown back the curtain and was addressing his housekeeper. 'Hello, Alice. How are you feeling?'

'Not too bad, thank you, Mr French. Sorry to be so much trouble.'

'Not at all. Now they're going to take you up to the operating theatre and sort that leg out.'

Alice's eyes widened in alarm and Chloe held her hand

tightly. 'It's okay, Alice. I'm sure you won't feel a thing.' Chloe sent a pleading look to her father.

'No, of course not. It will all be over before you know it.'

A nurse poked her head around the curtain. 'We're ready for Mrs Scully now, Mr French.'

'Very good. See you later then, Alice. Don't worry about a thing.'

Chloe kissed Alice's forehead. 'I'll light a candle for you in the chapel, Alice.'

'Thanks, love.'

'Good luck, Alice,' Toni added.

Alice smiled weakly and was wheeled away.

'Let's go to my office,' Theo said. 'We can make a few phone calls from there.'

'Phone who?' Chloe asked.

'Convalescent homes,' Theo told her leading the way.

'Oh no, Dad! You can't put her into one of those places. She'd hate it!'

'Chloe, the woman is not going to be able to manage alone and she has no relatives or friends to take care of her. There really is no alternative.'

Chloe shook her head miserably. 'She'll never agree.'

'She doesn't have much choice.' Theo nodded absently at Emma, led the way into his office and sat down at his large desk.

'Couldn't we look after her?' Chloe suggested, perching on the windowsill.

Theo looked at her with raised eyebrows. 'I thought you wanted to go to Tuscany?'

Chloe had finally worked up the courage to tell them

about Mark although she'd played down the relationship and said nothing about how long it had been going on. Theo had been dead against them going away together until she explained that they were going as part of a larger group of students. He'd finally agreed to consider it and after letting Chloe sweat for a few days he had eventually said yes.

'That's two weeks away,' she said now.

Theo shook his head impatiently. 'Chloe, Alice is going to be laid up a lot longer than that.' He buzzed Emma and asked her for a list of convalescent homes in the area. 'And bring us some tea,' he added.

Toni saw her plans go out the window. There was nothing she could do. She couldn't let this poor woman go into a home. She'd been too good to Chloe. It meant another few months with Theo but it couldn't be helped. She took a deep breath and looked her husband in the eye. 'Maybe Chloe's right. Alice will only need help getting washed and dressed. When Chloe's in Italy I could probably go in late in the mornings and pop back and check on her every so often.'

Chloe beamed at her. 'And I'm sure Mrs Donnelly would come and visit.'

'Who is Mrs Donnelly?'

'Alice's neighbour,' Chloe explained to her father.

'Why can't she look after her? If she lives next door it's the perfect solution.'

'She's over eighty and she's got arthritis, Dad,' Chloe said impatiently.

'But where would we put her?' Theo asked irritably.

'We could bring a bed down and put it in the back

lounge,' said Toni. 'The room is never used and it would be much more convenient.'

'Toni, you're a genius!' Chloe said delightedly.

Toni tried to smile back but she actually felt closer to tears.

Theo started to relax as he slowly realised the ramifications of Alice's injury. Toni would stay and Chloe would go off to Italy in ignorance of their problems. 'That's very considerate of you, darling. Okay, Chloe, why don't you tell Alice the good news when she gets out of surgery?'

Chloe ran around the desk to kiss her father. 'Thanks, Dad. Alice will be thrilled.' She hugged her stepmother. 'Thanks, Toni.'

Toni returned the hug and closed her eyes to Theo's gloating expression. 'No problem, love.'

Chapter Fifteen

Tuesday, 18th July, 2000

'Profits are down again. I think you may have to re-address the consultation limitations, Daniel.' Toni struggled to suppress a yawn.

'And won't Robert love that,' Daniel said moodily.

'How about changing the time limit to two weeks for the smaller procedures with only one consultation unless a second is requested?'

Daniel pulled on his beard. 'I don't like it. It's open to abuse.'

She sighed. 'I don't think you've much choice. We're losing business to the other Dublin clinics' – just as Theo had said they would – 'and we have no UK appointments for next month. Robert has only two consultations tomorrow and he's taking Friday off because he has no operations.'

'Oh, all right. We'll do as you suggest but only for the minor stuff. Draw up a list so that when we tell Robert the good news there are no misunderstandings.'

Toni nodded, made the note and rubbed her eyes wearily.

'Is looking after your housekeeper proving a bit of a strain? You know you can take a few weeks off if you like. Like you say, it's not as if we're run off our feet.'

Toni shuddered at the thought. Things hadn't been too bad when Chloe was there, but now she had left for Tuscany the atmosphere was a bit strained.

'I couldn't stay at home with her all day, Daniel. I'd throttle the woman! But I might take an extra couple of hours here and there if that's okay? I could make it up in the evenings.'

He shrugged. 'You do what you have to, Toni. As long as the clinic doesn't suffer I don't mind what hours you work.'

She stood up. 'Right. I'd better get going. I have to get the old dragon her lunch.'

'Don't put any arsenic in it. It will show up in the pathology report.'

Toni grinned. 'Thanks for the tip.' She left Daniel's office and went down to reception. 'Sandra, I'm heading off in a minute. I should be back in an hour or so.'

'Okay then, Toni. By the way, I'm really looking forward to our night out.' She smiled shyly at her boss.

Toni smiled brightly. 'Me too.' She collected her bag and car keys and left, wondering what on earth had possessed Jade to invite Sandra to go out with them. She'd been quite annoyed about it. She looked forward to her evenings with Jade but it would be completely different with Sandra tagging along.

'I'm sorry, Toni, but she just seemed so lonely,' Jade had said lamely.

Toni had been surprised at Jade's softness. She didn't

usually listen to sob stories. In fact, she rarely encouraged Sandra to talk at all! And what was Jade doing round at Sandra's house in the first place? It all seemed very odd. Still, a night out – even with Sandra in tow – would be a welcome break from Alice Scully. The ungrateful old bag hardly said two words to her unless she had to. And she positively hated having to accept Toni's help when washing and dressing. Theo didn't get involved in his housekeeper's care at all apart from popping his head around the door occasionally to inquire politely after her health. In fact he was rarely at home since Chloe had left – a fact that Toni was grateful for. The atmosphere when he was there was unbearable.

'Is that you, Toni?'

Toni shut the front door with an irritable sigh. 'Yes, it's me.' *Who else would it be?* She went into the lounge that was now Alice's bedroom. 'How are you?'

'Not too bad.'

'Good.' Toni pasted on a bright smile. 'It's a lovely day today. Why don't I help you into the conservatory and I'll bring you your lunch there?'

Alice looked slightly taken aback. 'Well, if it's not too much trouble . . .'

'Of course not.' Toni put the walking frame in front of Alice and then slipped a strong arm around the woman to lift her.

'Am I too heavy for you?'

'You're as light as a feather.'

Alice gave a small smile and they proceeded slowly out into the hall.

'It's a good job this is such an old house,' Toni

remarked conversationally. 'The wide doorways come in handy in situations like this.'

Alice nodded but said nothing as she concentrated all her efforts on manoeuvring herself forward.

Toni watched in reluctant admiration. The woman was obviously in a lot of pain, but she never said a word. Her only complaints were that Toni wasn't looking after Theo or cooking him proper meals.

Toni blatantly ignored Alice's culinary tips.

'Mr French loves a bit of smoked salmon with that rye bread I get in Tesco's.' Or 'Mr French enjoys a nice bit of hake – the fishmongers in Finglas are the best.'

And so Alice would watch with obvious disapproval when Toni unpacked some frozen foods and TV dinners after her infrequent and unplanned shopping trips on the way home from work.

Toni found it hard enough dealing with Alice's meals. She certainly wasn't going to worry about cooking for an ungrateful husband.

To be fair, Alice's needs were simple. A boiled egg and some toast, soup and brown bread or some cold meat and salad. She was also partial – Chloe had confided – to cod and chips and sometimes Toni would stop off at the local chip shop on her way home. While Alice protested that there was really no need for Toni to go to such trouble, she always ate every morsel with relish.

As Alice finally reached the conservatory, Toni moved ahead of her to plump the cushions on the most comfortable chair. Then she moved the walking frame carefully out of the way and lowered the woman down. Once Alice was settled, Toni carefully raised the injured leg on to a footstool.

Alice sank back and closed her eyes. 'Thank you,' she said breathlessly.

Toni felt a pang of pity. She looked so frail and tired. The short trip from the study had exhausted her. Toni realised that even when the plaster came off it would be a while before Alice was properly mobile again.

'You rest there for a moment. I'll get your lunch.' Toni switched on the radio to the classical channel that Alice liked so much and went on out to the kitchen.

When she carried back in the tray of barbecued chicken and salad that she'd picked up at the local deli, Alice opened her eyes and smiled. 'Aren't you having any?'

Toni looked surprised at the question. 'Yes, it's in the kitchen.'

'Why don't you join me? I'd appreciate the company.'

Toni nearly fell over in shock. 'Oh, right. I'll just get it.'

She carried in her plate and sat down opposite Alice and started to eat in slience.

'I haven't been very fair to you, Toni, have I?' Alice said, cutting her chicken into smaller pieces.

'Sorry?' Toni kept her head down. Alice had invited her to eat with her, used her name and now she *seemed* to be apologising.

'You see, I've always felt very protective of Chloe,' Alice continued, 'and though I approved of Mr French re-marrying –'

'You didn't think it should be to me,' Toni said bluntly.

Alice had the grace to look embarrassed. 'It was nothing personal. It's just that I felt Chloe needed a mother and you were – are – so young. But I was wrong.'

Toni nearly choked on some coleslaw and reached for her glass of water.

Alice seemed amused. 'Are you all right, dear?'

Dear? Toni nodded dumbly.

'You've been a great friend to Chloe, more like a big sister really and she obviously loves you.'

'I love her too.'

'I can see that now. You have brought stability and common sense into her life and been there for her when her father hasn't.' She shook her head sadly. 'He doesn't seem to understand the girl or accept the fact that she's growing up.' Alice felt disloyal discussing Mr French like this but it had to be said. Lying here for the last few weeks she'd had a lot of time to think and, more importantly, to observe. She had also had some very frank conversations with Chloe.

'He thinks she should concentrate on university and a career,' Toni was saying.

'What nonsense! The girl needs to have a bit of fun. I'm so glad she's gone off on this trip. And Mark Wheeler is a lovely young man. He'll take care of her.'

'I agree though I don't think Theo does. He might be happier if Mark wasn't Daniel's son.'

'Ridiculous. At least he knows the boy is from a good family. If he tries to clip her wings she'll fly the first chance she gets,' Alice warned.

Toni nodded soberly. 'I think she might get a place of her own when she turns eighteen.'

'And gets her trust? Yes, you're probably right. You don't think she'd move in with Mark, do you?'

Toni burst out laughing. 'I don't know who'd throw more of a fit. Theo or Daniel!'

Alice smiled. 'And the funny thing is the boy would probably be a better influence on her than that girl Ollie.'

Toni nodded. 'She's a wild one all right.'

Alice sighed. 'I think it's up to you and me to look out for Chloe, Toni. She needs us both.'

Toni looked away. If things went as planned, she would be leaving Theo once Chloe got home and Alice was on her feet again. She wondered if she should take advantage of the moment and confide in Alice.

But Alice was way ahead of her. 'You know, I have a feeling that Chloe might not be the only one thinking of taking flight.'

Toni looked up in alarm. 'What do you mean?'

Alice sighed. 'I'm not blind *or* stupid, Toni. I can see what's going on. Be honest. If I hadn't had that stupid fall you'd be gone by now, wouldn't you?'

Toni's voice was barely a whisper and her eyes were large in her pale, drawn face. 'How did you know?'

'Like I say, I've got to see things from a different perspective since I moved in.'

'I did try to make it work, Alice.'

'I'm sure you did but then Mr French isn't any easy man to live with.'

Toni looked at her, amazed. 'I thought you worshipped the ground he walked on!'

Alice smiled. 'I've known him for a long time and I do admire and respect him but I am aware of his faults. He gave Marianna a tough time too, you know.'

'But, but I thought they had the perfect marriage,' Toni stammered. She couldn't believe her ears. Theo's first marriage hadn't been as perfect as he'd always led her to believe?

'Yes, well it was better for Chloe to believe that,' Alice said matter-of-factly, 'but Marianna was very unhappy for a long time before she got sick.'

'I don't understand. I thought he was disappointed in me because I didn't measure up to *Her*.'

Alice smiled. 'Marianna was a wonderful girl but quite human, I assure you. And she hated entertaining as much as you do.'

Toni shook her head, trying to make sense of it all. 'I wish you'd told me this before. I've been trying to live up to an image all these years that didn't exist!'

'What difference would it have made?' Alice said, almost philosophical.

'Then why tell me now?' Toni said, feeling frustrated and angry at the other woman's calm demeanour as she dropped her bombshell.

'Because I think you should leave him. You've done your best for Chloe. It's time to live your own life.'

Toni took a moment to absorb this. Was the woman serious? 'I didn't think the Catholic Church approved of separation,' she finally retorted.

'It doesn't, but *I* do. The priests don't have an idea what goes on inside a marriage. It's God you'll have to answer to at the end of the day and I don't believe in a vengeful God.'

Toni rested her head back against a cushion, suddenly drained. Alice had managed to impress, amaze, shock and annoy her all in the space of one conversation – probably the first they'd ever had.

'I've said more than enough for now. But I just want

you to know that if you want to talk, I'll be happy to listen. But I'm afraid now I need to have a little nap.'

Toni looked at her tired, strained face and quickly stood up to help her.

'I would like to talk again,' she said carefully after she'd helped Alice back into bed, 'when I've had some time to think. But in the meantime, please keep all of this to yourself.'

Alice looked mournfully around the empty room. 'Who would I tell? The only people I ever see are Mrs Donnelly – and she's as deaf as a post – and Mr French, and he doesn't exactly stay to chat, does he?'

Toni shook her head sadly. 'Thank you. See you later.'

'Goodbye, dear.'

When Toni phoned Dotty that evening, the older woman suggested that she come straight over as Francis was away. Toni jumped at the invitation. She was dying to talk to someone and she wouldn't be able to confide in Jade tomorrow night, what with Sandra coming along. Anyway it was time she went to see Dotty. Their long-planned lunch had never happened because Dotty was kept in hospital longer than expected and when she came out she kept to her bed most days.

'I'm fine, Toni. Don't worry,' she'd assured her friend. 'It's just I'm so bloody tired all of the time.'

But thankfully, when Toni had talked to her earlier, Dotty had sounded like her old self and seemed to be looking forward to their evening together.

'It's like something out of a movie!' Dotty said delightedly as Toni filled her in on events.

Toni smiled but she found it hard to concentrate on

her own situation now that she'd seen Dotty. The woman was wasting away in front of her eyes.

'I must say, I'm not entirely surprised that you're leaving Theo, though I do think you're making a meal of it.'

Toni sighed. She could always rely on Dotty to speak her mind. 'What could I do? Between Chloe's Leaving Certificate and Alice's accident –'

'There are times when you have to think of yourself,' Dotty insisted.

'Oh, really? And do *you* think of yourself at all, Dotty?' Toni said bluntly.

'Of course I do. I'm a completely selfish old woman. All I do is stay in bed all day and watch TV.'

'You're sick,' Toni pointed out sharply.

Dotty shook her head impatiently. 'I'm fine. Don't start to fuss. It's bad enough having Francis fuss over me. It took me ages to persuade him to take a break and visit his brother for a few days. But the truth is, Toni, I need the break as much as he does. He's driving me mad. Eat this, drink that, take this tonic, have a nap – he's treating me like a child!'

'He loves you.'

Dotty's eyes were suspiciously bright. 'I know that, but I have to deal with this in my own way.'

Toni watched sadly as her friend drained her glass. She'd hardly touched any of the chow mein Toni had ordered for them.

'I ate a huge lunch,' she'd explained apologetically, 'but I'll gladly drink your wine!'

Dotty picked up the bottle now and reached over to top up Toni's glass.

'Actually, I wouldn't mind something a bit stronger if you don't mind.'

Dotty laughed. 'I wondered why you didn't bring the car. Well, what will you have? Francis must have every drink under the sun in this cabinet.'

'Just Scotch, please. I'll go and get some ice.' Toni walked quickly from the room. It was too hard to watch Dotty pour the drink with hands that were almost skeletal. Why hadn't Francis called her and told her things were this bad?

'There you go,' Dotty handed her a very large glass of whisky when she came back into the dining-room. 'Let's leave all this and go out into the garden. I hate sitting inside on such a lovely evening.'

Toni followed her outside, trying not to notice Dotty's skinny little ankles in the large, furry slippers.

'So what now?' Dotty asked when they were settled side by side on the large garden swing.

Toni shrugged. 'Oh, I don't know, the woman has thrown me into a complete spin. Why did she decide to talk to me now? After all these years?'

Dotty studied her glass in silence for a moment. 'Because suddenly she's feeling old, vulnerable and dependent. And the person she least expected to has taken control and come to her aid. You've made her think. Her saintly lord and master wanted to put her in a home, for God's sake!'

'She doesn't know that,' Toni pointed out.

'Don't kid yourself. You can bet she knows a lot more than she lets on.'

Toni thought of some of Alice's comments earlier. 'Yes, you're probably right. Poor woman.'

Dotty threw back her head and laughed. 'I never thought I'd hear you say that!'

Toni started to laugh too. 'No. Me neither. Isn't it amazing how quickly things can change?'

Dotty's eyes were sad as she watched the sun sinking into the trees. 'Amazing.'

Chapter Sixteen

Wednesday, 19th July, 2000

'That was lovely.' Sandra smiled at Jade and Toni.

'Yes.' Jade smiled back.

'The chicken was a bit tough,' Toni said moodily.

Jade frowned at her. Toni had hardly spoken throughout the meal and when she did it had been to complain or moan. Okay, she wasn't pleased about Sandra coming along, but she didn't have to make it quite so obvious.

Toni caught Jade's dirty look and looked down, shamefaced. She'd been terrible company and ratty with Sandra and for no real reason. Other than she'd loved to have got Jade on her own. To tell her about Alice and about Dotty. Poor Dotty. Toni felt depressed as she remembered the slight little figure that had waved her off, her other hand gripping tightly to the doorpost for support. 'I'm sorry for being such bad company,' she said finally.

'You're not,' Sandra assured her. 'I'm not always in the mood for chatting myself.'

Toni avoided Jade's eyes. 'Thanks. Anyway, let's have some more wine.'

Sandra looked alarmed.

Jade grinned at her. 'Don't worry, Sandra. I promise we won't bring you home drunk.'

'Your mother would be shocked,' Toni laughed.

'My mother would be delighted,' Sandra said drily. 'She's always nagging me to go out and have a good time.'

'My mother used to nag me to stay in!' Jade rolled her eyes expressively.

Toni laughed. 'I can imagine. I bet you were a right terror as a teenager.'

'I don't know what makes you say that, I'm sure.' Jade pretended offence. 'Anyway, Sandra isn't a teenager.'

'No, it's a long time since I was one of them,' Sandra agreed mournfully.

'So why don't you go out more?' Toni asked.

Sandra shrugged. 'I've nothing in common with the gang I used to hang around with.'

'What about men?' Jade's eyes twinkled.

'What about them?'

Jade winked at Toni. 'I think your mother's right. You should get out more. We need to find you a date.'

Sandra's eyes widened in panic. 'I don't think so . . .'

'Jade's right,' Toni agreed cheerfully. 'There must be someone we know that would be suitable. What about Johnny?'

Jade looked blank. 'Who's Johnny?'

Sandra gasped. 'The guy who delivers the medical supplies? He wouldn't give me a second glance.'

Jade nodded. 'Oh, *him*. Yeah, he's not bad. How old

would you say he is? Thirty, thirty-five? And why wouldn't he give you a second glance? You're attractive and around his own age –'

'I'm sure he has a girlfriend already,' Sandra said hurriedly.

'Ah, so you *do* like him then,' Toni teased.

'He's okay but, like I say, he's seeing someone. Excuse me. I really must go to the loo.'

Jade's eyes were thoughtful as she watched her leave. 'I think our Sandra is a very lonely girl.'

Toni sighed. 'She's not the only one.'

'Oh, yes?'

Toni's smile was twisted. 'I know I'm married, but I feel lonelier in that house than I think I would if I was all on my own.'

Jade's face darkened. 'Don't bet on it.'

'Sorry. That was tactless.'

'Aidan's mother died.' Jade said suddenly. She'd been putting off telling Toni. She should really have told her before the funeral. Toni and Aidan had always been good friends.

'Oh, no! When?'

'A couple of weeks ago.'

Toni looked dumbfounded. 'But why on earth didn't you tell me?'

Jade looked uncomfortable. 'There was a lot to organise and it was a small funeral. I didn't think –'

'No, you didn't!' Toni's eyes flashed angrily but she said no more as Sandra returned to the table.

'Oh, I'm glad I'm not in work in the morning.' Sandra eyed the full wine glass in front of her.

'Have you any plans?' Jade asked politely to cover the angry silence emanating from Toni.

'Mam is spending the day with her sister so I thought I might give the house a good clean. She gets all depressed if I do it when she's there.'

'Because she can't help?' Toni asked gently.

Sandra nodded. 'Though it doesn't stop her trying. And then I get worried and tell her to rest and then she gets annoyed with me.'

'It can't be easy,' Jade said simply.

'Oh, we do okay. What about you, Jade? How are you? You've had a tough time what with Aidan's mother and all.'

Toni's eyes widened in astonishment and Jade looked away. Sandra carried on oblivious, her tongue loosened by the wine. 'You've been great to stand by him the way you have.'

'Indeed you have.' Toni looked at her friend reproachfully. She was furious that Jade hadn't told her about Barbara Peters – Aidan must be disgusted with her for not attending the funeral or at least sending flowers. But she was completely dumbfounded that Jade had confided in Sandra and not in her. It was almost laughable.

Jade sighed. It looked like she would have to explain herself. Toni looked furious and with good reason. 'Aidan came to the clinic to tell me about his mother. Sandra met him then.'

Sandra nodded and sipped her wine happily. 'He was very nice. I'd say you made a lovely couple.'

'They did,' Toni retorted.

Jade's fingers tightened around her glass. 'Please, Toni.

172

Don't do this. I'm sorry I didn't tell you before. It was wrong of me. But it was all so sudden and there was so much to organise.'

'How come you were doing the organising?' Toni said grumpily. 'You're *supposed* to be separated.'

Jade shot her a beseeching look and then glanced at Sandra to see what she was making of all this. But, thankfully, Sandra seemed to have gone into a daze. God bless alcohol.

'He needed me, Toni. And there was Ann to consider.'

Toni nodded. 'Yeah. Sorry. How is Ann?'

'Bearing up quite well, really. Though I think she may still be in shock.'

'How did it happen?'

'Her heart. It was very sudden. She was healthy up until the end.'

Sandra's eyes grew misty. 'It's good that she didn't suffer.'

'I think it's time we got you home,' Toni said gently and signalled for the bill.

'Oh, but I'm enjoying myself,' Sandra protested, wiping her eyes.

'I think Toni is right, Sandra. It's getting late.'

Sandra focused with difficulty on the Swatch on her wrist. 'Oh, I had no idea it was that time! Mam will think I've been kidnapped.' She giggled. 'I'd love to do this again. It's been really nice.'

Jade buried her head in her bag.

'Then we will,' Toni said magnanimously.

'We will?' Jade repeated faintly.

'We will.' Toni smiled and Jade knew she was forgiven.

'Why don't you two share a taxi?' Toni said after they'd paid the bill.

Jade's face fell. 'Oh, eh, no need for that. If we hurry we can catch the last bus. We'd probably be waiting ages for a taxi anyway. What do you say, Sandra?'

'Okay,' Sandra smiled vacantly in her direction.

'You don't mind us leaving you, do you, Toni?'

Toni shook her head. 'Go for it. I'll see you tomorrow."

Jade nodded. 'Yeah.' She bent to give her friend a quick hug.

'Bye, Toni. See you.'

'Bye, Sandra. Safe home.'

Toni drained the last of the wine into her glass. No point in wasting it and sitting here alone was preferable to going home. Though Theo would no doubt already have retired for the night. Unless, of course, he was out on one of his nocturnal drives.

He could never be called a party animal that was for sure! His idea of socialising was having drinks parties that would usually be coming to a close by ten o'clock. Or another favourite of his was Sunday brunch. That way he'd have met his obligations but be rid of everyone by two.

Theo's entertaining was never spontaneous and the guest list was always carefully thought out. Toni had suggested Daniel or Jade or even her parents might come along but he had dismissed the suggestion out of hand.

'Not their sort of thing at all,' he'd said of her parents. Though how would he know what her parents were into, Toni thought bitterly? He'd never taken the trouble to find out. As for inviting anyone other than Robert from the clinic, he'd just laughed. Though it was unlikely that Jade would have accepted anyway. The dislike was entirely mutual. They had never gone out as a foursome the way they had when she was dating Ian.

She sighed as she thought back to the day of Alice's accident and the chance meeting with him. She could remember the feel of his fingers on her face and the wistful look in his eyes. But she must have imagined that. He had a new woman in his life now and they'd been together a while. She'd seen them together at many of the hospital functions and they looked very much a couple. No, she must forget all about Ian Chase and start planning for the future. Maybe she would even have to consider leaving the clinic. She didn't want to and she certainly wouldn't bow to any pressure from Theo but it might make things a lot easier for everyone in the long run. How could she ever get on with her new life if she still had to deal with Theo on a regular basis? She stood up to leave, thanked the waiter and wandered out on to the street. It was the first time she'd been in the city centre at this time of night for quite some time. She normally met Jade in her local Chinese restaurant. Instead of making her way to the taxi rank on Dame Street, she walked around into Grafton Street and headed towards Stephen's Green. She'd pick up a taxi there, after she'd had a breath of fresh air and breathed in the ambience of the vibrant city. It was after eleven but there were still a couple of hardy buskers on the street and she had to step nimbly aside a couple of times to avoid being mowed down by passing rickshaws.

She was standing waiting at the taxi rank for several minutes before she realised that the white BMW that had pulled up across the road was beeping at her. She peered across and gulped as she saw Ian Chase gesturing to her. Talk about timing. She waited for a gap in the traffic and hurried across to the car.

'I thought it was you.' Ian grinned at her. 'Hop in. I'll drop you.'

'There's no need –'

'Oh, come on, Toni! You could be waiting there for ages and it's not as if it's out of my way.'

Toni smiled. Ian still lived in his apartment in Beaumont, just ten minutes' drive from Theo's house. Now why, she mused as she climbed in beside Ian, did she still think of it as Theo's house? It was hers too now. Her home.

'Toni?'

'Oh, sorry, what was that?' Toni busied herself with her seat belt as he pulled back into traffic.

'I was just asking what an old married woman is doing wandering the streets of Dublin on her own at this time of night.'

'Less of the "old" please. I was out with Jade.'

'Oh, how is she?'

'Great. I think.' Toni frowned as she thought back on the tension earlier in the evening.

Ian glanced at her. 'You think?'

'Aidan's mother died a couple of weeks ago.'

'Oh, I'm sorry. Why didn't you let me know?'

Toni grimaced. 'I would have if I'd known. Jade never mentioned it until this evening.'

'You're annoyed with her?'

'Well, of course I am. I should have been there!'

'Yeah, me too. I always liked Aidan. Remember the night in the Indian restaurant on George's Street?'

Toni laughed. 'God, I'd forgotten all about that.'

'He'd been to the dentist that afternoon and the anaesthetic hadn't quite worn off –'

'And he ordered the Vindaloo!' Toni finished for him, laughing.

'Extra hot,' Ian reminded her. 'And then halfway through the meal the anaesthetic started to wear off.'

Toni shook her head as she remembered the sweat standing out on Aidan's red face. 'I've never seen anyone consume so much water.'

Ian chortled. 'I did try to warn him.'

Toni grinned. 'Not too hard, if my memory serves me right,'

Ian sighed. 'We had some good times with those two.'

'Yes.' Toni didn't dare look at him. Sitting so close together in the dark, she could almost feel the electricity crackle between them. She inhaled deeply. He still wore the same cologne. The one she'd first bought him.

'We had a lot of good times.' Ian put his hand on hers.

Toni snatched her hand away. 'Don't.' This was ridiculous! What was Ian playing at? For years he'd treated her like something that had crept out of the woodwork. And now this.

'Don't what?' Ian's voice was soft and caressing.

Toni sighed. 'I think I preferred it when you were horrible to me.'

'Did you?'

'Oh, stop this, Ian. What exactly are you trying to achieve? Have you had a little tiff with Carla and you're looking for something or someone to amuse you?'

Ian's fingers tightened on the steering wheel. 'I was just

making conversation actually. And no, Carla and I haven't had a "tiff". In fact she's probably waiting up for me. She doesn't like going to bed alone.'

Toni closed her eyes and tried to ignore the red-hot jealousy coursing through her.

'No doubt Theo is waiting up for you too.' Ian turned on to Griffith Avenue and pulled up sharply in front of the house.

Toni looked at him sadly. 'Goodnight, Ian. Thanks for the lift.'

Ian looked as if he were about to say something but changed his mind.

'What?' Toni prompted hopefully. She couldn't help it. She didn't want him to go like this. She wanted to grab his hand back.

He just shook his head. 'Nothing. Goodnight, Toni. Take care of yourself.'

Toni nodded dumbly and stumbled out of the car. 'Goodnight,' she said softly as he drove off into the night.

Chapter Seventeen

Wednesday, 19th July, 2000

Jade had insisted on walking Sandra to her bus stop. She was a little unsteady on her feet and Jade felt responsible. But the girl had enjoyed herself and, thankfully, seemed oblivious to the tense atmosphere at the end. Jade plunged her hands deep in her pockets and wandered back in the direction of her flat. It wasn't that far and walking on a beautiful night like tonight was preferable to a stuffy bus. She reflected on the evening as she walked. It had gone very well until Aidan came up. She couldn't really blame Toni for being annoyed. She had thought of inviting her to the funeral but dismissed the idea almost immediately. She didn't need Aidan and Toni getting reminiscent over a few drinks. Who knows what skeletons might have come out of the cupboard? And with the likes of Aidan's aunt around to listen in, it would have been asking for trouble. No, she had done the right thing.

But, on the other hand, Toni *was* her best friend and had trusted her with all the miserable secrets surrounding her marriage. Was she being disloyal not returning the confidence? Jade sighed as she turned into the narrow street that was home. It went against every grain in her body to talk about herself and her problems. And even though Aidan had let her down, she didn't want other people passing judgement on him. She would do anything to protect him from that.

* * *

'Please stay, Aidan. What's the point of us living separately? Two can live as cheaply as one.' Ann smiled brightly at her brother.

Aidan shrugged uncomfortably. 'Like I say, Ann. I'm doing a lot of travelling at the moment. There's a lot of work in Cork.'

'Which is all the more reason for you to sell your place in Dublin.'

Aidan scratched his head. This was getting very complicated. Ann was under the impression that he had a flat on the north side of the city. Probably because that's what he'd told her.

Ann watched him speculatively. She had been convinced that he was living with another woman and that's why he'd stayed away so long. Their mother had made it quite clear that she thought he was mad to have broken up with Jade and he wouldn't have dared bring home a replacement. Still, there had been no girlfriend at the funeral – just Jade. And they had seemed quite comfortable together. So the other woman – if she'd ever existed – seemed to be gone. Ann thought there might be some hope of reconciliation and that was more likely if he was living here at home where she could keep an eye on him.

'I'm a bit nervous on my own,' she said quietly, trying a different tack.

'Oh, love, there's nothing to be nervous about. You have the alarm and Caesar to look after you.' He reached down and fondled the Alsatian's ear.

'Yes, of course. And you have your own life to lead.'

Aidan sighed. Now he felt like a right heel. Maybe he should just give in and stay. Like Jade said, he couldn't sleep on Gerry Carson's sofa indefinitely. And if he lived here, he'd be nearer to his wife. Maybe . . .

'I'll go on up.'

'You're right, Ann. It makes sense for me to move in. I'll get my stuff tomorrow.'

Ann flew across the room and threw her arms around him. 'Oh, thanks, Aidan! I'll feel so much safer with you here. And it won't be as lonely.'

Aidan held her in his arms and stroked her hair. 'No problem, love. You've always got me no matter what happens.'

* * *

Toni undressed and paused before putting on her pyjamas. She studied herself critically in the mirror. Had Ian seen much of a change in her? She had put on a few pounds since he'd last seen her in the flesh, but other than that she hadn't changed much. The hips were a little fleshy and slightly broader, but her breasts were still small and high. And her waist was narrow, though not as narrow as

Carla's. That woman was like a tiny little doll. And though
Toni knew she was a few years older, she didn't look it. She
probably had wrinkles under all that make-up, she
thought as she dressed for bed and then laughed at herself
for her childishness. But when she turned off the light and
curled up in bed she wasn't laughing. She was
remembering Ian's smell and the look in his eyes and
wondering, if she'd left his hand on hers and hadn't
mentioned Carla, how would the evening have ended?
Would he have turned into a dark alley or asked to see her
again? Did he still have feelings for her? She plumped the
pillow angrily and closed her eyes. He was living with Carla
and she was still married – why was she even thinking like
this? Even when she did finally leave Theo, the last thing
she needed was another relationship. Suddenly, she felt a
strong urge to talk to her mother. The feeling took her by
surprise. Toni and her mother had grown apart since her
marriage and were more like polite strangers than mother
and daughter. Maybe she should go and visit her. Yes,
that's what she would do. Toni's heart lightened at the
prospect of seeing her. She closed her eyes and slept.

* * *

Ian let himself into the apartment and threw his keys on
the hall table. Walking through to the kitchen to fix
himself a drink, he flicked the switch on the answering
machine as he passed.

Carla's voice filled the room. 'Hi, honey, it's me. You said
you'd call.' Her sexy voice was reproachful. 'But I forgive
you. Come over tomorrow evening. We can catch up. Bye.'

Ian sighed as he poured a large whisky. Sometimes he found Carla a little too clingy. She wanted him to spend every free moment with her when sometimes all he wanted to do was fall asleep in front of *Match of the Day*. He'd lied to Toni, deliberately letting her believe that he and Carla were living together. God forbid. He chuckled as he carried his glass into the bedroom. As if Toni cared. She'd made her feelings quite clear seven years ago when she'd walked out on him. He threw back the drink, stripped naked and threw himself down on the unmade bed. He was a pathetic old man. Nearly forty-three years of age and still clinging on to dreams that the true love of his life would come back to him. He'd only stayed in this flat because if he closed his eyes and concentrated really hard he could see Toni floating around the bedroom in one of his shirts. Or standing beside him in the kitchen, barefoot, drinking a mug of coffee while he made breakfast. He sighed heavily. It was time he grew up. And maybe it was time he showed Carla a bit more consideration. They'd been together for over a year now. Maybe he should move in with her. She was quite a nice woman once you got past the hard veneer. He turned over on his side and closed his eyes. He'd call her in the morning and arrange for them to spend the weekend together. And then, maybe . . . he slept.

* * *

Sandra turned off the light in the kitchen and carried her cocoa upstairs, very slowly. She was feeling decidedly groggy. It wasn't exactly a bad feeling, just different. It had been a long time since she'd had more than a couple of glasses of wine and tonight she hadn't a clue how much she'd had to drink. Either Jade or Toni seemed to be topping up her glass every time she looked. It had been red wine, which she never drank, but she didn't like to say. It was actually quite nice, giving her a nice warm glow. She tiptoed past her mother's door and went into her bedroom. It was so nice of Jade to see her to the bus stop. There had been no need, of course. She was a bit unsteady but that was all. Still, it was nice having someone fuss over her. It was just so weird that it should be Jade. She had never thought they would be friends. She'd hoped that she'd get on with all the staff at the clinic but hadn't seen herself socialising with any of them. Vicky hardly talked to her and when she did it was usually to make a smart comment or to tell her a dirty joke. She didn't like either. And while she liked Toni, she was still the boss. Jade she was rather in awe of. The woman was so attractive, gutsy and clever, she seemed to have everything. *You know different now though,* she thought as she undressed. Jade had problems, just like everyone else. She was just better at hiding them.

Sandra considered going back out to the bathroom to take off her make-up, but she was too tired and anyway she might disturb her mother. She got into bed and took a sip of her cocoa. Maybe it would stop her having a hangover in the morning. Still, it was a small price to pay for the great night she'd had. It had been so different to her nights out with Susan and Caroline. No drunken flirting with men half their age. No moaning and bitching about their partners. Though she was a bit disappointed that Toni hadn't talked about Theo French. She was fascinated by that marriage and would have loved it if Toni had chatted about her husband. But she'd hardly mentioned him. Sandra hadn't found out any more about Aidan Peters either. Though she thought it very strange that Jade hadn't told Toni about his mother passing away. Maybe they weren't as close as she had thought. Maybe she and Jade were destined to become close friends. She smiled as she finished her cocoa. She was quite chuffed at the thought. And it would be nice to go out on a regular basis again. Her mother was right. She did need the break. She'd talk to Jade tomorrow about arranging another night out next week.

Sandra turned off the light, closed her eyes and snuggled down under the covers.

Chapter Eighteen

Saturday, 12th August, 2000

Jade watched Aidan sit down in her chair while she perched on the edge of the bed.

'How are you –'

'You look well –'

They both broke off and laughed awkwardly.

'You first,' Aidan prompted with a gentle smile.

'I was just asking how you were doing. And how is Ann?'

Aidan nodded sadly. 'We're doing okay. Ann is going through Mother's clothes at the moment.'

'That can't be easy.'

'No. Margaret offered to help but Ann wouldn't hear of it. She said Mother would haunt her!'

Jade laughed. 'She's probably right. Your mother would hate the thought of Margaret going through her private things. But tell Ann if she wants any help to give me a call.'

'Thanks, I'll do that.'

Jade stood up and went to the press. 'Would you like a drink? I'm afraid this is all I've got.' She took down the bottle of vodka and two glasses.

'I'd prefer a cup of tea.'

Jade glanced at him with raised eyebrows but said nothing. She put on the kettle, fiddling around with the plug until she was sure it was working.

Aidan frowned. 'I'll take a look at that for you. It could be dangerous.'

Jade laughed. 'Everything in this place is dangerous.' She put away the vodka and took down two mugs instead.

When the tea was made, Jade sat down again and stared into her mug. Any of their meetings in the last two years had been acrimonious, angry or emotional. It was very strange to be sitting here like two polite acquaintances.

'Ann wants me to stay.'

Jade looked up. 'And will you?'

'I may as well. I can't stay in Gerry's forever.'

Jade nodded. It made sense for Aidan to go home but she wondered if it would be the end of him altogether. Ann would wait on him hand and foot. And he'd probably sit in front of the TV all day and let her.

'You don't think I should?' Aidan read her thoughts.

'It's none of my business, Aidan. You're a grown man.'

'But you think I'll just sponge off her, don't you?'

'I never said that!' But Jade couldn't look at him.

Aidan put down his mug and rubbed his eyes wearily. 'I know that I've made a mess of my life, Jade, but I think this might be a chance of a new start for me. Ann thinks I'm working – I told her that I travel around the country a lot. So, that's what I'm going to do.'

'Oh?'

Aidan nodded. 'There's a guy I went to college with – Dave Bell. He has his own business in Thurles and he needs someone to cover the Leinster area for him.'

'He's offered you the job?'

Aidan nodded. 'It's mine if I want it.'

'But can you . . . do you think . . .' Jade searched for the right words.

'I'm going to try, Jade. I owe it to you, to Ann –'

'You owe it to yourself, Aidan. You have to do this for you and no one else.'

'That's what they say in the meetings.'

'So you are still going?' Jade felt guilty. She had always been ready to believe the worst of him. But then, she reminded herself, he'd given her good cause to.

'I did miss a few,' he admitted. 'Sometimes it got on top of me. I'd lost you, my business, my family and I didn't see the point in making an effort.'

'And now?'

'Now I've got Ann to think of. She needs me.'

'Ann may not be on her own forever,' Jade warned him. 'She's a lovely girl and she won't always want to live with her big brother.'

'I'm not stupid, Jade. Of course I realise that. But for the moment, right now, she needs me. I'm not going to let her down.'

Jade saw the determined set of his jaw and her eyes filled with tears. She was happy for him but at the same time she felt bitter. He hadn't thought twice about letting her down. His wife and home hadn't been good enough reasons to keep him from going off the rails in the first place. When times were tough, he didn't think of her and the effects his actions would have on their marriage. No, he'd just slunk off to the racecourse or the bookies and lost their home and their life savings.

'I want to repay you too,' Aidan said looking around in disgust. 'When I see you living in this dump it makes me sick. I've dragged you down to this. You should be living in luxury.'

Jade's eyes hardened. 'I should be in the house that you built for us.'

'I'm sorry, Jade. I'm so sorry. What more can I say?'

Jade pulled herself together and managed a brief smile. 'Nothing. I'm glad you're going to make the effort for Ann. I wish you the best of luck. Just don't hurt her . . .'

'The way I hurt you,' Aidan finished the sentence.

Jade said nothing.

'I haven't gambled since the day my mother died, Jade. And I hope I never will again. I'm going to try and I'll keep going to the meetings. I can't say more than that.'

'No. No you can't. What is it they say? One day at a time.'

Aidan smiled. 'Yes. One day at a time.'

* * *

Toni stood in arrivals and watched the screen. Finally, the flight from Rome had landed. An hour later than it was supposed to. She'd already phoned Alice to tell her to hold off on dinner. She'd call her again from the car when they were finally on their way.

'Toni?'

Toni swung around and smiled as Daniel pushed his way to her side.

'God, it's bedlam here.'

'It always is. Is Meg not with you?'

'Lord, no. She's at home preparing the fatted calf!'

Toni laughed. 'Alice is the same. You'd think they'd been away for years instead of six weeks.'

'Still, I missed Mark,' Daniel admitted.

'Yeah. I missed Chloe too.' Toni sighed. She was looking forward to seeing her stepdaughter again. But at the same time she was dreading the conversation that they would have to have.

'Here they come!' Daniel moved forward as a large group of teenagers came through the doors. There was a lot of laughing and hugging before they turned to seek out parents and family.

'Toni!' Chloe hurried forward.

Toni stared at the sophisticated young woman approaching her. 'Chloe?'

Chloe laughed and put a self-conscious hand up to her cropped hair. 'Do you like it?'

'Yes! Yes, I do.' Toni couldn't stop staring at Theo's daughter in her black jeans and tight black, sleeveless T-shirt. The sleek haircut showed off her wonderful bone structure and large blue eyes. 'You look marvellous!'

Chloe in turn inspected her stepmother, eyes narrowed. 'You've lost weight. Are you working too hard? Has minding Alice been too much for you?'

Toni shook her head and laughed. 'Everything's fine. But I'm glad you're home. And Alice can't wait to see you.'

'Hi, Toni,' Mark came over and slipped an arm around his girlfriend.

Toni smiled at the tall, handsome young man. 'Hello, Mark. Did you have a good time?'

'Well, it was hard work. But we did manage to fit in a bit of sightseeing.'

'And some socialising, no doubt,' Daniel said drily.

'We always seemed to be laughing,' Chloe told him. 'There was a great atmosphere at our vineyard. And the *craic* was great.'

'Well, I'm glad to hear it went well. But I better get you home, Mark, or your mother will go mad.'

Mark bent to kiss Chloe lightly on the lips. 'I'll call you later.'

Chloe smiled up into his eyes. 'Okay. Bye.'

Toni took command of the trolley and led the way out to the car.

'How's Dad?' It hadn't occurred to Chloe that her father would be at the airport to meet her. He wouldn't have the time.

'Great,' Toni replied lightly. 'Unfortunately he has to go out tonight but he said he'd try to get home a bit early to say hello before he went.'

'I'm honoured.'

Toni looked at her but there seemed to be no acrimony behind Chloe's sarcasm.

'And Alice? How's she doing?'

'Wonderful. She's come on in leaps and bounds literally since the plaster came off. And she's very good about doing her exercises. The hardest part is stopping her from doing too much!'

'You two seem to be getting on much better.'

Toni nodded. 'Yes, we are. We've spent so much time together since you left.'

Chloe grinned. 'So I did you a favour by going to Tuscany.'

'Maybe.' Toni stopped beside the car and switched off the alarm. 'I hope all your stuff fits.' Chloe had left six weeks ago with a large haversack but seemed to have accumulated a few more bags in Italy.

'I went a bit wild in Rome,' Chloe admitted. 'I hardly spent any money in the country so I had a major spending spree when I hit the city.'

Toni laughed. 'That seems reasonable.'

'The shops are just amazing. And the shoes – the shoes were just gorgeous.' She giggled. 'It's just as well Ollie didn't come with us. She'd have spent a small fortune.'

'I'm sure Ollie could manage to do that on a desert island!' Toni retorted as she crammed the last bag into the back seat. 'Okay. Let's go. I hope you're hungry. Alice has been cooking all day.'

Chloe smiled. 'I promise to eat every morsel. Oh, it's nice to be home.'

'Will you be saying that next Wednesday?' Toni asked with a concerned frown. The exam results would be out and she thought Chloe might be apprehensive.

'What, you mean my results? Well, there's nothing I can do now so there's no point in worrying about it.'

Toni was surprised at her composure. 'Well, Tuscany has had a very settling effect on you. Or is Mark responsible for the new-laid back Chloe French?'

Chloe blushed happily. 'A little of both. He's so great,

Toni. It would be really great if we could go to the same college.'

Toni sighed. 'Let me guess. He wants to go to UCD.'

Chloe nodded glumly. 'I don't suppose Dad has changed his thinking on that subject, has he?'

'We haven't discussed it,' Toni replied honestly. She had hardly seen Theo in the last few weeks, let alone talked to him.

'Well, maybe I won't get enough points to go to Trinity.'

Toni glanced sharply at her. 'I can't believe you're hoping not to do well.'

'I'm not, not really. A few points wouldn't matter. But it might solve all my problems.'

'Look, Chloe. You are very young. And if you seriously want to do medicine you have to give it your best shot. Even if you and Mark attend the same college you're not going to be able to spend much time together. It's going to be very hard work.'

'Yeah. That's what Mark says.'

'Well, thank goodness he's being sensible about it.'

'Oh, Toni. Don't nag. You know what I'm saying. If we were in the same college we could have lunch together, meet for coffee. But if I'm in the city and he's all the way out there we'll never see each other.'

'Don't be so dramatic,' Toni said briskly as she turned on to Griffith Avenue. 'And if you expect to have any hope of persuading your dad to let you go to UCD, you'd better come up with a better argument than that.'

'Speak of the devil,' Chloe murmured as Theo's Mercedes turned into the driveway in front of them.

'Daddy!' she cried jumping out of the car and running to greet him.

Toni grinned as she watched Theo's pleased expression as he hugged his daughter. 'Now, that kind of behaviour will get you a lot further, Chloe!' She climbed out of the car and started to unload her stepdaughter's bags.

Chapter Nineteen

Tuesday, 15th August, 2000

'Hello, Blessington Clinic. Can I help you?' Sandra said into the phone.

Jade flashed her a smile as she walked through reception. 'Morning.'

'Jade?' Toni stuck her head out of the office. 'Have you got a minute?'

'Sure,' Jade said easily and followed. 'How are things?'

Toni walked back around her desk and sat down. 'Not bad. Chloe's home.'

'You don't sound very happy about it.'

'Oh, I am. It's just . . .'

'You're not looking forward to telling her you're leaving.'

Toni threw her pen down on the desk and looked miserably at her friend. 'I'm dreading it. But I've decided to wait until after she gets her results.'

'You're just finding reasons to put it off, Toni. Are you sure you want to leave?'

'Yes! That is, I'm sure I want to leave Theo. But I wish it didn't mean leaving Chloe too.'

'She might decide to move in with you.'

'Over Theo's dead body,' Toni said darkly. She could think of nothing that would enrage Theo more than for his daughter to choose her over him.

Jade shrugged. 'He'd get over it.'

'Anyway, that's not what I wanted to talk to you about.'

'Oh?' Jade raised an eyebrow.

'It's Vicky.'

Jade groaned. 'What now?'

'She's asked for a few days off.'

'What?' Jade exploded. 'She can't! That's not on, Toni. Anyway she's just back from a long weekend.'

'Yes, I know that. But she says she has problems at home.'

'Yeah, right.'

'Look, I can't exactly call her a liar, can I? I'll phone the agency and get someone in to cover for her.'

'Good, because I'm not going to.'

'Okay, okay. Keep your hair on.'

'Sorry. It's just that she's always taking advantage. We'd be better off without her.'

'The thought had occurred to me,' admitted Toni. 'Though I'm not sure Robert would agree.'

'Tough. We shouldn't have to put up with this!'

Toni put her head on one side. Hiring and firing *was* her responsibility once she agreed it with Daniel. 'You're right, Jade. But I'll have to go through the proper channels first. I need to give Vicky a formal warning. In writing. Can you put together a note detailing any cock-ups she's been responsible for? And I'll go through her attendance record.'

Jade stood up, a broad smile on her face. 'It would be my pleasure.'

Toni's phone rang. 'Hello? Toni Jordan.'

'Hi, Toni. It's me. Ian.'

'Oh, hi.'

'I'll go,' Jade mouthed and left the room.

'Toni?'

'Yes, sorry. There was someone with me. What can I do for you?'

Ian laughed. 'Well, I'm not looking for a nose job if that's what you're asking. This is a social call.'

Toni smiled. 'Oh, I don't know. A nose job might not be such a bad idea.'

'Cheek. I have a Roman nose, I'll have you know –'

'Roaming all over your face, yeah I know. Lord, your jokes don't get any better, do they?'

'But I made you laugh.' Ian's voice was soft and warm.

Toni held the phone tight to her ear and closed her eyes. 'I'm sorry I was a bit narky with you the other night. It was very nice of you to give me a lift.'

'I'm a very nice guy.'

'Yes, yes, you are.' Toni's voice was barely a whisper.

'I want to see you, Toni,' Ian said quickly.

'Oh, I don't think –'

'No, don't think, Toni. Just say yes. Please?'

'Yes.'

'What?'

'I'll meet you.'

'The Beachcomber, tomorrow night?' Ian said hurriedly.

Toni looked at the diary in front of her. 'No, I can't. Look what about lunch on Friday? One o'clock?'

'Fine. See you then. Bye Toni.'

'Bye.' Toni put down the phone. What on earth had

she done? A shiver of excitement ran through her. Quickly followed by one of guilt. What was she doing meeting her ex? 'It's only lunch,' she murmured in an effort to calm herself. 'There's nothing wrong with having lunch with an old friend. Once it's all above board.' But she knew she wasn't going to tell anyone she was meeting Ian. Not even Jade.

* * *

'It's a bit drastic, isn't it?' Daniel stared at Toni. He'd been just about to head home when she'd come to him with her findings.

After Ian's call, Toni had thrown herself into researching Vicky Harrison's record and was not pleased with what she'd found. 'Read it, Daniel. The girl has screwed up a number of times – she could even have put lives in danger. She's always late and her attendance record has been getting steadily worse –'

'Okay, okay.' Daniel sighed. 'What do you want me to do?'

'Nothing.'

'Oh?' Daniel looked surprised and relieved.

'I just need your agreement. I want to have a chat with her. Present her with a written warning and give her a month to sort herself out.'

Daniel tugged on his beard. 'Seems reasonable.'

'Right.' Toni stood up. 'I'll talk to her as soon as she gets back. Goodnight, Daniel, and thanks.'

* * *

'Did you enjoy that?' Mark held Chloe's hand tightly as they walked out of the cinema.

'Not really.' It had been her idea to go and see *The Patriot*. She thought it would take their mind off the exam results. It hadn't worked. She couldn't concentrate on the story at all. 'Did you?'

'Mel Gibson was good,' Mark replied without enthusiasm.

'What time are you going in tomorrow?' Chloe returned to the subject preoccupying them both.

'First thing. I couldn't wait any longer.'

Chloe nodded. 'I know what you mean. Will you meet me afterwards?'

'Of course! But won't your dad expect you to come straight back?'

'Dad will be at work,' Chloe said dismissively. 'I have to phone him. *And* Toni. *And* Alice.'

Mark laughed. 'Yeah, I have to call Mam and Dad too.'

'Do you think you did well?' Chloe hadn't asked before. Mark was so clever and he'd worked hard.

'I think so. Whether it will be good enough to get me into computer science in UCD is another thing.'

'You'll get in,' Chloe told him confidently. 'Though I wish you'd apply to Trinity. That would sort out all our problems.'

Mark laughed. 'Some chance! I'll be bloody lucky if I get enough points to make UCD. I wouldn't have a hope of getting into Trinity. You're the brainy one in this partnership.'

'Rubbish.' Chloe punched him lightly in the arm.

'It's true. And it's nothing to be ashamed of, Chloe.' He hugged her affectionately. 'I'm proud of you.'

Chloe smiled. 'I'm not sure there's anything to be proud of. Sometimes I feel really confident that I did well. And then I start to have doubts.'

'That's only natural. Look, let's go for a beer and then I'll bring you home.'

Chloe glanced at her watch. It was only ten o'clock. 'Okay. Just one though.'

* * *

Theo put his head around the sitting-room door. 'Isn't Chloe home yet?' His voice was cold and accusing.

'No.' Toni didn't take her eyes off the TV screen.

'Well, where is she? Didn't you ask where she was going?'

Toni sighed and wondered when *his* daughter's whereabouts had become her sole responsibility. 'She and Mark went to the cinema.'

Theo snorted as he paced in front of her. 'She spends too much time with that boy.'

'He seems very nice.'

'I don't care how nice he is. He's a distraction. She's too young to be in a serious relationship.'

'So you'd prefer her to be out clubbing with a different guy every week like Ollie?'

'Chloe would never do that.'

Toni switched off the TV and stood up. She wasn't going to have yet another pointless argument. 'Look, Chloe will be out celebrating with her friends tomorrow night so I was going to organise a family dinner for Friday. Do you think you could squeeze that into your busy schedule?'

Theo smiled broadly. 'How could I resist a cosy dinner with my daughter and my loving wife? Of course I'll be there. But please leave the cooking to Alice.'

'I'm booking a restaurant,' Toni said stiffly resisting his attempt to draw her into a slanging match. 'Alice deserves a night off too.'

Theo stared at her. 'Why the hell would we bring her?'

'Because Chloe wants her there and it's her night. Now I'm going to bed.'

'Shall I come with you?' he moved closer to her, tucking a tendril of hair behind her ear and running his fingers down the length of her neck.

Toni shivered. 'Go to hell.'

Theo tut-tutted. 'My dear Toni, be careful. You might hurt my feelings.'

'What feelings are those?' Toni asked and walked out of the room, his harsh laughter ringing in her ears.

'Sick bastard,' she muttered as she climbed the stairs. She went into her room and after a moment's hesitation turned the key in the lock. Sometimes, she realised, he actually scared her. She hoped he didn't sense it. That would give him a real kick. She took off her clothes, tugged her hair out of its tight little bun and massaged her neck. She froze as she heard him come upstairs and quickly pulled on her sloppy pyjamas. She held her breath when his step paused outside her door and watched the door handle nervously. But Theo retraced his steps and moments later she heard his own door closing. She fell back against the pillow and closed her eyes, pulling the duvet protectively around her. It seemed unbelievable that she was lying here trembling, her door locked against her husband. A man she'd once loved but now despised and feared. She turned off the light and buried her face in the pillow and banished Theo from her thoughts. Instead, she thought about lunch on Friday with Ian. She was looking forward to it like a teenager to her first date. But it wasn't a first date. She had a long history with Ian Chase. And it seemed all she could think about today – when she wasn't trying to bury Vicky Harrison – was the love she'd shared with the man. The incredible, fierce passion when they'd first met that had them pulling off each other's clothes almost as soon as they touched. There was one occasion – which still made her blush – when they were having dinner together in The Grand Hotel in Malahide. But they were barely eating, because they couldn't take their eyes and hands off each other. Finally, Ian excused himself and came back a few minutes later with a key.

Wordlessly, Toni had stood up and taken his hand. She laughed as she remembered them calling room service several hours later when their appetites mysteriously returned.

She tossed and turned, long after she heard Chloe come home. Her thoughts tumbled between Theo and Ian, one moment feeling guilty, then sad and then angry. Finally, exhausted, she drifted into a fitful sleep, her dreams as troubled as her thoughts.

* * *

Wednesday, 16th August, 2000

'Chloe! Chloe! I did it! I can't believe it!' Ollie danced Chloe around the corridor.

Chloe pulled away laughing. 'That's great, Ollie.'

'What about you?'

'Not bad,' Chloe admitted shyly. 'I haven't figured out the exact number of points yet so I'm not sure if I've enough for Trinity.'

'You will,' Ollie said confidently and then understanding dawned as she saw the look on Chloe's face. 'You were *hoping* that you'd only have enough to get you a place in UCD, weren't you?'

Chloe grinned sheepishly. 'Well . . .'

'You know you were kidding yourself, don't you?' Ollie said matter-of-factly. 'Even if they didn't offer you a place immediately, you'd definitely be included in the second round.'

'I suppose.'

Ollie shook her head at Chloe's downcast expression. 'For God's sake, Chlo, look around you! There are girls devastated because they didn't do well and you're moaning because you did *too* well!'

'Sorry. It's just that –'

'You want to be with Mark. I know, I know.' Ollie grabbed her arm and led her out into the sunshine. She was heartily fed up with Chloe going on and on about her beloved boyfriend. 'But it's unlikely that's going to happen. So forget about it and let's concentrate on where we're going tonight.'

'I need to ask Mark –'

'Give me a break, Chloe!' Ollie exploded. 'Tonight is a girls' night. Anyway, I'm sure Mark will want to be out with his own friends.'

'I'll check. I'm meeting him in town in an hour.'

Ollie sighed. 'Well, okay then. I have to go home now anyway. Mum will be in a tizzy wondering what's happening.'

'You can use my mobile and call her if you want,' Chloe offered.

'Nah.' Ollie grinned delightedly. 'I want to see the look on her face!'

Chloe watched her friend bounce off towards the bus stop and sighed. Ollie was going to DCU to do a B.Sc. in multimedia.

'Next stop, daytime TV. Then, I think, my own talk show,' Ollie had told her confidently.

Chloe didn't doubt it. With Ollie's personality and extraordinary hard neck, success was a certainty. Chloe sighed as she phoned her father's office and waited for Emma to put her through. With Ollie in Glasnevin and Mark in Clonskeagh, she was going to be very lonely. Very lonely indeed.

'Hello, Dad? Yeah. Yeah, I got it.'

* * *

Mark stared moodily into his coffee and his mother and Chloe exchanged worried looks.

'I'm sure you'll get in, Mark,' Chloe repeated desperately.

'Of course he will.' Meg Wheeler said smiling. 'Daniel says it's a given. You have four hundred and twenty points –'

'Four hundred and fifteen,' Mark corrected.

'That's plenty.' Chloe assured him.

Mark glowered at her. She'd be completely desolate if she was in his position.

Chloe saw his expression and hurriedly changed the subject. 'Where are you going tonight? Ollie says all the girls are heading for the Red Box.'

'I don't think I'll bother.'

'Don't be ridiculous,' his mother said briskly. 'Ryan and Justin will be expecting you to go out with them.'

'I'm looking forward to it,' Chloe lied. 'There should be a great atmosphere in town.'

Meg nodded approvingly. Thank goodness Mark was going out with such a nice girl. Daniel wasn't too keen on her, but that was because she was Theo French's daughter. But Meg thought they made a lovely couple. She sighed. Mark was still very young but then she had only been seventeen when she started to date his father.

'You listen to Chloe,' she told her son gently. 'There's no point in worrying until the places are offered next week. You may as well enjoy yourself tonight.'

Mark smiled reluctantly and nodded. 'Okay, Mum. But when the cops haul me home for being drunk and disorderly, remember it was your idea!'

Meg tousled his hair affectionately. 'Tell them to keep you in a cell till morning. I need my beauty sleep!'

Chapter Twenty

Friday, 18th August, 2000

'What about Monday?' Sandra asked patiently.

Toni looked blank. 'Sorry?'

Sandra sighed. 'For our night out. How about Monday?'

'Oh, eh, I'm not sure. Chloe is all worked up about her college applications and the first offers come out on Monday. I'd better not make any plans.'

'Okay. Then how about Tuesday? Jade said that either Monday or Tuesday were good for her.'

Toni stood up abruptly. 'I just don't know, Sandra. Why don't you and Jade go ahead? If I can make it, I will.' And she went into her office and closed the door.

Sandra stared after her. Every time she thought she was getting close to Toni, the shutters would come down again.

'What's up?' Jade put down a pile of files on Sandra's desk and looked at the girl's glum expression.

'Oh, nothing. I was just asking Toni about going out next week.'

'Oh right. Is Monday okay with her?'

'No, and she's not sure about Tuesday either. She said we should go ahead without her.'

Jade frowned. It had been Toni's idea to invite Sandra out with them again. Surely she wasn't still annoyed about the business with Aidan? 'I'll have a word with her.' She smiled brightly at Sandra. 'Why don't you go ahead and book the restaurant?'

'China World?' Sandra asked, knowing it was Jade's favourite.

Jade sighed and thought of her bank balance. 'Yes, China World.' She crossed reception to Toni's office, tapped perfunctorily on the door and walked in.

Toni looked up irritably. 'What is it, Jade?'

'Just wondering about dinner next week.'

Toni looked pointedly at her watch. 'I told Sandra. I'm not sure if I'm free. Look, I have an awful lot to do –'

'Have I done something? Is this about Aidan?'

Toni shook her head. 'No, of course not. Honestly, Jade, I just have a lot on my mind at the moment.'

Jade nodded, not completely convinced. 'Want to talk about it?'

Toni shook her head. 'No, look, I just need some space at the moment.'

'Fine. You know where I am. Seeya.' Jade left the office, closing the door with an angry snap.

Toni sighed. She hadn't meant to be ratty. It was this damn lunch that had her so worked up. That and the thought of trying to pull off a cosy little family dinner tonight. She picked up the phone and dialled. 'Mr Ian Chase, please.'

'I'm afraid Mr Chase isn't in today,' the receptionist replied pleasantly. 'May I take a message?'

'No, I'll call again.' Toni put down the phone and stared at it. Then she picked it up again and dialled Ian's home number. After two rings she got the answering machine. She thought of leaving a message but what if Carla heard it? She hung up and looked at the clock on the wall. Twelve o'clock. It looked like she'd have to meet him. But she wouldn't stay. She'd just explain and apologise and get out of there as quickly as possible.

* * *

'I wish Mark was coming with us tonight,' Chloe said moodily as she watched Alice place the soda bread in the oven and wipe her hands in her apron.

'Don't be silly, love,' Alice said, ignoring the girl's sulky pout. 'There's a time for boyfriends and a time for family. Anyway, I doubt he'd enjoy it much. Your father would probably spend the evening grilling him about his intentions.'

Chloe giggled. 'Yeah. Poor Mark gets an earful every time Dad answers the phone. He saw him in the hospital last week but Mark scarpered down the corridor before Dad could collar him.'

'Sensible lad,' Alice said drily and then remembering her position added, 'although it's only natural that your father wants to get to know the boy.'

'I suppose. But I still don't think tonight's going to be much fun.'

Alice eyed her over her glasses. 'Of course it will. Won't I be there?'

Chloe hugged her affectionately. 'Yeah, sorry. And at least we're not going to one of Dad's fancy restaurants.'

'Where are we going?' Alice had been told the name of the restaurant but her memory wasn't what it used to be.

'Jasko's Bistro in Dame Street. You'll love it, Alice. There's a great atmosphere. Ollie's folks took us there a couple of times.'

'Sounds fancy,' Alice said dubiously.

'Fish is their speciality,' Chloe assured her.

'I do like fish,' Alice admitted.

'There you go. Now I'm going to call Ollie. She's going out tonight too. Maybe we could all meet up afterwards. That would be cool.'

Alice smiled as she watched her leave. It was unlikely that Mr French would think it was 'cool' to meet up with Olivia and her family. Although given how bad things were between him and Toni at the moment, he'd probably welcome anyone as a distraction.

'Are you sure this is a good idea?' Alice had asked Toni, as they strolled home from Mass the previous Sunday, when she'd told her of the dinner she was planning.

Toni had shrugged and linked her arm through Alice's as they came to some rough pavement. 'Probably not, but what choice have I got? We have to celebrate Chloe's exam results and it might be easier in a restaurant.'

'Where everyone's forced to be on their best behaviour?'

'Exactly.'

'You're going to have to talk to the girl soon. She's already suspicious.'

Toni had frowned. 'Do you think so?'

212

'I know it. And once all the fuss about college has died down she's going to start asking questions.'

'Then I'd better figure out some answers,' Toni said worriedly.

'You're definitely going then?'

'I don't see what else I can do, Alice. Things have gone from bad to worse.'

'Then you must do what you think best, dear, and don't let anyone tell you otherwise.'

'Thank you, Alice. You've been a tower of strength these last few weeks.'

Alice had shrugged off her thanks, embarrassed. 'Sure what have I done?'

'Well, I'm going to Mass again – something I haven't done in years!'

'You only started going again because I couldn't walk and you brought me in the car. And I'm very grateful.'

'You're welcome. And, maybe that was true to begin with, but now I actually enjoy it.'

'The Lord works in mysterious ways.' Alice had smiled knowingly.

'My mother would be amazed!'

'How is your mother?'

'We haven't spoken in a while,' Toni had admitted.

'That's a pity.'

'Alice, how come you can be so non-committal and still make me feel as if you're scolding me?'

'That's not me. That's your conscience talking.'

'You're wasted on housekeeping, Alice Scully. You should have your own chat show. Or at the very least be writing a problem page for one of the tabloids.'

Alice had allowed herself a small smile. 'I just speak as I find.'

'I must introduce you to my friend Dotty Price. You two would get on like a house on fire!'

* * *

Toni walked into the pub and blinked as her eyes adjusted to the gloom after the bright sunshine outside.

'Toni? Over here.'

She swung around to see Ian sitting in 'their' corner. At the table where they had sat the first time Ian had asked her out. She stared at him and for a moment considered turning tail and running.

Ian stood up and came towards her. 'What can I get you?'

'I'm not sure . . .'

'It's only lunch, Toni,' he said gently leading her over to the table. 'I'm not going to eat you. Not unless you ask me too!' He grinned wickedly at her.

'Ian!' Toni hissed, looking around nervously.

Ian held up his hands. 'Sorry, sorry. Just a joke. A bad one. Now, come on, what would you like?'

'Eh, a ham and cheese sandwich and a mineral water.'

Ian sighed as he watched her perch awkwardly on the edge of the seat. She looked as though she might take flight at any moment. 'Wouldn't you like something a bit stronger?'

'I have a lot of work to do this afternoon,' she said curtly. 'In fact I can't stay long at all. I shouldn't even be here.'

'I'm very glad you are,' Ian said dropping a light kiss on her cheek before going up to the bar.

Toni touched the spot where he'd kissed her and stared after him. He hadn't changed at all. Still charming, still funny and still very, very handsome. Some grey hair at his temples, the only indicator of his advancing years. His body was still lean, his eyes sparkled with the same good humour and his voice, if anything, had just got deeper and sexier.

Toni tore her eyes away from him and began to systematically shred a beermat. *Stop it. You're still married and he's attached. This is just a friendly lunch between two old friends.*

She jumped as Ian placed her glass in front of her and took the chair opposite. She tried not to look disappointed. He had always sat beside her. Very close beside her. Sometimes he'd even-

'Toni?'

Ian was staring at her.

'Sorry! I was miles away. Just thinking about work.' She picked up her water hoping she could trust her trembling fingers.

'How is everything at the Blessington?'

'Good.' She sighed. 'Well, no, to be honest. Things aren't going well at all at the moment.'

'Oh?'

She explained Daniel's new procedure and Robert's feelings about it while Ian nodded attentively.

'It's a difficult one,' he said when she'd finished. 'Your patients are paying a lot of money and they don't want to have to wait weeks for these procedures.'

'But don't you see –' Toni paused as their food was brought. An unimaginative sandwich for her and a cottage pie with chips for him. She looked at his plate longingly.

Ian grinned at her. 'Would you like a chip?'

'No, thank you. As I was saying. I think the problem is – especially with some of our younger patients – they haven't really thought it through. Often it's just an attempt to quick fix something else. A husband has walked out or is suspected of having an affair. A girl is teased at school. Surgery isn't going to solve their problems.'

'But that's not *your* problem, ' Ian pointed out. 'I hate to say it, but Robert is right. They are adults and it's up to them to make the decision. All you can do is make them aware of the dangers.'

'But what about Robert operating on overweight people and diabetics?'

Ian's face sobered. 'That's not on. If I were Daniel I'd tell him the next time he stepped out of line he was out. There are plenty of surgeons who'd jump into Robert's shoes. The Blessington is a very cushy little number. Especially given its central location.'

Toni nodded thoughtfully.

'Aren't you going to eat that?' Ian looked at her untouched sandwich.

Toni looked down at it and grinned. 'No. Maybe I'll have a chip after all.'

Ian laughed. 'This is like old times, sitting here putting the wrongs of the world to right while you eat my chips!'

'It seems like a lifetime ago,' Toni murmured. When

they had started seeing each other, they'd agreed to keep it quiet. The hospital was a hotbed of gossip and a senior doctor dating a secretary would definitely have set the tongues wagging. So The Beachcomber had become their hideaway. It was far enough from the hospital to avoid meeting anyone. But near enough to allow them to escape for brief lunches.

'I miss you,' Ian said suddenly, his grey eyes intent.

'What about Carla?'

'Carla has nothing to do with us.'

Toni shook her head, bewildered. Where was he going with this? What did he expect? 'I doubt she'd see it that way,' she said in an effort to break the spell he was casting over them.

'I don't want to talk about Carla,' he murmured taking her hand and kissing the tips of her fingers. 'I want to talk about you. About us.'

Toni snatched her hand away, alarmed at the effect he was having on her. 'There is no us.'

'Isn't there?'

'No, there isn't. I'm married.' *Just about*, she added to herself. 'And you're attached. We were over a long time ago.'

Ian sighed and sat back in his chair. 'Okay then. We'll just be friends.'

Toni looked at him suspiciously. 'What?'

'What's to stop us keeping in touch, having a bite of lunch occasionally? Let's be friends again, Toni. I miss talking to you.'

'We could never just be friends. We have too much history –'

Ian looked at her with raised eyebrows. 'Don't you trust yourself? Are you afraid that you won't be able to keep your hands off me?'

Toni sat on her hands, her cheeks red. 'You should be so lucky.'

'Then there isn't a problem, is there? Come on, Toni.'

Toni looked into his eyes and felt her resolve weaken. 'Okay, then. Friends.'

* * *

'I wish I had more time before college started,' Chloe complained after their main courses had been set in front of them. 'I really could do with a rest.'

Alice laughed. 'You're only just back from holiday.'

'That was hard work, Alice.'

'And you never enjoyed a minute of it,' Toni chimed in with a tolerant smile.

Chloe grinned back at her. 'Yeah, well, I suppose I might have.'

'You should count yourself lucky, young lady,' Alice said gravely. 'There are plenty less fortunate than you.'

Chloe rolled her eyes at Toni. 'Yes, Alice.'

'Look at that poor woman who was in that terrible accident last night.'

'Where?' Chloe asked.

'Oh, I don't know, somewhere around Mount Street. It was on the news. The car was in a terrible state.'

Toni nodded. 'Yes, I heard about that. It's a wonder she got out alive.'

'She's alive?' Theo said faintly.

'Yes. Serious but stable, whatever that means. Apparently she just ploughed into a parked car.'

'She was probably pissed,' Chloe said knowingly.

'You don't know that, Miss,' Alice said reprovingly.

'No, sorry,' Chloe said meekly. 'How is the hake, Alice?'

'Lovely. Everything's lovely.'

'What about you, Dad? Are the scallops good? Dad?'

Theo looked blankly at his daughter. 'Sorry?'

'Your dinner? Is it okay?'

'Oh, yes, fine.' He pushed the fish around his plate in a distracted fashion.

'What about more wine?' Toni suggested hopefully. Dinner hadn't been quite the trial she'd expected but she could still do with another drink.

'Of course.'

And to Toni's surprise he signalled the waiter to bring another bottle.

'So what about it, Alice? Shall we go dancing?' Chloe swayed in her seat and giggled happily.

Alice smiled. 'I think I might slow you down just a bit. You should meet up with Ollie and go on somewhere with her.'

Chloe shot her a grateful look.

'Where were they eating?' Toni asked.

'The Clarence,' Toni said eagerly. 'And then they were going on to the Shelbourne for drinks.'

Toni smiled. Clever Chloe. Theo loved the Shelbourne hotel. 'What do you say, Theo? Shall we go to the Shelbourne and meet Ollie and her parents?'

Theo watched the waiter top up their glasses and took a long drink.

'Theo?'

'Sorry, what was that?'

'I was suggesting that we meet Ollie and her parents in the Shelbourne for a drink.'

He looked momentarily disconcerted and then managed a polite smile. 'You go. But I'm afraid I have to go home.'

'Oh, Dad!'

'I'm sorry, Chloe, but I have a very early start in the morning.'

'But tomorrow is Saturday!'

'Sorry, darling, but I have to go to a conference in Oxford this weekend.'

Toni looked vaguely surprised. She didn't remember him saying anything about a conference. Still, she cheered up. It would be a lot easier for her if he did go home early. 'You go on, Theo. We can get a taxi.'

'I'll escort you to the Shelbourne first and say hello to Ollie and her family.'

Toni looked at him from under raised eyebrows. That was very big of him. The wine must have gone to his head.

They left for the Shelbourne an hour later and after Theo had made a little small talk and bought a round of drinks, he made his excuses.

'Thanks, Dad. It was a lovely evening.' Chloe reached up to kiss his cheek.

Her father hugged her tightly. 'I'm very proud of you, Chloe,' he said gruffly. 'Never forget that.'

Chloe looked up, surprised to see tears in his eyes. 'Thanks, Dad. I love you.'

Theo gave her another quick hug, pecked his wife's cheek and left.

Toni visibly relaxed once he'd left and chatted animatedly to Ollie's parents while Chloe and Ollie gabbled nineteen to the dozen. Alice took a sip of her port, closed her eyes and within seconds was dozing peacefully.

Chloe nudged Toni with a giggle. 'Maybe we won't go dancing after all.'

'Maybe not,' Toni whispered back.

Chapter Twenty-one

Monday, 21st August, 2000

Toni put down the phone and sat staring into space. Theo had disappeared and she had no idea where he was or why. She shook her head in an effort to clear it. She should do something, but what? Should she call the police or was that going too far? There was no point in calling anyone at Sylvester's. If Emma didn't know where Theo was then no one else would either. She picked up the phone to call Alice. Maybe Theo had phoned home. Of course! If there was a problem he would have called home first. The phone rang and rang until finally the answering machine cut in. 'Alice, hi, it's Toni. Would you give me a call when you get in? Thanks, bye.' She hung up and stared at the phone accusingly. Damn you, Theo, where are you? What are you up to?

She thought about ringing Chloe on her mobile. She must have gone to meet Ollie or Mark. But then if she hadn't heard from her father she would just start to worry. No, best not to phone her yet.

'Hey, what's happening?' Jade breezed in.

Toni looked up at her. 'Theo's gone.'

Jade sank into a chair. 'What? He's moved out?'

'No, well, I don't think so – oh, I don't know. He seems to have disappeared into thin air.'

'Okay, slow down. When did he leave?'

'Saturday morning. He was supposed to be going to a conference in Oxford but he never got there.'

'And he hasn't been in touch?'

'Nope. His secretary was expecting him in this morning as usual. Unless he's called Chloe but I'm afraid to call and ask her in case –'

'Yes, of course. Where is she?'

'I'm not sure. The college places came out this morning so she's probably with Ollie or Mark.'

'He might have phoned home.'

'Yeah, he could have. I've been trying to reach Alice but she's not there.'

'Why don't you go home and check? You're not going to get anything done here until you get to the bottom of this.'

Toni glanced at her watch. 'I was supposed to have a meeting with Daniel in an hour.'

'I'll tell him you had to go. Do you want me to tell him why?'

Toni shrugged. 'I don't mind. With a bit of luck Theo will either be at home or he'll have been in touch and we'll all be laughing about this tomorrow.'

'Yeah, I'm sure he's fine. Go on, you take off. I'll fill Daniel in and keep an eye on Sandra.'

Toni smiled gratefully. 'I don't know why your title is nurse. It should be chief all-rounder!'

'Hey, whatever your needs, Jade Peters can take care of them.' And with a little bow, Jade was gone.

Alice looked up in surprise when Toni walked into the kitchen. 'That was a very short day,' she joked and then stopped when she saw the preoccupied look on Toni's face. 'What is it? What's happened? Is it Chloe?'

'No, no nothing like that. Have you heard from Mr French today?'

'Well no, but then I've been out for most of the afternoon.'

'And did you check the answering machine?'

'Yes, yours was the only message. I was just about to call you – why, Toni? What's wrong?'

Toni took her arm and steered her towards a chair before sinking into the one beside her. 'It's Theo. He's . . . missing.'

Alice took off her glasses and wiped them absently in her apron. 'What do you mean he's missing? Isn't he in Oxford?'

'No. Well, at least I don't think so. Apparently Theo never went to the conference at all.'

'But he told us on Friday night he was going.'

'Yes, I know. It's all a bit of a mystery. I just hope there hasn't been an accident.'

'Now don't think like that, love. I'm sure there's a reasonable explanation.'

'That's what Emma said,' Toni said grimly, 'but I don't know what it could be.'

'Look, why don't you check his study and see if you can find any clues? I'll look in his bedroom if you like.'

'Good idea, Alice.' Toni hurried off in the direction of Theo's study.

The first thing that struck Alice when she went into Theo's room was its untidiness. She hadn't been in here for a while as Toni had banned her from cleaning upstairs until her leg was completely better. But even so Mr French was a very tidy man and usually she only had to flick a duster over the furniture, and hoover. She looked around her for clues. There was nothing on the dressingtable or bedside locker and something didn't look right, but Alice couldn't figure out what it was. She slid back the mirrored door of the wardrobe and gasped. Half of his clothes were gone – much more than he'd need for a weekend away. She moved on to the chest of drawers and noticed that his sock drawer was almost empty and the best of his ties were missing too. Looking around the room again, Alice finally realised what was different. All the photos of Chloe and Marianna were gone. She checked the drawers of the dressing table but the only photo she found was the one of him and Toni taken on their wedding day. The glass was cracked and the frame marked. Alice set it down and went out into the hallway. 'Toni?' she called. 'I think you'd better come up here.'

Toni stirred when she heard Alice's voice. She looked back again at the letter in her hand, shaking her head in disbelief. Alice didn't have to tell her what she'd found in Theo's room. Toni already knew. Theo had left her. But why?

'What on earth are we going to tell Chloe?' Alice asked yet again, as she sipped the brandy that Toni had shoved into her trembling hands.

Toni stared into her own glass. 'I don't know. I could show her the letter, I suppose.'

'But that makes it look like you're to blame,' Alice protested.

'Maybe I am.'

'Rubbish! This has nothing to do with you, Toni, you know it doesn't.' Alice said vehemently and read out the note again. Characteristically it was short and to the point.

Toni

I've decided I can't live like this any longer. Tell Chloe I'm sorry and I'll be in touch as soon as I get settled.

Theo.'

'Settled where?' Toni wondered aloud. Where would he go? Surely he wouldn't leave Dublin? She couldn't imagine him just walking away from his high-powered position in Sylvester's. But then she couldn't understand why he'd left his daughter or his home either. She had told him she'd be leaving soon. She shook her head, baffled by his behaviour.

'Live like what any longer?' Alice asked. 'Is he talking about the pressure of work? Is he talking about your marriage? It's a very cryptic note. And it's completely out of character for Mr French to act on impulse like this.'

Toni nodded. 'You're right. He plans everything. And this couldn't have been planned. Why would he leave without knowing if Chloe got into Trinity? That was so important to him. Oh, Alice, maybe something *has* happened to him?'

'How could it have?' Alice said reasonably. 'Wasn't he able to write that note?'

'Someone might have *made* him write it.'

'And allowed him to pack his bags and take his photographs? I don't think so.'

'No. You're right of course. I'm being melodramatic. But what the hell am I going to tell Chloe?'

'Did I hear my name mentioned?' Chloe pushed open the door and dumped all her bags on the sofa. 'Oh, I'm knackered. Any chance of a cup of tea?' She noticed the empty brandy glasses on the coffee table. 'My, you two are hitting the bottle early, aren't you?'

Alice and Toni looked bleakly at each other.

'What is it? What's wrong?' Chloe looked worriedly from one to the other.

'Sit down, love. We have something to tell you.'

'We've got to do something,' Chloe said again some hours later when they were still trying to fathom Theo's actions. 'Why don't you call the police?'

'As I said, love, there's no point,' Alice said gently. 'They can't do anything about it. Your dad has left of his own free will.'

'I'm sure he'll call you tomorrow,' Toni tried to reassure her. 'He can't have gone far. He has his work to think of.'

'What did you do to him?' Chloe flung at her angrily. Against Alice's advice, Toni had shown her Theo's note. 'Are you having an affair or something?'

'No, Chloe! Of course not!' she reached out a hand to her stepdaughter but Chloe had turned away.

Alice shot her a sympathetic look. 'You're both upset. I think we should get some sleep. I'm sure your father will be in touch tomorrow, Chloe. Now go on upstairs and I'll bring you some hot chocolate.'

'You shouldn't be using the stairs,' Toni said automatically.

'Oh, don't be silly.' Alice flapped her hands and went out to the kitchen while Toni steered an unresponsive Chloe towards the stairs.

Toni helped Chloe to undress and put her to bed. Chloe begged her to stay with her, her earlier animosity forgotten. 'He'll be okay, won't he, Toni?' she asked tearfully, clinging to her stepmother.

Toni stroked her hair. 'Of course he will, love. He'll be fine. And he'll be so proud that you got offers from both colleges.'

As Chloe drifted into sleep thanks to Alice's heavily laced hot chocolate, Toni tucked the duvet around her and tiptoed from the room. Please God let Theo call tomorrow. If he didn't she didn't know what Chloe would do. Thank God she hadn't told her that she too had been planning to leave. Maybe that's why Theo was gone. Maybe he was playing games, knowing full well that Toni would never leave Chloe on her own. But what good was it to him if Toni stayed and he left? She went into her own room and flopped down on the bed. Why was she trying to make sense of anything that Theo French did? The man was a law unto himself. He, no doubt, had his reasons for leaving. And he would make them known in his own good time and not before.

Chapter Twenty-two

Tuesday, 22nd August, 2000

'Mrs French?'

'Speaking?' Toni frowned. Only someone from the hospital would call her Mrs French. To the rest of the world she was Toni Jordan. 'Speaking.'

'Mrs French, this is Mary Legge, Mr Allen's secretary?'

'Oh, yes of course, Mary, how are you?' Toni wondered why Sylvester's general manager was phoning her. Unless of course they'd heard something from Theo.

'Very well, thank you,' the secretary continued politely. 'I wonder could I speak to Mr French?'

Toni gulped. 'Eh, well, I'm afraid he's not here.'

'Oh, well, do you know where I could reach him? His mobile is off.'

'Sorry, I'm afraid I don't.'

'Well, this is very odd. He was supposed to attend a board meeting here at ten.'

Toni looked at her watch. It was almost eleven now. 'I see.'

'And you've no idea where he might be?' the secretary persisted.

'No. I'm very sorry I can't be of more help, Mary.'

'Maybe you'd ask him to call as soon as he gets in?'

'Yes. Yes, of course. Goodbye, Mary.'

'Goodbye, Mrs French.'

'Was that Dad?' Chloe ran downstairs and rushed to her side.

Toni shook her head. 'No, sorry. Come on. Let's have a cup of tea.'

Chloe followed her into the kitchen where Alice was ironing.

'Don't worry about that now,' Toni told her.

'I have to keep busy,' Alice said distractedly.

'Where is he, Alice?' Chloe said desperately. 'Is there anyone you can think of that he would go to? Someone from his past? A friend of Mum's?'

'I'm sorry, love. I really don't know,' Alice said sadly. 'I've been racking my brains but I can't think of anyone.'

'Maybe Robert Perkins would know something. They're friends, aren't they?' Chloe looked hopefully at Toni.

'I'll call him.' Toni went back out to get the phone. She didn't really think Robert would know anything. They weren't that close. That was the problem. Theo wasn't really close to anyone – including his wife and child. 'Sandra? Hi, it's me.'

'Toni, hi. We were worried about you. Is everything okay? Are you sick?'

'No, I'm fine. But I won't be in today. Is Daniel or Robert there?'

'Daniel is in theatre but Mr Perkins is free. Would you like me to put you through?'

Toni sighed. Looked like she'd have to talk to Perky. 'Yes, please.'

'Okay then. See you tomorrow.'

The phone clicked and then Toni heard Robert's deep throaty voice. 'Robert Perkins?'

'Robert, it's Toni.'

'Yes, Toni?'

'I just wondered . . .' Damn! She hated having to tell him anything but Chloe was standing beside her watching and waiting expectantly.

'Yes?' Robert prompted impatiently.

'Well, it seems Theo has gone away. I wondered if he'd said anything to you.'

'Gone away? Where?'

'That's just it,' Toni admitted with difficulty. 'I don't know.'

Robert burst out laughing. 'Well, that's a turn-up for the books!'

Toni bit her lip. 'So he didn't tell you he was going?'

'Not a word. Has he left the hospital? Don't tell me he's gone abroad?'

'I really don't know,' Toni cut him off abruptly. 'Sorry for bothering you, Robert. If you do hear from him please ask him to call home. We're very worried.'

Robert laughed again. 'I'll bet.'

Toni hung up angrily and shook her head at Chloe's questioning look. 'He doesn't know anything.'

'This is crazy! Somebody has to know where he is? Call Emma again. He has to let the hospital know where they can get hold of him.'

Toni dialled the number obediently. 'Emma? It's Toni. Any news?'

'Not a dicky-bird,' Emma said irritably, 'And there are a lot of people looking for him. He was supposed to attend a very important board meeting at ten. They're not impressed.'

'So I gathered. Mary Legge phoned here too. Okay, thanks, Emma. Please keep in touch.'

Emma's voice softened. 'I realise how worried you must be. I'll call as soon as I hear anything.'

'Thanks, Emma. Goodbye.'

'Well?' Chloe asked impatiently.

'No news yet, I'm afraid. Look, I'm just going to nip down to the chemist. I have the most awful headache. I'll be back in ten minutes.' She grabbed her keys and bag and left before Chloe could offer to come with her. She drove to the shops and when she'd parked she pulled her mobile out of her bag and dialled.

'Hello? Yes, may I speak to Mr Ian Chase please?'

* * *

At exactly midday, Ian walked into the pub and strode towards Toni, a broad smile on his face. 'This is nice. I hadn't expected to hear from you so soon.'

'What would you like to drink?'

'Coffee for me too, I'm afraid. I have an operation in an hour.' He signalled the waitress and ordered fresh coffee for them both. 'So. How are you? You sounded a bit tense on the phone.'

'Theo has left me,' she blurted out.

Ian stared at her. 'What?'

234

Toni looked away. 'He's gone. He said he was attending a conference in Oxford at the weekend but he never turned up.'

'Perhaps he's had an accident.'

Toni shook her head. 'No, I found a note in his study saying he couldn't live with me any more.'

Ian stood up as the coffee arrived, pulled some change out of his pocket and threw it on the girl's tray. 'Thanks.' He waited for her to leave before turning back to Toni. 'I don't know what to say, Toni. Are you . . . upset?'

Toni shrugged. 'I don't know. I'm furious with him for walking out on Chloe and I'm completely baffled as to why he's gone now. Why would he leave Chloe? Why would he leave his work?'

'Why would he leave you?' Ian countered.

'We haven't been getting on very well,' Toni admitted. 'A few months ago I asked him for a divorce.'

'And what did he say?' Ian asked gently.

'He went mad. Said I could whistle for it.'

'Then it doesn't make much sense for him to leave you.'

She shook her head. 'Nothing makes sense, Ian. You know how much his position in Sylvester's means to him. Why would he walk away from that?'

'Maybe he's moved on to something better.'

'If that's the case then why would he do it in such a cloak-and-dagger manner?'

'So what are you saying?'

'He didn't plan this. He couldn't have. He was expected at that conference. He was expected at a board meeting in the hospital this morning, for God's sake.

Emma hasn't a clue what's going on either. Why would he keep us all in the dark? Unless . . .'

'Unless?'

'Unless he had something to hide.'

'What are you suggesting?'

'Maybe he was afraid of being fired. Afraid of being disgraced.'

Ian held up a hand. 'Hold on a minute, Toni. Don't you think you're jumping to conclusions?'

'Have you a better reason?' she snapped back.

'Okay. What do you think he might have done to disgrace himself?'

'Well, I don't know, I haven't figured that out yet. Maybe he botched an operation or something.'

'For God's sake, Toni, you can't go around saying things like that. You could ruin the man's reputation.'

'And God forbid I do that! He's only trying to ruin my life and his own daughter's!'

Ian put a placating hand on her arm. 'Look, Toni, you've had a shock and you're upset. I think you need some time to cool down before you do anything.'

Toni shook her head in disbelief. 'I should have known it. It's like some kind of old boys' club. Any sign of trouble and you all stick together.' She jumped to her feet and grabbed her bag, knocking over her cup in her haste. 'Well, thanks a lot, Ian! Thanks for nothing. It's so good to be friends again!'

Still trembling, Toni almost ran out of the pub, climbed into her car and pulled out of the car park with a screech of brakes. She was about to head for home but the thought of Chloe staring at her with large, mournful eyes made her change her mind. She'd go in to work after all. At least she'd be able to make some calls without her stepdaughter listening in on every word.

Sandra looked up and smiled as Toni came through the door. 'Toni! I wasn't expecting you.'

'Change of plan,' Toni said briskly. 'Is everything okay?'

Sandra nodded. 'No problems. Have you thought any more about going out tonight? I heard that the college places came out yesterday so I thought –'

'No, Sandra. It's out of the question,' Toni said abruptly.

She had only closed the door of her office when her mobile rang.

'Toni Jordan, hello?'

'It's me. Is there any news?'

Toni sighed at the hope in Chloe's voice. 'No, sorry, love, nothing.'

'We can't just do nothing, Toni! We have to try and find him.' Chloe's voice was rising steadily.

'Calm down,' Toni said firmly. 'I've no intention of doing nothing. I'm in the clinic and I have a list of people I'm going to call this afternoon.' She stared at the blank page in front of her.

'Who are you going to call?' Chloe demanded.

'Well, his solicitor, his bank manager maybe his doctor –'

'Oh, Toni you're a genius! Oh, thank you. I'm sorry for being bitchy – it's just that I'm so worried.'

'I know, love. But I'm sure your dad is fine wherever

he is. I'll call you later. And remember. Your dad is going to be so proud of you when he hears your news.'

'Thanks.'

Toni put down the phone and pulled out a telephone directory. She had only been bullshitting when she'd told Chloe about the calls she was going to make. She'd only planned to call John Allen, the general manager at Sylvester's. But maybe it wasn't such a bad idea to call the bank and Theo's solicitor. She found the solicitor's number first and dialled.

'Mr Stringer is not available at the moment,' his secretary told her. 'Would you like to leave a message?'

'Please ask him to call Toni Jordan . . . French.'

'Certainly Mrs Jordan-French and your number?'

'No, it's just Jordan. But my husband's name is French. Theodore French.'

'Oh. Right, Mrs Jordan. And your number?'

Toni sighed and gave her number. Then she called the bank. She wasn't sure who to ask for. Though Theo had given her access to all his accounts she rarely used them. Her salary was still paid into her own current account and she used that to cover her day-to-day expenses. Theo took care of Alice's salary, the housekeeping account and any bills that came in.

'I wanted to talk to someone about my husband's accounts. His name is Theodore French.'

'One moment please.'

Toni listened to *Für Elise* and tapped her fingers impatiently.

'Mrs French? I'm just putting you through to the manager, Mr Shilling.'

She should have realised that Theo would only deal with the top man. Mr Shilling! She giggled. What a name for a bank manager!

'Mrs French? This is Tom Shilling. How can I help you?'

Toni thought quickly. 'Eh, I was just wondering if my husband had been in touch with you. We have been thinking of opening an account for our daughter now that she's starting college.' It was pretty lame, but all Toni could come up with on the spot. She could hardly tell the man she was trying to find her missing husband!

'An excellent idea, Mrs French, but no, I haven't heard from Mr French in quite some time.'

'Oh I see.' That had to be good news, Toni thought.

'If you would like to make an appointment to come in and discuss the matter I'd be delighted to take you through the options. We would be very happy to do business with you again. I must say, I was very upset that Mr French felt he had to move his business to another bank. If there was a problem with our service I wish he had told me.'

Toni closed her eyes. 'Sorry?'

'I'm referring to Mr French withdrawing most of the funds from his current and savings accounts.'

'Oh, right, of course. Sorry, when was that again?'

'Just let me check on the computer. Oh, yes, that was the fifth of June.'

'Ah, yes, I remember. I can assure you, Mr Shilling, that it wasn't because of bad service.'

'Well, that's nice to know.'

'How much is left in those accounts?' Toni asked casually.

239

'Fifty-three pounds in the current account and twenty-one pounds and seventy-three pence in the savings account.'

'Great,' Toni said grimly. 'Well, thank you very much for your help, Mr Shilling. We'll be in touch.'

Chapter Twenty-three

Tuesday, 22nd August, 2000

Toni was sitting at her desk with her head in her hands when Jade came in.

'Toni?' Jade took in at a glance her friend's faded blue jeans, T-shirt and trainers. Her hair was pulled back into an untidy knot. 'Toni, what is it?'

Toni looked up vacantly and then glanced at her watch. She'd been sitting here in a daze for over an hour.

'What's happened now? Have you heard something?'

'Yes.'

Jade looked at her expectantly. 'It's not good, is it? Has something happened to him?'

Toni laughed bitterly. 'Other than that he seems to have gone out of his mind? No.'

'Tell me.'

'There was a note in his study. It said he couldn't live like this any longer – whatever the hell that means. We checked his bedroom and he's taken a lot of clothes and some photos with him. It doesn't look like he's planning on coming back too soon.'

'Jesus! How's Chloe taking it?'

'She's in a terrible state. And it should be such a happy time for her. You know she got a place in UCD and in Trinity?'

Jade smiled. 'No surprise there.'

'No. Oh, and there's more. Theo's cleaned out our bank accounts.'

'So he must have planned this.'

Toni shook her head. 'No, he did this a while back. The Monday after I asked him for a divorce, to be specific.'

'The bastard!' Jade gasped. 'But there must be more money somewhere. Theo has to be loaded.'

'All tied up in bonds, shares, pension plans.' Toni shrugged helplessly.

'Don't you have money of your own?'

'There's a couple of hundred in a building society and whatever is in my current account but that's it. I always let Theo take care of our finances.'

Jade sighed. That's exactly what she'd done and look where it had got her.

'Oh, why did he do it, Jade? I just don't understand.'

'Maybe he just wanted to dump you before you dumped him.'

'I don't buy that. He wouldn't have chosen to leave now. Just before the college offers are made? No. He didn't plan this.' She stood up and started to pace. 'It has to have something to do with the hospital, I don't care what Ian says.'

Jade turned to stare at her. 'Ian?'

Toni nodded, too preoccupied to care about her friend's questioning look. 'Yes. I talked to him earlier. I thought he might be able to help.'

'And?'

'I was wrong,' Toni said abruptly.

'So, what now?'

'I'm going to phone John Allen to see if he knows anything.'

Jade shook her head. 'If his secretary doesn't know anything it's unlikely that John will.'

'But I'm going to have to tell him what's going on, Jade. I'm surprised he hasn't called me.'

'Yes, they're going to have to find a replacement for him,' Jade agreed. 'Maybe you should go and see him. It's not really a conversation for the phone.'

Toni nodded and picked up her keys. 'You're right. Thanks, Jade.'

'Is there anything I can do while you're out?'

'Actually, there is, if you can spare the time.'

'I'm free for the next hour or so. What do I do?'

'Theo's solicitor, Timothy Stringer is due to return my call. Pretend you're me and find out if he's had any dealings with him recently.'

Jade's eyes widened. 'Concerning wills and things?'

Toni shrugged. 'You never know. And could you phone Bill Thompson, Theo's GP? Just in case there's a medical reason for his behaviour.'

'He's not going to tell me – that is, you,' Jade pointed out.

Toni grinned. 'You'll figure out a way to extract the necessary information, Ms Peters.'

Jade smiled back. 'Okay, boss. I'll do my best.'

'I'll be back as quick as I can.'

'Okay then. Good luck.'

* * *

'Well, this is all very strange,' John Allen shook his head worriedly. 'I had no idea that Theo had gone away. It's really most irregular. He has given no notice to this hospital. It leaves me in a very awkward position.'

Toni glared at him. 'Well, I'm afraid I'm more concerned about the effect this is having on his daughter.'

'Yes, yes, of course. It must be a very distressing time for you both.'

'It is,' Toni said, slightly mollified. 'Maybe you could talk to his staff and colleagues and see if anyone can shed some light on this mystery, John.'

John nodded emphatically. 'I can assure you I will leave no stone unturned. If Theo's departure has anything to do with this hospital I'll soon know what it is, you can depend on that.' He stood up indicating the interview was at an end. 'I'll call you later, Toni.'

Toni shook his hand. 'Thank you, John. I appreciate your help.'

* * *

When she got back to the office, Jade had left a note on her desk.

In theatre until five, I'll drop back then to fill you in. J.

So, Toni interpreted, Jade had obviously found out

something. Whether it was good or bad she'd have to wait thirty minutes to find out.

Sandra pushed open the door and carried in a tray with a large pot of tea, a plate of sandwiches and a packet of chocolate biscuits. 'I doubt if you've eaten all day,' she said kindly as she put the tray on the desk. 'But you have to keep your strength up and a nice cup of tea always makes me feel better.'

Toni looked at her curiously. Surely Jade hadn't told her what was going on?

Sandra saw the look. 'Chloe was on. She told me about her dad. She's terribly upset, poor girl.'

'Yes.'

'But I told her that he'd turn up when he was ready. Maybe a patient died on him or something and he flipped. Sure don't we all crack up from time to time?'

Toni stared at her. 'You may have something there, Sandra. Listen, thanks. And thanks for being so kind to Chloe.'

Sandra smiled shyly. 'Not at all. Don't mention it. Now I'll go and leave you in peace. You make sure and eat some of those sandwiches.'

Toni smiled. 'I will. Thanks.' She bit into a sandwich and poured a cup of tea and was surprised to find that she did have an appetite. The sandwiches were gone and she'd started on the biscuits when Jade arrived.

She grabbed a biscuit and sat down. 'Well?'

'No luck,' Toni reported. 'It was a total surprise to John. He's going to suss out the other staff to see if anyone knows anything. How about you? Did you talk to Stringer?'

Jade cocked her head on one side. 'I don't think I talked to him. It was more like he talked *at* me.'

Toni sighed. 'Solicitors.'

'Indeed. Well, what he did admit is that Theo was in touch with him on Monday.'

'Monday! So he's still in Dublin.'

Jade shrugged. 'Ah, we don't know that. Stringer wouldn't say if he made a personal appearance or not. He did tell me that there were letters on the way to both you and Chloe.'

Toni brightened. 'Well that's got to be good news, hasn't it?'

Jade was sceptical. 'I wouldn't get your hopes up.'

'What about the doctor?'

Jade shook her head. 'Hasn't seen him in months and Theo was in perfect health when they did his annual check-up back in April.

Toni nodded. 'Yes, I didn't really expect anything else. Though Sandra said something that made sense.'

Jade looked at her with raised eyebrows. 'You told Sandra?'

'No, Chloe did. Anyway, Sandra thought that maybe one of his patient's died and it upset him.'

'Well, it should be easy enough to find that. Get Emma to check.'

Toni picked up the phone and dialled. 'You're right. It will give her something to do. I think the poor girl is going round the bend without Theo belting out orders at her every five minutes. Hello, Emma? It's Toni.'

'Oh, Toni! Has he been in touch?'

'Nope. Anything at your end?'

Emma lowered her voice. 'Well, I've overheard some stories. They're probably not true but I thought you should know about them.'

'Go on.'

'Not over the phone. I could drop over to the house on my way home.'

'No, Chloe will be there. How about we meet at six in the Gresham for a quick drink?'

'That's fine. I'll see you then. Goodbye, Toni.'

'Goodbye, Emma.' Toni was frowning when she hung up.

'What?' Jade asked.

'There's some gossip doing the rounds.'

Jade gave a short laugh. 'Glad to hear nothing's changed.'

'Yes but you know the problem with gossip, Jade. There's usually a tiny percentage of truth in it.'

* * *

'Thanks for coming.' Toni handed Emma a gin and tonic and took a sip of her whisky.

Emma took a gulp of her drink. 'I hope you're still saying that when you hear what I have to say.'

'I've no intention of shooting the messenger, Emma. I want to know what people are saying. I talked to John Allen but he seemed to be completely in the dark.'

'Oh, I don't know. He probably wouldn't tell you anything anyway. You know what they're like.'

'Maybe you're right.' Toni thought of Ian's reaction when she'd said that Theo's disappearance might be connected to Sylvester's. 'So tell me what you've heard.'

Emma shifted uncomfortably in her seat. 'I doubt if you could believe a word of it. The sources aren't exactly reliable –'

'Just tell me, Emma.'

The other girl sighed. 'Well, the first one I heard – but I don't believe – is that he botched an operation and is afraid of being struck off.'

Toni gulped. That was one of the reasons high on her list.

'But I don't believe that,' Emma said loyally,

'Well, it's easily checked. Anything else?'

Emma looked down. 'There's a horrible rumour doing the rounds. I'm so sorry, Toni. But they're saying that he was on drugs.'

Toni laughed. 'Rubbish. Theo wouldn't touch them. It's hard enough to get him to have a few drinks, for God's sake! He's always preaching about the importance of moderation.'

Relief flooded Emma's face. 'Yes, you're right, it's ridiculous.'

'Next?'

'There was one suggestion that he might be involved in some kind of fraud.'

'Why?' Toni was genuinely surprised.

'Well, he was always going on about his shares and investments.'

Toni shook her head. 'No, I don't believe he'd get involved in anything dodgy. His position in the medical community was too important to him.'

'I suppose. Well, I'm afraid the only other story is that

he –' Emma paused to take a gulp of her drink, '– ran away with another woman.'

Toni laughed again. 'You know your boss, Emma. Do you think the woman has been born who'd be able to drag Theo away from his beloved career?'

Emma smiled. 'I suppose not. He'd only leave Sylvester's if he had a much better position to go to or –'

'Or?'

Emma's smile faded. 'Or he had no other choice.'

Chapter Twenty-four

Tuesday evening, 22nd August, 2000

Toni walked nervously up the narrow, dark street, regretting her decision to leave the car at the clinic. She'd obviously got the address wrong. There was no way Jade could live here. She paused outside number 67. It was the last house in the terrace and looked as uninviting and bleak as all the others. There was a light on in the front room and Toni decided to admit defeat and ask for directions. She walked up the uneven path and pressed the bell. When there was no response she banged the knocker, sending a flurry of dead paint to the ground.

'What is it? What do you want? I've no rooms. Can't you see the sign?'

Toni looked from the tiny wizened woman to the yellowing sign in the front window.

'Em, I'm not looking for a room and I am very sorry to disturb you. I'm looking for an address, I wondered if you could help me?'

Patsy Stewart inhaled deeply on her cigarette before

throwing the butt out into the garden. 'Where was it you were looking for?'

'It's an apartment block on Manor Court. Number 67.'

'This is 67 Manor Court.' Patsy cackled. 'Apartment block, is it?'

Toni smiled. 'I must have made a mistake. Sorry.'

'Who are you looking for?' Patsy asked as Toni turned away.

'A Mrs Peters,' Toni said politely.

'Jade? Ah you've come to the right place, love. Apartment block,' she muttered with a broad grin. 'Maybe one day, love. When I win the lotto!' She hollered up the stairs and Jade leaned over the bannisters. 'What is it Mrs Stewart? – Toni!'

'Hi.'

Patsy looked from one to the other before shuffling back down the hall. 'Apartment block!'

Jade looked solemnly down at her friend. 'You'd better come up.'

Toni climbed the stairs and let out a small gasp as Jade led her into the cold, shabby little room.

Jade turned to face her, her eyes defiant. 'Well, now you know. Welcome to my luxurious pad.'

Toni sank down onto the edge of the bed. 'I had no idea, Jade. Why didn't you tell me?'

'Because it's my business and I don't want pity from you or anyone else.'

'Jade, I'm your friend!'

Jade looked away. 'Do you want a drink? I can offer you black tea, coffee or,' she reached into the press, 'a sniff of vodka.'

'Yes, I do want a drink, but I need a large one. Let's go down to that pub on the corner.'

'In case you hadn't figured it out yet, Toni, I can't really afford to go out drinking every night.' Jade's voice dripped with sarcasm.

Toni's eyes flashed angrily. 'Then you're just going to have to accept some charity, aren't you? Now come on. I'm not in the mood for an argument.'

Toni marched out of the room and, after a moment, Jade picked up her bag and followed.

Toni got the drinks and carried them over to the corner table where Jade was sitting.

'Any news? Had Emma heard anything?'

Toni shook her head. 'Not from Theo. But she's heard plenty from everyone else in the hospital. But never mind that for the moment. I think you should be doing the talking.'

Jade nodded, almost relieved that Toni been finally found her out. 'Well, the reason for my salubrious surroundings is simple. I'm broke.'

Toni blinked. 'I don't understand. You must have got a fortune for your house.'

Jade sighed. 'Well, the banks did. Aidan and I were up to our eyes in debt when we separated. I'm still paying off some of the bills now, though thankfully I should be in the clear soon.'

Toni stared at her flabbergasted. 'But you never said anything. All this time, Jade – I can't believe it. Why didn't you tell me? I would have helped.'

'I know you would have. And I would have been very

grateful but I'd also have hated you. I couldn't risk that, Toni. Your friendship is the one thing that's kept me going. I'd go nuts if we didn't have our nights out.'

Toni smiled and drained her glass. 'Let me get a refill and then you can tell me all about it.'

'No, I'll get this,' Jade protested.

'Shut up, Jade.' Toni said equably and went to the bar.

'It all started a couple of years before we separated,' Jade began when Toni returned, 'although I didn't realise it at the time. Aidan had been going through a rough patch. He was building this amazing house out in Malahide for a couple, but they broke up and neither one of them wanted the house. Anyway, to cut a long story short, Aidan never got paid. He got a bit depressed and started to slack off work – though I didn't know that then. And to cheer himself up he started going to the bookies or the racecourse.'

Toni gazed at her horrified. 'Oh, my God. How did you find out?'

'I was in his study one day and I found all the unpaid bills. I couldn't believe it. Aidan never owed anyone a penny in his life. When I confronted him he told me that he was owed money by a major developer and he was strapped for cash.'

'And you believed him.'

Jade shrugged. 'He'd never done anything like it before. Of course I believed him. We talked to the bank and worked out payment plans and cut back on all the non-essentials. No holidays, no nights out . . .'

'But he did it again?'

Jade's eyes were dark with sadness. 'I don't know that

254

he ever stopped. But one day I found out how much he was lying to me and I knew that I couldn't live with him any more.'

Toni took her hand and held it tightly. 'Oh, Jade. Why did you go through this all alone?'

'I was embarrassed. I felt ashamed of Aidan. And I was furious that I'd been taken in so easily. How could I have been so stupid?'

'Because you loved him and he loved you.'

'He couldn't have loved me,' Jade spat out bitterly. 'You don't do that to someone you love. Take away their home, their life, their good name.' She rummaged in her bag and pulled out a crumpled pack of cigarettes.

'Can I have one?' Toni asked miserably. What on earth had they done to deserve men like Aidan and Theo? Wasn't there such a thing as a trustworthy man any more? Did they all lie and cheat?

'You don't smoke,' Jade pointed out as she lit their cigarettes.

'No,' Toni agreed, inhaled deeply and coughed until tears streamed from her eyes. She stubbed out the cigarette and waved at the waiter who ignored her. 'Maybe I'll have another drink instead.'

Jade stood up. 'I'll go. I think I can just about afford one round.'

'I'll buy the fish and chips on the way home,' Toni offered. While Jade was at the bar she dialled home. 'Chloe? Hi, have you heard anything?'

'No, Toni. Where are you? I've been worried sick.'

'I'm still in work,' Toni lied. She didn't think Chloe would understand it if she said she was in a pub.

'Did you find out anything? Did you talk to Dad's solicitor?'

'No.' At least that was the truth, Toni thought. 'He's to call me. And so is John Allen. I got hold of Theo's doctor but he hasn't seen him in ages. And he says your dad is as fit as a fiddle.'

'Well, I suppose that's something.'

'Is Mark there with you?'

'Yes.'

'Good. Ask him to stay until I get home. I'll pay for his taxi.'

'Okay, Toni. Thanks. Will you be late?'

'Jade and I were just going to grab a bite to eat. Is that okay?'

'Sure. See you later.'

'Who was that?' Jade set the drinks down carefully.

Toni sighed. 'Chloe. I've just told her I'm still at work and then I'm going for something to eat with you.'

'Well, that part is true. But why the lies?'

Toni looked grim as she remembered her talk with Emma. 'Because I'm just not ready to face her.'

Jade put down her drink. 'What's happened?'

Toni bit her lip and pushed an untidy curl back off her face. 'I'm not sure, Jade, and I don't know what to believe. But it's not good.'

'Just tell me,' Jade said gently. 'You'll feel better.'

Toni's eyes were bright with tears. 'I doubt that.' But slowly, her voice trembling, she related the rumours that Emma had heard.

'There is no foundation behind any of these stories. If he screwed up an operation or did anything dodgy in connection with the hospital John Allen will soon hear about it.'

'Yes, but will he tell anyone?' Toni said sceptically. 'The reputation of their precious hospital is more important than anything or anyone.'

'You can't sit on a story involving your chief of surgery, Toni,' Jade pointed out. 'Especially when he's done a bunk.'

'I suppose.'

'And as for the other stories, they just don't make sense. Theo is as straight as they come!'

'That's what I thought, Jade, but something made him leave. And leave in a hurry.'

'Maybe when you get his letter it will explain everything.'

'Maybe. Jade, do you think he's been seeing other women?' Toni asked suddenly.

'Probably,' Jade answered without hesitation. 'Oh, come on, Toni. You weren't born yesterday! His beautiful young wife wants a divorce and you're surprised that he might be seeking comfort elsewhere? I'll be amazed if he doesn't replace you with a younger model.'

Toni digested this in silence and drained her glass.

'Toni? Shit, am I being too blunt here? It's your own fault, though. Three vodkas on an empty stomach bring out the honesty in me.'

'No, it's okay. I suppose I never really thought about it – him with another woman. I was so wrapped in what would happen to me that I never gave much thought as to what would happen to him. Poor Chloe. At this rate she could end up with someone younger than she is for a stepmother.'

Jade laughed. 'Oh, well, they'll be able to watch Top of the Pops together!'

'Jade!'

'Ah, you've got to laugh, Toni. If you don't laugh you cry.'

Toni sighed at the sadness in her friend's eyes. 'Come on. I'll buy you that supper. Now do you have any bread in your flat or are you too poor to even buy that?'

Jade pondered the question. 'I have a couple of slices of bread. Just no butter.'

'Eh, lass, in my day if yer had a piece of dry bread, ye thought all yer birthdays had come together.'

'That's nothing,' Jade scoffed. 'We used to have to wait until our Da ate his dry bread and we'd be lucky if we got a bit of the crust!'

Toni linked her arm through Jade's. 'Come on, you daft old bat. Let's go.'

* * *

Toni climbed into the cab, waved at Jade and gave her address to the driver. Then she changed her mind. 'No, actually, can you bring me to Ashgrove in Beaumont?'

'Is that the posh apartments off Shantalla Road?'

'Yes.' Toni stared blindly out of the window. Why on earth was she going to Ian's apartment at this time of night. He was probably asleep. In bed with Carla. Shit, this wasn't a good idea. 'No, no, take me to Griffith Avenue.'

'Look, love, make up your mind will ye? Now is it Beaumont or Glasnevin?'

Toni took a deep breath. 'Okay, Beaumont. But I want

you to wait for me. I'll just be a few minutes and then you can take me to Glasnevin.'

Toni ignoring the driver's muttered expletives, tidied her hair and straightened her T-shirt. She didn't want to look pissed and emotional when Ian answered the door. Five minutes later, the taxi pulled up in front of the apartment block.

'I won't be long,' she promised.

The driver pulled out a newspaper. 'Take as long as ye like, love. You're paying.'

Toni stood in the doorway, her finger hovering over the button.

'Are you going to stand there all night?'

Toni jumped as Ian loomed out of the darkness behind her. 'Ian! God, you scared the hell out of me!'

'Sorry. Here, let me.'

He leaned across her to open the door, so close that she could smell the familiar tang of his aftershave. 'I can't stay long,' she said shakily.

He took her hand and pulled her towards the lift. 'Oh, and I hoped you were here to stay.'

He swayed slightly as he stepped into the lift. 'You're drunk!' Toni exclaimed.

Ian gave her a broad sloppy grin. 'I think you've had a few yourself, Toni. You have tomato ketchup on your chin.' He leaned forward and licked it off, his tongue hot on her skin.

'Ian, don't!'

The lift doors slid silently open on the next floor and trapping her wrist in a vice-like grip he pulled her firmly towards the door of his apartment. 'Come on, Toni. Let's not play games. We both know why you're here.'

'No! No way, Ian! Fuck off!' Toni kneed him in the groin and he folded in two.

'Jesus, Toni! What the hell did you do that for?'

Toni jumped back into the lift and pressed the button. As the doors closed he looked up and she saw a mixture of pain and fury in his eyes. When the lift opened again she ran out to the waiting taxi, tears flooding down her cheeks.

'Hey, love? What's wrong?'

'Nothing! Just drive!' she gasped before collapsing into a corner and sobbing all the way home.

Chapter Twenty-five

Wednesday, 23rd August, 2000

'I'm sure she'd tell you if there was anything to tell,' Mark insisted, nodding his thanks as Alice put a mug of tea in front of him.

Chloe paced the kitchen moodily. 'No, she's definitely keeping something from me. They must have had a row. Why else would Dad just up and leave like that?'

'I'm sure it would take more than a row with Toni to make your dad leave,' Mark said matter-of-factly.

Alice nodded in agreement. 'You're quite right, Mark. I'm sure your dad had his reasons for going and he'll tell you soon enough. It's only been a few days.'

'But I'm so worried, Alice. What if something terrible has happened to him?' Chloe sniffed miserably, tears filling her eyes.

Mark groaned and gathered into his arms. 'Don't cry, Chloe. Please don't cry.'

'I think I heard the post,' Alice murmured and discreetly left the room. She shuffled out into the hall and bent slowly to pick up the post. Perching her glasses on her nose she flicked through the letters. Three junk mail, two for Mr French, one for Toni and one for – 'Oh!' Alice threw the other letters on the hall table and hurried back to the kitchen. 'Chloe! There's a letter for you.'

Chloe pulled away from Mark and wiped her eyes. 'It's probably from one of the colleges,' she said dismissively.

'I don't think so.' Alice held it out to her.

'Dad! It's from Dad!' Chloe almost snatched it out of her hand and tore it open, pulling out a single sheet of paper.

'Well?' Mark prompted anxiously after Chloe had read it several times and still said nothing.

'Here.' She shoved it into his hand.

Mark read it aloud.

My dearest Chloe,

I'm sorry to leave so suddenly and without saying goodbye. Things were becoming unbearable and I just had to get away.

I hope you will forgive me for leaving at such an important time in your life but I know that you are strong and well able to stand on your own two feet.

I have set up a standing order for you that will sustain you through university – Tim Stringer will be in touch with the details. And of course you will have your mother's inheritance in October.

Use it wisely, my dear, and study hard.

Make me proud.

Love,

Dad.

'Well, at least we know he's all right,' Alice smiled reassuringly at Chloe.

'Yes, he is, isn't he?' Chloe said fiercely. 'God, what

could be so bad for him to just take off like that? How could he leave me? He's been moaning on and on at me about exams and college. And now, when I need him most, he disappears.'

'You don't need anyone, Chloe. You're strong, intelligent and beautiful. And you're apparently rich too.' Mark grinned at her.

Chloe smiled reluctantly. 'I suppose you're after me for my money now!'

'Hey, I'm a poor student. I need all the help I can get. If it wasn't for you I'd probably have to become a toyboy.'

Chloe laughed reluctantly.

Alice smiled. 'Why don't you two go for a walk and I'll have a nice lunch ready when you get back?'

Mark took Chloe's hand. 'How about it?'

Chloe nodded. 'Yeah. I could do with clearing my head. Thanks, Alice.' She bent and hugged the woman. 'What would I do without you? Promise you won't ever leave me?'

Alice swallowed the lump in her throat. 'Not a chance.'

* * *

'Toni, could I have a word?'

'What is it, Sandra? I'm busy, ' Toni asked irritably, not even looking up from her work.

'It's about Mam,' Sandra murmured timidly.

Toni's head jerked up. 'Is she sick? What's wrong? Oh, sit down, Sandra. Sorry for snapping.'

Sandra smiled gratefully and sat down. 'Oh, that's okay, Toni. You have a lot on your mind.'

'Never mind me. Tell me what's wrong.'

'Well, Mam won't admit it, Toni, but she isn't at all well. Her speech is slurred when she's tired and her balance isn't great either.'

'Has she seen the doctor?'

'Oh, yes. I asked him about putting her on this new drug, but apparently it's only proven to be effective in milder forms of the disease.'

'I'm sorry.'

Sandra shrugged, well used to disappointment. 'He said he'd change her medication and see if that helped. But the fact is, Toni, I don't think I should be working full time. At least not at the moment.'

'No problem, Sandra. I told you that before. You can take a few weeks off if you like, or I could get someone in to job-share.'

Sandra brightened. 'Oh, that would be great. The job-share, I mean. Mam would be furious if I gave up work completely. She feels guilty enough as it is. If I could just be there in the mornings to help her wash and dress and make some lunch . . .'

'No problem. I'll call the agency today. In the meantime, I can sit at your desk in the mornings and I'm sure Jade will help out too.'

Sandra beamed at her. 'Oh, thanks, Toni. I really appreciate it.'

'Not at all, Sandra. Family comes first.'

Sandra saw the dark misery in Toni's eyes. 'Is there no news?'

Toni shook her head. 'It's Chloe I feel sorry for. She's so worried.'

264

'But at least she's got you, Toni.'

Toni smiled weakly. 'Yes.'

Sandra stood up. 'If there's anything I can do . . .'

'Thanks, Sandra, but there's nothing we can do but wait. Anyway, I think you've got enough on your hands.'

'Well, I'm still on for going out some night. A break would do us all good.'

'Yeah, I'd like that. Maybe next week if things have settled down.'

Sandra waved her hands as she headed for the door. 'Whenever. Seeya later, Toni, and thanks again.'

The smile faded from Toni's face when the door had closed, and she slumped back in her chair. It was only two days since they'd learned of Theo's disappearance but it felt like months. Jade kept pestering her to do something about her financial situation but Toni couldn't summon up the interest. All she could think about was the look on Ian's face when she'd left him last night. He was completely out of line accusing her of coming there for just One Thing. Toni sighed. Or was he? Maybe he was right. Maybe she was kidding herself that she'd gone there to talk. Maybe she wanted him. Wanted to feel his arms around her. Wanted to feel his lips on her skin and taste the saltiness of his. She shuddered. She'd made a fool of herself and he would probably never even talk to her now. Although he had been very drunk. Maybe he wouldn't remember exactly what had happened. She brightened at the thought.

The phone on her desk rang making her jump guiltily. 'Hello, Toni Jordan speaking.'

'Toni? It's Alice.'

'Alice! Is there anything wrong? Have you heard something?'

'Not directly.'

'What do you mean?'

'Chloe got a letter from her father.'

'Oh, thank God. What did it say?'

'Much the same as the first note and that he's set up a standing order for her.'

'That's something, I suppose. Is she happier? Can I speak to her?'

'She's gone for a walk with Mark. She was a bit upset.'

'Well, I suppose the relief –'

Alice sighed. 'I'm afraid it's not relief she's feeling, Toni. She's angry with him for leaving her.'

'She's not the only one. Poor Chloe. I think I'll take her out to dinner tonight. We need to talk.'

'Why don't I make you something before I go home? Then you would have more privacy.'

'That would be better. Thank you, Alice. You're an angel.'

'You're welcome, dear. Good luck.'

* * *

'Ollie? Can you hear me?' Chloe closed over the door to the kitchen where Alice was busy chopping vegetables.

'Barely. Why are you whispering?'

'Oh, Ollie! It's Dad. He wrote me a letter and it sounds like he's never coming back.'

'Crikey. Where is he?'

'He doesn't say,' Chloe sniffed. 'He says he left because life was unbearable.'

Ollie whistled. 'Wow. What on earth could be unbearable in his life?'

Chloe bristled. 'What do you mean?'

'Well, he's got everything. A big job, lots of money, a gorgeous wife and a clever daughter.'

'Maybe he was under a lot of pressure. Stress does funny things to people.' Chloe didn't really believe that her dad was one of them. He always seemed in control.

'Nah, he must have run off with someone else.'

'Why would you say that?' Chloe protested. 'I don't know where you get these ideas from, Ollie. I really don't'

'Stands to reason. But he doesn't want you to hate him so he's lying low for a while. He'll probably call you in a few weeks and tell you. Then you'll be so relieved that he's okay and he's coming home you won't mind the fact that you're getting a new stepmother!'

Chloe chewed on her thumb nail. She hated to think there might be any truth in Ollie's rather dramatic version of events but there was something weird going on.

'Chlo? Are you still there?'

'Yeah.'

'Do you want to come over to my place?'

'Maybe later. Can I call you?'

'Sure,' Ollie said kindly. 'Don't worry about it, Chlo. I'm sure everything will work out.'

'Yeah. Right. Bye.'

* * *

'I'm not hungry,' Chloe pushed her plate away.

Toni tucked into her coq-au-vin with false gusto. 'That's

a pity. Alice has outdone herself tonight. This is gorgeous.'

Chloe sniffed appreciatively. It did look good. She should probably have some. Just so as not to offend Alice.

Toni suppressed a smile as Chloe served herself from the casserole. 'I'm so glad that your dad finally wrote to you. It's wonderful to know that he's okay, isn't it?'

'Oh, wonderful!' Chloe said sarcastically.

'Look, Chloe, I know you're angry.'

Chloe laughed. 'Angry? Why would I be angry? I'm getting my own allowance. I'll get my mother's inheritance in a few weeks. I'm free.'

Toni sighed. 'I'm sure it must have been very hard for your father to leave you.'

Chloe looked her straight in the eye. 'Why did he leave? You know, don't you, Toni?'

Toni held her gaze. 'No, honestly, Chloe, I don't.'

'Did you have a row?'

'No, but it's true that we've being going through a difficult patch.'

Chloe put down her knife and fork and pushed her plate away. 'How difficult?'

Toni shrugged uncomfortably. She was tempted to tell Chloe that she'd asked Theo for a divorce but decided against it. The girl had enough to cope with at the moment. 'We've just been getting on each other's nerves lately. It happens.'

'I think you know something you're not telling me,' Chloe accused.

Toni nodded silently.

'I knew it! Tell me, Toni. I'll find out sooner or later.'

'Okay then. There are a lot of nasty rumours about

your dad doing the rounds. They're all rubbish, of course.'

'What kind of rumours?'

Toni sighed. 'Oh, the usual. He ran off with a patient, he was involved in some kind of fraud, someone died unnecessarily on his operating table –'

'That's a load of crap,' Chloe said angrily.

'Yes, I'm sure it is and you must ignore it all. It's nothing but vicious gossip.'

'But why did he go, Toni? Was it because of you?'

Toni looked her straight in the eye. 'No, I don't believe that either.'

'But what's left? What other reason could there be? Why has he left me, Toni? Why?'

'I wish I could answer that, love. Look, he will be in touch, I'm sure he will. In the meantime why don't you fill out your college application and send it back? He'll be thrilled to hear all about it when he does phone.'

'I'm not going,' Chloe said stubbornly.

'I know you'd prefer to go to UCD and if you really want to –'

'I'm not going to either of them. I've decided. I don't want to be a doctor. I don't want to be anything. I'm going to take a year out, see the world and think about what I want to do with my life.'

'I don't think you've thought this through, Chloe,' Toni said gently. 'This is a very big decision and not one you should make lightly.'

'Hell, my dad made a decision to walk out on me pretty lightly, so why should I be any different? He doesn't care so why should I?' And she ran from the room crying.

Toni pushed her plate aside and rested her head in her

hands. This was so unfair and so completely selfish of Theo. What kind of a man was he to leave his own daughter like this? *A guilty one*, an ominous voice in her head answered and she stood up abruptly and poured herself a large Scotch. Draining it in one gulp she ignored the dishes and went out into the hall to set the alarm and lock up. She was too tired to think any more about this tonight. As she reached up a hand to turn off the light, she noticed the envelope on the hall table. She took it up and peered at it in the gloom. Yes, it was for her. She tore it open as she went up to her room and turned on the bedside lamp to read it. The thick notepaper looked expensive and official. She scanned the gold pre-printed name at the top. Timothy Stringer, Theo's solicitor! She started to read, stopping halfway to turn on the main light. She re-read the document several times before it finally sank in. 'You bastard, Theo. You vicious, cold, miserable bastard!'

Chapter Twenty-six

Thursday, 24th August, 2000

Jade paced Toni's office in cold fury as she read the letter the next morning. 'God, he's a clever bastard.'

'He certainly has had the last laugh.'

'But how did he get everything organised so quickly?'

'I've no idea. What am I going to tell Chloe?'

'The truth,' Jade said firmly. 'You can't protect her from everything.'

'Oh, right. Let me see, how does this sound? "Your Dad's taken all our money, put the house up for sale. Oh and yes, I nearly forgot, he's filed for divorce on the grounds of irreconcilable differences." Yes, that should go down well.'

Jade sat down and stared at her. 'I'm not saying it will be easy, Toni. But you have to tell her. An estate agent is going to turn up on your doorstep any day now.'

Toni groaned. 'Oh, Lord, just when I thought things couldn't get any worse. You know she says she won't go to college now. She's talking about taking a year off and travelling. How am I going to talk her out of that one?'

She took a sip of her tea and then pushed the cold liquid away in disgust.

'That's another day's work. Right now you need to get yourself a solicitor. You live in the house, and possession is nine-tenths of the law.'

Toni tapped her pen anxiously. 'I haven't got time for bloody solicitors and all of that bureaucratic nonsense. I need to get to the bottom of this. Maybe if I find out why Theo really did a runner it will help in the divorce courts.'

'The divorce courts won't care,' Jade said cynically.

'Well, sod them and Theo. I've got a job and Chloe has her allowance and her inheritance. We'll survive.'

'What about the clinic?' Jade asked suddenly.

'What do you mean?'

Jade frowned. 'Well, Theo is a major investor – or was.'

Toni stared at her. 'Jesus! I'd forgotten. I wonder has he sold out to Daniel. No, he couldn't have. Daniel would have told me.'

'Oh, bloody hell,' Jade muttered. 'You know what he's done, don't you?'

'What?'

'Well, think about it. How does he get more money and get back at you at the same time?' He sells his shares to Robert.'

Toni frowned. 'But that would make Robert the majority shareholder – oh, shit!'

'You may not have a job after all,' Jade said glumly.

'No way! Why would Robert fire me? What would be the point?'

Jade blinked and then shook her head. 'This is silly. We don't even know that Theo *has* sold his shares.'

Toni stood up. 'There's only one way to find out.'

Jade's eyes followed her to the door. 'Just keep your cool,' she cautioned.

Toni paused in the doorway, a smile playing around her lips. 'Sorry? Is that Jade Peters telling *me* to keep my cool with Perky?'

Jade made a face and Toni laughed and went down the corridor to Robert's office. She knocked briefly and walked in. 'Robert? Could I have a word?'

Robert beamed at her. 'Toni, my dear. Of course you can. Do sit down. Tell me, have you heard anything from the Scarlet Pimpernel?'

Toni sat down and looked at the amused twinkle in the surgeon's eye. He's enjoying all this, she realised. The bastard thinks it's funny. Or maybe he's happy because he's just become the majority shareholder.

Toni shook her head solemnly. 'Not directly, Robert. He wrote to Chloe but that's all.'

Robert frowned. 'Didn't he write to you?'

Toni watched him carefully. 'No, he let his solicitor do that.'

Robert laughed out loud and then looked slightly shamefaced at Toni's shocked expression. 'I'm sorry, my dear. I'm not being very sensitive. It's just that you've got to hand it to the man. He really knows how to make an exit.'

'Have you any idea *why* he left?'

Robert smirked. 'I'm afraid not, my dear. If there's another woman, I haven't met her.'

Toni ignored the remark. 'I think something must have happened at the hospital. There have been a lot of rumours flying around.'

Robert shrugged. 'There's always talk in that hospital.'

'But there must be some truth in it for Theo to leave,' Toni persisted.

'Maybe he got a better offer,' Robert suggested. 'There are a lot of other countries that would welcome a surgeon of Theo's calibre.'

Toni nodded. If Robert knew anything, he obviously wasn't going to tell her. 'Did Theo sell you his shares in the Blessington?' she asked bluntly.

Robert smiled. 'Now what makes you say that?'

Toni stood up. 'Thank you. That answers my question. Does Daniel know?'

Robert shrugged. 'I leave paperwork to solicitors but he has probably received notification by now.'

Toni walked to the door. 'I doubt it. I'm sure he'd have been straight up to congratulate you if he had.' She banged the door and walked down the corridor, his booming laughter following her. Even if he didn't fire her, Toni couldn't see herself staying on with Robert at the helm. She went straight to Daniel's office, tapped on the door and walked in. The first thing she noticed was the pile of untouched mail on his desk. Daniel was sitting back in his chair, engrossed in an article in *The Lancet.*

'Hi Toni,' he said vaguely and waved her to a chair.

'For God's sake, Daniel, don't you ever open your post?' she said in exasperation.

Daniel looked faintly surprised at her tone. 'There's plenty of time. Do you know there's the most amazing research going on in Wales –'

'Daniel! Theo has sold his shares to Robert.'

Daniel put down the magazine. 'What shares?'

'His shares in the Blessington, of course'

Daniel blinked. 'What are you talking about?'

Toni rubbed her eyes wearily. 'Chloe got a letter from Theo. It doesn't look like he's coming back. And then I got a letter from his solicitor and he wants a divorce. And he cleaned out our accounts and I think he's sold his shares in the clinic to Robert and . . . and . . .' Toni broke off as her eyes filled with tears of frustration.

Daniel came around to sit on the front of his desk and took her hand. 'Oh, Toni! I'm so sorry. This is terrible. What on earth has possessed the man? I always thought he'd a screw loose – sorry, my dear – but this is a bit extreme even for him.'

Toni blew her nose. 'I'm convinced this has something to do with Sylvester's, Daniel, but no one is taking me seriously. Would you see if you can find out anything?'

Daniel squeezed her hand. 'Of course, my dear. Did you talk to Francis Price? He is on the board, after all.'

Toni jumped up and kissed him. 'Dotty's husband! Of course, why didn't I think of that?'

Daniel smiled and walked back around his desk pulling his post towards him. 'Well, you do that, dear, and I'll try and find out if we still have jobs.'

Toni's smile faded. 'Do you think Robert would want to get rid of us all, Daniel?'

'Not until it suited him.'

Toni looked at his downcast expression. 'I'm so sorry Daniel. This is *your* clinic and you're going to lose it because of me.'

Daniel smiled suddenly. 'Don't be silly, my dear. It's just business.'

As Toni walked back to her office she thought about those words. They were exactly the ones Theo had used. 'It's just business.'

'Well?' Jade jumped to her feet and looked at Toni anxiously.

'You were right. Robert's grinning like the cat that's got the cream. I've just broken the news to Daniel.'

'How did he take it?'

'Remarkably well.'

Jade sat down again and sighed. 'Oh, well. At least if Perky wants to get rid of us, we could always start again somewhere new.'

Toni brightened. 'Do you think so?'

'I don't see why not. Daniel must have a few bob tucked away by now. And Robert would probably pay a good price just to get him out.'

'I can't imagine us leaving the Blessington,' Toni said sadly.

'It's only a building,' Jade retorted matter-of-factly. 'Nothing more. It's people that make a place. Not bricks and mortar.'

'Ian, it's me.' After everyone had gone, Toni had finally realised who she wanted to talk to.

'Toni?'

'Look, I'm sorry about the other night. I overreacted.'

'I was a bit out of order myself,' Ian admitted. 'I'm afraid I'd had one too many.'

Toni smiled. 'Me too. So are we still friends? I could really use one right now.'

'Theo hasn't turned up then?'

'No, not personally, but he sent Chloe what seemed like a goodbye letter.'

'Did he say any more about why he'd left?'

'No. But he's been talking to his solicitor. He wants a divorce.'

'How very strange,' Ian murmured. 'I wonder what's happened to change his mind.'

'God knows,' Toni said with a tired sigh. 'Nothing is making sense. He never even let the hospital know that he was going. John Allen is in shock.'

Ian chuckled. 'Our John is a very organised man. Having his chief of surgery disappear is enough to put him on the operating table himself!'

'There's more, Ian. I haven't told Chloe. He's taken all of our money with him. And he's sold his shares in the Blessington to Robert. He also wants to sell the house so that he can have half of the proceeds.'

'Oh, Toni, I'm sorry. This is turning into a nightmare for you.'

'It wouldn't be so terrible if I could understand why he's doing it. As it is I don't know what to think and I haven't a clue what to say to Chloe. And there are some horrible rumours doing the rounds.'

'I've heard them,' Ian said grimly. The gossip in Sylvester's had always bothered him. 'I wouldn't pay any heed to them, if I were you, Toni. Theo's disappearance is as big a mystery to everyone in the hospital as it is to you.'

'I'm sorry about what I said,' Toni mumbled. 'You know about the old boys' club stuff.'

Ian laughed. 'Don't worry about it.'

'Oh, Ian, what should I do? I seem to be going down a blind alley.'

'Well, it's interesting that Theo needs cash. He's wasting no time realising all of his assets. That means he's in some kind of trouble.'

'I hadn't thought of that. I just thought he was out to get me.'

'That's possible too. Look, why don't I do a little detective work? I could talk to the other doctors that got involved in the same investment schemes and brokers, that sort of thing.'

'I'd be grateful for anything you could do,' Toni said fervently. 'Because I'm at a loss what to do next.'

'Okay then, leave it with me. I'll call you when I get news.'

'Thanks, Ian. And again, sorry for –'

'Oh, Toni, shut up.'

Toni smiled. 'Okay. Bye.'

Chapter Twenty-seven

Thursday night, 24th August, 2000

'This is nice.' Aidan smiled at Jade and looked around the busy pub.

'It's okay,' Jade replied, wondering why they were here. When Aidan had phoned and asked her to meet him she'd instinctively refused.

'Please, Jade,' Aidan had pleaded. 'I need to see you.'

Jade had agreed reluctantly and wondered how much money he was going to tap her for this time. But so far Aidan hadn't mentioned money and he had bought the first round too. He also was looking rather nice in his black chinos, new blue shirt and his trusty leather jacket.

'How's the job going?' she asked.

'Actually that's what I wanted to talk to you about.'

Jade sighed. Here we go.

'It's going really well. In fact Dave is so pleased he's given me a rise.'

Jade stared at him.

'Jade? Did you hear me?'

'I'm not sure,' she murmured.

Aidan grinned. 'Dave has given me a rise, Jade. He thinks I'm doing a good job.'

'I'm very happy for you.'

'Be happy for us.' Aidan reached into his jacket and pulled out an envelope. 'This is for you. It's only a fraction of what I owe you but it's a start.'

Jade stared at the envelope on the table. 'Oh, I don't know, Aidan. Maybe you should keep it. If something were to go wrong . . .'

The smile faded from his face. 'You mean if I were to start gambling again.'

'I didn't say that –'

'But it's what you meant,' he said bitterly.

Jade said nothing.

Aidan sighed. 'Sorry. I know it must be hard for you to believe that I'm back on the straight and narrow. All I can do is prove it to you. And this is the first step.' He pushed the envelope towards her. 'Please take it, Jade.'

Jade picked it up and slipped it into her bag. 'Thank you.'

He smiled again. 'Why don't we go and get something to eat?'

'Oh, I'm not sure I have time. I was expecting Toni to drop around.'

'Just a quick bite in the steakhouse on the corner,' Aidan said persuasively.

Jade smiled suddenly. 'Why not? I haven't eaten a thing since breakfast. I'm starving.'

Aidan's brow wrinkled in concern. 'You are very thin. I hope you're taking care of yourself.'

'I'm fine,' she said breezily. 'In fact, at the moment I'm probably the most trouble-free person in that clinic.'

'Toni must be in a bad way. I can't believe that Theo would just leave like that. He was always a bit weird but this is even strange for him.'

'I know. Chloe's taking it very hard. And she doesn't even know the half of it.'

'Why not?'

'Toni doesn't want to upset her so she hasn't said anything about the money or the divorce. And the funny thing is that while Toni is protecting her, Chloe suspects that it's all Toni's fault and is taking it out on her.'

'Toni just happens to be in the firing line. You always hurt the one you love.' Aidan's eyes met hers and held them.

Jade coughed and stood up. 'Must just nip to the loo before we go.'

Aidan watched her hurry away with sad eyes. He'd lost so much when he'd lost Jade. Though his life was improving and he was feeling stronger and more confident than he had in years, it still wasn't the same without her. As he felt the depression start to creep up on him he took a deep breath and forced himself to smile. This was no time to feel sad. He'd persuaded Jade to go for a meal with him and he was going to enjoy every minute. And then when he was lying alone in bed tonight he would at least have something pleasant to think about.

* * *

Friday morning, 25th August, 2000

Ian shoved Carla's make-up bag out of the way and reached for his shaver. He hated the way she took over the place when she stayed the night. In fact everything she did these days seemed to set his teeth on edge. Especially the way she hung out of him in public. He wasn't against holding hands or even the odd kiss, but when she was with him it was like having an extra limb.

'Ian, honey? Are you nearly ready?'

And he hated it when she called him honey.

'I've got a meeting in Sylvester's later. Do you want to meet up for lunch?'

He scowled at his reflection in the mirror. He also hated the fact that she spent so much time at the hospital.

'No, I'm going to be tied up.'

Carla walked in and slipped her arms around him from behind, her pouting face appearing beside his in the mirror. 'Oh. Couldn't you get out of it? For little old me?' She planted a kiss on his cheek.

'Afraid not,' Ian smiled apologetically and went back into the bedroom to put on his shirt.

'Not to worry.' Carla followed him. 'I'll take Lynn out instead and get all the juicy gossip about Theo French.'

Ian groaned inwardly. The Sylvester's buyer was a nosy loudmouth and the last thing he needed was for Carla to team up with her. 'I wish you wouldn't talk to that cow. She's just a vicious gossip.'

'There's no smoke without fire,' Carla told him as she carefully put on a stocking.

Ian said nothing. If he made too big a deal out of this it would only arouse her curiosity. Instead he sat down on the bed beside her and ran a finger playfully around the top of her stocking. 'You smell gorgeous,' he murmured, kissing her neck. 'Maybe I *could* get away at lunchtime. We could come back here for a . . .' he nibbled her earlobe. '. . . bite to eat.'

Carla twisted her head around and kissed him hungrily. 'That would be nice,' She murmured, surprised and pleased at his sudden interest.

Ian pushed her back on the bed and began to kiss her neck and throat.

Carla groaned. 'I'm going to be late.'

'Then I'll see you at lunchtime?' Ian's lips moved down to trace the lacy edge of her bra.

Carla shivered. It was nice to know that he hadn't completely lost interest. Their sex-life lately had become predictable and brief and she was getting quite bored. She bent her head to kiss the hand caressing her breast. 'I'll be here at one.'

'I'll be waiting,' he promised and watched as she finished dressing.

The things he did to protect Toni, Ian mused, as he watched Carla dress. But she didn't need the likes of Carla sniffing around. If anyone was likely to beef up the rumours it was her. He looked on objectively as she put in her contact lenses. She was a tough businesswoman who had got to the top because she wasn't afraid of making enemies and stepping on anyone who got in her way. Carla had joined the sales team in *Medway*, the large pharmaceutical distributor, at twenty-eight. Just five years later, she was the head of sales for the Dublin area. And a year after that, when her boss joined that big sales team in the sky, she was made sales director.

There was absolutely no reason for her to involve herself so deeply in the Sylvester's account – Ian knew she didn't pay half as many visits to the other hospitals in the city. The fact made him uncomfortable. He was convinced she was just keeping tabs on him. Though that was irritating – he hated possessive women – it was also hilarious. He didn't have time to see other women – he didn't get a chance to eat most days!

Carla slipped on the jacket of her suit and came over to kiss him goodbye. 'See you later, honey.'

Ian pasted what he hoped was an enthusiastic smile on his face. 'Bye, Carla.'

When she'd left he finished getting dressed, collected a can of coke from the fridge and his battered, bulging briefcase from the hall and went out to the car. As he pulled into the early morning rush-hour traffic his thoughts turned to Theodore French.

When he'd offered to help Toni he hadn't really figured out how he'd go about it. The more he thought about what Toni had told him the more likely it seemed that Theo had got himself into some kind of trouble. The question was what? He drummed the wheel thoughtfully as he drove up the North Circular Road. The man needed money that was for sure. Did he owe someone? Was he being blackmailed? Did he have some rather expensive habits? He didn't believe Theo would be taking such drastic action because of Toni. He would have been a lot more organised if that was the reason and he certainly wouldn't have been the one to leave. No, if he was out for revenge he would have kicked her out of his house and then ensured that she was forced out of the clinic too. So Toni as a reason could be ruled out. So he would concentrate for the moment on Theo's penchant for the stock market. He'd decided that Stuart Beecher was the man to talk to. Like Theo, the cardiologist loved to dabble in stocks and shares, taking some amazing risks. He and Theo shared information and brokers so if there was anything going down Stuart would know about it. Well, he was a start. And right now, Ian's only lead.

Ian blasted his horn at a guy in a Honda who cut in front of him. The other driver stuck his finger in the air and sped away into the distance. Ian sighed. In his younger days he'd probably have torn after him like a madman but now he couldn't be bothered. 'You're getting old, Chase. You're not up to it any more. No wonder Carla's fed up with you.' He knew he'd completely taken his girlfriend by surprise with his advances this morning. He'd surprised himself too. He'd never seen himself as an actor. But once he started to make love to Carla his body took over. She was a beautiful woman and damn sexy. Once he forgot what a total bitch she could be he quite enjoyed himself. But tricking her like this just to keep her away from the hospital was a bit cheap. Especially if it got her hopes up that their relationship was going somewhere. Ian groaned as he pulled into the hospital car park. She'd probably start talking about moving in together again. Damn it, maybe he'd ring her later in the morning and tell her he couldn't make it at lunchtime after all. But at the same time it would be best to keep her away from Sylvester's as much as possible. It was only a matter of time before someone told her that he was asking questions about Theo. And it wouldn't take long for Carla to work out that he was back in touch with Toni. And then she'd want to know why he was going to so much trouble for his ex. And he knew he wouldn't be able to answer that question honestly. If he said he was just helping a friend it would be a lie, he admitted to himself as he grabbed his briefcase and got out of the car. But he didn't want to dwell on his reasons for wanting to help Toni. It was much better to concentrate on the job at hand and worry about that later.

Chapter Twenty-eight

Friday night, 25th August, 2000

'Oh, hello Toni. How are you?'

'I'm okay, Francis. How's Dotty?'

Francis sighed heavily. 'Not good. Not good at all.'

Toni clutched the phone tighter to her ear. 'Can I come and see her?'

'Not just now, my dear. She's in a lot of pain so she's under sedation most of the time.'

'Oh my God. I had no idea . . .'

'That's the way she wanted it, Toni,' he said gently. 'Everything to be as normal as possible for as long as possible. You know how she loves a laugh. And she said that if everyone started creeping around her with long faces she'd go mad.'

Toni smiled. 'She's so brave.'

'Yes. Yes, she is.'

'You must tell me, Francis, if there's anything I can do.'

'Thank you, dear, but I must say the nurses are very good. And Mrs Caulfield, our housekeeper, has been marvellous.'

'Well, the offer is there. If ever you need me.'

'Did you want me for something in particular, my dear?' he asked, ever the gentleman.

'Eh, no, Francis. I just called to say hello.'

'Well, it's always nice to hear –'

Toni heard Dotty's frail voice in the background.

'Sorry, my dear, I've got to go. Thanks ever so much for phoning.'

Toni sighed. 'Tell Dotty I was asking for her.'

'I'll do that. Goodbye.'

Toni put down the phone and crossed the conservatory to stare out into her garden. Poor Dotty. Poor Francis. She felt so completely helpless. It was so difficult to stand back and watch someone you loved slip away like this. Francis would probably go to pieces when Dotty was gone. And that's when Toni would be able to help. She tidied up in the kitchen, locked up and was just going up the stairs when the doorbell rang. She retraced her steps and peered through the window beside the door. Who on earth could be calling so late? 'What is it?' she called nervously.

'Mrs French? Police.'

Toni threw open the door. 'God, what is it? Is it Theo?'

The older of the two men stepped forward and showed her his badge. 'I'm Detective-Inspector Morrisey. And this is Sergeant Doyle. Is your husband in?'

'No.'

'May we come in?' he said and stepped into the hall before she could reply.

'Of course,' Toni said faintly and brought them into the living-room. Well, Theo was obviously all right because it was him they wanted to talk to. 'Why do you want to talk to my husband?'

'Where is Mr French?' Morrisey asked, ignoring her question.

'I don't know,' Toni said, watching the sergeant wander around the room looking at photographs.

'Do you expect him home this evening?'

Toni sighed. 'No. He's left me.'

The two policemen exchanged a look. 'I see,' Morrisey said. 'When was this?'

'Monday, no, actually, Saturday.'

'Which was it, Mrs French? Monday or Saturday?'

'I didn't find out until Monday but he'd been gone since Saturday.'

The sergeant smirked. 'Didn't you notice he was missing?'

Toni scowled at him. 'He left early on Saturday morning to attend a conference in Oxford. When he didn't return on Monday we started making enquiries. It turned out that he never went to the conference.'

'And weren't you worried about him?' The DI studied her with razor-sharp eyes.

'Of course I was bloody worried,' she snapped, 'but then I found a note in his study saying that he had left me.'

'I see. May we see his study?'

'No, you may not. Not until you tell me what this is all about.'

'Sergeant?' Morrisey nodded to his junior who flipped open his notebook.

'We would like to interview Mr French about an accident that took place at approximately one o'clock on the morning of Friday, the eighteenth of August last.'

'What? Theo wasn't in any accident.'

'You were with him on that night, Mrs French?'

Toni cast her mind back and then nodded vehemently. 'Yes. He was at home. I remember because it was the night before we went out to celebrate our daughter's Leaving Certificate results.'

'And he stayed in the whole night?'

Toni hesitated.

'Well, Mrs French?'

'I'm sure he must have –'

'You don't know?'

'Well, we have separate bedrooms.'

'So he could have gone out after you were asleep?'

'I suppose, but I'm telling you he couldn't have been in any accident. His car is in the garage and there isn't a mark on it. Take a look at it if you don't believe me.'

'It wasn't his car that he crashed,' the sergeant informed her.

Toni shook her head in confusion.

'Do you remember what time you went to bed, Mrs French?' the DI persisted.

'Probably about eleven.'

'I see,' the detective said solemnly. 'So he could have gone out and you would never have known about it?'

'I probably would have heard him.'

'You sleep in separate bedrooms, Mrs French. It is quite possible that he went out and you never heard a thing, isn't it?'

'Well, yes, but I'm sure he wouldn't have –'

'We have a witness that says otherwise, Mrs French.'

'Who?'

The detective ignored her once more. 'And he went away on Saturday morning?'

'Yes. I heard the taxi. That would have collected him about six.'

'I see. And you have no idea where he might be?'

Toni shook her head.

'He hasn't made any contact since he left?'

'Well, yes. He wrote to his daughter and he was in touch with his solicitor to instruct him to begin divorce proceedings.'

'Did that come as a shock to you?'

'Yes – no, look, I don't see what this has to do with you. You're only investigating a car accident. You don't need to know all the ins and outs of my marriage to do that.'

'That's not necessarily the case, Mrs French. Other charges may follow.'

'Charges?'

'Mr French was the driver of a car in which a woman was badly injured. He had no insurance, is believed to have been under the influence of drink and drugs at the time and he left the scene of an accident. Yes, there are quite a few charges stacking up against Mr French.'

Toni stared at them. 'You're making a mistake. Theo is a surgeon and very careful about drinking. And he'd never touch drugs.'

'Really?' The detective shot her a pitying look. 'I have the feeling that Mr French got up to a lot more than you realise.'

'Who is this woman? Is she all right.'

'I can't tell you her name, Mrs French, but suffice it to say she is well known to the Gardai. And yes, she is going to be all right, although no thanks to your husband who left her for dead.'

Suddenly Toni had a flashback of the conversation at dinner that night. 'This was the accident on Mount Street? The woman was in a coma?'

'That's right. But, unfortunately for your husband, she's now very much awake and has a perfect recollection of the events of that night.'

'Was she, is she a . . . prostitute?'

'Yes, Mrs French. And apparently your husband was one of her regulars.'

'I can't believe it. Theo would never –'

'If I had a fiver for every time a wife told me that,' the detective said with a melodramatic sigh. 'Now, Mrs French. May we have a look around Mr French's study? We don't have a search warrant but if you insist we will get one and be back in the morning.'

Toni shook her head and stood up. 'No, there's no need for that. But please be quiet. Chloe is asleep upstairs.'

'That's your daughter?'

'Stepdaughter,' Toni corrected automatically.

'Best prepare her for the shock, Mrs French,' the sergeant said kindly. 'You don't want her to read about this in the paper.'

Toni stared at him. 'But surely you won't release his name? I mean you haven't even talked to him yet. It's not as if he's under arrest.'

'Only because he isn't here,' the detective assured her. 'Now I'll need something with Mr French's fingerprints on it. The sergeant will issue you a receipt, Mrs French. and you can have it back in a couple of days.'

Toni led the way into the study. While they looked around she picked up the silver letter-opener that she'd bought him for their first wedding anniversary. 'His prints should be on this.'

The sergeant produced a bag and carefully wrapped it before stuffing it into his pocket. Then he wrote her a receipt and tore it from his notebook. 'You should know, Mrs French, that once we have established that his prints match the ones in the car it will be public knowledge that we are looking for Mr French to help us with our enquiries.'

'Oh my God,' Toni sank into Theo's leather chair. 'Oh, my God.'

* * *

Saturday morning, 26th August, 2000

Mark rang the doorbell twice before a dishevelled Toni came to answer it.

'Thanks for coming, Mark,' she said with a ghost of a smile and led the way into the kitchen. 'Do you want some coffee?'

'Yeah. What is it, Toni? What's happened?'

Toni poured the coffee and handed it to him. 'Sorry for getting you over here so early but I wanted you to be here before Chloe woke. The police were here last night, Mark. They came to arrest Theo.'

'Jesus, why?'

'He was involved in an accident but I won't go into the details now. You'll hear soon enough. I'm sorry for dragging you into this, Mark, but Alice isn't due in till this afternoon

– she has an appointment with the physiotherapist and I didn't want to do this on my own.'

'That's okay. So, are you going to wake her?'

Toni glanced at the clock. 'I'll give her another few minutes,' she said knowing that she was just trying to postpone the inevitable. 'God, I don't know how she's going to take this.'

'I'm sure it will be all right, Mrs French. The police have probably made a mistake.'

'I don't think so, Mark. I don't think so.'

When she finally called Chloe and asked her to come downstairs, the girl stopped short when she saw her boyfriend. 'What are you doing here? What's going on?' She turned to Toni. 'God, what's happened now?'

Toni led her to a chair and knelt at her feet. 'The police were here last night, Chloe.'

'Oh, God, has something happened to Dad?'

'No. They came to see your dad. They wanted to question him about an accident that took place last week.'

Chloe frowned. 'Dad never said anything about being in an accident.'

'No,' Toni said quietly. 'He didn't tell anyone, Chloe. That's part of the problem. He left the scene of the accident and there was a woman seriously injured.'

Chloe gasped. 'He knocked her down?'

Toni wished she could let Chloe believe that, it would be a lot simpler, but the sergeant had warned her that every gory detail would be spread across the newspapers before the day was out. 'No, he didn't knock her down. She was in the car with him. It was her car, apparently.'

'I don't understand.' Chloe looked at her, scared eyes in a pale face.

Toni held her hands in hers. 'I'm sorry love. I don't know all the details but your dad was driving, she was in the passenger seat, he lost control and drove into a parked car.'

Chloe gasped. 'That was the accident that Alice was telling us about.'

'Yes, that's right.'

'But they never said anyone else was in the car.'

'They didn't know until the woman woke up from her coma yesterday.'

'But who is she?'

Toni glanced at Mark. 'I don't know.'

Chloe frowned. 'The accident happened in the middle of the night. What was dad doing out at that hour? And why wasn't he in his own car?'

'I don't know all the details,' Toni was able to answer honestly.

'Was he having an affair?' Chloe thought about what Ollie had said.

Toni took a deep breath. 'No, Chloe. She's a prostitute.'

Chloe laughed. 'Don't be ridiculous! What would dad be doing with a prostitute?'

'I'd say that was pretty obvious,' Mark said drily.

Chloe shot him a venomous look. 'How dare you? Dad would never do anything like that, would he, Toni?'

Toni turned away.

'Toni?' Chloe pulled her back around and looked anxiously into her face. 'You don't believe this, do you?'

Toni shrugged. 'Why would the woman lie?'

'God knows. She's a prostitute! How can you believe her over Dad?'

'We'll know for sure very soon,' Toni said quietly. 'The police are checking his fingerprints.'

'Jesus,' Mark breathed. 'He could be in serious shit here. He's lucky she didn't die.'

'There you go again presuming he's guilty,' Chloe cried. 'Why are you both so ready to believe the worst of him?'

'Because he's left the country, Chloe. Because he's taken all our money with him. Because he's sold his shares in the clinic.'

Chloe sank into a chair. 'You never told me.'

'I'm sorry, love. I didn't want to upset you. And I was hoping that I could figure out why he'd left. I thought it had something to do with Sylvester's. I never imagined that it would be anything like this.'

'He won't be coming back now,' Mark warned Chloe. 'He'd be arrested as soon as he set foot in the country.'

Chloe shook her head in disbelief, silent tears rolling down her cheeks. 'It can't be true.'

'It doesn't look good,' Toni told her. There was no point in trying to shelter Chloe from this. 'And I should warn you that it will be all over the news and the papers before long.'

'Oh, God.'

'We'll get through this, Chloe. We'll get through it together.'

* * *

Saturday afternoon, 26th August, 2000

Alice crossed herself. 'Oh dear God!'

Toni patted her hand. 'I'm sorry, Alice.'

'I just can't believe it's true. What kind of a man does something like that?'

Toni didn't reply. She thought she'd known every evil twist of her husband's mind but obviously not.

'So what happens now?'

'Once the police have established for definite that Theo was driving the car there will be a warrant out for his arrest and his name will be released to the papers.'

'Oh, poor Chloe. Is there anything I can do?'

'Keep an eye out for journalists and send them packing before they get to Chloe.' Toni sighed. 'Other than that, Alice, I don't think there's anything we can do to protect her now.'

Chapter Twenty-nine

Saturday evening, 26th August, 2000

'My God, Chloe, what's going on? I saw the six o'clock news. They said the police are looking to talk to your dad in connection with an accident last week.'

Ollie had finally got through to her friend on her mobile. Toni had taken off the phone hours ago after the first journalists started to call.

'Oh, Ollie, it's a complete nightmare. They're making Dad sound like some kind of dangerous criminal.'

'But why?'

'They said he was driving the car in that accident on Mount Street last week. They said he left her for dead.'

'Oh, Chloe. Look, I'm sure it's not true,' Ollie said with uncharacteristic sensitivity. 'They've got the wrong man.'

'The journalists don't seem to think so,' Chloe told her, her voice shaky. 'God, Ollie, you wouldn't believe the questions they asked.'

'It's not often they get such a juicy story,' Ollie said blithely. 'And your dad is kind of well known. That makes it even better. Don't worry, Chloe. It'll be forgotten in a couple of days.'

'I don't know about that, Ollie. The police told Toni that once they've checked the fingerprints in the car are Dad's they'll be issuing a warrant for his arrest. Then the press will have a field day.'

'So are you going to stay holed up until this calms down?'

'I suppose we'll have to. Toni says it's only a matter of time before the press set up camp on our doorstep.'

'Look, why don't you come around here for a while? If it's going to get that bad you should get out while you can.'

'I don't know, Ollie.'

'Oh, go on. Take a taxi. You need a break.'

'Yeah, you're right. Just let me check with Toni. I don't like leaving her. I'll call you back in five.'

Toni was sitting in the conservatory staring blankly out into the garden when Chloe came to find her. 'Toni, would you mind if I went over to Ollie's for a while?'

Toni summoned up a smile. 'No, of course not, love, but take a taxi. There's a twenty-pound note in my purse.'

Chloe bent and kissed her cheek. 'Thanks. I won't be late.'

Toni was relieved that Chloe wanted to go out. Mark had asked her this morning but she'd said no. Toni was afraid she was going to go into her shell and talk to no one. Time with the very down-to-earth Ollie would do her good. But would it be enough to get her through the awful time ahead? Toni dreaded the thought of the press harassing her. And the thought of the girl reading sordid details about her father's secret sex life in the newspapers didn't bear thinking about. If only she could get her away from here for a few days. On impulse she picked up the phone. 'Hello, Mum? It's me.'

* * *

Sunday morning, 27th August, 2000

Toni glanced around the bright sitting-room. It had changed since she was last here. The sofas were covered in heavy dark green brocade and the curtains and carpet were a pale cream. The bookcases however still stood against the wall and were as stuffed with books as they'd always been. Toni smiled as she fingered her school copy of *Hamlet*.

'Here we are,' her mother announced as she arrived back with a tray.

'I could have come out to the kitchen,' Toni protested.

'Oh, no, it's a mess out there.'

'Where's Dad?'

'Oh, he's pottering around somewhere. We didn't think you'd be down quite so early.'

Toni glanced ruefully at the clock. It wasn't even nine yet. 'Sorry. I just wanted to get back before Chloe got up. She's a bit nervous.'

'I'm not surprised. And how are you?' Mary asked gently.

'Fine. No. No, Mum, actually I'm not fine at all.' She put down her cup and promptly burst into tears.

Mary Jordan abandoned her sponge cake and sat down

next to Toni taking her awkwardly in her arms. 'Oh Toni! My poor girl. This is so unfair.'

Toni clung to her and breathed in her perfume. That wonderful scent that had always made her feel safe as a child. She closed her eyes and willed it to work its magic again.

Mary smoothed the dark hair off Toni's face and looked into her troubled hazel eyes.

'Aren't you going to say "I told you so"?' Toni murmured, pulling out a tissue.

Mary stared at her. 'Of course not! My God, Toni, we thought he was too old for you. We never for one moment thought that he was capable of, of . . .'

'I have a feeling that this is just the tip of the iceberg,' Toni said miserably. 'From what the detective told me, Theo was involved with some very strange people. And it's been going on for quite some time.' Toni's voice turned into another sob.

Her mother stood up and took the brandy bottle from the cabinet in the corner and poured a generous dash into Toni's tea. 'Here, I think you need this. It's been a terrible shock for you. For someone you love to let you down so badly!'

'That's something else you don't know,' Toni said apologetically. 'I had asked Theo for a divorce.'

Mary stared at her. 'But I thought you were happy.'

Toni shook her head. 'I haven't been happy for a very long time. You and Dad were right,' she said with a shaky laugh. 'I should never have married him.'

'Oh, love, I'm so sorry. I've missed you so much and the only thing that kept me going was the thought that you were content.'

'I should have kept in touch more. My God, you're only an hour's drive away. And at this hour on a Sunday morning,' she added with a tremulous laugh, '– only half that. I'm sorry, Mum. I should never have let him come between us.'

Mary hugged her fiercely. 'Nothing and no one can ever come between us, Toni.'

'I just wish I understood why he did it.'

Mary's mouth was a grim line. 'Some men have strange . . . needs.'

'Maybe I drove him to it.'

'Don't talk nonsense. What he did has nothing to do with you.'

Toni looked nervously at her watch. 'I should get back soon. If those bloody journalists get to Chloe I think I'll strangle them.'

'Why don't you send her to stay with us for a while?' Mary suggested. 'No one knows her down here and it would be a break for her. And it would mean one less thing for you to worry about.'

Toni considered the idea. Chloe did get on very well with her parents – the few times they'd met – and she loved the old house in Skerries. 'Are you sure you could cope with her?'

Mary laughed. 'After all my years as a district nurse I think I can cope with one teenager. Especially one who is hurting as much as she must be.'

Toni hugged her. 'I don't deserve you. I've been a lousy daughter and as soon as I turn to you for help, you're there for me.'

Mary hugged her back. 'We've always been here for you, Toni. I'm just glad that you've finally realised it.'

'I don't think you can speak for Dad,' Toni said bitterly.

'You and your dad are too alike, both as stubborn as mules. I should have bashed your heads together a long time ago and made you see sense. Now why don't you go and find him?'

'Oh, I don't know –'

'Toni Jordan, you are not leaving this house without speaking to your father.'

Toni nodded, aware that her mother wasn't going to let her off the hook this time. 'Okay, Mum. But I'm not staying if he starts going on at me.'

'He'll be delighted to see you.'

'Right,' Toni said doubtfully and followed her out to the kitchen.

'Try the shed,' Mary suggested. 'He usually ends up in there fixing things. Or,' she chuckled, 'reading the sports pages.'

Toni smiled back uncertainly and went out into the garden. It was months since she'd seen her father. The obligatory Easter visit, all polite conversation and awkward silences. She hated these occasions with Theo politely complimenting her mother on her fruit cake and her father asking him stiffly about the hospital. The last real conversation Toni had had with her father was the week before her wedding when he'd refused to give her away.

'Give you away to a man nearly as old as me? I'd cut my own arm off first!'

And no matter how much her mother had pleaded with him, he'd stuck to his guns. Toni had stared at him defiantly, her eyes bright with unshed tears. 'Fine, Dad.

It's your decision. But if you don't give us your blessing then I don't want you at my wedding.'

Her mother had looked at her horrified. 'Toni!'

'Sorry, Mum.' She'd given her a quick peck on the cheek and run out of the house. And that had been that. The wedding in the registry office on Stephen's Green had been a sad little affair. With only her mother, Jade and Aidan there to wish her well. She knew her mother hadn't approved either. But there was no way she would stay away from her own daughter's wedding. Even though it had caused a huge row with her husband.

Toni walked slowly down the path towards the shed and paused with her hand on the door handle.

'Looking for me?'

Toni swung around to see her dad standing behind her, a pair of clippers in his hands.

She smiled weakly. 'I was but I'd feel happier if you put *them* down.'

Peter Jordan looked at the clippers thoughtfully. 'They're so rusty they wouldn't cut butter.'

'The garden looks well.' Toni looked around at the neatly manicured flowerbeds and the tightly clipped lawn.

'Your mother says you can tell I was an actuary just by looking at this garden. All the flowers are colour-coded and lined up like columns of figures.'

Toni's laughter was genuine. It was true her father had always been a precise man and her mother had always slagged him about it. 'I like it,' she said shyly.

Peter looked up at the house. 'Are you on your own?'

'Yes. It was just a spur-of-the-moment thing. I wanted to see . . . how you both were.'

His short laugh was bitter. 'Still alive, I'm afraid.'

'Dad!' Toni looked at him horrified.

'Sorry. But it's hard to believe you give a damn these days. We haven't set eyes on you in months and you never pick up the phone.'

'The phone works in both directions,' Toni shot back angrily.

Peter held up his hands. 'Okay, okay. Don't get on your high horse. I don't have the energy for a row.'

Toni sneaked a look at him as he hung the clippers back on a nail in the shed. He looked older and greyer. And he'd lost weight. 'You're all right, aren't you?' she asked gruffly.

'Fine.'

'How's young Chloe?' He switched to a subject they could usually discuss without fighting.

'Not great. But she did brilliantly in her Leaving Certificate.'

Peter shook his head. 'She's left school? I can hardly believe it. The years have flown by.'

'Yes.'

'So what's she going to do now?'

'Probably medicine in Trinity.'

'I should have guessed,' her father said drily.

'Actually, she's talking about taking a year off first.'

'And what does Mr French think of that?'

Toni stared at him. 'Mum hasn't told you?'

'Told me what?'

And with a heavy heart, Toni sat down on the edge of his bench and told him her story.

* * *

Sunday night, 27th August, 2000

'Toni?'

'Ian?'

'Yeah, sorry for ringing so late. I did try earlier but I couldn't get through.'

'We've left the phone off the hook all day. There are only so many times you can say "no comment". And then I was talking to Jade for the last hour.'

'So, is it true?'

'It seems to be. We'll know for definite after the police have checked fingerprints.'

'I just can't believe it. I realised that there had to a serious reason to make him leave in such a hurry, but this!'

'It is a bit hard to take in.'

'And is it true that she – that this woman is a prostitute?'

Toni sighed. 'Oh, yes. The police told me that. And they say that Theo was one of her regular clients. And I can believe it. Theo had a habit of going out driving late at night.'

'What? Didn't you ask him where he was going?'

'He said he just drove,' Toni said feeling foolish. 'That it relaxed him. Lord, I was terribly gullible, wasn't I?'

'You were terribly trusting,' Ian corrected. 'Why would you suspect him? I can't believe the man went to a prostitute when he had you at home.'

'Well, thanks but you don't have to worry about my ego. It's reasonably intact. I'm more shocked that Theo left her to die. He's a doctor, for God's sake. How could he do that?'

'Shock? Panic? Think about it. A respected surgeon found drinking and driving – possibly even under the influence of drugs – with a prostitute. His reputation would be in tatters. His career would be over.'

'Well, it's over now anyway, isn't it?'

'In Ireland maybe. But there's nothing to stop him starting again somewhere else.'

'But how? Wouldn't he need papers? Wouldn't he need a visa to work abroad?'

'Yeah, you're probably right. And of course that's why he would need the money. Well, it looks as if my job as a detective is over before it even started. The professionals have taken over.'

'I hope they find him,' Toni said grimly. 'He shouldn't get away with this.'

'But it would be terrible for Chloe if they did catch up with him and drag him back in handcuffs.'

'Yeah, you're right. But the least he could do is call her and explain himself.'

'Maybe he doesn't know that the cat is out of the bag yet. He could be anywhere in the world by now.'

'Yeah, but I bet he's keeping in touch with someone. He'd want to know if she died, wouldn't he? Because if she had, without regaining consciousness, then he'd be off the hook.'

'True. Maybe he calls the hospital.'

'Or maybe he just keeps in touch with Mr Stringer,' Toni replied.

'Who?'

'Theo's solicitor. He's the last person that Theo talked to.'

'Did you tell the police that, Toni?'

'Yeah. Would he have to tell the cops everything he

knows or is there such a thing as client confidentiality?'

'I think there might be. Maybe I shouldn't hang up my deerstalker just yet.'

'What do you mean?'

'Why don't we try to track him down?' Ian suggested.

'Do you think we could?'

'You know his family, I know his medical background – we must have as much chance as the police, probably more so.'

'Then let's do it. I'll start by writing to him,' Toni announced. She felt better now that they'd decided to do something.

'I don't understand.'

'I'm going to write to him care of Timothy Stringer. If we're right and they are keeping in touch then Theo will get it eventually.'

'And what are you going to say?'

'I'm going to tell him that he's destroyed his daughter's life. That she's talking about bunking out of college and that the least he owes her is an explanation.'

'There's no harm in sending it,' Ian agreed. 'Let me know what the solicitor says when you give it to him.'

'Will do.'

'How come you're able to talk so freely, Toni? Where's Chloe?'

'Out cold. I poured a couple of glasses of wine into her over dinner and gave her a sleeping tablet going to bed.'

'Not a bad idea. Maybe you should take one to.'

'Maybe. But first I'm going to write this letter. Goodnight, Ian. Thanks for being . . . a friend.'

'No problem. Goodnight, Toni.'

Chapter Thirty

Monday, 28th August, 2000

'Toni! I wasn't expecting you in.'

'Hi, Daniel. I've been here since six-thirty. I figured journalists wouldn't be up that early.'

Daniel smiled sadly. 'You shouldn't have come in at all. It's been a lousy weekend for you, I'm so sorry.'

'I have a lot to do and it keeps my mind occupied.'

'Have the police been in touch since?'

Toni shook her head. 'No, but they probably will be before the day is out. I must say your son has been great, Daniel. Chloe would have totally cracked but for him.'

'They seem to be pretty close, don't they?'

Toni smiled. 'That's an understatement.'

Daniel frowned. 'They're very young to be so serious but Meg keeps reminding me how young she was when we married.'

'And they're both so level-headed. I don't think either of them would rush into anything before they finish college.'

'I hope you're right. Look, I'd better go and scrub up. Talk to you later.'

'Bye, Daniel.'

Toni smiled as Sandra walked into reception. 'Morning, Sandra.'

'Toni!'

'Yes, I know. You didn't think I'd be in today.'

'How did you get past that lot?' Sandra nodded at the throng of press at the gates.

'I got up early. I'm afraid this situation is going to be a bit of a pain for you for a few days, Sandra. But please don't put anyone through who phones from the papers or TV stations.'

'No problem. And should I call our security firm and ask them to put a man on the gate?'

Toni nodded. 'That's a great idea.'

Sandra flushed with pleasure. It wasn't often that she was told that.

'Right, then, let's get to work and try to keep today as normal as possible.'

'Yes, boss.'

When morning surgery was finished, Jade arrived in with two sandwiches and two coffees. 'I didn't think you'd want to go out to lunch today.'

Toni smiled. 'Thanks.' She unwrapped the salad sandwich and took a bite.

'Any more news?' Jade settled herself in a chair and took a sip of her coffee.

Toni shook her head.

'I expect the police will be talking to staff at the hospital today,' Jade mused.

Toni stared at her. 'I suppose so. They asked me for a list of friends and relatives – anyone that Theo might have gone to stay with or know where he'd gone.' She gave a wry smile. 'It was a very short list.'

'Has he any family?' Jade asked.

Toni shook her head. 'He had an older sister but she died a couple of years ago. His parents are dead a long time.'

'And you have no idea where he might have gone?'

Toni shook her head. 'I'm pretty sure he's left the country though. He took his passport.'

Jade noticed the faraway look in her eye. 'What are you thinking?'

'I want to talk to her,' Toni said.

'Who?'

'The woman.'

'Oh, no, Toni, that's a *really* bad idea.'

'Why?' Toni demanded. 'She's the only one who can tell me what really happened that night.'

'The police have told you what happened.'

'The police told me as little as possible.'

'But why do you think she would talk to you?'

Toni shrugged. 'Maybe she won't but I have to try.'

'Is she in Sylvester's?' Jade asked.

'Yes.'

'Then not only will the place be crawling with police but the staff know you.'

'Only some of them do,' Toni argued. 'And I was thinking I could go in after visiting time tonight when it's quiet.'

'I really think it's a mistake,' Jade told her.

Toni looked her in the eye. 'Are you telling me that you wouldn't want to do the same?'

COLETTE CADDLE

Jade grinned ruefully. 'I would have been up there first thing Saturday morning,' she admitted.

The ward was in darkness when Toni stepped out of the lift. It was nearly ten-thirty but she had been in the hospital since nine trying to find the woman and then get to her without being spotted. Toni made her way quietly down to room four and put her head around the door. 'May Darcy?'

The woman in the bed lifted her head. 'Who wants to know?'

Toni closed the door quietly and walked towards her. 'Theo French's wife.'

The woman looked her up and down and smiled broadly. 'So yer the little wife, are ye? Yer not a bit like I was expecting.'

'Likewise,' Toni said faintly. She'd been expecting a skinny little blonde for some reason, someone not much older than Chloe. But May Darcy was at least fifty, probably weighed in at fourteen stone and had a mop of dyed auburn hair.

'I suppose yer here to warn me off.'

'Sorry?'

'Well, it's too late, love, I've told the police everything. I wouldn't have said a word if the stupid bastard had at least called an ambulance for me. I'm loyal to me regular punters, ye know. But the stupid gobshite just left me there.'

'I know. I'm sorry. How are you feeling?'

May looked taken aback. 'Eh, all right. I won't be working for a while.' She indicated her left leg, which was encased in plaster. 'But me head is all right. A tough nut to crack, that's me.'

314

Toni smiled faintly.

'He should pay through the nose for this, ye know. I'm going to be out of pocket and I'll probably lose some punters. They're not going to sit playing with themselves for a couple of months until I'm ready to do business again.'

Toni winced at the thought. 'You should be able to make a claim. You need to get yourself a solicitor.'

May's eyes widened. 'Are you for real?'

Toni nodded. 'Yep. You see I was planning to divorce the man anyway.'

May threw back her head and laughed. 'Well, that's a good one! Yer divorcing him?'

'I've wanted to leave for months now. But after what he's done to you . . .' She shook her head. 'I didn't think he could sink this low.'

'He probably just panicked, silly bugger,' May said generously.

Toni shook her head in wonder. 'You're a very forgiving woman.'

May shrugged. 'Life's too short. So tell me, was he terrible to live with?'

'Recently, yes.'

'I'm not surprised. He's a bit of a weirdo, if ye ask me.'

'How long has he, have you . . . known him?'

May screwed up her face. 'Oh, it must be nearly eight years now.'

Toni gasped. 'Eight years!'

'Yeah. He first came to me when his wife got sick.'

'Oh, my God. And, eh, how often?'

'Sometimes every week, then I wouldn't see him for a

couple of months, then he'd be back again!' She shrugged. 'Some fellas are like that.'

'Did you do it – in the car?'

May laughed at her. 'We did it everywhere, love. Ah, no, I'm just kidding ye. No, we usually went back to me flat. And sometimes I brought him to parties.'

Toni looked incredulous. 'Parties?'

May nodded. 'Very select, only regulars – people ye could trust. Theo only came along a couple of times a year. He was very careful. He wouldn't go unless I knew everyone who was going to be there.' She laughed. 'But they weren't half as exciting as it says in the papers. There was never more than six or eight people and most of them just wanted to get high or drink.'

'What did Theo want?' Toni asked quietly.

'He did a little coke and had a few drinks.'

Toni shook her head in amazement. 'He was always giving out about drugs – he even hated smoking. And he never drank more that a couple of glasses of wine when we were out.'

'A lot of punters are like that,' May confided. 'They behave like naughty schoolboys when they're with me and like priests at home.'

Toni heard voices in the corridor and stood up. 'I'd better get out of here.'

May grinned. 'The papers would have a field day if they caught ye up here with me!'

Toni smiled wryly. 'Wouldn't they just? Look, thanks for talking to me.'

May shrugged. 'It's not yer fault he did what he did. And if ye want my opinion yer better off without him.

A fine-looking girl like ye – sure ye could have any man!'

Toni smiled. 'Thanks. Bye.'

'Bye, love.'

Ian was walking out to the car park at the back of the hospital when he caught sight of Toni. He was about to call out and just stopped himself in time. She would have really appreciated that! Instead he quickened his pace and within moments was walking at her side. 'Good evening, Ms Jordan. Can't keep away from me, eh?'

Toni looked around nervously and kept walking. 'For God's sake, Ian, don't draw attention to me.'

'It's hardly the place to come if you're trying to keep a low profile,' he murmured. 'Why on earth are you here anyway? Were you visiting someone?'

Toni shot him a guilty look.

'Toni? Oh, jeez, Toni, tell me you didn't.'

Toni said nothing and kept walking.

'Are you crazy? What if someone had seen you?'

Toni paused at the exit and glanced around. 'Well, they didn't.'

Ian shook his head impatiently. 'Are you driving?'

'No, of course not. The press and the police know my car.'

'Then come on, I'll give you a lift.'

'No, if I'm seen with you –'

'You can stretch out on the back seat. Now, come on. Let's get out of here before you're spotted.'

'I still can't believe you did that,' he said again, after draining the last of his pint.

Toni's lips twitched. 'I still can't believe I didn't get caught.'

'And so what did this woman have to tell you?'

'Nothing much.'

'What was she like?' he asked curiously.

'Actually very nice. I quite liked her.'

Ian stood up to go to the bar. 'Women! I'll never understand any of you!'

Chapter Thirty-one

Thursday, 7th September, 2000

'My goodness did you see this?' Vicky pored over the paper. *'Prostitute Tells of Surgeon's Kinky Habits.'*

Sandra scowled at her. 'I don't think you should be reading that in here. It would upset Toni.'

'She isn't here, is she? Probably skiving off again,' she added loudly.

Sandra glowered at her. She'd done that deliberately because Mr Perkins was passing. 'Of course she isn't,' she replied equally loudly. 'Toni is in a meeting with Daniel.'

Robert paused and turned to Sandra with a silky smile. 'Are they in Daniel's office, Sandra?'

Sandra could have bitten her tongue off. Whatever the meeting was about she knew that Mr Perkins's presence wouldn't be welcome. 'Yes, Mr Perkins. Actually they should be finished any minute. I think they were just going through Daniel's schedule for next week.'

Robert nodded and carried on to his own office. Sandra sighed in relief.

Vicky looked at her with narrowed eyes. 'What are you

up to, Sandra? Or, more to the point, what are Toni and Daniel up to?'

Sandra busied herself with the post. 'Nothing. Why would they be up to anything?'

Vicky grinned smugly. 'Because they're wondering how long more they're going to have jobs.'

Sandra glared at her. 'I'm sure Mr Perkins will keep things the same as before. Why would he change anything?'

Vicky smoothed her blue uniform and gazed proudly down at her breasts. 'Why not? But don't worry, San. I'll put in a good word for you if you like.'

Sandra bristled at her cocky tone. 'No, thanks. I'll let my work speak for itself.'

Vicky threw back her head and laughed. 'Then you'd better start looking for a new job!'

Sandra buried her head in her work, too choked up to reply. What had she ever done to Vicky? Why was she always so bitchy and cruel?

'Jade can certainly start looking,' Vicky continued. 'I'm going to make damn sure she gets the sack.'

'And how can you do that?'

'Robert listens to me. He'll do whatever I ask him.'

Sandra looked at her pityingly. 'And why would he listen to a tart like you?'

Vicky stared at her in shock. Little timid Sandra had never been bitchy. 'How dare you?' she blustered.

'I dare because you're getting too big for your boots.'

'Well, your days are numbered, that's for sure,' Vicky said angrily.

Sandra shrugged. 'Whatever.'

Vicky stormed off in disgust. It was no fun being able

to lord it over Toni and Jade unless she had someone to brag to. To hell with them all. When they were gone, she'd be in charge and anyone she hired would damn well show her some respect. She marched straight up to Robert's office to discuss it with him.

When she barged in, Robert looked up and smiled. 'Good morning, Vicky.'

Vicky smiled sweetly and perched on the chair in front of him, making sure to hike her skirt up a few inches.

Robert watched appreciatively.

'I just wondered, Rob, if you'd thought any more about staff.'

Robert sighed. Vicky had been going on and on since he'd bought Theo out. It was very tiresome. The perils of screwing someone you worked with, he realised. Perhaps he should do something about that. But for the moment he smiled charmingly. 'There hasn't been time, my dear. I've been so incredibly busy.'

Vicky's eyes flickered in disbelief to the pile of newspapers spread out on the desk. 'You *are* going to put me in charge, aren't you, Rob?' she persisted.

Robert laughed gently. 'Oh, my dear, you don't want to be bothered with all the humdrum work involved in running this place. You're much too pretty for such a dreary job.'

'You don't think I can do it,' Vicky accused.

'Of course I do,' Robert said placatingly although he was getting a bit tired of Vicky's whinging. 'But I need to keep Toni on for a while. Until I've got this place under control. Then, we can start making some real changes around here.'

Vicky relaxed slightly. He'd said 'we'. She was being too paranoid. Of course Robert would look after her. Hadn't he always said he would? It was the one reason she'd stayed with him – it certainly wasn't for his body! No, within a few months she'd be running the Blessington. And then, once she had some money and experience she could wave Robert and the clinic goodbye. She stood up and came around the desk to plant a kiss on his cheek. 'We'll make such a wonderful team,' she murmured in his ear.

Robert fondled her bum and buried his face in her cleavage. 'We already do, my dear. We already do.'

* * *

Toni left Daniel's office and walked slowly back to her own. She didn't feel any better for the meeting, even though Daniel had assured her that Robert had no immediate plans to change anything. And it seemed Daniel had no immediate plans either. He was completely resigned to Robert becoming the boss. Toni threw her pad down on the desk in frustration. She had hoped this meeting was about them joining forces to ensure either the continued integrity of the clinic or a decision to start up somewhere else. But Daniel, like Jade, had suggested she concentrate on getting her personal life in order.

She had finally gone to see a solicitor – a nice girl from an old firm that her dad had recommended. But her sympathy and kindness had got on Toni's nerves. She had explained her situation to Teresa Neil in a cool calm voice and sat patiently as Ms Neil told her what she already knew. Divorce was a long and complicated business and it didn't help that her husband was not traceable.

'I'm sure his solicitor knows where he is,' Toni had said.

'I will write to Mr Stringer and let him know that I am representing you. Then we need to agree an official separation. That's only a formality as Mr French is the one who filed for divorce. We need details of his financial status of course.'

'Well, I can supply part of that,' Toni had told her bitterly. 'He took most of the money from our joint accounts.'

'Right, then that's about it for now.' Teresa had stood up and held out her hand. 'I'll set the wheels in motion and be in touch.'

Toni didn't share Ms Neil's confidence that everything would be plain sailing. Theo had shown no signs of playing ball so far. Why would he start now? There was still no sign of him answering her letter. The discreet Mr Stringer wouldn't even reveal if Theo had received it.

'But why ever not?' Toni had demanded.

'It's my duty to keep my client's confidence,' Stringer had said self-importantly.

'Fine!' Toni had slammed down the phone. Now, as she stared out of the window of her office and watched a woman struggle with a brolly in the car park, she regretted her temper. She would probably get a lot further if she batted her eyelashes and wept prettily. That's what Jade would have done. Now there was a woman that could be one hell of an actress when the situation called for it. Toni had seen her in action. There was that memorable occasion when Perky had accused her of deliberately not booking him into the black-tie dinner that he attended every year along with the other ambitious movers and shakers.

'Oh, Robert, I'm so terribly sorry,' Jade had said her eyes wide and full of remorse. 'I must have forgotten. Well. It was that time of the month and you know what we women are like. Completely unreliable when our hormones come into play.'

Robert had looked at her suspiciously but Jade's expression was completely innocent.

'I'm completely ashamed of myself,' she'd continued. 'If there's anything I can do to make it up to you . . .'

'Oh, forget it,' Robert had said grumpily and strode back to his office.

After the door had shut behind him Toni and Jade had burst out laughing.

'You didn't forget that dinner at all,' Toni had accused.

'I don't know how you can say such a thing!' Jade had said with mock outrage. But as she sashayed down the corridor she'd turned to deliver a broad wink.

'Nutter,' Toni said now, thinking of her friend. Mind you, it would be great to be more like her. No one got the better of Jade. And yet everyone seemed to like her. Well, except Perky and Vicky but then that was almost a compliment.

The phone interrupted her thoughts and she was thrilled to hear her stepdaughter on the line.

'Chloe, how are you? How's life in Skerries?'

'Fine, did you hear the news? Mark got a place in UCD on the second round of offers on Monday.'

Toni smiled. 'Daniel told me. I'm delighted for him.'

Chloe sighed. 'I miss him. I miss you too,' she added hurriedly.

'And I miss you, love.'

'Any word from Dad?'

'No, I'm afraid not.'

'I saw the papers. Your folks didn't want me to but I needed to know.'

'Yes.' Toni's mother had called to let her daughter know that Chloe had seen every article there was to see about her father.

'Do you think it's all true, Toni?'

'No, love,' Toni was able to say quite honestly thanks to May Darcy.

'Me neither.' Chloe sounded relieved. 'Okay then. I'd better go. I'll put you on to your Dad. He wants a word.'

'Eh, okay. Hi, Dad.' Toni still couldn't get used to this new relationship with her father. In the past when he'd answer the phone they'd exchange some stiff pleasantries and he'd hurriedly pass the phone to his wife. At least some good had come of this sorry mess.

'Hello, love. Did you go and see that solicitor?'

'Yeah, I did. She's going to get in touch with Theo's guy.'

'It's for the best,' he said reassuringly. 'Now just try and put it out of your mind and leave it to her.'

Toni said her goodbyes and turned back to the pile of files on her desk. Her dad was right. She'd be better off concentrating on more mundane issues at the moment. If she just looked after the day-to-day running of the clinic and put Robert and Theo and Daniel all out of her mind she'd be a lot better off.

But Toni had only just got down to work when the phone rang.

'Toni Jordan?'

'Toni, it's Francis.'

Toni's heart skipped a beat. 'Francis? Is everything all right?'

'I'm afraid not, my dear.' His voice was faint and shaky.

'I'll be right there,' Toni assured him.

'We're at the hospice, Toni. Do you know where that is?'

Toni swallowed back the tears. 'I'll be there in half an hour.'

* * *

Toni tried to smile at the tiny shape in the bed, but it didn't matter – Dotty's eyes were firmly closed. Toni looked in alarm at Francis.

He came over and kissed her cheek. 'She sleeps most of the time now. But she isn't in any pain. Do you mind if I just pop out for a moment?'

Toni shook her head unable to speak.

Francis squeezed her hand and left the room.

Toni sat down by the bed and took Dotty's thin hand in hers.

Dotty's eyes fluttered open.

'Oh, I'm sorry, Dotty. I didn't mean to disturb you.'

Dotty grinned and for a moment she looked just like her old self. 'I'll have plenty of time to sleep, love. Help me sit up a little. Oh, it's good to see you. How are things?'

Toni fixed some pillows and eased the woman up carefully in the bed.

Dotty lay back against them and looked up at her. 'I don't suppose you've heard from the old sod yet.'

Toni smiled. 'If you mean my dear husband, then no I haven't. Anyway, let's not talk about him. Tell me about you.'

Dotty scowled at her. 'I'm in a bloody hospice, Toni. What do you want me to say? That I'm feeling much better?'

Toni felt the tears prick her eyes and bowed her head to hide them from her friend. 'I'm sorry.'

'Oh, don't be,' Dotty said impatiently. 'It's actually very nice here. I'm much better off and at least Francis isn't fussing around as much.' She looked around, suddenly realising her husband wasn't in the room. 'I suppose he's off having a smoke?'

Toni grinned through her tears. 'I think so. Are you in any pain?'

'No. To be honest I feel high as a kite most of the time. If only I'd had these drugs in my student days!' She chuckled softly.

'Dotty Price! Shame on you.'

Dotty sighed. 'Ah, you've got to laugh, don't you? Don't forget that, Toni. How is Chloe holding up?'

'She's a lot better. She's spending some time with my parents at the moment.'

Dotty's eyes widened with interest. 'You're kidding?'

Toni shook her head. 'Nope. I finally took your advice and went to see Mum. She's been wonderful.'

'And your father?'

Toni smiled. 'He's been great too. We've actually managed to have several conversations without rowing.'

Dotty clutched her hand tightly. 'Oh, I'm so glad, Toni. You need your family at a time like this. And I'm sure they've missed you terribly.'

'I think they have,' Toni said guiltily.

'Never mind. You're friends now and that's all that matters.' Dotty closed her eyes again.

'Do you want me to go?'

'No, dear. I'm afraid I'm always dozing off these days. But I'd like you to stay for a while, if you don't mind. It's nice to know you're here.'

Toni bent over to kiss her forehead. 'I'll stay as long as you like.'

As Dotty slept, Toni sat and held her hand and prayed that her friend's death would be a quick and painless one.

Chapter Thirty-two

Sunday, 10th September, 2000

Three days later Dotty passed away with her husband by her side. Toni had gone home for a shower, remarkably cheered up by how bright and lively Dotty had been that afternoon. She had entertained Francis and Toni with stories from her student days, although Francis insisted she was making most of it up.

'It's hard to believe now, Toni, but Dotty was a very shy, timid girl when I met her first.'

Dotty had winked at Toni. 'That was all technique. Francis was terrified of women and I knew I'd have to play the part of the meek little girl to get him.'

'So you set your cap at him?'

'Absolutely! We were meant for each other. But the silly man would never have realised that. I had to nudge him along.'

Francis smiled. 'You were so pretty.'

Dotty snorted. 'It's a wonder you noticed. He always had his head buried in his damn books, Toni.'

'Ian used to be the same.' Toni had laughed.

'Ian Chase?' Francis looked vaguely surprised. 'Lord, I'd forgotten that you two had been an item. Nice chap.'

Toni stared at her hands. 'Yes.'

Dotty looked on speculatively. Sickness had not dulled her sensitivity and she was quite sure that Toni still had feelings for Ian Chase.

'How do you feel about fulfilling an old woman's dying wish?'

'Dotty!' Toni looked horrified. 'Please don't talk like that.'

'Oh don't be so bloody silly, girl. It won't be long now. So will you make me a promise?'

Toni nodded, not trusting herself to speak. She knew Dotty didn't have long but it was just so hard to accept. Especially when she was as animated as she was today.

'I want you to go and see Ian Chase and have a nice long chat.'

'Now, Dotty,' her husband warned.

'I'm not asking her to jump on him, Francis,' Dotty protested.

Toni laughed. 'Actually, Dotty, we've already made our peace. Ian has been a tower of strength over the last few weeks.'

'Excellent! So will you be moving in together?'

'Dotty!'

'Oh, leave me alone, Francis! I'm not going to be here to see it all played out. I'm entitled to a preview.'

Toni laughed. 'You are but I'm afraid Ian already has a girlfriend.'

'I wouldn't worry about her,' Dotty said dismissively. 'He'd go back to you like a shot if he had the chance.'

Toni grinned. 'We'll just have to wait and see.'

'If only,' Dotty said with a wistful sigh. 'Now off you go, Toni and let me and my fella have a kiss and a cuddle before I nod off again.'

Toni bent to kiss Dotty and smiled at an embarrassed Francis as she collected her coat and went to the door. 'I'll bring you back some marshmallows.'

'Lovely.' Dotty smiled though her bedside table was full of tempting treats that she hadn't eaten.

And when Toni returned a couple of hours later it was to be told by a nurse that Dotty had slipped away twenty minutes earlier and Francis was still with her. Toni sat in the waiting-room for him, not wanting to intrude on this very private moment. When he finally came to look for her she took his hands in hers and kissed his cheek. 'I'm so sorry, Francis.'

Francis nodded and gripped her hands tightly, smiling through his tears. 'It was very peaceful. She told me what suit and shoes I should wear for the funeral, who I should invite back to the house and then she just said "I love you," and she was gone.'

Tears rolled unchecked down Toni's cheeks. 'She was a wonderful woman.'

'Yes.'

'Why don't you sit down, Francis. I'll get us some tea.'

Francis sat down obediently and Toni was about to go in search of a nurse when one appeared in the doorway carrying a tray.

'I thought you could do with some tea,' she explained kindly. 'We're all very sorry for your loss, Mr Price. Dotty was a lovely woman. She was a pleasure to look after.'

Francis stood to shake her hand. 'Thank you for everything, Nurse. I really appreciate all you did to make Dotty comfortable.'

When they were alone again and Toni had handed him a cup of tea, he looked at her worriedly. 'Dotty has given me very definite instructions about the funeral and she wants me to have people back to the house. Lots of them. She said it should be like a party.'

Toni smiled. No surprise there. Dotty's only regret would not being there to enjoy it.

'But I don't know if I can cope with all that,' Francis said distraught. 'I want to follow her wishes but I just don't know if I'm up to it.'

'Why don't you let me organise it all?' Toni said taking charge. 'You take care of the church and the service and leave the rest to me.'

Francis brightened marginally. 'Really? I'm sure Mrs Caulfield will help.'

'Between us we'll make sure it's a credit to Dotty.'

'Oh, thank you, my dear. This is so kind of you. Dotty would be happy to know that you were looking after things. You were like a daughter to her.'

'She was a wonderful friend to me. I'll never forget that.'

* * *

Tuesday, 12 September, 2000

The funeral went off exactly as Dotty would have wanted, Toni thought as she looked around the large living-room full of people talking and laughing. Though there were a few people from the hospital, most of the guests were Dotty's friends and relations and there were – not surprisingly – quite a lot of them. Dotty had left lists of people to be informed of her demise. Some of the comments that she'd scribbled in beside certain names had had Toni rolling around laughing.

Beside Ivy O'Brien's name she'd written. 'Nosy old cow who'll be trying to figure out how much the coffin cost! Make sure she sees all my best silver!'

Dotty, much to Francis's embarrassment, had even left instructions for 'I Did It My Way' to be sung when she was being carried out of the church.

Toni watched Francis now, surrounded by friends and family. There was a polite smile on his face but he had a distant look in his eye. He had, as Dotty had stipulated, worn his new tweed suit with a loud, garish tie that she'd bought for him.

'You've never worn it,' she'd complained from her sickbed. 'So it's the least you can do for me.'

Francis had been totally shocked. 'But it's so . . . inappropriate. What do you think, Toni?'

'It's, eh, very colourful.'

Francis sighed resignedly. 'Indeed.'

Dotty's eyes had twinkled mischievously. 'It will give them all something to talk about.'

Toni smiled at the memory.

'A penny for them?'

Toni swung around to see Ian smiling down at her. 'I was just thinking how much she made me laugh. She always made me laugh no matter how miserable I was. Poor old Francis. He looks so lost without her.'

Ian moved closer. 'It can't be easy for you either. And after all that's happened – I'm so sorry. '

Toni blinked back the tears. 'I'll miss her advice,' she admitted. 'She never steered me wrong. Do you know that one of the last things she said to me was that I should make my peace with you? She was thrilled when I'd told her that we had already talked.'

'I'll take that as a compliment.'

'You can,' Toni assured him. 'She liked you. And Francis does too.'

'He's a good man. Look, Toni, I know this isn't the time or the place but I just wanted you to know that I'm getting close to a lead.'

'I thought you'd forgotten. It's been a while since I've heard from you.'

'Yes, sorry about that. I forgot to tell that I was going away for a couple of days.'

Toni had a mental image of him rubbing oil into Carla's back.

'A conference down in Cork. Total waste of time.'

Toni smiled broadly. 'Oh, well, no problem.'

'Anyway I hope to have some news for you soon.'

'Great.'

He lowered his voice as he saw Francis approaching. 'I think you're needed. I'll call you.'

'Hello, Ian.'

'Francis.' Ian shook hands with the older man. 'How are you holding up?'

Francis held up his glass. 'As long as I've got one of these in my hand I can cope,' he joked.

Toni smiled at him but she felt nothing but pity for the

man. He was only a shadow of his former self. His shoulders drooped and there were dark circles under his eyes. 'Have you had anything to eat?'

'Oh, I ate some of those sandwiches,' he waved his hand vaguely.

'Let me get you some smoked salmon and brown bread. It will soak up some of that Scotch.'

'That would be a damned shame,' he told her. 'I'd prefer it if you filled up your own glass and joined me for a chat in the library.'

'I'll leave you to it,' Ian said discreetly and moved away to join his colleagues.

'Thank you for all your help, my dear.' Francis handed her a Scotch, took his own glass and went around to sit at his desk.

'It's the least I could do,' Toni said sadly.

He smiled at her over his glasses. 'I just wanted to have a word with you before I get too squiffy to talk. Dotty left me very specific instructions about a lot of things, as you know.'

Toni smiled at the sheaf of paper in front of him covered in Dotty's slanting scrawl. 'She was a very organised lady.'

'A very bossy one,' Francis retorted but his tone was warm. 'Anyway she wanted me to distribute some of her personal items – ornaments, jewellery and the like. And she wanted you to have this.' He took a black, velvet box from the desk drawer and walked around to hand it to her.

Toni opened the box and gasped. 'Oh, Francis! I can't take these.'

'You must, my dear. Or I'll be haunted until the day I die.'

'But . . . but . . .'

Francis looked at the heavy ruby earrings and matching necklace. 'But she loved them and she loved you. She wanted you to have them, Toni. Please don't argue.'

Toni went around the desk to hug him to her. 'Thank you, Francis. It is nice to have a keepsake.'

'Toni, I wonder if I could ask you to do me yet another favour?'

'Of course. Anything.'

'Well, Dotty left some gifts for the nurses at the hospice. And though I'm extremely grateful to them, I just can't face going back . . .'

'I'll take care of it. Don't worry about a thing.'

'Thank you, dear. I knew I could rely on you.'

'What will you do now, Francis?' Toni asked quietly.

Francis stared into his glass. 'I don't know. I suppose I'll muddle along somehow.'

'You must take care of yourself, eat properly.'

Francis laughed. 'I don't have a choice. Mrs Caulfield shoves food down my throat every chance she gets.'

'Good. And you must get out and about too. Dotty wouldn't want you moping around in the house on your own.'

'Indeed.'

Toni looked at the bleak look in his eyes and immediately felt stupid. How could she talk such utter crap? The man had just lost the love of his life. His partner, his friend and his confidante. And she was telling

336

him to get on with it. If he weren't so incredibly polite he'd probably tell her to bugger off and rightly so! 'Don't mind me, Francis. I don't know what I'm talking about. All I can tell you is that there's always an ear at the end of the phone if you want it.'

'What about a drinking partner?' Francis asked with a twinkle in his eye.

Toni raised her glass. 'No better woman!'

'Oh, Toni. You're a tonic. Thank you so much.'

'I only wish I could do more,' Toni said helplessly.

'I know that, dear. But there's nothing more to be done.'

Chapter Thirty-three

Friday, 15th September, 2000

Chloe pulled on a sweatshirt and went out to the garden. 'Hi, Mr J,' she said shyly.

Peter Jordan turned and smiled at her. 'Hello there. Have you come to help?'

He waved towards the flowerbeds where he was digging up bulbs and placing them carefully in crates. Chloe laughed. 'I think I'd be more of a hindrance than a help. Toni's tried to get me interested in gardening but I'm just no good at it.'

'Toni has green fingers all right,' Peter said proudly.

'Yes, you should see our garden. It used to be a total wilderness but now it's gorgeous.'

Peter nodded silently. Though he'd grudgingly accepted him into his home, Peter had always vowed that he would never step inside French's door. And hadn't he been proved right? When Toni had told him what Theo had done he felt physically sick at the thought of his daughter being married to such a man.

'Are you okay?'

He looked up to see Chloe's sweet, concerned face. 'Just daydreaming, love. Why don't you pick a few flowers for Mary?'

Chloe smiled. 'Okay. Shall I just gather a selection?'

'Yes, that would be grand. Lots of pink. She likes pink.'

He watched the young girl as she went off to the shed for the secateurs. She was very pretty and no doubt would become a beautiful woman. A strong, kind and intelligent one at that. It was hard to believe that she was French's daughter. Though there was no denying she had his eyes. But she had a gentle, sweet nature and loved a laugh. In fact she could almost be Toni's own daughter. Although – he chuckled – Toni was a lot more temperamental. She got that from him. They both lost their temper too easily. Said things that weren't easily taken back. He sighed heavily. So many years had been wasted because of Theo French. And now he'd not only hurt Toni but his own daughter too. It was time that Peter put all the arguments and hurt behind him and looked after his daughter. And his step-granddaughter. He laughed aloud as she approached.

'What is it?' She smiled shyly.

'I was just wondering if there's such a thing as a step-grandfather.'

'Sure there is. His name's Peter Jordan!'

Peter smiled back at her. She was really a lovely girl. He felt as if he'd been given another chance. He'd screwed things up with Toni. Maybe he could make things up to her by looking out for Chloe. The girl needed some kind of father figure in her life. His heart had nearly broken as he watched her read the details of her father's accident and worse his weird sex life. As if it wasn't bad enough that he visited a prostitute, according to reports from 'a reliable source' he also indulged in occasional group sex. And there were always drugs at these sessions. The man was obviously sick.

It couldn't be easy for Toni. The shame and embarrassment was overwhelming. But all she seemed to be concerned about was Chloe. He swallowed the lump in his throat and bent over the flowerbed. He was very proud of the way his daughter was handling this situation. Very proud indeed.

* * *

Jade was rushing back from the bank when she saw Ian climbing into his car outside the clinic. 'Hello, Ian. What on earth are you doing here?'

Ian got back out and hugged her. 'Jade, great to see you. How are things?'

'Very well. Were you here to see Toni?' she asked innocently.

Ian grinned. 'No, actually, I was here to see Robert. We're organising a rota of anaesthetists for the clinic.'

Jade's eyes widened. Ian had refused point blank to have anything to do with the clinic before and they'd had to use anaesthetists from a hospital across town.

'Well, that's great. Toni will be pleased.'

'How is she? She was very upset at Dotty's funeral on Tuesday.'

'Oh.' Jade looked surprised. Toni hadn't mentioned Ian being at the funeral. But then she'd been walking around in a daze since Dotty's death. 'Yeah, they were close. But you know Toni. She's getting on with things.'

'I was sorry to hear about you and Aidan,' he said suddenly.

Jade looked up in surprise at the turn of conversation.

'Sorry,' Ian looked embarrassed. 'It's just I've never had an opportunity to say that before. I've missed you both. We had some good times.'

'Yeah, we did.'

'Do you keep in touch?' Ian asked.

'We didn't, but that changed lately when Aidan's mother died.'

'Yes, I heard about that too. I'm sorry. Is he coping okay?'

Jade shrugged. 'Seems to be.' She hadn't seen Aidan since the night they'd had dinner together and he'd been on a high that night. 'He's got a new job so that's probably a good distraction.'

Ian frowned. 'Oh. Isn't he working for himself any more?'

Jade bit her tongue. It wasn't like her to make such a slip-up. 'No, he was fed up worrying about accounts and tax. He wanted to get back to doing the job he was qualified for.'

Ian laughed. 'Sensible man. Give him my best.'

'I will. Well, I'd better get inside or Perky will have a fit.'

'It was good to see you again, Jade.'

Jade smiled. He really was a very nice man. 'You too.' She reached up to give him a friendly peck on the cheek. 'And one other thing.'

'Yes?' Ian walked her to the door.

342

'Don't quote me but I'd say Toni regrets ever marrying Theo French.'

Ian shrugged. 'It's a bit late for regrets. Goodbye, Jade.'

'Bye.' Jade hurried inside. It was such a pity Toni had broken up with that man. He was so nice. And he was still a fine thing too – for his age. There was a slight beer belly but then that was to be expected. He was a forty-something bachelor after all. She knew he was seeing Carla but from what she'd heard from her sources at the hospital, the relationship didn't seem to be going anywhere. Maybe there was still a chance that he and Toni would get back together. After all, how did Ian know that Aidan's mother had died unless Toni had told him. Jade smiled slowly. My God, they were seeing each other again! Well, well, well!

* * *

'That bitch has been driving me mad.' Sandra banged the filing cabinet drawer.

Jade looked at her with raised eyebrows. It wasn't often you heard Sandra curse. 'Let me guess. Are you talking about my lovely colleague Vicky Harrison? What's she done now?' She took her coat off and sat down beside Sandra.

'Oh, nothing . . . everything. She's just acting as if she's already running the place. It makes my blood boil. She doesn't do half as much work as you do.'

Jade smiled. 'I'll take that as a compliment. Is Toni in?'

'You just missed her. I think she had another meeting with the solicitor.'

'Poor Toni. She seems to spend her life in meetings these days.'

'We ought to organise another night out to cheer her up,' Sandra said brightly.

'You're becoming quite a party animal, Ms Tomkins.'

Sandra grinned. 'That's what Mam says. She's delighted.'

'How is she?'

'Brilliant!' Sandra's eyes danced in her head and Vicky was forgotten. 'She's steadier on her feet than she's been in years and her speech is perfect – well, unless she's very tired.'

'That's wonderful. Is there any reason for this improvement?'

'Nothing I can put my finger on. Her medicine is the same. Her diet is the same. The only difference is she's been going out more. There are a few social events a month in the parish and one of our neighbours started taking her along. She drives so it's very handy.'

'Maybe your mother's got herself a fella,' Jade said, her eyes twinkling.

'Don't be silly. Oh! You don't think . . . no.'

'She's not that old, Sandra.'

'And she's great company,' Sandra said thoughtfully. 'I often thought she must be lonely. It's almost fifteen years since Dad died.'

'She was a very young widow.'

'Yes. And she never looked at another man – and there were plenty that were interested. But Mam would have nothing to do with any of them.'

'Maybe she's ready for some companionship now,' Jade suggested gently. 'And if she thinks your social life is improving then she probably feels more comfortable about going out.'

Sandra's eyes widened in horror. 'Oh, Jade! Do you think she's been staying in just because of me?'

'Don't be silly, Sandra. Your mother has been very sick. All I'm saying is that she will enjoy herself more if she knows you're having a good time too.'

Sandra thought about this for a moment.

Jade looked at her worriedly. What had she started? 'Sandra?'

'There's only one thing for it,' Sandra said firmly. 'We're definitely having a night out next week. And it's going to be a late one!'

'I don't think I'm going to be able to keep up with you at this rate.' Jade laughed in relief.

'It could be worse. You could be trying to keep up with my mother!'

* * *

'Mr Stringer still hasn't supplied me with financial statements,' Teresa Neil told her client.

'Because the money is all in offshore accounts,' Toni said, tapping her nails impatiently on the arm of her chair.

'Have you any proof of that?' Teresa had asked calmly.

'Of course not. He'd hardly call me with the account numbers!'

Teresa put down her pen and fixed her with a cool stare. 'Ms Jordan, this isn't an easy time for you and separations can get very ugly and costly. It would help if you remembered that I'm on your side.'

Toni sighed. 'I'm sorry but surely it's a clear-cut case. He stole all of my money.'

'No he didn't. He withdrew money from your joint account. You could have done the same. There is nothing illegal about it.'

Toni rubbed the bridge of her nose wearily. 'Well, if Stringer won't co-operate what do we do?'

'Mr Stringer is co-operating as much as he can. But he says he cannot contact his client and his hands are tied until Mr French contacts him.'

'He knows where he is. I'd stake my life on it!'

'Be that as it may, Ms Jordan. I can't call the man a liar. It was Mr French who asked for the divorce. We have to assume he will be in touch with his solicitor to progress matters.'

'And until then we just twiddle our thumbs?'

'No. I have written to Mr Stringer and told him that we will not agree to the sale of the house until financial arrangements are in place.'

'Oh,' Toni said slightly mollified. 'Great. Thanks.'

Teresa smiled at her. 'Like I say, Toni. I'm on your side.'

Chapter Thirty-four

Saturday, 16th September, 2000

Jade sipped her wine and looked around her appreciatively. It was so nice to sit in Coopers Café instead of her usual Chinese restaurant. A more upmarket restaurant, it was in one of the nicer parts of the city and populated in the evenings by the beautiful people. It was also very nice to look at the menu without worrying about the prices – although of course she'd still be careful in her choice. And it was a definite plus to be able to order a glass of wine while she waited for Toni and Sandra. She glanced at her watch. It had only just gone eight so they weren't exactly late. Though Jade didn't mind. She was enjoying people-watching and absorbing the atmosphere.

'Jade!' Sandra handed her coat shyly to a waitress and hurried over to the table. 'Sorry I'm late. Ooh, it's very posh here, isn't it?" She looked around her wide-eyed.

'You're not late. I was early.' Jade smiled at Sandra as she sat down. 'You're going to have to learn to stop apologising all of the time.'

'Sorry . . . oh!' Sandra giggled.

'Let me get you a drink. What would you like?'

'Oh, whatever you think.' Sandra shrugged looking around her wide-eyed. 'It's very flash here, isn't it?'

'I like it. This Chardonnay is nice, would you like some of that?'

'Lovely.'

Jade beckoned a passing waiter and ordered a bottle. 'I'm sure we'll get through it,' she said to Sandra with a wink.

'Oh, I don't think I should. It goes straight to my head.'

'Good! That's exactly what you need.'

'What's exactly what she needs?' Toni appeared beside them and sat down.

'Hi, Toni. Jade's trying to get me drunk.'

'Well, she'll have no problem getting me drunk at all,' Toni said drily. 'I'm ready to drown in the stuff.'

The waiter appeared with the wine and filled their glasses.

Jade held up her glass. 'Here's to forgetting all of our problems.'

'I'd have to get completely rat-arsed to manage that,' Toni assured her. 'But I would like to make a toast to you two. Thank you for putting up with me these last few weeks and thanks for talking me into coming out tonight.'

'You're welcome.' Sandra sipped her wine and smiled. 'Oooh. This is nice.'

Jade laughed. 'I can see I'm going to have a couple of drunks on my hands.'

Sandra giggled. 'This is a nice place. It must be very expensive.'

'Don't you worry about that, Sandra. This is on me.'

Toni's eyes were large under arched eyebrows. 'Jade?'

'Aidan's doing really well in his new job. And he insisted on giving me a little . . . gift.'

Toni smiled at the look of pride on Jade's face and the twinkle in her eye. 'That's great, Jade. I'm delighted for him. But you shouldn't be spending your money on us.'

'Absolutely not,' Sandra agreed stoutly.

'Oh rubbish! I'm entitled to a little treat. Anyway it was my idea to come here – I really think if I eat another Chinese meal I'll change colour!'

Toni laughed. 'Well, okay then. But at least let me buy the next bottle.'

Sandra shook her head. '*Another* bottle! Oh dear.'

'I'm afraid you're in very bad company, Sandra.'

'True,' Jade agreed. 'You'll learn nothing but bad habits from us pair.'

'And how to screw up your life,' Toni added.

'Oh stop that,' Sandra protested. 'I didn't have a life at all until you two took pity on me. Now, top up my glass, Jade. The night is young.'

Toni tossed back her hair and laughed. 'Sandra, you're a tonic.'

'It's nice to see you laugh. And you should wear your hair loose more often. It's gorgeous like that.' Sandra would kill to have Toni's silky mane.

'But not very practical.'

Jade made a face at her. 'Oh, who cares about practical, Toni? You're not at work now.'

'And I probably won't be at work at all very soon if Robert has his way.'

Sandra's smile disappeared. 'You don't really believe that, do you?'

'No, of course she doesn't, Sandra,' Jade said quickly. 'She's just feeling sorry for herself.'

'Yeah, sorry, Sandra. Don't mind me.'

'I suppose Vicky will get promoted,' Jade added morosely.

'Well, put it this way,' Toni told them. 'I don't think I'll be giving her that formal warning.'

Sandra's eyes were on stalks. 'You were going to give Vicky a formal warning?'

Toni nodded. This was very unprofessional but it probably didn't matter any more. 'She's been messing us around so much lately. Her attendance record is lousy –'

'And when she is in she makes mistakes all the time,' Jade chipped in.

Toni nodded. 'It's a wonder she hasn't killed someone. Oh well. She'll probably be running the place soon! Actually, that would be fun. She might do some work for a change.'

Jade's eyebrows disappeared under her fringe. 'No chance. She'd just sit in your chair and bark out orders all day.'

Toni smiled. 'I don't think I'd care. She's welcome to my job and all of the hassle that goes with it. I bet her little affair with Robert won't last long once she starts to ruin his business.'

Sandra choked on her wine. 'Perky – Mr Perkins – and Vicky are having an affair?' She gasped after her cough had subsided.

Jade rolled her eyes. 'Oh, Sandra! Where have you been?'

'In a different world by the sound of it. I know she flirts with him but I had no idea they were at it!'

Toni laughed. 'And how!'

Sandra shuddered. 'How can she?'

'I wonder will Daniel start again somewhere else?' Jade mused.

'Oh, wouldn't it be lovely if we could all stay together?' Sandra said wistfully as the waiter arrived with their starters. She eyed her plate dubiously. 'I asked for cheese,' she whispered when he'd gone.

'It's deep-fried Brie,' Jade told her. 'Go on, try it.'

Sandra took a cautious nibble. 'Oh, it's gorgeous,' she said with her mouth full. 'Oops, sorry.'

Jade shook her head in despair. 'That word is going to be etched on your gravestone.'

Toni laughed. 'Don't mind her, Sandra.'

Sandra barely glanced up from her food. 'I won't.'

'God bless booze and its liberating powers.' Toni laughed, raising her glass to her friends. It was nice to get out of the house for a while. With Chloe staying up with her parents and Alice only coming in once a week Toni found the place more depressing than ever.

'So, Sandra, what's new in your life?' Jade asked. 'Any men?'

'Don't be silly, Jade. Where would I meet men?'

'You do work in reception,' Toni pointed out with a grin.

'Yes and the only men I meet are either coming to get tummy tucks or hair implants. Very attractive!'

Jade laughed. 'Well, maybe it's not the best place to get a date,' she conceded. 'You should let us set you up.'

'We've been through all this and I'm still not interested,' Sandra said firmly. 'I'm quite happy as I am. Anyway, I don't have time for a boyfriend.'

'How is your Mum?' Toni asked gently.

Sandra smiled. 'She's doing really great. It's amazing. Every time I think she's not going to recover from an attack, she bounces back again.'

Toni nodded. 'She's a very determined woman, your mother. I'm convinced it helps to be positive.'

'And that herbal tea is great too,' Jade winked at Sandra.

Toni looked puzzled. 'Really?'

'Absolutely! Oh look, here's our food. Shall I order that second bottle?' Jade emptied the dregs into their three glasses.

Toni grinned. 'Why not?'

'Another Irish coffee anyone?' Toni waved her empty glass in the air. It was a good job Chloe wasn't here to see the state she was in!

'Not for me,' Sandra said sleepily and then hiccuped. 'Oh. Excuse me,' she said with a giggle. 'I think I'm a little bit tipsy.'

Jade looked at the receptionist stretched out on Toni's sofa, one foot waving about and her skirt riding up her hips. 'No, are you?'

'What about it, Jade?' Toni asked.

'Just a little one.'

Toni took her glass and weaved her way out to the kitchen. There was only a little cream left so she made a drink for Jade, a straight coffee for Sandra and poured a large Scotch for herself. Not trusting herself to balance the drinks in her current state, Toni put them on a tray adding a large packet of chocolate biscuits to go with them.

'Oh, yummy.' Sandra pulled herself up when she spied the biscuits.

Jade eyed the Scotch with narrowed eyes. 'You shouldn't mix your drinks, Toni. You'll be dying in the morning.'

Toni shrugged. 'So? God, you sounded like Ian there. He was always giving out to me for mixing my drinks.'

'Ian Chase never gave out to you in his life,' Jade retorted.

Toni collapsed into an armchair smiling. 'No. He didn't, did he? Not until . . .'

'Maybe you two will get back together,' Jade suggested lightly. Toni still hadn't told her there was anything going on but Jade had a feeling . . .

'Don't be silly, Jade. There's no going back after all these years.'

'Why not?' Sandra asked curiously. She might be drunk but she was still capable of sniffing out gossip. It was great to finally hear Jade and Toni talk openly about their love lives. 'I think life's too short for that kind of attitude.'

Jade smiled. 'Well said, Sandra.'

Toni scowled at the pair of them. 'Stop ganging up on me. I've enough on my plate at the moment. Romance is the last thing on my mind.'

'Really?' Jade smiled at her but before Toni could comment she'd turned back to Sandra. ' I think you and I should be making a move.'

Sandra snuggled back into the sofa. 'But I'm so comfortable.'

Toni stood up. 'I'll phone for a taxi.'

Jade looked at her with raised eyebrows. 'That's pushing the boat out a bit.'

'Maybe you could make it to Cabra,' Toni said drily, 'but there's no way this girl could walk to Kilmainham.'

'Maybe not,' Jade conceded with a grin. God, it was good not to have to worry about money. If only she could believe it would always be like this. But it would be a long time before she could trust Aidan again. He'd hurt her too badly and the wounds hadn't healed yet. But they were improving, she acknowledged. And given time, maybe . . .

'I think I'm going to be sick,' Sandra groaned.

Jade jumped to her feet and hauled her out to the bathroom. 'Okay, love. I've got you. Let's go talk to God on the big white telephone. Back in a mo,' she called to Toni who was standing in the hall with the phone in her hand.

Toni shrugged, gave her address and hung up.

Jade reappeared in the doorway.

'Is Sandra okay?'

'No, but she'll live. I just hope she doesn't throw up in the taxi.'

'Maybe I should get her some water.'

'Good idea. And a couple of painkillers might be an idea too. In fact I'll have some of those too.' Jade yawned widely and looked at Toni's tossed hair and smeared mascara. 'And you should join us. I don't think any of us are going to feel too bright in the morning.'

Chapter Thirty-five

Saturday, 23rd September, 2000

Mark stood smiling as the train pulled into Connolly station. He couldn't wait to see Chloe again. It had been almost a month since they'd met although they'd spoken nearly every day. He scanned each carriage as the train slowed in front of him and then there she was, waving at him from behind a young family who were unloading buggies at an incredibly slow pace. Chloe hopped from one foot to the other impatiently and when they'd finally sorted themselves out she moved quickly past them and ran into Mark's arms.

'I thought you were never going to get off,' he said pulling away to smile at her, his eyes caressing every inch of her beautiful face. 'Your hair's longer.'

Chloe made a face. 'I was going to get it cut again just to annoy Dad. Then I thought he'd probably never see it anyway. You prefer it longer, don't you?'

'I'd like you if you were bald,' he assured her. He took her backpack, slung it easily over his shoulder and led the way to the car. 'So, did you have a good time?'

'It was great. I thought it would be really quiet and boring but Mary and Peter have a great life. They socialise more than we do.'

Mark laughed. 'One of the perks of being retired. Money.'

'It's a nice thought, isn't it?' Chloe said dreamily. 'To be that old and still enjoying life. Still enjoying each other.'

'That's the way we'll be. We'll have his and her Zimmer frames and we'll roll down to the pub together.'

Chloe smiled but said nothing.

'I'm so glad you're back. I didn't know what to do with myself while you were gone.'

'But it won't be for long, Mark.'

'What do you mean?'

'I'm going to travel. I told you that.'

Mark's smile faded away. Chloe had talked about taking a year out to travel but he'd never really taken it seriously. He thought that she'd calm down after a while and change her mind. He certainly hadn't expected her to be still talking about it after her break in Skerries.

'But I thought you were just saying that because you were upset.'

'I still am,' Chloe said, a steely note creeping into her voice.

'Of course you are,' Mark said placatingly. 'And that's all the more reason why you should stay with the people who love you. Don't run away, Chloe. It won't solve anything.'

'I am not running away,' she said angrily. 'I'm taking a year to weigh things up and decide what I really want.'

'But now that you don't have to worry about your dad's opinion you could come to UCD with me.'

Chloe wavered for a second but then her mouth set in a firm line, very like her father's. 'No. It just doesn't feel right. I've got to get away and clear my head. And I need to stand on my own two feet for a change. I've been dependent on Dad for too long.'

'Well, that won't change,' Mark pointed out sarcastically. 'It's his money you'll be using to travel. Poor little rich girl.'

Chloe stopped in her tracks and slapped his face. Then stared in shock as the side of his face reddened. 'Oh, I'm sorry!'

Mark touched his face with a rueful smile. 'Me too. Look, I don't want us to fight, Chloe. It's just that I don't want to lose you. You're only just back and you're talking about leaving again.'

'Please don't make it any harder than it already is, Mark. I have to do this.'

Mark nodded and opened his mother's car. They were halfway home when he finally had the courage to ask the question uppermost in his mind. 'When will you go?'

Chloe sighed. She'd thought about this a lot. 'After my birthday. It would upset Toni and Alice if I went before then.'

Mark swallowed hard. 'That's only a few weeks away.'

She nodded and stared out of the window, her eyes bright with tears.

Mark squeezed her knee and smiled brightly. 'Then we're going to have to make it one hell of a birthday, aren't we?' he said with forced enthusiasm.

Chloe put her hand over his and held it tightly. 'Thanks, Mark.'

When they reached the house Alice had laid on a huge spread.

'Roast stuffed chicken,' Chloe squealed in delight. 'And peas and gravy. Oh, Alice, you're a pet.'

The woman blushed happily. 'It's nice to have you home, love. We've missed you.'

'It's great to see you moving around so easily.'

'Oh, I'm fine now. Who knows? I might even enter the Marathon!'

Chloe laughed. 'Toni isn't home then?' She'd expected her stepmother to be here. It was six o'clock after all. She shouldn't be still in work at this hour on a Saturday.

The hall door banged and Toni rushed into the kitchen, laden down with bags. Mark rushed to help her.

'Oh, thanks, Mark. Chloe, love!' Relieved of her burden she threw her arms around her stepdaughter.

Chloe allowed herself to be hugged. 'Hi, Toni. You're only just in time. Alice has made us a lovely dinner.'

Toni noticed the reproachful tone and decided to ignore it. 'Sorry, Alice. It took longer than I thought.'

'Shall I get the glasses?' Alice smiled.

Toni nodded and produced a bottle of champagne from one of the bags. 'This is what kept me. I couldn't get the damn cooler to work!'

Alice arrived back with the champagne glasses just as Toni popped the cork.

'Welcome home, love.' Toni handed Chloe the first glass.

Chloe flashed her a guilty smile. 'Thanks, Toni. This is great.'

Mark took his glass and clinked it against hers. 'Cheers, Chloe.'

Alice took a small sip. 'I think it would be safer if I saved mine until I've served up dinner. This stuff goes right to my head.'

Chloe laughed. 'I don't think I've ever seen you drunk, Alice.'

'Well, today could be the day,' Toni said with a wink and produced a second bottle from the bag. 'I figured you're nearly eighteen so what the hell.'

'And what's in here?' Chloe went over to inspect another bag. 'Oh, Toni! Cheesecake, gorgeous!'

'Don't expect this treatment every day,' Toni warned but she was smiling happily, delighted to have Chloe home.

'Come on, everyone. Sit down,' Alice called as she carried the plates to the table.

'This looks great, Mrs S.' Mark eyed his plate hungrily.

'I hope your mother won't have anything prepared for you,' Alice said worriedly.

'He'll eat it as well,' Chloe assured her. 'He's like a dustbin.'

'Excuse me, I'm a growing lad,' Mark protested.

Toni attacked her plate hungrily. She hadn't been eating well while Chloe was away and it was so nice to sit down to a home-cooked meal and a relaxed atmosphere. She raised her glass towards Alice. 'God bless the cook.'

'Hear! Hear!' Chloe smiled at Alice.

Alice took a sip of her champagne. 'You're welcome – ooh, this is nice.'

'Get used to it,' Toni told her. 'You'll be drinking buckets of it when this lady turns eighteen.'

Chloe's smile faded. How did she tell them that she didn't really want a party any more? And that she'd be leaving home soon after.

Mark shot her a meaningful look but she kept her head down and pretended not to notice.

Toni saw the exchange and had a pretty good idea what it meant. Though she and Chloe hadn't discussed college since she'd gone to stay in Skerries, her mother had told her that Chloe was still adamant that she wanted a year off. Toni wondered how soon she planned to leave. They hadn't even discussed where she would go although Toni knew that she had some cousins in Sydney. That should be far enough away for Chloe. She sighed heavily at the thought of losing her stepdaughter.

Alice glanced sharply at her. 'Everything all right, Toni?'

'Yes, fine. I've just eaten too much. It's so delicious.'

Chloe watched them, amused. 'You know, Mark, you'd never believe it now but these two barely passed the time of day up until a few months ago.'

Toni looked up sharply but relaxed when she realised that Chloe was just teasing. 'That's rubbish,' she retorted, poker-faced.

'Absolute nonsense,' Alice chipped in. 'I don't know where she gets these ideas, do you Toni?'

Toni gazed back innocently. 'I've no idea, Alice. It's probably going to all these clubs, you know. They say that strobe lighting has a funny effect on the brain.'

Chloe threw her head back and laughed and Toni thought it was a wonderful sound.

'You're both certifiable,' Chloe said finally. 'I think

you've been at the booze while I've been away! What do you think, Mark?'

'Probably,' he grinned. It was nice to see Chloe so relaxed. Maybe now she was home she'd give up this idea of travelling the world.

Toni shooed Chloe and Mark from the kitchen and made Alice sit down and have a cup of tea while she stacked the dishwasher.

'She seems a lot happier,' Alice remarked.

'Isn't it great? I must phone Mum and Dad later and thank them. I'm not sure what they did but it definitely worked.'

'The poor girl just needed some time to herself. Now she'll be ready to start college.'

Toni sighed. 'She doesn't want to start college. She wants a gap year.'

'A what?'

'She wants to take a year out to travel.'

'Can she do that?'

Toni shrugged. 'Oh, yes, it's quite common. I just wish I could believe that she's doing it for the right reasons. I think she sees it as a way of getting back at Theo.'

'Damn that man,' Alice stormed.

Toni's eyes widened. To hear Alice curse her beloved boss was very weird.

'He's ruined that poor child's life. I would dearly love to give him a piece of my mind.'

'I'm going to find him, Alice, if it's the last thing I do. I don't care if he never comes back to Ireland but he at least should keep in touch with Chloe.'

'She may not want him to any more,' Alice said sadly.

'She should at least have the choice.'

Chloe let her head slide down on to Mark's shoulder. 'It's so nice to be home.'

'I think you'd be better off in bed,' Mark laughed. 'That champagne has gone right to your head.'

'I feel wonderful,' Chloe said sleepily.

'You look beautiful,' Mark murmured bending his head to kiss her.

Chloe kissed him back passionately. When they came up for air she smiled shyly at him. 'Mark? There's something I wanted to ask you.'

'Oh?' He tucked a tendril of hair back behind her ear and kissed the tip of her nose.

'Before I go away I want you to . . .'

'What?' he prompted looking into her wide blue eyes.

'I want you to make love to me. Properly.' Chloe's face reddened but she held his gaze, her eyes full of love.

Mark stared at her. 'Are you sure that you want –'

She pressed a finger to his lips. 'I've never been more sure of anything in my life. But I don't want it to happen in the back of your mother's car.'

'We could go somewhere,' Mark said racking his brains.

'No. We'll do it here. In my room.'

Mark stared at her as if she'd taken leave of her senses. 'And will Toni bring us some hot cocoa afterwards?'

Chloe giggled at the thought. 'No, silly. Toni goes out nearly every week with Jade and Sandra. We'll plan it for

362

one of those nights. Then we'll have the whole place to ourselves until at least eleven.'

'Oh.' Mark stared at her. He could hardly believe that after all this time they were finally going to do 'It'. 'And you're sure?'

Chloe kissed him tenderly. 'I'm sure.'

Alice tied a headscarf under her chin and followed Toni into the sitting-room.

She smiled at Chloe as she put on her coat. 'I'll be off now, love. It's wonderful to have you home.'

Chloe jumped up from the sofa. 'We'll drop you home, won't we, Mark?'

'Sure.'

'I've already offered,' Toni told them, 'but apparently Alice's got a hot date!'

'Go away out of that.' Alice rolled her eyes. 'Don't mind her, Chloe. I'm just going to bingo and Mr Reilly said he'd give me a lift.'

Chloe grinned as she remembered the skinny little man who lived down the road from Alice. 'So you and Tommy Reilly have finally got together.'

'I hope I've got better taste than that!' Alice sniffed. 'He wouldn't even keep me warm at night.'

'Alice!' Toni looked scandalised.

Alice grinned back as a horn beeped outside. 'That will be him. Goodnight, everyone. Wish me luck!'

'Night, Alice.' Chloe hugged her.

Mark went in search of his jacket after Alice had left. 'I should be making tracks too.'

'It's only eight-thirty!' Chloe exclaimed.

'I've got football training,' he explained.

Toni laughed. 'I don't know how you're going to run around a football pitch after eating one of Alice's dinners.'

'And drinking all that champagne.' Chloe giggled.

'I know. I'll probably get thrown off the team. Or throw up!'

Chloe squirmed. 'Ugh, don't say that! Will you call me tomorrow?'

'Of course I will,' he murmured. 'Goodnight, Toni.'

'Night, Mark.'

Chloe walked Mark out to the door. 'I hope the next night Toni goes out there isn't football practice,' she said lightly.

Mark stopped and pulled her to him. 'I don't care if Man U want me to try out for them. If it's a choice between them and you, you win every time.'

'Oh Mark.' Chloe sighed.

Toni sat watching television, smiling at the romantic mumbling punctuated by long silences in the hall. Maybe Mark would persuade Chloe not to take a year out. She seemed so crazy about him it was hard to imagine her leaving him. He might not be willing to wait for her. After all, he was only nineteen and he was a handsome enough lad.

Finally the hall door closed and Chloe wandered back into the room and curled up on the sofa.

'Glad to be home?' Toni asked.

'Oh yes.'

'Well, I'm glad you're back. I've missed you.'

'I've missed you too,' Chloe grinned. 'Although I had

a great time in Skerries. You're so lucky, Toni. Your parents are really great.'

'I didn't always think so.'

'Was it because of Dad?' Chloe asked.

Toni looked up sharply. Surely her folks hadn't said anything to Chloe? 'Why do you say that?'

Chloe's gaze was candid. 'Well, he was a lot older than you. There can't be that many years between my dad and yours.'

'Seven,' Toni admitted. 'My father was furious.'

'And now?' Chloe prompted.

'Now we're okay.' Toni smiled at her stepdaughter, knowing it was the truth. 'Chloe, about this travelling –'

Chloe sighed. 'Oh please don't start, Toni.'

'Will you hear me out, please?'

'Sorry.'

'I won't object to you going if you really want to but I have an alternative suggestion for you.'

'I'm listening.'

'Well, I understand why you don't want to go to college at the moment. My God, it would be impossible to concentrate and even though things have quietened down in the press, it might still be awkward for you.'

'Yeah, kids pointing at me saying "There's the daughter of that perv surgeon".'

Toni sighed. 'Whatever. But I think you need your friends and family right now. I hate the thoughts of you in some crummy hostel in the middle of nowhere all on your own.'

'I'll make friends,' Chloe said more confidently than she felt.

'Of course you will but I'd still like you to postpone the trip for a few months. Sandra is only working part-time at the moment. How would you feel about working at the clinic?'

Chloe stared at her. 'What?'

'Well, think about it. You would have a salary – not an enormous one – and you'd get some work experience. You get to see Mark and Ollie all the time. And you would still have your year out to think about what you want to do.'

Chloe nodded slowly. 'And I could still go abroad later?'

'If you wanted to,' Toni agreed. 'I just hate you going right now, Chloe. It's been a very unsettling time. I'd feel happier if you were here with me.'

'Can I think about it?'

Toni smiled. 'Of course. There's plenty of time.'

Chapter Thirty-six

Monday, 25th September, 2000

Jade bit back a smart retort as Vicky put on her coat and tottered out of the room on those silly heels she insisted on wearing. The girl was thoroughly enjoying winding Jade up at every opportunity and Jade was doing her best not to retaliate.

But it wasn't easy. Jade was finding it very hard to keep her temper in check these days. In fact she was feeling very down lately and she'd no idea why. She didn't owe anyone any money – Aidan had finally paid off all of their outstanding debts last week. And she could probably afford to find herself a nice little flat now. But somehow she couldn't summon up enough enthusiasm. Maybe she'd get Toni or Sandra to come flat-hunting with her. It would be more fun than doing it alone. Jade smiled wryly, thinking how much she'd changed in the last few months. There was a time when she insisted on doing everything on her own, shunning any intervention or offers of assistance from her friends.

The phone buzzed and she picked it up. 'Yes?' she said briefly, knowing it was Robert.

'Jade, could you drop in to me, please?'

Jade raised an eyebrow at his polite tone. 'Certainly.' She hung up and walked down the corridor, tapping on his door before going in. 'What can I do for you, Robert?'

Robert smiled and gestured for her to sit down. 'It's a bit delicate, Jade,' he said, steepling his fingers and looking very serious.

'Oh yes?' Jade said calmly. *This is it. I'm getting the push.*

'There have been a lot of slip-ups lately. Files misplaced, case-notes missing . . .'

'I hope you're not pointing the finger at me,' Jade said hotly.

'Oh, no, no, not at all, my dear.'

My dear. Jade watched him suspiciously.

'I'm afraid it's Vicky who has let us down.'

Jade stared at him in astonishment. 'Vicky?'

'Yes. I'm sure you'll agree that she hasn't exactly been pulling her weight recently.'

'I can't say she ever did,' Jade said candidly.

'Quite. Well, I think Daniel has probably been too soft on the girl.'

Jade blinked.

'And Toni too,' Robert added seriously. 'But now that I am in charge I think it's time for a clean sweep.'

'Clean sweep?' Jade echoed faintly.

'Indeed,' Robert said more confidently. 'There's no room in my clinic for layabouts. I've looked at Vicky's file and her attendance record has been abysmal lately. She's got to go.'

'Oh.'

'I need to know, Jade, if you'll be able to manage things until we find a replacement. Of course, I'll get Toni to organise a temp in the meantime. What do you think?'

Jade gaped at him wordlessly and felt a sudden rush of pity for Vicky. The bastard was dumping her. And how! 'I, eh, it's up to you of course, Robert. I'll manage the workload no problem.' *I always have before, she added silently.* 'Once I get some kind of backup.'

'No problem. Well then, I'll discuss the matter with Toni and set the wheels in motion. Needless to say, Jade, keep this to yourself for the moment.'

Jade stood up and flashed him a false smile. 'Of course.' *You cold, conniving bastard,* she thought as she walked back to the office she shared with Vicky. The poor bitch thought she was going to be running the place and he was planning her downfall. Though it was hard to feel sorry for Vicky. She was a lazy, two-faced cow and they'd be better off without her. And she'd pick up work easily enough. There was a shortage of nurses in Dublin and some other unfortunate was bound to offer her a job. But it was Robert's ruthlessness that had taken Jade's breath away. Maybe she was next for the chop.

She was still sitting musing over the sudden turn of events when Toni walked in.

'You'll never guess.' Toni shut the door and sat down, her eyes dancing in her head.

'Perky is sacking his girlfriend?'

Toni looked disappointed. 'You know?'

'He just told me. Poor bitch.'

369

'I can't believe you! You've never had a good word to say about the woman.'

'Still,' Jade looked uncomfortable, 'to be fired by your own boyfriend.'

'I suppose. I wonder what she'll do?'

'Probably take a knife to him. I can't imagine her going quietly, can you?'

Toni chuckled. 'No, I suppose not. I just can't believe it. I thought you or me would be the first ones he'd get rid of.'

'Robert's a businessman first,' Jade said shrewdly. 'As long as we keep this place running smoothly and he keeps making money, he'll be happy.'

'You're right,' Toni agreed. 'I never thought about it like that before. Thank God that's one less thing to worry about.'

'Any news?' Jade asked, noting the dark circles under her friend's eyes.

'From Theo? Not a word. But Chloe's in much better form.'

'Is she still planning to go away?'

Toni smiled. 'Hopefully not. I've suggested that she come and work here instead.'

'Doing what?'

'Standing in for Sandra in the mornings. She can't be any worse that the temps we've had.'

'That's a great idea, Toni. And it would still give Chloe a year to think about college.'

'That's what I said but she hasn't said yes yet.'

'She will. She must be upset about leaving Mark.'

Toni shrugged. 'I'm not sure but it does seem serious between them.'

'There you are then. She's probably looking for a reason to stay but she's too stubborn to back down.'

Toni nodded. That actually made sense. Chloe could be as stubborn as her father, or, she smiled, as her stepmother. 'You should set up a counselling service.'

'I might have to when Robert gets around to firing me.'

Toni paused in the doorway. 'You know? I don't think that's going to happen. I've a feeling everything is going to work out just fine.'

After the conversation with Jade, Toni couldn't wait to get home to talk to her stepdaughter. She was delighted to find a good-humoured Chloe in the kitchen talking to Alice as she put the finishing touches to a casserole for their dinner.

'Hi folks,' Toni said cheerfully, pulling off her coat.

'Hello, love,' Alice smiled.

'Hi, Toni.' Chloe blew her a kiss.

That was a good sign, Toni thought happily. 'That smells good, Alice. Are you staying to eat with us?'

'No, I promised to drop in and see my neighbour. She hasn't been too well. I thought I'd bring her some of this,' she gestured to a smaller dish, 'and keep her company for a few hours.'

'Well then, I'll drop you home.'

'Thanks,' Alice said gratefully. 'Now, Chloe love, turn the temperature down in about ten minutes.'

Chloe hopped off the counter. 'Will do. See you tomorrow.'

'It's nice to see her in such good form,' Alice said as they walked out to the car.

'Yes, it is. I'm hoping to persuade her not to go away, Alice. Wish me luck.'

Toni entertained Chloe over dinner with the tale of Vicky's impending departure.

'What a horrible man he is,' Chloe mused. 'I don't know what Dad sees in him.'

'Have you thought any more about my suggestion?' Toni asked lightly.

'A bit,' Chloe mumbled.

'Wouldn't you miss Mark if you went away?'

'He could come with me but he wants to start his course.'

'You can't blame him for that.'

'If he loved me, he'd come,' Chloe said sulkily.

Toni laughed. 'And if you loved him, you'd stay. Don't be silly, Chloe.'

Chloe looked slightly shamefaced.

'Why not compromise,' Toni said lightly and stood up to clear away their dishes.

Chloe frowned. 'How?'

'You take the job at the Blessington and maybe when Mark gets his holidays you could go away together.'

Chloe brightened. 'I suppose, but he doesn't get that long a break.'

'No,' Toni agreed as she stacked the dishwasher. 'Well, it's just an idea.' Deciding not to push her luck any further, she changed the subject. 'You know, we need to plan your birthday party soon.'

'I don't think I should have one.'

Toni turned to stare at her. 'Why on earth not?'

'Well, with this whole thing with Dad it just doesn't seem right. And it would probably bring the journalists back in droves.'

Toni's eyes hardened. That man was not going to screw everything up. She wouldn't let him. She came back to the table and sat down. 'They won't know about your birthday, Chloe, and you can't let your dad affect all your decisions. It's time that we got on with our lives.'

'That's not so easy for me,' Chloe said sadly. 'No. I've decided. No party.'

Toni saw the determined look in her eye and decided not to argue the point. 'It's up to you. Let me know if you change your mind.'

'You're not annoyed with me, are you, Toni?'

Toni paused to give her a quick hug. 'Of course not, love. Maybe we'll just have a quiet dinner.'

'We'll see,' Chloe said evasively.

'Fine,' Toni said brightly and threw down her dishcloth. 'Now, I'm going to have a soak in the bath. I'll be back down in time for *Who Wants To Be A Millionaire*.'

'Okay. I think I'll go over to Ollie's.'

'Right. Don't be too late.'

'I won't.'

Toni went upstairs wondering if she'd made any headway at all. At least she'd got Chloe thinking. Maybe it was best to leave it at that for the moment. But it was an awful pity about the party. Damn Theo. She'd murder him if they ever met up again!

The phone rang just as Toni was about to step into the bath. Luckily she'd brought the phone upstairs with her but where she'd left it was another matter.

'Yes?' she said breathlessly after finding it under the towel.

'Hi, Toni. It's me.'

'Oh, hi, Ian?' Toni tightened the towel around her and then smiled at her silliness. 'How are you?'

'Fine. Any news?'

'Nothing. You?'

'Maybe. I was talking to a few people about Theo's old college buddies. One name that came up I thought might interest you. Eric Levinson.'

'Eric! Of course – he was the New Zealander. He was the one who was at our wedding. God, do you think Theo might have gone over to him?'

'It's worth checking out,' Ian said cheerfully. 'I'm afraid I've found no one else who hails from far-off climes.'

'Then it must be Eric.'

'Now, don't get your hopes up too soon, Toni.'

'I won't.'

'So do I get a reward for my good work? How about dinner some night?'

'Oh, I suppose so,' Toni said teasingly. 'And I suppose it should be on me.'

'Well, yes, if you insist! How about next Friday?'

'Fine. Where shall we meet?'

'Why not in the usual place at eight? I'll book somewhere for dinner.'

'I'll look forward to it.' And as she put down the phone and climbed into her bath she realised just how much she was looking forward to it.

Chapter Thirty-seven

Tuesday, 26th September, 2000

'There's a new nurse starting today,' Jade told Sandra.

'Has to be better than the last one,' Sandra said cheerfully. There had been two temps sent to replace Vicky and they had been a disaster. The first, Ruth, a thin girl with an acerbic tongue had shouted at everyone including the patients for no apparent reason. And the second, Milly, a good-tempered plump woman in her early fifties had pumped everyone for gossip.

'And this is not the sort of clinic where that's going to go down too well,' Jade had said drily when explaining the problem to Robert. 'I've told them we'll give them one more chance and then we're taking our business elsewhere.'

'What time is she due in?' Sandra asked, looking at the clock. It was just gone eight.

'He,' Jade corrected with a wink. 'Matthew Little. And he's due in at eight-thirty.'

Sandra's eyes were like saucers. 'A man? Is that a good idea?'

Jade shrugged. 'I'm willing to give him a go if he's got

half a brain. We're desperate. I just wish we had someone decent to help you out, Sandra. Although I have a feeling that Toni has found someone suitable.'

'Bev was great,' Sandra said with a sigh. 'It's a pity she had to leave. Why is it whenever we find any decent workers they leave?'

Jade laughed. 'Maybe it's us! Listen, I'm just going in to see Toni. Give me a shout when Matthew gets here, would you?'

'No problem.'

Left to herself, Sandra turned her attention to sorting the post and was completely engrossed when there was a polite cough behind her. She swung around to face the incredibly tall young man at the desk. 'Yes?'

'Hi, I'm Matthew Little. The agency sent me.'

Sandra smiled vacantly. His eyes were huge and a very dark brown. Like a faithful dog, she thought dreamily. In fact everything about him was big. He was built like a rugby player with hands like shovels. She giggled. 'Sorry, it's just your name . . .'

Matthew gave a wry grin. 'Yeah. Everyone says that.'

'Sorry.'

'That's okay.'

'I'm Sandra, by the way. I run reception.'

Matthew nodded shyly. 'Nice to meet you.'

'I'll just get Jade Peters. She's the senior nurse.' Sandra buzzed through to Toni's office, her eyes never leaving his face. He was gorgeous, in a cuddly bear sort of way. Everything about him seemed brown and fluffy. His hair was brown and stood on end in soft curls. He wore a brown leather car coat that looked years old, teamed up with faded brown cords. Sandra figured he must be about her age but she'd get the exact details from Jade.

Jade came out a couple of minutes later to collect Matthew. She stopped dead in her tracks halfway across reception when she saw this mountain of a man. Collecting herself, she stuck out her hand and pasted on her professional smile. 'Matthew? I'm Jade Peters.'

Her hand disappeared into Matthew's huge one. 'Nice to meet you, Jade.'

'Okay then. Why don't you come down to my office and we'll have a chat.'

Matthew ambled down the corridor after her.

'I'll bring you some tea,' Sandra called after them, eager to get another look at this gentle giant. 'Matthew,' she breathed softly and went off to the kitchen to put on the kettle. 'What a nice name!'

'So, Matthew. You seem to have all the relevant experience. Do you mind me asking you why you're temping?'

Matthew's face clouded over. 'I gave up my permanent job to look after my dad. He had cancer.'

'Oh, I'm sorry. Is he . . .' Jade searched for the right words.

'He died last month,' Matthew said simply. 'But I haven't done anything about getting a permanent job yet.'

'There's plenty of time for that,' Jade said gently. 'When could you start?'

'Right away,' he assured her, the nice smile returning to his eyes. 'I can't wait to get started. So any overtime that's going, you just throw it my way!'

Jade grinned. 'I think you're going to fit in very well here.'

'I hope so.'

'Here we are,' Sandra bustled in and set a tray down on the desk.

'Meet our latest recruit, Sandra.'

Sandra beamed at him. 'Oh, congratulations, Matthew. Welcome to the Blessington.'

Matthew grinned back. 'Thanks.'

Jade stared at him. He was blushing! And Sandra was positively glowing. Wait until Toni heard about this. Jade sent up a silent prayer that Matthew would work out. Sandra would probably throttle her if she let him go!

'You're kidding?' Toni goggled at her when she was filled in. 'Love at first sight, eh?'

'Looks like it,' Jade said happily. 'Sandra's positively floating around the place. And it's all "any questions, Matthew, and you just come to me."'

Toni smiled. 'And what's this Matthew like?'

'He's got this gorgeous, sexy Donegal accent. He's quite shy, nice-looking and very big. And get this, his surname is Little.'

Toni laughed. 'It sounds like they're made for each other.'

'Except we'll have to get her a box to stand on when she's kissing him.'

'Oh, I do hope he works out,' Toni fretted. 'For our sake and Sandra's.'

'And his,' Jade added and told Toni about his background.

Toni shook her head in wonder. 'He took care of his father and she's looking after her mother. This is uncanny.'

'It is a bit weird,' Jade agreed. 'Maybe there's such a thing as fate after all.'

The phone buzzed and she picked it up. 'Yes, Sandra?'

'Jade, Aidan's in reception for you.'

Jade stared at the phone. 'Aidan?'

'Yes. Can you come down?'

'Eh, right, yes. I'll be there in a moment.' She hung up the phone and stared at Toni. 'I wonder what he wants.'

'Perhaps it's just a social call.'

Jade shook her head. 'I don't know. It's all been going a bit too well lately. I've been waiting for reality to return.'

'That's a bit harsh. He's done very well. Look at all the money he's given you.'

'I know. It's just hard to trust him after all that's happened.'

Toni patted her hand. 'Just go and say hello and stop reading so much into it. Maybe he's got another brown envelope for you!'

Jade laughed as she stood up. 'You're right. I'm being too bloody suspicious. Look, if Perky's looking for me tell him I won't be long. We have surgery in thirty minutes.'

'No problem. Now go on, before he gets fed up waiting.'

Jade hurried down to reception, straightening her uniform and slicking back her hair as she went.

Aidan stood up and smiled. 'Hello, love. You look well.'

'Hi, Aidan. You too.'

They stood awkwardly looking at each other.

Sandra sat watching as the silence grew. 'I've just got to go up and show Matthew where, eh, where we keep the, eh, cups and things.' She hurried away. 'Back in a sec.'

Aidan laughed. 'Very discreet.'

'She thinks we want to be alone.'

Aidan smiled into her eyes. 'Clever girl.'

Jade looked away. 'So what can I do for you?' She walked over to one of the sofas and sat down.

'Well, I was looking for a favour,' Aidan admitted.

Jade felt a knot forming in her stomach. 'Oh, yes,' she said, the smile frozen on her face.

Aidan sighed. 'It's not about money, Jade.'

Jade looked down at her hands. 'Sorry.'

'That's okay.'

'So what is it?' Jade asked brightly.

'I wanted your opinion on something.'

Jade arched an eyebrow. 'Are you sure?'

Aidan laughed. 'I think so. I'm going to look at an apartment this evening and I wanted you to come too.'

'An apartment? Are you selling your mother's house?'

'No, but Ann's got a man in her life and it's looking very serious. I think I'm in the way.'

'So you're moving out on your own?'

Aidan looked nervous. 'Eh, I think so.'

Jade bristled at the thought of him moving into a fancy new pad while she still lived in a hovel. 'So where is the apartment?'

'In Clontarf.'

Jade's blood began to boil. 'Clontarf? That's a very exclusive area. Apartments must be expensive there.'

'I'd get a good deal. I know the estate agent.'

'Right.' Jade said flatly.

'So, will you come?'

'When?' Jade was curious despite herself.

'I could pick you up at six-thirty.'

'Okay then.' Jade stood up. 'See you later.' She stalked off down the corridor, leaving Aidan staring after her baffled.

'The cheek of him!' She paced up and down Toni's office.

'I don't see . . .'

'I'm living in dire poverty and he wants to show off the swanky new apartment he's buying himself!'

'You could afford to move too,' Toni pointed out.

Jade scowled. 'That's not the point.'

'Oh,' Toni said confused. 'What exactly *is* your point, Jade?'

'He's being irresponsible,' Jade retorted stubbornly. 'He's only just getting back on his feet and he's throwing all his money away on a fancy bachelor pad.'

Toni's lips twitched as realisation dawned on her. 'How much is it?'

'I don't know.'

'You're not worried about the money. You just don't want him setting himself up as an eligible bachelor.'

'Rubbish,' Jade scoffed.

'Is it?'

'Of course. I just wish he'd be more practical. If he's not careful he'll end up in the gutter again.'

'But,' Toni pointed out, 'he ended up in trouble because he was gambling. He's not doing that now, is he?'

'Well, no, I don't think so,' Jade conceded.

'Then why don't you just wish the man well instead of waiting for him to fall flat on his face?'

Jade looked at her horrified. 'I'm not!'

'Aren't you?' Toni said softly. 'Leave the past in the past, Jade. Go along and see this flat, wish him good luck and look to the future. Hasn't there been enough heartache?'

'It's not that simple.' Jade flopped into a chair feeling sad and defeated.

'I think it's up to you how simple it is.' Toni stood up. 'Anyway, enough of this preaching. I'm beginning to annoy myself!'

Jade smiled. 'Only beginning?'

Toni hit her with her pen as she left the room.

'Ouch!' Jade rubbed her head.

'That'll teach you not to appreciate my words of wisdom!'

Jade sat staring into space long after Toni had left. Was there any truth in what her friend had said? Did she begrudge Aidan some happiness? A Future? That wasn't like her. Usually. But the circumstance of their separation was still a raw memory. That must be it. But, damn it, she'd do her best to rise above it all. She was forty-three years of age not some naïve little teenager. She would go along with Aidan tonight and wish him well. She knew he wished her nothing but happiness.

'Jade?' Robert barked at her as he stuck his head around the door. 'Are you planning on assisting me or shall I call Sandra?'

'Sorry, Robert, I got sidetracked,' Jade apologised hastily as she followed him to the theatre.

'Don't you start letting me down too, Jade.' The threat in Robert's words was implicit.

Jade smiled tightly. 'Of course not. It won't happen again.' There might come a time when she had enough of Perky and his silly ways but she was damned if she'd give him reason to fire her!

Aidan picked her up at six-thirty sharp and they chatted amicably as they drove to Clontarf. But when Aidan turned off the Howth road and guided the car in through the security gates of an exclusive apartment block Jade had to swallow hard. How could he even bring her here knowing the way she lived?

Aidan, seemingly oblivious to the dark mood that had descended over his wife, led the way to a discreet doorway on the side of the building. He pressed a button and Jade heard the estate agent greet him and buzz the door open. Going inside, Jade was immediately aware of the silence created by the thick carpeting. Guiding her into the lift, Aidan pressed the button for the fourth floor. 'Well?' he said excitedly.

Jade shrugged. 'It seems very nice so far.'

'Wail till you see the view, Jade. It's amazing.'

Jade didn't doubt it. And she expected the price was equally amazing.

'Aidan! Good to see you.' The man shook Aidan's hand warmly. 'And you must be Jade.'

'Jade, this is Alan Kiely.'

'Nice to meet you,' Jade said formally.

'I'll go outside – I've a couple of calls to make – and leave you two to wander around in peace.'

'Cheers, mate,' Aidan said, darting a nervous look at Jade.

'He seemed to be expecting me,' she remarked, wandering over to the window to see this 'amazing' view.

'Yes. I told him I was bringing you with me. Come on. You have to see the kitchen.'

Jade followed him into the large room done, rather unusually, in dark greens and browns. The effect was both

383

warm and sophisticated and Jade loved it immediately. She ran her hand along the tiled worktop.

'Well?' Aidan said expectantly.

'It's lovely.'

'Okay, now the bathroom. There are two en-suites as well.'

Jade arched an eyebrow. 'A two-bedroomed apartment with three bathrooms!'

Aidan laughed. 'It's far from en-suites I was reared!'

Jade followed him into the blue and white bathroom and stared at the obviously expensive tiles, the power shower and the Jacuzzi switch by the bath. 'Don't you think this is all a bit . . . much?' she said unable to keep her feelings to herself any longer.

'Maybe . . . for one.' He crossed the room and took her by the arms, looking down into her eyes. 'But not for two. Share it with me, Jade. Let's start again –'

'No!' Jade pushed him away. 'What are you talking about, Aidan? You want me to move in with you? As if the last two years haven't happened? You think that a flashy apartment with amazing views and fancy tiles is going to wipe the slate clean?'

'But Jade . . .'

Not trusting herself to say any more without bursting into tears – something she would never do in front of this man again – she ran from the apartment and stabbed the button for the lift. In the lobby Alan Kiely moved forward, smiling broadly until he saw the look on her face.

'Thanks for your time,' she said coldly, 'but it's not my style.'

Chapter Thirty-eight

Wednesday night, 27th September, 2000

Toni and Chloe sat in companionable silence watching television. Toni wasn't really taking in much of the storyline of the medical drama. She was too busy thinking about Ian and how he was getting on with his investigations.

Chloe wasn't much better. She couldn't stop thinking about Toni's proposal. Now that Mark had started in college she saw a lot less of him and it was killing her. If she was finding that hard to cope with how would it be if she were in a different country with only the occasional telephone call to look forward to?

'Toni?' she said as the credits rolled.

'Yes, love?'

'Is that offer still open? You know, the job at the clinic?'

'It certainly is.'

'Then I'll take it. Can we just do it on a temporary basis, though, because, well, I might change my mind?'

'I was only offering a temporary position,' Toni assured her. 'As soon as Sandra wants to work a full day again the position is gone.'

'That's fair. Okay, so when do I start?'

'How about tomorrow morning?'

Chloe grinned. 'Okay. I'll go and phone Mark and tell him.'

'And then go straight to bed. You've got work in the morning!'

When Chloe was gone Toni poured herself a large Scotch to celebrate. Looking at the golden liquid in her glass reminded her of Francis. Maybe she'd give him a call. She hadn't talked to him in a couple of weeks. She carried her drink back into the study and dialled his number. It rang for some time before he answered.

'Hello?'

'Francis? It's Toni.'

'Toni, my dear. How nice.'

'Did I wake you?' Toni asked anxiously. He sounded rather groggy.

'Not at all, my dear. I was just going through some old photo albums. Goodness, there are dozens of the things.'

'That's nice.'

Francis sighed. 'I'm not so sure. It just reminds me of what I've lost.'

'Poor you,' Toni said inadequately and wished she could think of some words of comfort.

'How are things with you, my dear? Any word from French?'

Toni brightened. Well, if nothing else, she'd be able to distract him with her story. 'We're trying to track him down, Francis.'

'We?'

'Ian Chase is helping me,' she admitted.

'Well, he's a sensible chap. I'm sure if anyone can find French it's him. Just make sure that when you get hold of him you get some money out of him.'

'Well, the solicitor says he will have to give back half of what was in our accounts —' Toni started.

'No, no, my dear. I'm talking about *real* money. Theo was a great one for the stock market.'

'Yes, I realise that. It's a pity I can't prove that he made some successful investments. It would be very useful when we're sorting out the financial arrangements.'

Francis laughed. 'That should be easy, my dear. Ask anyone who worked with him. He was always boasting about his success on the market.'

'That wasn't very discreet.'

'Bloody stupid,' Francis agreed. 'But he couldn't resist it. He wanted everyone to know how brilliant he was. The man has an incredible ego.'

Toni smiled as she remembered Dotty saying the exact same thing about Francis. 'Well, thanks for telling me, Francis. It could make things a lot easier for me.'

'My pleasure, dear. Now keep me posted. I want to know all the gory details.'

Toni laughed. 'I promise. You look after yourself, do you hear me?'

'I'm fine. Don't you worry your pretty head about me, bye bye.'

'Goodnight Francis. God bless.' Toni hung up and took a long drink before phoning Ian.

'Hi, I wasn't expecting to hear from you tonight. You're not cancelling our dinner, are you?'

Toni smiled at the warmth in his voice. 'No, I'm not cancelling. I just have another job for you.'

'Slave-driver! What is it now?'

'Remember you were going to check out Theo's pals in the stock market?'

'Yeah.'

'Well, I'd really appreciate if you did that. According to Francis Price, Theo made quite a lot of money. If I had any proof of that it would help my solicitor a great deal.'

'Okay, then. Leave it with me.'

'Thanks, Ian. I really do appreciate your help.'

'Maybe you'd like to show me how much sometime?' Ian's voice was hopeful.

'Ian!' Toni admonished but she was smiling.

'Okay, okay, I'll settle for dinner. But I want to pick the wine.'

Toni laughed. 'Deal.'

* * *

Thursday, 28th September, 2000

'Sandra? I'd like you to meet your new assistant.'

Sandra pasted a smile on her face before turning around. She wondered how long this one would last. 'Chloe!'

'Yes, reporting for duty – if you'll have me.'

Sandra beamed at her. 'Of course I will! How marvellous. But I thought you were off on your travels soon.'

Chloe and Toni exchanged smiles. 'I've put that on hold for the moment. So tell me what to do?'

'Right, then,' Sandra steered her towards the canteen. 'Let's start with the most important job.'

Toni laughed. 'I'll leave you to it,' she called after them and went into her office. After a few moments Jade stuck her head around the door. 'Did I just see what I thought I saw?'

'If you mean Sandra showing her new assistant the ropes, then yes.'

'Oh, Toni, that's wonderful. So, Chloe isn't going away?'

'Not for the moment. She probably will at some stage and, hopefully, then it will be for the right reasons.'

'I'm delighted things are working out for you both.'

'They're not working out too bad with Robert either, are they?'

'Only because he still needs us. As soon as he's got into a routine he'll start looking for replacements.'

'Oh, I don't know.'

'Do you think Daniel will stay?' Jade swirled her drink.

'Probably. Once Robert lets him get on with his job without too much interference. If he wants him to take on some of the cosmetic stuff I'd say Daniel will be out the door before you can say collagen!'

'Perky won't ask him to do that. Could you imagine it? Daniel would spend all of his time trying to talk the patients out of it!'

Toni laughed. 'That's true. And Robert will probably be happy to let Daniel get on with it. He lends a certain . . . credibility to the clinic.'

'So life goes on pretty much as before. Suits me.'

'What about Aidan?' Toni asked. 'You never did tell me. Did you go and see that apartment with him?'

Jade nodded grimly. 'Oh, yes.'

'And?'

'And it was amazing. Very flash. Just perfect for a rich young architect about town.'

Toni sighed. 'Why are you so angry with him, Jade?'

Jade flashed her a look of total disbelief. 'Why? You have to ask that after everything he's put me through? I know you say I should put all of it behind me, Toni,' she added as Toni went to interrupt, 'but it's easier said than done. The man is living in cloud-cuckoo-land.'

'Did you tell him that?' Toni asked, feeling a bit sorry for Aidan.

'I was too angry to say anything much. Especially after he . . .' Jade trailed away and stared silently into her glass.

Toni's ears pricked up. 'Especially after he what?'

Jade sighed. 'He asked me to move in with him.'

'What? But that's wonderful! Jade? You still love him, don't you?'

Jade shrugged. 'I'm not sure what I feel, Toni, other than anger. After all we've been through . . .'

Toni shook her head bewildered. 'I'm sorry, Jade. I'm not sure what I'm missing here. I just don't understand.'

'Okay. If he'd asked me if we could make another go of it, then I might well have said yes. If he suggested then that we look at apartments together, I might have agreed – after an awful lot of conditions. But to go from being practically on the streets to something so plush, present me with a *fait accompli* – it's just so ridiculous. He's being completely unrealistic. He wants to make up for the last couple of years in a couple of weeks. I'd much prefer to keep things on a more down-to-earth footing. How can I trust him like this? He's behaving like Donald bloody Trump!'

'Oh, Jade. I'm sorry. Did you tell him this?'

'No, like I said, I just got the hell out of there. My blood was boiling. I thought I might actually hit him.'

'Maybe you should have. It might have brought him to his senses. Look, promise me you'll talk to him,' Toni pleaded. 'It would be a shame to let things go back to the way they were. You could at least still be friends.'

Jade searched Toni's face. 'Do you really believe that? That it's possible to be friends with a man you once loved? Once shared a bed with?'

Toni felt the colour rise in her cheeks. 'It's worth a try,' she said evading a direct answer.

Chapter Thirty-nine

Friday evening, 29th September, 2000

'What are you up to?' Ollie asked curiously as she sat on her bed and watched Chloe try on her clothes.

Chloe fidgeted with the hem on Ollie's rather skimpy psychedelic shift dress. 'What do you mean?' she asked innocently. She pulled off the dress in disgust. Ollie was much smaller than she was and the dress looked positively indecent. Mark would be shocked if she wore that.

'You heard,' Ollie persevered. 'You go out with Mark most nights of the week. What's so special about tonight?'

'He's taking me somewhere special,' Chloe improvised.

'Where?'

'I don't know. It's a surprise. He just said I should dress up.'

'So what's the occasion?'

'Dunno.'

'Well, it's not long till your birthday,' Ollie said thoughtfully. 'Oh!'

'What?'

'Maybe he's going to ask you to marry him!'

'Don't be ridiculous.' Chloe laughed.

'It's not ridiculous,' Ollie said sulkily. 'He's crazy about you.'

'Mark couldn't afford a ring never mind a wedding and a mortgage.'

'The bride's family pay for the wedding,' Ollie reminded her. 'And you're going to be rich very soon.'

'Mark is not going to propose,' Chloe said emphatically.

'You sound very sure.' Ollie looked at her curiously.

Chloe reddened. 'I am.'

'So what is going to happen? And why are you picking all of my sexiest clothes – oh my God! You're going to do it, aren't you?'

'Ollie!'

Ollie rolled around the bed laughing uproariously. 'Finally Miss French is going to lose her virginity!'

'For God's sake, Ollie,' Chloe hissed nervously, mindful of Mrs Coyle hoovering outside the door.

'Oh, don't worry about Mum. She can't hear a thing when she's got that thing on. So, how are you going to do it? Are you going to seduce him?' Ollie hopped off the bed and started to scan through the pile of clothes with a critical eye. 'You need something sexy but subtle.'

'Then I won't find it here,' Chloe remarked looking at the flimsy garments that made up Ollie's wardrobe.

'Cheeky! You'd better be nice to me or I won't help you.'

Chloe sighed. She wasn't sure she wanted Ollie's help – still, she had to talk to someone. Suddenly she felt so nervous about the whole thing. A night of passion with Mark before she went away had seemed very romantic at the time but now she wasn't going anywhere it didn't seem quite so momentous. And what if she was disappointed? Or worse, what if she disappointed him? What if she was no good at sex? She was tempted to ask Ollie about it but she knew her friend would only tease her mercilessly and then pester her for details afterwards. Mind you, that would happen anyway.

'So where are you two going?'

'My place,' Chloe mumbled. 'Toni's going out.'

'Excellent! So you need to set the scene. Some low music, lots of booze and some nibbles.' She giggled. 'Although Mark will probably be happy enough with you!'

Chloe put her head in her hands and groaned. 'Oh, why did I tell you? I knew you'd be like this.'

'Like what?' Ollie asked innocently.

'Smart-assed.'

'Oh come on, Chlo. I'm only having a laugh.'

'At my expense.'

'Will you lighten up? I'm not as dumb as you seem to think, you know. I realise this is a very big deal for you.'

'Honest?'

'Of course. But you'll feel a lot more comfortable if you plan it all and if you feel sexy. Jeans and trainers just won't cut it.'

Chloe sighed. 'That's why I came over here. Nothing in my wardrobe seems . . . right.'

'More suitable for a convent than a club,' Ollie agreed.

'But I don't want to go overboard either. I'm not going to be comfortable if I'm tarted up to the nines. It's just not me.'

'I've got the very thing. You know those black velvet hipsters you have?'

Chloe nodded.

'Well, how about this to go with them?' Like a magician, Ollie produced a black, sparkly belly top from the wardrobe. It had a round neck – quite demure by Ollie's standards – but it was nothing but thin, lacy straps at the back.

'Gosh!' Chloe breathed.

'Gorgeous, isn't it?'

'Yeah, but I'm not sure I could get away with it.'

Ollie sighed. There was no point in telling her friend that she'd look good in a sack. 'Just try it on,' she pleaded instead.

'Okay,' Chloe agreed, knowing it was easier just to give in. But there was no way she'd wear it.

'Wow!' she breathed when Ollie spun her around in front of the mirror.

Ollie grinned widely. 'Wow is not the word. You look sensational!' The plain neck of the top emphasised Chloe's long neck and the narrow sparkling straps revealed the perfect creamy skin of her back.

'It is nice,' Chloe acknowledged.

'Nice!' Ollie rolled her eyes in exasperation. 'You're wearing it.'

'Do you think I should?'

'Yes.'

'But it's brand new, Ollie. I couldn't. It must have cost you a bomb.'

Ollie shrugged carelessly. 'You can make it up to me when you're rich.'

'Deal,' Chloe said and meant it. She'd bring Ollie on a shopping day to remember when she got her inheritance. Ollie would love that. 'I hope Mark doesn't think it's too much.'

'Mark will love it.'

'You think so?'

'I know so.'

* * *

'And Mrs Dunne is fasting and will be operated on in the morning.'

'Right,' Matthew scribbled in his pad, his large hand almost obscuring the page.

'You don't have to write everything down,' Jade said, amused.

'Oh, I always write everything down for the first few days,' Matthew said seriously. 'I don't want to forget anything.'

'Fair enough,' Jade said impressed. 'You can assist Daniel in surgery on Monday.'

'Really?'

Jade frowned. 'Well, you have assisted on that operation before, haven't you?'

Matthew nodded enthusiastically. 'Oh, yes. I just didn't think you'd let me jump straight in.'

'I wouldn't with Robert – Mr Perkins. But Daniel is a lot more patient. Just do as he tells you and you'll get along fine.'

Matthew nodded and continued to write furiously in his notebook.

'Okay then, I think that's everything. I'll be in here for another thirty minutes – excuse me.' Jade broke off to answer the phone. 'Jade Peters?'

'Jade, I have Aidan for you.'

'No, Sandra, don't –' But the phone clicked as Sandra put the call through. 'Hello?'

'Jade? Hi, it's me.'

'Yes?' Jade said coolly, turning slightly away from Matthew.

'Jade, I'm so sorry about the other day. I can see it was bloody insensitive of me –'

'Aidan, I'm very busy at the moment.'

'Then meet me tonight. Give me a chance to explain.'

Jade hesitated. It was impossible to talk on the phone and it wasn't as if she had anything else to do when her shift finished. 'Okay, then. Where shall we meet?'

'Why don't you come over here? Ann's going out. I could cook.'

Jade grinned. 'If you make threats like that I'm definitely not coming.'

Aidan laughed. 'Fair enough. We'll order in. See you about eight?'

Jade looked at her watch. 'Make it half past. Bye.' Jade hung up the phone and turned back to Matthew. 'Now, where were we?'

* * *

Toni got out of the car and let herself into the silent house. Chloe had gone straight to Ollie's after work and probably wouldn't be in before Toni left and Alice was off today. She had the place to herself. She checked her watch as she threw her coat on the bannisters and went upstairs. Six-thirty and she was meeting Ian at eight. She went into her bedroom and sat down in front of the mirror, looking critically at her reflection. There was no chance of Ian getting any romantic ideas – at least not if he saw her like this. Her grey suit and white blouse drained her face of colour. Her hair was pulled back in a tight, unbecoming knot and there were bags the size of suitcases under her eyes. 'You're getting old, Jordan,' she sighed wearily. She went into the bathroom and turned on the taps to fill the large tub. She looked idly through Chloe's range of Body Shop bath products on the shelf. Lavender to help you relax. That would do. She poured a large dollop into the running water and breathed in the scent.

Going back into the bedroom she took off her suit and blouse and opened her wardrobe to search for something suitable to wear. Every instinct inside screamed out that she should make herself look as feminine and attractive as possible. But what if he got the wrong idea? Maybe she should just wear jeans. But Toni had never really been a jeans kind of person. She went for more feminine clothes. Probably because she'd always worn suits for her job. Light grey or navy in summer. Charcoal grey and black in the winter. Always teamed with a crisp white shirt. Boring but practical and professional. She pulled out a red wool dress with a high neck. It always looked well if a little on the formal side. 'And old,' Jade would probably say. She thought Toni dressed much too old for her age.

'You've got a beautiful figure, Toni,' she was always saying. 'For God's sake show it off while you can!'

Toni lay the dress to one side and rummaged deeper into the wardrobe. Her hand came to rest on a warm rich fabric. She pulled out the pair of black suede trousers she'd bought last year and hardly worn. She'd forgotten all about them. She usually teamed them with a white silk shirt but looking at it she realised it was something that would look more suitable on her mother. Going to the chest of drawers she pulled out a thin chocolate-brown sleeveless top. She had always loved it and knew it made the best of her hazel eyes and dark hair. But Theo hadn't approved of it.

'You should give it to Chloe,' he'd remarked scathingly when he first saw it. 'It's more her age group.'

Toni's lips settled into a firm line. This was definitely the outfit for tonight! She hurried back into the bathroom and turned off the taps. Dropping her underwear on the floor she lowered herself into the hot water and closed her eyes. She couldn't believe the excitement bubbling up inside her. It was like she was going on her first date. The thought of spending an entire evening with Ian, looking into those fathomless grey eyes of his . . . she shivered despite the warmth of the water. She had forgotten what it was like to feel excited, turned on. And that was just thinking about dinner. She sat up abruptly and reached for the soap. This was ridiculous. She was behaving like some kind of sex-starved nympho. And it wasn't like she'd even have a chance with Ian. He had the lovely Carla to keep him warm at night. How could she compete with her? The woman positively oozed sex, from her long red fingernails to her tight expensive short suits and legs that went all the way up to her armpits. And Ian was a leg man. Toni stretched one of her legs out of the water and scrutinised it. Ian had always said she had lovely legs. In fact he complained that she didn't show them off enough with her long skirts and tailored trousers. She splashed it back down into the water. Well, he wasn't going to see them tonight. Unless of course . . .

* * *

Toni had left by the time Chloe got home. Hurrying upstairs, she showered and dressed and was just putting on some lip gloss when the doorbell went. Her stomach churned and she stared at her reflection, panic filling her. The bell went again. 'Oh, God, coming. I'm coming.'

'Hi.' Mark smiled into her eyes.

Chloe smiled back. 'Hi.' It was only Mark, for God's sake. Why was she getting herself into such a state?

'Can I come in?'

'Oh, yeah, sorry.' Chloe turned and led the way in, stopping when she heard Mark's gasp. 'What? What is it?'

'That's some top.'

Chloe pulled at the neckline. 'Oh, this thing?'

'You look wonderful, Chloe,' he said running his hands up and down her arms. 'Just beautiful.'

Chloe smiled weakly. 'Thanks. I'll go and get some drinks. Do you want coke or something stronger? There's no beer I'm afraid.' She was aware that she was prattling on but she couldn't seem to stop.

'Coke will be fine.'

'Right. Well, make yourself comfortable. Back in a minute.' She escaped into the kitchen, grabbed two cans of coke from the fridge and held them against her burning cheeks. Oh, God, what was she doing?

'I brought a video with me,' Mark said calmly, when she returned with the drinks. '*Sliding Doors*. You wanted to see that, didn't you?'

'Oh, eh, yeah. Great.'

Mark set up the video and sat down on the sofa next to Chloe. She snuggled up against him and allowed herself to relax. It wasn't until it was over and the credits rolled up that she stiffened again.

'Just relax, love,' Mark said sensing her withdrawal. 'We don't have to do this if you don't want to. I'll understand. I love you.'

Chloe turned to him and smiled. 'I love you too. And I do want to . . . it's just that I'm a bit nervous.'

'I promise I'll be very gentle and if you want me to stop at any stage it's no problem.'

Chloe put a finger to his lips. 'Let's go upstairs.'

Mark bent his head and kissed her. When he pulled back he looked into her eyes. 'I want you so much.'

Chloe turned and led the way out of the room and they climbed the stairs in silence, their hands tightly entwined.

* * *

'That was lovely,' Jade pushed her plate away and smiled at Aidan.

'Yes, there's nothing quite like a number twenty-six with fried rice.'

Jade laughed and stood up to clear the plates.

'No, no, you sit down. I'll have these done in a jiffy.'

Jade sat down obediently and watched as he carried the

plates to the sink, dumped the empty cartons in the bin and put on a kettle.

'I'm afraid I can only offer you instant coffee.'

Jade looked shocked. 'That's terrible! You know I'm used to better than that, Aidan.'

Aidan smiled but his eyes were sad. 'I'm only too well aware of the life you've become used to.'

Jade bent her head and twirled her glass between her fingers.

'That's why I wanted to do something about it,' Aidan continued, 'although I made a total botch of it.'

'You did,' Jade confirmed but there was no longer any anger in her voice.

'I've no excuses. I suppose I was just looking for a quick fix to blot out the past.'

'That's just not possible.'

'Yes. Yes, I realise that now. God, did you ever see anything like that apartment?'

Jade burst out laughing. 'It was a bit . . . much.'

'I'd have been afraid to walk on those cream carpets.'

'Yes, they were very suitable for a man who spends most of his time wandering around building sites,' Jade said drily.

Aidan finished drying the dishes and made two cups of coffee. 'I don't know what I was thinking of.'

'You meant well,' Jade said kindly.

'Yes.' He set the coffee in front of her and sat down. 'And though I got the location wrong, Jade, the proposal still stands.'

'Proposal?'

'I want you to move in with me. We'll find somewhere

together, a flat, a house, whatever you want. And if you don't want to share a bedroom, I'll understand.'

Jade shook her head. 'That would never work.'

'Which bit?'

'The last bit . . . all of it . . . oh, I don't know.'

Aidan reached over and took her hand, kissing the palm, his lips soft and warm. 'I have to agree I'd prefer you to share my bedroom, my bed. I've missed you so much, Jade.' He leaned over and kissed her hungrily.

Jade didn't pull away as quickly as she probably should have. This was madness. There was no way she was getting back with Aidan. She certainly wasn't going to bed with him. 'No, Aidan, we can't . . .'

'Why not? We're married, aren't we?' Aidan smiled into her eyes before his lips descended on hers once more.

Jade groaned and gave herself up to the sensations that were engulfing her. She wound her arms around his neck and moulded her mouth to his. Maybe this wasn't the answer, maybe she'd regret it tomorrow, but right now she knew exactly what she wanted.

Chapter Forty

'I never talked like that!' Toni protested laughing.

'Oh yes you did,' Ian told her. 'It was your telephone voice when you first started in admin. Very mid-Atlantic indeed.'

'Oh, leave me alone. I was young and trying to make an impression.'

Ian's eyes twinkled. 'You made an impression on me.'

Toni looked down at her hands. This wasn't going at all as she'd imagined. They'd hardly talked about Theo all night. In fact all they'd done was reminisce about old times and, Toni realised with some pain, those had been very good days indeed.

'You're not eating,' Ian remarked.

Toni flashed him a quick smile and turned her attention back to the enormous steak in front of her. 'I'm struggling. I shouldn't have had those chicken wings to start with.'

'Nonsense. You can't come to Sale E Pepe and not have the chicken wings.'

Toni had been delighted when he'd told her that he'd booked a table in the cosy Malahide restaurant. 'Then I probably should have had a salad for my main course,' she replied.

'Toni Jordan eating rabbit food! Hah!'

'I eat healthily.' Lord, Theo would laugh his head off if he heard her!

'You do,' Ian agreed, munching happily on his steak. 'And there's nothing healthier than a fine piece of Irish beef.'

Toni laughed. 'Well, maybe I could eat a little bit more.'

'You just need to wash it down with plenty of red wine. It helps the digestion.' Ian caught the waitress's eye and held up the empty bottle.

'It's just as well I took a taxi,' Toni said. She was feeling more than a little bit tipsy already.

'When did you ever drive when you were out with me?'

'Well, I didn't but that was usually because I was staying over . . .' Her voice trailed off and she kept her eyes firmly on her plate.

Ian smiled lazily. 'Oh, that's right. I'd forgotten.'

Toni shot him a suspicious look.

The waitress brought the wine. 'Just pour away,' he told her. 'I'm sure it will be fine.'

'So have you any news for me?' Toni asked after the waitress had gone.

'I do. Firstly, good old Francis was quite correct. Theo had a major windfall at the beginning of the year.'

'Did he now?'

'And he talked to a few doctors about it so I suppose that's proof.'

'I'll tell my solicitor. His money really isn't that important to me but I like the idea of punishing him in some way for what he's done.'

'Damn right. I also managed to track down Eric Levinson.'

Toni put her glass down with a clatter. 'You didn't?'

Ian grinned. 'I did, although we haven't actually spoken yet. He's no longer in New Zealand. He's in Cape Town.'

'South Africa? The man gets around. Do you know where?'

'I don't know where he's living but I do know the hospital he's working in. I'll call him on Monday.'

Toni frowned. 'What are you going to say?'

Ian laughed. 'Yes, I was wondering about that myself. What could I say that wouldn't frighten Theo off — that's if he's there.'

'And?' Toni prompted impatiently.

'Maybe I'll tell Eric that it's Theo's broker calling with news on some shares.'

'Will he believe you though?' Toni agonised. 'I mean would they go to the trouble of tracking Theo down? What's in it for them?'

'Fees,' Ian said, clearly pleased with himself. 'It's a gamble, yes, but Theo is probably greedy enough to take the bait. Especially if he needs money.'

'But he has plenty of money,' Toni protested. 'I'm the one who's broke.'

'It takes a lot of money to buy your way into a new practice. Especially if you don't have the correct papers.'

'God, you've got it all worked out,' Toni gasped.

Ian shrugged. 'A lot of it is guesswork. I could be completely wrong.'

'We'll know on Monday, won't we?'

'Maybe. I wouldn't expect to get much out of Eric straight off. But if I'm right, either he or Theo will be in touch very soon. What you have to decide is "what then?"'

Toni frowned. 'I don't understand.'

'Are you going to tell the police?'

Toni swallowed hard. She knew that she should, and that she wanted to, but –

'Toni?' Ian's voice was sharp.

'Oh, Ian, how can I do that to Chloe?'

'Don't then.' He shrugged. 'I will.'

'Oh, Ian, please.'

'Please what? Please protect your beloved husband?'

'You know that's not what I mean.'

'I'm beginning to wonder, Toni. Why do you really want me to track Theo down? Is it getting lonely in that big old bed all on your own?'

Toni laughed. 'I've always been alone.'

'Yeah. Right.'

'Ian, listen to me. The only person I care about is Chloe. The girl has been, no, is going through hell. Hardly a day goes by but another nasty story appears in the paper. The journalists – if you could call them that – still phone. She has opted out of college because she can't face the thought of being laughed at. Now, do you think she needs to see her dad brought back here in handcuffs?'

'Maybe that's exactly what she needs to see. If he came back, he'd be tried, sentenced and that would be an end to it. At the moment she's in a kind of limbo. She doesn't know where he is and when or if he'll ever come back.'

'I suppose you're right,' Toni admitted reluctantly. 'But promise me something, Ian?'

He eyed her warily.

'Before we tell the police, let me talk to him.'

'I don't know, Toni.'

She reached over and took his hand. 'Please, Ian. Please trust me.'

Ian studied her silently for a moment then nodded. 'Okay. We'll do this your way.'

'Thank you. I promise it's only Chloe I'm interested in.'

'So your marriage is over?'

'It's been over a long time, Ian. It was a mistake from the beginning.'

'I'm sorry.'

'Are you?' She smiled.

He smiled. 'No, I suppose that was a lie. Was it my fault that you married him?'

Toni looked startled. 'No. Why would you say that?'

He shrugged. 'Well, I thought we'd been getting on just fine. I obviously missed something. Had you got bored with me?'

'Not with you, with us. We had settled into a predictable pattern and there was no sign of that changing. Theo came along and he was so different, so vibrant. When he looked at me I felt like I was the most important person in his world.'

Ian winced.

'Sorry, you don't need to hear this. Anyway why are we raking over the past?'

'So that we can have a future, Toni.' He stroked the back of her hand.

'How can we have a future, Ian? I may be free but I don't believe you are. What about the lovely Carla?'

Ian looked momentarily confused. He'd forgotten all about Carla. In his mind they were finished. But there was a minor complication in that he hadn't told her that yet. 'Ah,' he said softly.

Toni's eyes hardened. 'Yes, "Ah". I'm not into playing the part of the other woman, Ian. My life has been complicated enough.'

'I'll sort it out,' he assured her.

'Don't do anything on my account. After all, who are we kidding, Ian? We can't just turn the clock back. We've had fun tonight after too many glasses of wine. It doesn't mean we have a future.'

'Doesn't it?'

Toni had to look away from the intensity and warmth of his gaze. 'No, it doesn't. Now I think we should go.'

'Fine.' Ian signalled the waitress and after a brief argument with Toni paid the bill. 'You can pay for the taxi,' he told her.

Toni stared at him.

'Oh, for God's sake, Toni. It would be ridiculous to get separate taxis when we live so close by.'

Toni's cheeks reddened. He was hardly likely to jump on her in the back of a cab. She'd be so lucky!

They got their coats and went downstairs to find a fleet of cars at the rank outside the door. Ian gave a wry smile. 'One of the advantages of going home early on a Friday night.' It was only ten o'clock.

Toni said nothing and sat into the car. Ian climbed in the other side and gave the driver directions. She was a bit put out that he told him to drop him off first. Fine, she was paying but whatever happened to seeing a lady home after a date? But this isn't a date, she reminded herself miserably. Not unless you're willing to share him with Carla. God, he had some nerve! Coming on to her when he was still obviously involved with someone else.

'It's over between Carla and me, Toni,' Ian said as if reading her thoughts.

'Does she know that?'

Ian moved closer and slid his arm across the back of the seat. 'No, she doesn't. But I'll tell her on Sunday. I won't see her before then. She's been away for a few days.'

Toni digested this piece of information in silence, conscious of Ian's fingers fiddling with her hair. 'How can I trust you?'

Ian put a finger under her chin and turned her to face him, his eyes only inches away from hers. 'Have I ever given you reason not to?'

Toni shook her head, her eyes dropping from his eyes to his lips. No, Ian had been the honest and faithful one. She was the one who'd lied. And yet he was ready to give her another chance.

'Well?' he said softly before bending his head to drop a gentle kiss on her lips. 'Have I?' This time he kissed the tip of her nose.

Toni closed her eyes and leaned into him.

He kissed both of her eyelids. 'Do you trust me, Toni?'

She could feel his breath on her face and she breathed in the smell of him, that achingly familiar wonderful smell.

'Toni?' His lips touched hers lightly, teasing.

She opened her eyes and looked straight into his. 'I trust you.'

The cab pulled up outside Ian's apartment. 'We'll both be getting out here,' he said, his eyes not leaving her face.

The driver grinned at him in the mirror. 'Whatever you say, boss.'

Toni stumbled out of the car after Ian, too shocked and aroused to even realise he was paying for the taxi. Ian took her firmly by the hand and led her to the door, kissing her while he fumbled for his key. After they practically fell into the hallway, Ian tugged her on into the lift and pinned her against the wall after jabbing the button for the second floor.

Toni moaned as his hands moved in under her coat and touched her through the thin fabric of her top.

The lift opened again and Ian propelled her towards the flat, pulling her coat from her shoulders as they swayed wildly around the hall.

Toni giggled. 'For God's sake open the door before one of your neighbours comes out to see what's going on.'

'Fuck the neighbours,' Ian muttered opening the door of the flat and practically lifting her inside. 'I don't give a shit who sees us. I want you and I want everyone to know that I want you.'

Toni stepped away from him and slowly removed her top.

Ian gasped at the sight of her in the skimpy black bra. He reached for her but Toni sidestepped him, and reached back to open the hooks without taking her eyes off his face.

Ian stared at her mesmerised, his breathing heavy.

'Jesus!' He stepped forward but Toni backed away again and found herself pressed up against his table.

Ian smiled as he moved closer. 'I've got you now.'

Toni watched him through a haze as she slid the bra from her shoulders. 'Then take me,' she murmured allowing herself to fall back on the table.

Ian wrenched the bra from her body and bent his head to kiss her breasts, his hands busy with the zip of her trousers. 'God, I want you, Toni!'

Toni smiled through the haze. 'I want you too. I've wanted you for so long.'

Ian lifted his head to stare at her. 'We'd probably be more comfortable in the bedroom.'

Toni pulled him back down. 'Who wants to be comfortable?'

* * *

Chloe lifted her hand to stroke Mark's face. He turned his face to kiss it.

'Are you all right?'

She smiled. 'Yeah.'

Mark bent his head to kiss her.

'Was I . . . okay?' Chloe asked anxiously.

'You were fantastic!'

Chloe smiled happily as she settled back into his arms.

'And?' Mark prompted.

'And what?' Chloe replied innocently.

'You!' Mark started to tickle her mercilessly.

Finally she wriggled out from under him. 'Oh, stop, please.'

'Say it.'

Chloe gave an exaggerated sigh. 'Yes, well you were quite good too.'

Mark resumed his tickling. 'Quite good? Quite good? Bloody cheek!'

'You were brilliant!' Chloe assured him breathlessly. 'Now please stop tickling me.'

Mark released her with a triumphant grin. 'That's more like it.'

Chloe planted a tender kiss on his chest. 'I mean it,' she said softly. 'Look, you have to get dressed. Toni could be home at any minute.'

'It's only five past ten.'

'You don't have to go home yet. I'd just feel a lot more comfortable if we were downstairs and fully clothed.'

'Okay then but give me one more cuddle first.'

Chloe softened as he gave her his most charming smile. 'Just a quick one then,' she said allowing him to pull her back down under the duvet.

Chapter Forty-one

Early Saturday morning, 30th September, 2000

Jade let herself out of the house as quietly as she could and almost ran down the road. Aidan would be disgusted that she'd crept out while he was asleep but she just couldn't face him. And she certainly couldn't face Ann. There had been no sign of her when they got in last night but Jade knew Aidan's sister would be there this morning and the thought of her knowing, cheesy grin made Jade cringe. She reached the bus stop just as a bus pulled up and flung herself on to it gratefully, flopping into the nearest seat.

No, Aidan wouldn't be impressed with her but she didn't know what to make of last night and needed time to think. The sex had been amazing – just as it always had been. Aidan was a sensitive lover and she'd been thrilled that he'd remembered exactly how and where she liked to be touched. She'd often wondered if he'd had any other women while they'd been apart but usually dismissed it as highly unlikely. Aidan's mistress had been the gambling.

She'd never gone out with anyone else either. She'd been so hurt and shocked by Aidan's behaviour it was as if she'd

415

gone into a stupor for the last couple of years, concentrating all her energies on paying off his debts and living as cheaply as possible. There had been no time for other men. And she was too wary to let anyone close.

And now she'd slept with Aidan again. She shook her head as the bus pulled into her stop. She jumped off and walked the short distance to her bedsit. It was as if the last two years had just been some kind of nightmare. Spending last night with Aidan had felt right. Their lovemaking had been sweet, passionate and forgiving. It was like they'd been trying to purge themselves of the bitterness and hurt that had grown up between them. And, Jade admitted, as she let herself in to the dreary old house, it felt good. She'd got precious little sleep but she felt full of energy and . . . happy. Yes, she actually felt happy. So what now? She went into her room and put on the kettle. It was only six o'clock but she was much too hyper to sleep. What she needed was a large mug of creamy coffee. She went to the fridge and smiled as she took out the carton of cream – a luxury she would never have allowed herself a few short weeks ago. She made the coffee and carried it and a packet of biscuits to her chair. How long more would she spend in this hellhole, she wondered. Should she agree to get a place with Aidan? Could they really start again, could she trust him? She sighed as she bit into a biscuit. She wasn't getting any younger and she had no interest in looking for a new partner but she didn't want to end up alone. And she did love Aidan. And, whatever his faults, she knew he adored her too. 'So why not, Jade?' she murmured. 'What have you got to lose?'

* * *

Chloe snuggled deeper under the covers and closed her eyes. She'd heard Toni going downstairs but she couldn't face anyone just yet. She wanted some more time to herself. Some more time to think about last night. She smiled a secret smile. And it had been so right, not sordid or dirty, just perfect. They were meant for each other. And she was glad she'd decided not to go away. Like Toni said there was plenty of time for that. Once Mark got his holidays she could treat them both to a little break. Maybe in Amsterdam! Because before the week was out she was going to be a rich woman. Yes, woman. After last night she felt like a woman. A woman in love.

* * *

Ian rolled over in the bed, burying his face into the pillow. He sniffed appreciatively at the faint traces of Toni's perfume that remained – real evidence that last night had happened. It wasn't his imagination. What a pity she couldn't have stayed the night. It would have been wonderful to wake up beside her. But she'd had to rush back to Chloe.

'I can't stay out all night, Ian. What would she think?' Toni had insisted as he'd tried to pull her back into bed.

'I suppose she'd think you've got a life of your own.'

Toni had glared at him. 'She's just a kid, Ian, whose Dad has just done a bunk, in case you've forgotten. The last thing she needs is for me to leave her too.'

'But you're not leaving her . . .'

'But that's what she'd think.' Toni had wandered around the apartment collecting her clothes.

Ian had watched appreciatively. He hadn't thought he'd

417

ever see Toni Jordan walking naked around his apartment again.

She dressed hurriedly, gazing anxiously at the clock. 'I've got to go.'

Ian picked up the phone by the bed and dialled the local taxi firm. 'They'll be here in five minutes.'

Toni sat down beside him. 'Thanks.'

'When will I see you again?'

'I don't know.'

'How about lunch.'

'Today?' Toni stared at him.

'Why not? It's Saturday.'

'Well, I'm not sure. I'll have to see what Chloe's doing.' Ian sighed.

Toni glanced at him sharply. 'There's one thing you've got to understand, Ian. Things are different now. I have responsibilities. If you want me back you have to accept that my stepdaughter is part of my life. Theo's daughter.'

Ian looked away. 'She's almost an adult. She'll be going her own way soon.'

'Maybe. But she will always have a home with me. Maybe you should think about that.' Toni gave him a quick peck on the cheek and stood up. 'I'll wait downstairs for the taxi.'

'I'll call you later.'

'No,' Toni said quickly. 'I'll call you.'

Ian frowned now as he remembered the conversation. He was surprised at how devoted Toni was to her stepdaughter. It looked like he'd have to get to know her too if he was going to see anything of Toni. A cosy threesome, he thought with a sigh. Not quite what he'd had in mind. This wasn't going to be easy. The girl was sure to resent him. She might even blame him for the break-up of the marriage. And then there was Theo. He wouldn't want his daughter anywhere near Ian. Although, Ian chuckled, there wasn't much he could do about it if he was in South Africa. He jumped out of bed and headed for the shower, whistling merrily. Once he'd explained things to Carla – shit! Carla! He'd completely forgotten about her. He'd have to finish with her tomorrow and it was not going to be pleasant. Carla was the kind of woman who did the dumping and would be horrified and furious that he wanted to break up with her. Maybe he could do something to make her walk out on him. 'You wimp,' he berated himself and turned the cold tap on full. Carla would have to be told and he would have to take the consequences. He just hoped they didn't involve his genitals and any large surgical instruments!

* * *

Feeling like a young girl in love and unable to keep it to herself, Toni phoned Jade and asked if she could come over. Jade was delighted. They could wander down to the pub and have a nice lazy lunch.

When Toni arrived, bright and bushy-tailed, Jade shot her a suspicious look. 'You seem in very good mood.'

'I am. I had a date last night.'

Jade looked at Toni, wide-eyed 'With who – crikey it was Ian, wasn't it?'

Toni nodded happily.

'I just knew you were seeing him again.'

Toni flopped down on to Jade's lumpy mattress. 'I wanted

to try and track Theo down and he's been helping me.'

'That was nice of him but I'm sure he's not doing it for the good of his health. So are you back together or was it just a one-night thing?"

Toni sighed. 'He seems to think everything's back on.'

'And you don't.' Jade leaned against the fridge and studied her friend's face.

'Things are so complicated at the moment, Jade. How can I possibly think about a new relationship at a time like this?'

'But it wouldn't really be "new" now, would it?'

'And that's another thing. How can we just turn the clock back and pretend that nothing has changed?'

'You don't. But you don't let something really good slip through your fingers either.'

Toni gazed at the tender expression on Jade's face. 'Is there something *you* want to tell me by any chance?'

Jade smiled. 'Let's say that while you and Ian were in the throes of passion, Aidan and I were . . . getting reacquainted too.'

'You're kidding!' Toni hopped off the bed to hug her. 'Oh, Jade, I'm delighted for you.'

'Why?'

Toni looked confused. 'Well, because you belong together. You love each other.'

Jade laughed. 'Does that sound familiar to you?'

'Oh, stop trying to trick me!'

'I'm not. Just pointing out the obvious.'

'Except you don't have a stepdaughter to worry about.'

'Chloe will get used to the idea. Eventually.'

Toni sighed. 'I'm afraid I might be collecting my pension by then.'

Chapter Forty-two

Sunday lunchtime, 1st October, 2000

Ian looked at his watch. Nearly two. Carla would be here any minute. He looked around the busy restaurant. It had been his idea to meet in *Giovanni's*. There was less chance of a scene. Although, with Carla's fiery temper, a public place probably wouldn't stop her. She'd been surprised by his call. Normally she just dropped over to his place on a Sunday, they'd read the papers in companionable silence and then go out for a pub lunch. He'd noted the curious note in her voice at this change of arrangement. Carla was no fool. She'd probably already figured out what he was up to.

He was on his second glass of wine when she finally arrived in, breathless and smiling. Ian watched the appreciative glances from the waiters as she peeled off her leather jacket to reveal a slender figure in black jeans and tight red top.

'Sorry, hon,' she said and planted a long kiss on his lips, leaving a crimson stain. 'I didn't realise the time. Have you been waiting long?' Her eyes flickered smugly to the wine bottle. Ian knew she liked to think of him sitting around waiting for her.

'Not long.' He poured her a glass of wine.

Carla had a quick look around the restaurant and only turned her attention to him once she'd satisfied herself there was no one more important there. 'So how are things, hon? Did you miss me?'

'The place is never the same without you,' Ian said honestly.

'Oh, hon! You say the nicest things,' she purred.

Ian gritted his teeth in annoyance. Had she always been this false? How had he stayed with her so long?

Carla watched him from under her lashes. 'So what have you been up to while I was away?'

Ian swallowed hard. 'Eh, nothing, working, the usual.'

'Poor you, always working.'

Ian smiled guiltily.

'Any more on Theo French? Have they found a body in his back garden yet?'

'I don't read the rubbish they print. Half of it is probably made up. And I certainly don't listen to the bloody gossips in that hospital. They're worse!'

Carla's eyes widened. 'Okay, okay, keep your hair on. I was just making conversation.'

Ian smiled apologetically. 'Sorry, it's just that I'm sick of hearing about Theo French. Now can we change the subject?'

'Sure.' Carla smiled into his eyes. 'What would you like to talk about?'

Two hours later Ian sat sipping the last of a second bottle

of wine, his jacket on to cover the red wine stain spreading across his denim shirt.

'Can I get you anything else, sir?' the waiter asked sympathetically.

Ian shot him a brave smile. 'No, thank you. I'm fine.'

The waiter nodded and left him to his drink. Ian sat staring out of the window, his smile turning into a cheesy grin. He was free! And despite the wet shirt and the string of abuse that Carla had just hurled at him he felt happier than he had in months. He couldn't wait to talk to Toni. Maybe she could meet him for a drink this evening. Maybe even dinner. Perhaps there would be a repeat performance of Friday night. His spirits soared as he remembered the feel of Toni's bare skin under his hands. He pushed away the wine and laughed. He didn't need alcohol. He was high on life. 'The bill, please,' he called and paid in cash, incorporating a large tip. 'Thanks very much. Everything was lovely,' he assured the baffled waiter and strode out on to the street, oblivious of the curious stares from the other customers.

* * *

Toni was delighted and at the same time a little irritated when Ian called late on Sunday afternoon to tell her that it was all over with Carla. He obviously thought that once Carla was out of the way they could just take up where they'd left off all those years ago.

'Let's have dinner,' he said. 'Let's celebrate.'

'I can't,' Toni hissed back at him. She was standing in the hall and Chloe was in the living-room watching TV.

The house was much too quiet for confidential conversations. 'It's just not possible.'

'Oh. Okay, then. I'll call you after I've talked to Eric Levinson.'

'Okay, good luck. Bye.'

'Who was that?' Chloe looked when Toni walked back into the room.

'Oh, just work,' she'd said vaguely and buried her head in a newspaper.

Chloe left it at that and went back to staring blankly at the television. She was feeling decidedly left out because now that Ollie and Mark had started college they didn't like going out on Sunday nights. Whereas she was still full of energy and excitement from Friday night. She had spent most of yesterday and today with Mark but when she'd tried to persuade him to go out he was adamant. 'I've got work to do for tomorrow, Chloe. I haven't picked up a book all weekend.'

'But it's only the start of term,' Chloe had wheedled.

'Yes, and I'm starting as I mean to go on. I'll call you tomorrow night.'

And so she was sitting here bored out of her mind.

Toni, for once, was heartily glad that her stepdaughter was in a bad mood. There were so many things flying around inside her head she didn't think she was capable of intelligent conversation.

'I think I'll go to bed.' Chloe stood up and shuffled towards the door.

Toni smiled brightly. 'Good idea, love. An early night will do you good.'

Chloe rolled her eyes before carrying on out into the hall. 'Whatever.'

Toni dropped her paper in her lap, rested her head back against the chair and closed her eyes. Now she could think about Ian in peace and she didn't have to worry if there was a silly smile on her face.

* * *

Monday afternoon, 2nd October, 2000

Ian took a deep breath. 'Eric Levinson? Hi, how are you. Stuart Beecher, Sylvester's hospital in Dublin.'

'Stuart! How are you?'

Ian smiled with relief. Thankfully, it seemed Eric's memory for voices wasn't too good. 'Can't complain, Eric. Listen, I'll tell you why I'm calling. I've lost contact with a colleague and I really need to get hold of him –'

'If you're referring to Mr Theodore French, you've found him.'

Ian gulped. He certainly hadn't expected it to be this easy. 'Eh, he's there, then?'

'Certainly is. Oh, it took me a while to persuade him to sign on the dotted line. He insisted that he was only here on holiday. But I knew he was ready for a change.'

'Right. Well, that's great.'

'Look, he's not here right now. I could get him to phone you back.'

'No! Eh, no I won't be here. Can you tell me when would be a good time to call again?'

'Sure, Stuart, try between six and seven in the morning. He has surgery at seven-thirty so he should be around.'

425

'That's great, Eric, Thanks.' Ian hung up the phone and flopped into his chair. My God, he'd done it! He'd found Theo. The urge to pick up the phone and call the police was almost too great to resist. But he'd promised Toni. He picked up the phone again and dialled. When the receptionist had put him through he didn't bother with the niceties. 'I've found him, Toni.'

'Ian? You're kidding!'

'No. I just spoke to Levinson. Theo is working at the same hospital in Cape Town. Eric just persuaded him to sign up.'

'I'd say that was difficult,' Toni said dryly. 'My God, we've got him.'

'We should tell the police.'

'No, I want to talk to Theo first.'

'But what if he takes off? You could be in big trouble, Toni, if the cops ever hear about it.'

'Please, Ian. For Chloe's sake I have to give him the opportunity to do the decent thing.'

Ian doubted that French was capable of that but he didn't want to lose Toni a second time.

'You should be able to get him between six and seven in the morning. Get a pen and I'll give you the number.'

* * *

Tuesday, 3rd October, 2000

'May I speak to Mr Theodore French, please?' Toni asked hoping her voice wasn't trembling as much as her hands.

'One moment, please.'

Toni listened to a series of clicks and then she was listening to music. She hoped fervently that he was available. She wanted to finish this conversation before Chloe woke.

'Theodore French here. Hello? Hello?'

Toni took a deep breath. 'Hello, Theo.'

'Toni!'

'Surprised to hear from me?'

'How did you find me?'

There was something different about his voice. He sounded frightened. Yes, that was it, he was frightened. 'It wasn't that difficult.'

'Have you told –'

'The police? No, not yet. I want you to do that.'

'What?'

'For Chloe.'

'How is she?'

'Not good at all.' Toni crossed her fingers. 'She's not eating, stays in her room most of the time and is refusing to go to college. Oh, she got offered that place in Trinity if you're interested.'

'But she must go!'

Toni sighed dramatically. 'I'm afraid there's no hope of that. She's decided to leave home. She's planning to work her way around the world.'

'What, but that's ridiculous! She's too young to do that alone. Or is Mark Wheeler behind this?'

'No, Mark has started his course in UCD. He's tried to persuade Chloe to stay but she won't listen to him either.'

'You have to make her see sense, Toni,' he insisted.

'I've tried. But she says she wants to get as far away from Ireland and the Irish press as possible. She's fed up reading sick stories about her father every day. They upset her too much.'

This was greeted with silence.

'Why don't you come home, Theo?'

'I can't.'

'So what are you going to do? Spend the rest of your days alone in a strange country?'

'It's better than spending them in jail.'

'If you handed yourself in, I'm sure it would reduce your sentence. And it would mean you'd see your daughter.'

'But she's going away.'

'She wouldn't if she knew you were coming back.'

'But after all I've done surely she wouldn't have anything to do with me any more?'

'You're her dad, Theo. It won't be easy but she'll learn to forgive and forget.'

'It was an accident, Toni. You know that? And I just panicked. I thought she was dead.'

'I believe you. But I'm afraid it's the reports on your sex life that you're going to find harder to explain to Chloe.'

'God, no, I can't face her.'

'If you care about her, you will, Theo. You're the only one who can help her now.'

'I don't know.'

Toni took a deep breath. 'Let me make this decision easier for you, Theo. If you don't agree to come back, I will tell the police where you are.'

'I need time to think.'

'To think or to run? Look, Theo, it's only a matter of time before they catch up with you. Do the decent thing.

Wouldn't you like to win back the respect of your daughter?'

'Can I talk to her?' His voice was barely a whisper.

'Not now. I don't want you making things worse. If you agree to come back, then I'll let you talk to her. Otherwise I will make it my life's work to make sure you never get near her again.'

'You've grown very hard, Toni.'

Toni's laugh was harsh. 'I wonder why?'

Chapter Forty-three

Thursday evening, 5th October, 2000

It took Toni two more days before Theo agreed. Ian was frantic, convinced that he was using the time to plan his escape but Toni begged him to wait. And then Theo called. 'I need to give Eric some notice here and plan my flights but I should be back in Dublin before the end of the month.'

'For what it's worth, Theo, I think you're doing the right thing.'

'Can I speak to my daughter now?'

'Let me talk to her first. Call back at ten.' And she hung up the phone and went in search of Chloe. She was lying on her bed listening to music.

'Hi, Toni. What's up?'

'I have some news.' Toni sat down on the side of the bed and slowly began to explain.

'I know it's probably a shock, Chloe,' she said when she was finished and Chloe hadn't said a word. 'And you don't have to talk to him yet if you don't want to.'

'Of course I want to, I suppose. Oh, I don't know!' Chloe tugged nervously on the dark wisps of hair fanning her face. 'Why now? Why hasn't he been in touch before?'

'He didn't make contact with me. I found him.'

'When is he going to call?'

'At ten.'

'Okay. I think I'd like to be on my own for a bit.'

Toni nodded and stood up. 'Will you be okay?'

'Sure.' After Toni had left, Chloe curled up into a ball and tried to figure out how she felt about her dad. Reading the reports of his other life in the paper had disgusted her. And though she knew parts of it were probably fabricated she knew there was some truth there too. She was ashamed of him for leaving that woman to die, but Mark had said that he must have panicked. And that made sense. But she was disappointed that he hadn't come back of his own accord. And she was still angry that he hadn't thought of her before running away. At least he could have said goodbye. Even her mum had done that.

She still remembered that day. She had been sitting up on the bed, wearing her favourite blue dress while her mother gently brushed her long hair. As she brushed, she explained that she had to go away.

'Don't go, Mummy,' Chloe had begged tearfully.

'I must, love.'

'Then take me with you.'

'I can't do that. Anyway, you have to stay here and mind Daddy.' And she'd turned Chloe around to face her, gazing tenderly into her eyes. 'But I'll always be with you,

Chloe. Whenever you look up into the night sky, I'll be up there among the stars watching over you.'

Chloe wiped a tear away as she remembered her mother's words. 'Mind Daddy,' her mother had said. Maybe that's why he'd left. Maybe she hadn't looked after him properly. Maybe she'd let him down. Maybe he'd gone because of her. She started as the phone rang. Moments later, Toni walked in and handed it to her.

'Daddy?' Chloe said faintly, gripping the phone with trembling fingers.

It was more than an hour later when she went downstairs to a nervous Toni who was pacing the kitchen, only pausing to gulp down mouthfuls of coffee.

'How did it go?' she asked anxiously.

Chloe smiled weakly. 'Okay,' she said but the tears were already falling.

Toni held out her arms and Chloe rushed into them.

'He says he's sorry, Toni, that he made a terrible mistake and he's going to come home and face the music. He kept asking me not to go away,' she added, sounding slightly confused.

Toni suppressed a smile. 'I told him you were thinking of travelling. It's going to be very hard when he gets back, Chloe. Do you think you can be there for him?'

Chloe sighed. 'I know the papers will be all over us again and we'll have to go to court and he'll probably end up in jail –' her voice cracked and Toni held her tight. 'But I suppose I'm proud that he's coming back to face up to what he's done.'

'You know that he'll be arrested as soon as he steps off the plane, Chloe? And it's unlikely they'll give him bail.'

'He said that.' Chloe wiped her hand across her face and took a couple of shaky breaths. 'You know, you're right. He is going to need support. I don't suppose there's any chance of you two getting back together –'

'None, Chloe.'

Chloe nodded. 'I can't really blame you.'

Toni sighed. 'Look, there's something you should know, love. I asked your dad for a divorce a few months ago.'

Chloe sank into a chair. 'So you knew what he was up to all along?'

Toni shook her head. 'No, amazingly I didn't. We had just grown apart and I wanted to put an end to it. I had planned to leave after you finished your exams but then Alice had her accident so I stayed.'

'I see.'

'I'm sorry, love. I wanted to make it work for your sake.'

'Are you involved with anyone else?' Chloe asked in a small voice.

Toni pondered the question. 'Yes and no.'

Chloe looked alarmed.

'I didn't lie to you Chloe, when I said I never had an affair. But since your dad left I've started seeing someone that I knew a very long time ago.'

'An old boyfriend?'

Toni smiled. 'Yes, that's right.'

'And are you going to marry him?'

Toni laughed. 'My, God, Chloe, it takes four years to

get a divorce, it's a bit soon to talk about marriage! I've no plans to rush into anything. I'm going to move into an apartment in Clontarf. It has two bedrooms and I'd like to think that you would look on one of them as yours.'

'What about this house?'

Toni shrugged. 'It's up to your dad what he does with the house. He may want to sell it.'

'And what about Alice?'

Toni laughed. 'I think it's time that Alice retired, don't you? Anyway, she's part of the family, Chloe. We're not going to lose touch with her simply because she doesn't work for us any more.'

'I'm so glad you two are friends now.'

Toni nodded. 'Yes, I'm glad about that too. She's been very good to me over the last couple of months.'

'And you've been good to her too,' Chloe pointed out.

'God, we're beginning to sound like the *Waltons!* Enough of all this, I'm starving. How about we go down to the takeaway and buy lots of unhealthy food?'

Chloe laughed shakily. 'I am hungry,' she realised with surprise.

'Good.'

'Just let me go and wash my face.'

Toni let out a sigh of relief as Chloe disappeared. Thank goodness that the young were so resilient. Going out to the garden she phoned Ian on her mobile. 'It's all going to be okay, Ian. Theo's just talked to Chloe. He'll be home in a couple of weeks.'

'Do you think you can trust him?'

'Yes, I do.'

'You probably should tell the police, Toni –'

'I will, closer to the time.'

'Toni –'

'Oh, please, Ian, leave it at that. It's going to be all right.'

'I just don't want you to get in any trouble.'

Toni smiled in the darkness. 'I know and I'm grateful.'

'Can I see you tomorrow?'

'I think I can slip out for a quick lunch. Usual place?'

'Usual place. See you at one. Bye, love.'

Long after he'd hung up Toni stood staring at the phone. 'Bye, love.'

* * *

Friday morning, 6th October, 2000

The next morning, Toni was up early, scribbling away on a notepad when Alice arrived. 'Morning, Alice. Beautiful morning, isn't it?'

Alice took off her raincoat. 'Morning.' She looked curiously at Toni's tracksuit. 'Aren't you going in to work today?'

'Later but first I wanted to talk to you about Chloe's birthday.'

'A little dinner party you were saying.' Alice put the kettle on and dropped two slices of bread in the toaster.

'No, Alice. We're going to have a party. A huge party. In fact you can bring all your bingo buddies if you like!'

Alice frowned. 'But didn't Chloe say that she didn't want a big do now that her father has gone away?'

436

Toni smiled. 'Ah, but that was before she talked to him.'

Alice sank down on to a chair. 'No.'

'Yes, Alice. It's all over. Theo's coming back and he's going to hand himself up to the police.'

'But how? Why?'

'Let's say when he heard how devastated his daughter was he decided it was the right thing to do.'

'You found him.' Alice shook her head in wonder.

Toni smiled. 'With a little help from a friend.'

'Where is he?'

'South Africa.'

Alice looked more confused.

'He has a friend there,' Toni explained.

'And how did Chloe take the news?'

Toni smiled. 'Unbelievably well. I wouldn't say she's forgiven him but she's ready to stand by him.'

'She's a good girl,' Alice said tenderly. 'And she wants to have a party?'

Toni shook her head. 'We haven't discussed it. It's going to be a surprise.'

Alice looked dubious. 'Is that wise?'

Toni nodded confidently. 'I think so. When Theo gets back, we're going to be skulking around trying to avoid the press again. I think we're all entitled to one big bash before that happens. We'll have it next Saturday.'

Alice frowned worriedly. 'We don't have much time to organise everything. We have to decide on what food to have and then there's the cake to make.'

'You don't have to worry about a thing,' Toni promised her. 'I'm going to get caterers in.'

'Oh, but I could manage –'

'Absolutely not, Alice. You're going to be a guest at this party. And we're not going to breathe a word of this to Chloe. We'll go along with the quiet dinner story and I'll get Mark and Ollie to arrange for all of her friends to come along.' Toni stood up took a slice of toast and her mug of tea and headed for the door. 'I'll go and start making some phone calls right now. If Chloe comes down keep her away from the study.'

'Leave it to me. I'll keep her well out of your way.'

Toni put down the phone and ticked another item off her list. She was almost halfway through it at this stage. The food was sorted – good old Liz Connolly never let her down. Ollie was in charge of inviting all of Chloe's friends. Mark was charged with keeping Chloe out of the house all day. Next, Toni decided, she'd phone her parents. They would have to stay the night – the first time ever, and go home the next day. Toni smiled happily. It was so good to have her parents back in her life. She phoned them now at least twice a week and her Mum had been up for a day's shopping. Even conversations with her father were no longer stilted. In fact, when Toni had told him about her conversation with Theo he had been very supportive.

'You're handling all of this very well, Toni. I'm proud of you,' he'd said gruffly.

Toni had been surprised at how happy the words had made her feel. She hadn't realised that her father's approval meant so much.

Mary Jordan told her daughter they'd be delighted to

come to the party and started to quiz her about what Chloe would like for a birthday present. After a long chat Toni put down the phone and went back to her list. She planned to invite everyone from the clinic and partners, though she was hoping that Matthew wouldn't bring anyone. He and Sandra seemed made for each other. She wondered if Jade would bring Aidan. She'd love to invite Ian, but that was out of the question. Although, Chloe didn't know him so maybe – she'd have to think about it. Next, Francis Price. It might seem rather unseemly to invite someone so recently bereaved to a party but then Francis and Dotty had never been "ordinary people". And Francis would tell her quite bluntly if he didn't want to come along.

'Lovely, my dear!' was the delighted reply. 'I shall bring the Scotch. I know the youngsters won't want it but we'll probably need it if we have to listen to their ridiculous music.'

Toni laughed. 'Good idea. I'll provide the paracetemol!'

Chapter Forty-four

Friday, 13th October, 2000

'I can't wait for this party, can you, Jade?' Sandra asked excitedly.

'Shush, Sandra. What if Chloe hears you?'

'She and Toni have gone out to lunch. So are you going?'

'Wouldn't miss it. Is Matthew going?'

Sandra shuffled the papers in front of her. 'How would I know?'

'Would you like me to find out for you?'

'Jade!'

'Oh, come on, Sandra. There's nothing wrong with me asking him if he's coming to Chloe's party. And anyway, you know you fancy him. It will be a great opportunity for you to get to know each other outside of work.'

'I do not fancy him,' Sandra hissed looking anxiously over her shoulder.

'You like him though,' Jade persisted.

'He's very nice,' Sandra agreed lamely.

'He likes you too, you know.'

Sandra stared at her. 'Don't be silly. What makes you say that?'

Jade grinned. 'Because he watches you when you're not looking. Just the way you watch him.'

'I do not – oh, okay. I do. But I'm sure you're wrong. He's not interested in me. He probably has a girlfriend.'

'I doubt it. I'm sure he would have mentioned her by now. I'll tell you what, I'll ask him.' Jade stood up and stretched.

'You can't do that!'

'Why not? I'll just tell him that Toni says we can bring our partners to the party if we want to.'

'Oh, right,' Sandra said miserably. Matthew was bound to have a partner. How could someone so handsome and nice not have? And he'd bring her along to the party and Sandra would have to watch them being lovey-dovey all night.

'Stop worrying,' Jade said as she walked across reception. 'It's going to be a great night.'

Sandra watched her retreat down the corridor. If only she had Jade's confidence. Then maybe Matthew would be interested in her. He was always very nice to her but then, Sandra thought with a tender smile, he was nice to everyone. She sighed heavily.

'Penny for them?' Daniel asked as he came through the door and breezed past her desk.

'I was just thinking about the party.'

'Oh, young Chloe's eighteenth? Should be a good night. Although I'm sure Mark would prefer it if his folks weren't there.'

Sandra laughed. 'You probably won't even see each other in the crowd. Toni seems to have invited just about everyone.'

'Good on her. I think it's just what's needed after all that's happened.'

Sandra smiled. 'Yes. Poor Chloe, I hope she enjoys herself.'

'I'm sure she will. Now, Sandra, give me five minutes to sort myself out and send in my next patient.'

'Yes, Daniel.'

* * *

Toni and Chloe were strolling back to the clinic after a sandwich and some shopping when striding towards them, shoulders hunched, hands deep in the pockets of his jacket was Ian Chase. Toni considered walking past him. If he kept his head down -

'Toni!' Ian's face lit up when he spotted her. 'Hi.'

Chloe, who'd fallen a step behind as she rummaged in her bag, came up beside her stepmother and stared at him curiously. 'Hello.'

Ian's smile faltered slightly. 'Oh, hi.'

Toni looked awkwardly from one to the other. 'Eh, Ian, this is Chloe, my stepdaughter. Chloe, this is Mr Chase. He's consultant anaesthetist at Sylvester's.'

Chloe smiled warily. 'Pleased to meet you, Mr Chase. You must have worked with my dad.'

'Eh, yes, I did. And Toni, of course, before she became such an important person.'

'Wow, that must have been years ago! I never knew her when she worked in Sylvester's.'

Toni laughed awkwardly. 'I barely remember it myself. We'd better be going. Good to see you again, Ian.'

Ian frowned at her cold formality. 'And you. Nice to meet you, Chloe.'

'Yeah, you too. Bye.'

They walked on in silence for a moment and then Chloe stopped as realisation hit her. 'That's him, isn't it?'

'Sorry?' Toni did her best to look confused.

'That's your old boyfriend. I'm right, aren't I? He was positively beaming at you before you introduced me.'

'Okay, Chloe, that was him.' Toni started to walk on.

Chloe hurried after her. 'Were he and dad friends?'

Toni laughed. 'Hardly.'

'Why not?'

Toni sighed. 'Because I was going out with Ian when I met your dad. I left Ian to be with him.'

'And now you're sorry you ever broke up with him, aren't you?'

Toni sighed miserably. Just when things were getting back to normal. 'I have no regrets, Chloe.'

'That day that Dad disappeared I asked you why you had married him.'

'I remember,' Toni said softly.

'You didn't give much of an answer. It was a mistake from day one, wasn't it?'

'No, of course not,' Toni said but she couldn't look at Chloe.

'I don't believe you.' Chloe's eyes were full of tears.

Toni put a hand on her arm. 'Chloe, you mustn't think –'

Chloe shook her off. 'I've got to go. Sandra will be wondering where I am.'

Toni watched her almost run the rest of the way back. 'Shit, shit, shit.'

When Toni arrived into reception, Chloe kept her head bent over her desk. Toni half expected that there would be a message waiting from Ian. She cringed at the thought of Chloe hearing Sandra say he'd called but thankfully he hadn't. She went into her office and shut the door, wondering what she should do next. The idea of a surprise party didn't seem such a good one now. Chloe would probably walk out. She jumped as the phone rang loudly by her ear. She let it ring a few times before finally picking it up.

'Hello, Toni Jordan speaking.'

'Hello, Ms Jordan. This is Mr Chase.'

Toni sighed. 'I'm so sorry, Ian. It was such a shock seeing you like that.'

'I could see that.'

'Chloe guessed who you were.'

'Oh. I take it she's not too happy?'

'That's putting it mildly,' Toni said grimly.

'Look, I can't talk now, Toni. I have an operation in five minutes. Meet me this evening for a drink.'

Toni thought of all the things she had to do for tomorrow night's party but she wanted to see Ian. 'Okay then. I'll see you in the Beachcomber at eight.'

'Eight it is,' Ian said. 'Bye.'

'Bye.'

She was staring into space minutes later when Jade walked in. 'Hi, Toni – oh, what's the matter?'

'Nothing.'

'It looks like it,' Jade said sarcastically sitting down on the edge of Toni's desk. 'Let me guess. Ian?'

'Yes and no.' Suddenly Toni felt very close to tears.

445

'Chloe and I bumped into him on the way back from lunch. She guessed who he was.'

Jade frowned. 'But you told her about him the other night, didn't you? I thought she was okay about it.'

'I think she was in theory. But when she saw him in the flesh –' Toni shrugged.

'What are you going to do?'

'I'll have to stop seeing him. At least for the moment. Even if Chloe learned to accept him, Theo will do everything he can to turn her against him when he gets back.'

'Chloe's not that stupid. You can't lose Ian again, Toni. You've got a life too. Chloe is eighteen. She'll just have to learn to deal with it.'

'But what if she doesn't want anything more to do with me?' Toni said glumly. 'Whatever I do or say I'm going to end up losing someone I love.'

'You should have more faith.'

'In who?'

'Both of them. If Ian loves you he'll learn to accept Chloe. And if Chloe loves you she'll want you to have a life of your own.'

'You really don't know the first thing about kids, do you?' Toni said drily.

Jade flinched. 'No, probably not.'

'Oh, Jade, I'm sorry. That was a horrible thing to say.'

Jade smiled faintly. 'No, no. It's true.'

Toni grabbed her hand. 'It was thoughtless and hurtful. I'm sorry.'

'Forget it.' Jade flashed her a broad smile and stood up. 'I'd better get back to work. Best of luck, whatever you decide to do.'

'Thanks.' Toni watched her leave. How could she have been so tactless? Jade and Aidan had always wanted children but for some reason it was not to be. Toni didn't know why and it was pointless asking Jade. It was a subject she was determinedly tight-lipped about.

'Toni? Sorry to bother you but I've been going through these figures and I just can't seem to make things add up.'

Toni looked up into Sandra's apologetic face. 'Let's have a look then.' She smiled at her receptionist and put her problems on the back burner.

* * *

'This is nice,' Ian said sarcastically after they'd sat in silence for what seemed like hours.

Toni looked blank. 'Sorry?'

'What's going on, Toni?' Ian said impatiently.

Toni sighed. 'I'm sorry. I need to say something to you but it's not easy to say.'

Ian's face darkened. 'Then don't say it, Toni. Please don't say it.'

'I have to –'

'No, you don't! You don't.' Ian lowered his voice as Toni looked round uneasily at the curious glances they were getting.

'It's not going to work.'

'But you're not giving us a chance! Can't you even do that? Do I mean so little to you?'

Toni looked at him desperately. 'You mean everything to me. I love you.'

Ian's eyes softened and he took her hand and held it

447

between his. 'Then let's give it a go, Toni. Chloe will learn to accept it.'

Toni smiled through her tears. 'I'll talk to her.'

Ian, oblivious to their surroundings, gathered her into his arms and kissed her tenderly. 'I love you, Toni. And I'll do whatever I have to do to make Chloe like me. I'll even bring her to the zoo!'

'I think she might be a little bit old for that. Now if you were to bring her to a nightclub. .'

'Okay.'

'Don't even think about it,' Toni warned with a shaky laugh.

'It will be all right,' Ian said softly.

Toni clutched his hand tightly and wished she could believe him.

When Toni got home Chloe was in bed. She tapped on the door and went in and sat on the side of the bed. 'Chloe? Chloe, are you awake.'

'Did you have a nice evening?' Chloe asked sarcastically.

Toni winced. 'Please, Chloe. Try and understand.'

'I understand, and hey, why do you care what I think? You're moving out and starting your new life. Now that you've persuaded Dad to come back you can go off into the sunset with lover-boy with a clear conscience.'

'Is that what you think? You think I only tracked your father down so that I could turn my back on you?'

'It's true, isn't it?' Chloe challenged.

Toni stood up wearily. 'No, Chloe, it isn't. But there's no point in talking about it. You've obviously made up your mind.'

Chapter Forty-five

Saturday, 14th October, 2000

Alice walked over to the table and sat down, dumping her dusters and polish in front of her. 'What is it now, Toni?'

'Sorry?'

'You've been polishing that glass for the last five minutes. What's wrong, love?'

'I had a row with Chloe.'

'What about?'

'I told her about –' Toni stopped suddenly remembering that Alice knew nothing about Ian Chase either. She stood up and went to fill the kettle. 'You'd better sit down. It's a long story.'

'She'll see sense when she calms down,' Alice assured Toni three cups of tea later.

'I'm not so sure. She went out very early this morning without even talking to me. Oh, God, Alice. What if she doesn't turn up for the party tonight?'

'Of course she will. Mark will see to that.'

'But what if she doesn't want it? She'll probably be furious with me.'

'Maybe,' Alice replied calmly. 'But your friend Jade is right, Toni. You're entitled to have a life.'

'But it's all so soon to be throwing this at her!'

'You didn't tell her you were getting married, did you?'

'No!'

'Or that you were moving in together?'

'No, of course not!'

'Then, I don't think you've got anything to apologise for. You were just being honest with the girl. You told her that you wanted to start seeing this man again. It's probably a bit of a shock, but she'll get used to it.'

'I'm not so sure. I think Theo has suddenly become the victim again in her eyes.'

'Well, that's just silly and I shall tell her so!'

'Oh, no, Alice, keep out of it. I want her to have at least one person that she can talk to. Oh, I wonder where she's gone?'

'She's probably with Olivia.'

'Yes, you're right. Should I call her?'

'Why don't you just polish those glasses, Toni.'

Toni sighed. 'Okay.'

* * *

Chloe spent the day wandering around town looking absently into shop windows. By the time she turned up on Ollie's doorstep her friend was almost frantic.

'Where the hell have you been?'

Chloe shrugged.

'Everyone is looking for you. Well, Toni and Mark are. You should give them a call and tell them you're okay.'

'But I'm not,' Chloe said moodily as Ollie led the way up to her bedroom.

'What's wrong?'

'Toni's involved with someone. It's the guy she was going out with before she met Dad.'

Ollie's eyes were round. 'Way to go, Toni!'

'Ollie!'

'Sorry, Chlo, but, you've got to admit, it's kind of romantic.'

'But what about Dad?'

Ollie laughed. 'What about him? Jeez, Chloe, I know he's your dad but he's not exactly saint material! I think you should be happy for Toni. You don't expect her to spend the rest of her life on her own, do you? I mean she's not that old. She could still have kids.'

Chloe paled. 'But what about me?'

Ollie rolled her eyes. 'What about you? Just 'cos she's dating someone doesn't mean she won't want anything more to do with you.'

Chloe scowled. 'I just think it's all a bit convenient. Probably the only reason she tracked Dad was so she could go off with this guy and not worry about me.'

'Chloe, you're eighteen in a couple of days. You don't need a guardian. She could walk away from you any time she likes. But she hasn't and she won't.'

Chloe chewed on a nail. 'She's bought an apartment. It's two-bedroomed and she says the other room is mine.'

'There you are then,' Ollie said triumphantly. 'I'm right, aren't I?'

'Oh, I don't know. It just all seems a bit quick.'

Ollie sat down and put an arm around her friend. 'Look, I know it's sad for you to see them split up but you knew it was going to happen. The fact that Toni is seeing someone else is incidental. Though I think you should wish her luck. The last few weeks must have been hell for her. Imagine finding out all those horrible things about your husband? Imagine the embarrassment?'

'I suppose.'

'It probably won't be long before your dad finds himself a new girlfriend. Some women are really attracted to jailbirds.'

Chloe stared at her in dismay.

'Sorry, just kidding. Look, I know it's not easy to accept, Chlo, but things change. People change.'

Chloe's eyes filled with tears. 'But I don't want them to, Ollie. I want everything to go back to the way it was.'

'Not possible, my friend.'

Chloe sniffed. 'No. It isn't, is it?'

* * *

'No, Mark, she still hasn't been in touch. Try Ollie again and phone me if you catch up with her, will you? And remember, back here for nine. Okay, Mark. Thanks. Bye.'

Toni hung up the phone and went back into the kitchen. Liz Connolly had arrived with two waitresses and gorgeous aromas were now emanating from the large oven.

'Any luck?' Alice asked as she put on her coat and scarf.

Toni shook her head.

'Don't worry, love.' Alice patted her arm. 'She'll be

here. Now, I must go and get my glad rags on. See you later. Good luck.'

'Thanks,' Toni turned to Liz. 'Anything I can do to help?'

'No thanks, Toni.'

'Okay then. I'll go and get ready. Shout if you need me.'

Toni went into the dining-room, poured herself a whisky and took it upstairs. She was tempted to bring the bottle but she couldn't hide behind the booze tonight. Whether or not the guest of honour turned up, she had nearly eighty guests arriving in two hours. Show time.

'Toni, you look fabulous!' Jade twirled her friend around in the hall, taking in the knee length black cocktail dress, with its low neck and clinging folds.

'Thanks.' Toni smiled vaguely. 'You look lovely too.'

Jade was resplendent in a green silk trouser suit that made her eyes look even more brilliant than ever.

'You're the first,' Toni told her leading her into the sitting-room. 'Isn't Aidan coming?'

'Oh, Yes. But I told him I wanted to come along early in case you needed any help.'

'Thanks, but Liz seems to have everything under control.' She went to the drinks table at the end of the room and made Jade a large vodka.

'What's wrong?' Jade asked as she took the glass.

'It's Chloe. We had a row last night and I haven't seen her since. She went out first thing this morning.'

'Was the row over Ian?'

Toni nodded. 'I wish I'd kept my mouth shut.'

'Don't be silly. You can't live like a nun forever.'

'Maybe not forever but I should have waited a bit

453

longer. I was silly thinking that she'd be able to handle it so soon.'

'Oh, shut up, woman. You're talking cobblers. It's not as if Chloe is a child and you're her only parent. Thanks to you she's going to have her father back in her life. And you will always be there for her too. I think she's doing pretty well considering.'

'Considering what?'

'Considering the way Theo's treated you. Toni, most women would have walked away from such a mess but you've been there for Chloe through all this shit.'

Toni shook her head. 'Chloe's like my own daughter. I couldn't ever leave her.'

'I know that and so does she, deep down. I'm sorry, Toni, but you have to toughen up. Chloe is out of order. She seems to have forgotten that Theo is both a pervert and a criminal –'

'Jade!'

'It's true. You are a better parent to her than Theo has ever been. You've put her happiness first every time.'

'I couldn't have done anything else,' Toni protested.

'No, you couldn't,' Jade said softly. 'That's because you're a good mum.'

The doorbell rang, echoing through the quiet room and Jade smiled warmly at her. 'Now it looks as if your guests are arriving. Why don't you go and let them in and I'll put on some music?'

* * *

'Great food,' Aidan said through a mouthful of vol-au-vent.

'Thanks.' Toni gazed around the room. It was almost full, it was ten past nine and there was still no sign of Chloe.

'She'll turn up.' Aidan smiled kindly at her.

'Oh, God, Aidan, I hope so. I'm going to look very silly if she doesn't.'

Jade appeared at her side. 'Mark just phoned. Chloe's at Ollie's dolling herself up. She thinks they're going clubbing. He's on his way to pick them up.'

'Oh, God. I feel sick.'

'You'll be fine. Drink up.'

'I'll just go and check that they have the champagne and glasses ready.' Toni hurried away.

'My but she's a bundle of nerves,' Aidan remarked to his wife.

'I can't say I blame her,' Jade muttered. 'This could all go horribly wrong.'

Toni moved across the room, stopping occasionally to talk and smile.

'Toni?'

'Hi, Mum. Is someone getting you a drink?'

'Your dad's gone to get me one although I don't know where he's got to. Where's the birthday girl?'

'Good question.'

Mary frowned at the worried look on Toni's face. 'Is there something wrong?'

'Can't go into it now, Mum, but we had words last night. I haven't seen her since.'

'Oh dear.'

'I'm not quite sure how she's going to react to this.

Maybe a surprise party wasn't such a good idea after all.'

Mary hugged her daughter. 'It was a lovely idea. Don't you worry. She'll be thrilled when she sees all her friends.'

'I hope you're right,' Toni mumbled and carried on towards the kitchen where she found her father and Francis deep in conversation.

'Hello, Dad.' She kissed her father's cheek. 'Mum was wondering where you'd got to with her drink. Hello, Francis.'

Peter rolled his eyes at Francis. 'Better get back. Nice to meet you.'

'And you,' Francis called after him. 'How are you, my dear? Looking lovely as ever.'

'Thank you, Francis. I'm so glad you came.'

'Wouldn't miss it. Dotty would have loved this. She adored parties. Once they had nothing to do with Sylvester's, of course!'

Toni laughed. 'Oh, I wish she were here. I could certainly do with her advice at the moment.'

'Oh?'

'Trust me, Francis, you don't want to know. Look, I must go and stand by the door. Just in case Chloe turns up.'

'Righto. See you later.'

'Can I have your attention, please?' Toni called and the room quietened.

'A car has just pulled up outside and we believe it contains our guest of honour. So quiet everyone, and lights out please.'

After several minutes when nothing had happened, Jade slipped out the back door and around the side.

Before she even got to the front of the house she could hear the raised voices.

'I'm not going in now,' Chloe was protesting. 'I'll talk to Toni when I'm ready. You can't force me –'

'I can.' Jade pulled open the door and tugged on Chloe's arm.

'What are you doing here?' Chloe looked puzzled.

'I'm one of the guests at the surprise party Toni is trying to give you. Now please get inside before I lose my temper.'

'Party?'

'Yes, party. And don't even think about not going in there. And when you do you'd better give Toni the biggest hug and kiss in the world!'

Chloe scowled. 'And I suppose you expect me to kiss her boyfriend too.'

'Not possible because he's not in there,' Jade said abruptly. 'Toni had too much respect for you to invite him.'

'Oh.'

'Yes, oh. And another thing, Chloe, Ian is the one who spent all of his spare time trying to track down your dad. And they were doing it for you. If you stopped and thought about it for a moment you would realise that life would have been a lot easier for them if Theo stayed in Cape Town. But they put you first. Now, don't you think it's time you showed a little gratitude?'

After a moment Chloe nodded. 'Okay, Jade. Let's go in.'

Jade beamed at her. 'I'll go in the back way. And remember, look surprised!'

Chapter Forty-six

Saturday night, 14th October, 2000

Toni held her breath as she heard Chloe turn the key in the front door.

'Surprise! Happy birthday!' Everyone shouted as Chloe reached a hand up to the light-switch.

'Oh!' Chloe blinked as her school friends descended on her with hugs and kisses.

'Happy birthday, love.' Alice fought her way through the crowd and hugged her.

'Oh, thanks, Alice. Did you do all this?'

'No, Toni took care of everything. She's been running around all week trying to get everything ready on time. She wanted it to be a very special night for you.'

Chloe looked from Alice's steady gaze to her stepmother standing at a discreet distance. She smiled tremulously and Toni smiled back. Alice squeezed her hand as she made her way over to Toni.

'Thanks,' she murmured and kissed her cheek.

Toni hugged her tightly. 'Oh, you're welcome, love. Happy birthday.'

'Champagne!' Jade appeared beside them with two glasses, while the waitresses distributed the champagne to the other guests. 'Happy birthday, Chloe!' Jade kissed her cheek. 'You look gorgeous, by the way.'

Chloe grinned sheepishly at Jade. 'Thanks. My best friend insisted on dolling me up to visit some new club in town.'

'Well, this is it, love.' Toni laughed nervously. 'I hope you're not disappointed.'

Chloe's bottom lip trembled. 'No. No, it's great. Thanks.'

'Chloe? Happy birthday, dear.' Mary Jordan came forward to kiss her, with Peter hot on her heels.

Chloe smiled at them affectionately at them. 'Hi! My goodness, you came all the way from Skerries! That's great.'

Mary laughed. 'It's not *that* far!'

Ollie tugged on her friend's arm. 'Let's go and talk to the gang from school. '

Chloe looked at Toni.

'Go on, love. It's your party, enjoy it.'

As Toni watched Chloe being swallowed up by the crowd Jade grabbed a bottle of champagne off a passing tray and filled Toni's glass. 'Drink. Everything's going to be fine.'

Toni gulped her wine and tried to swallow the tears that were threatening. 'I can't believe it! She seems to be okay.'

Jade smiled. 'Well, like I say, she's a sensible girl. She just needed time to think about things.'

Mark grinned at her and she shot him a warning look. 'Shouldn't you be with your girlfriend, Mark?'

'On my way.' He saluted obediently and went in search of Chloe.

'Well done,' he whispered in Chloe's ear when he finally got her alone for a moment.

'I've been horrible to her, Mark, haven't I? Maybe I should go and talk to her.'

'Leave it for now, Chloe. The easiest way to make Toni happy now is to enjoy this party. You wouldn't believe the planning that's gone into it!'

Toni sat slumped in a corner with her mother, Jade and Alice all assuring her that everything was going to be fine.

'I can't believe that you and Ian are back together,' her mother said for the third time.

'I can't believe that I haven't even met him,' Alice chipped in.

'He's lovely,' Mary said fondly.

'He is,' Jade agreed with a wink at her friend.

Toni winced. 'I wish you'd stop talking as if I'm not here.'

Jade pushed her glass towards her. 'You just drink and don't mind us.'

'You should have invited him along tonight,' Mary continued. 'Your dad would have loved to see him.'

Toni laughed. 'Oh, yes, Chloe would have loved that!'

'I suppose,' she acknowledged.

Jade stood up. 'Would you excuse me? I need to go to the loo.'

Toni stood up too. 'And I need to circulate.'

Alice shook her head and smiled as Toni moved away. 'She's gone to so much trouble to get everything just right and she still can't relax.'

'Well, it looks like Chloe's forgiven her.' Mary's eyes followed her daughter anxiously.

461

'They're very close. Toni's been like a real mother to that girl. You should be proud of her.'

Mary smiled. 'I am.'

Aidan reached out and grabbed Jade's arm as she hurried past. 'Hey, I've hardly seen you all evening.'

'Sorry, Aidan, I'll be back to you in a minute.'

He rolled his eyes. 'Where are you off to now?'

Jade grinned. 'Trust me.'

'Jade, there's something I wanted to tell you –'

'Later, Aidan,' Jade called over her shoulder and hurried away.

Aidan sighed and went off in search of another drink.

Following the noise, Jade finally found Chloe surrounded by her ex-school pals. 'Chloe? Could I have a quick word?'

Chloe eyed her warily as Jade led her to a quiet corner. 'Look, Jade, I'm sorry and I'll tell Toni so later –'

'Good,' Jade said with a bright smile, 'but why not do something to show her just how sorry you are.'

'Like what?'

'Follow me,' Jade said mysteriously and led her outside.

Toni was just crossing the hallway as Mark was opening the door to some late arrivals.

'Oh my God!' She stood gaping as Robert Perkins stood there beaming down into the face of Vicky Harrison. 'Sandra?' she hissed, and beckoned quickly to her receptionist. 'Look what the cat's dragged in!'

Sandra's mouth fell open as she looked at the smug grin on Vicky's face. Robert moved towards them.

'Good evening, ladies. Having a nice time?'

'Eh, yes thanks,' Sandra said faintly.

'Fine, Robert. Glad you could make it.' Toni looked pointedly at her ex-nurse.

Vicky grinned victoriously at them. 'Hi, girls! Bet you didn't think you'd be seeing me again. Still sweating away at the clinic, are you? I couldn't stand another day of that job.' She shivered dramatically. 'And Robert was worried about all the stress I was under. He's such a honey.' She planted a kiss on his cheek and Robert blushed.

'Well, come along, my dear. Let's get a drink.'

'Where's Jade?' Vicky looked around. 'Won't she be surprised to see me?' She giggled as she allowed Robert to lead her away.

'She'll be stunned,' Toni murmured, staring after them.

'I just don't believe it,' Sandra spluttered. 'How could she go out with him after he fired her like that?'

Toni shook her head and laughed. 'I don't think Robert exactly fired her somehow.'

'But what's he doing?'

'I think it's called having your cake and eating it.'

'I'm back.' Jade appeared at Aidan's side and smiled apologetically. 'Sorry about that – oh my good God, would you look at that!' She gulped as she saw Vicky and Robert laughing and joking by the bar.

'Jade, I –'

'Back in a minute, Aidan. I just need to talk to Sandra and Toni.' And she was gone again.

Aidan closed his eyes and counted to ten. Maybe he should just forget the whole thing and go home.

'Have you seen them?' Jade hissed in Toni's ear.

Toni turned away from the people she was talking to. 'I take it you're referring to Pinky and Perky?'

'The nerve of the woman,' Jade fumed. 'What the hell is Robert thinking of?'

Toni grinned as she watched the director fondle Vicky's bum. 'I think he's making the best of a situation. Oh, come on, Jade, you've got to laugh.'

'I suppose,' Jade smirked reluctantly. 'I always wrote her off as being stupid but I'm beginning to wonder.'

'She certainly seems to have got what she wanted,' Toni agreed with a laugh.

'Toni?'

She turned around to see Chloe at her side. 'Yes, love?'

'There's another guest arriving.'

Toni frowned. 'I thought everyone was here,' she murmured as she followed Chloe out to the hall.

Ian stood awkwardly in the doorway. 'Hi, Toni.'

Toni shot Chloe a look of alarm. 'Chloe, honestly, I did not invite him here –'

'No, I did,' Chloe said quietly and kissed her cheek. 'I'm sorry, Toni. I've been a silly little cow.'

Toni hugged her fiercely. 'No, you haven't. It's been a lousy time for you.'

'For both of us,' Chloe corrected, 'and I conveniently forgot that. But my friend and yours –' She nodded to Ollie and Jade standing grinning from ear to ear in the background '– talked some sense into me.'

Toni looked from them to Ian and back to Chloe. 'I don't know what to say.'

Chloe smiled. 'Well, you could offer him a drink.'

464

Ian came forward and held out his hand to Chloe. 'Thank you, Chloe. And happy birthday.'

Chloe shook his hand shyly. 'Thanks. Now, I'd better get back to Mark.'

'I need to go to the loo.' Ollie disappeared.

'I'd better check on Aidan.' Jade sped away with a little wave and soon Toni and Ian were alone.

'I can't believe you're here,' Toni murmured as he took her in his arms.

'Me neither,' Ian said with a chuckle. 'I nearly dropped the phone when she called. What caused the sudden change of heart?'

'I have absolutely no idea,' Toni said between kisses, 'but I'm not complaining.'

'Are you planning to stand still for a few minutes,' Aidan said sharply when Jade reappeared at his side.

She stared at him in surprise. 'What on earth's the matter, Aidan?'

'Nothing, it's just that I've been trying to talk to you all evening.'

'What about?' she asked nervously.

He took a gulp of his drink and looked her straight in the eye. 'Well, you know we were talking about getting a place together –'

'Oh, don't tell me you've gone and rented somewhere without me? Really, Aidan, will you never learn?'

'Please, just hear me out.'

Jade's mouth settled into a grim line. 'Go on.'

'The guy that I sold our house to, do you remember him?'

'Oh yes. I remember him,' she said drily.

'Well, he was just buying it as an investment.' Aidan hurried on ignoring her hostile expression. 'He rented it out to a few different people, and, well, it's been nothing but a headache for him.'

'My heart bleeds.'

Aidan ignored the jibe. 'The couple that are renting it at the moment, their lease is up in January and he's not going to renew it.'

'Why are you telling me all this, Aidan?'

'Because, love – if you agree, of course – I want to buy it back off him.'

Jade stared at him. 'What?'

He smiled. 'Wouldn't it be wonderful to have our home back?'

'Well, yes, but how could we possibly afford it?'

'Well, it needs a lot of work done to it.' Aidan grimaced. 'Some of the tenants weren't exactly house-proud. And he's looking for a quick sale.'

'My God, I don't believe it.'

'It's true, love. Just say the word and we can move back there in just a few months.'

Jade threw her arms around him. 'Oh, Aidan, thank you!'

'Is it what you really want, Jade?'

Jade's green eyes sparkled. 'Oh, yes, love. It's what I want. It's what I've always wanted.'

Toni led Ian shyly over to her parents.

'Ian!' Mary blinked. 'You're here.'

Ian bent to kiss her. 'Hello, Mary.'

'Nice to see you, lad.' Peter pumped his hand.

466

Ian grinned. It had been awhile since anyone had called him a lad.

'Does Chloe know that he's here?' Mary whispered to Toni.

'It's okay, Mum, she invited him.'

'Oh, Toni, love, that's wonderful.'

'Do I get an introduction?' Alice eyed the tall dark stranger with curiosity.

'Sorry, Alice, this is Ian Chase.'

Ian shook her hand. 'I've heard a lot about you.'

'And I about you – although only since this morning.'

Ian laughed. 'It seems to have been quite a day.'

'You wouldn't believe.' Alice exchanged a look with Toni and they laughed.

'Hello,' Sandra advanced on them. 'You're Ian, aren't you? We've talked on the phone.'

Toni grinned. 'This is Sandra, Ian.'

'You work at the Blessington, don't you?'

Sandra blushed. 'That's right. Nice to meet you.'

'And this is our new nurse, Matthew Little.' Toni drew the big, shy man forward.

Ian shook hands with him. 'How are you getting on, Matthew, surrounded by all these women?'

Matthew's blush matched Sandra's. 'Fine, thanks. They're all very nice.'

'I'll go and get you a drink.' Toni smiled at Ian and took the long way around the room so that she could check on her guests. She was thrilled to see Jade and Aidan locked in each other's arms. And in another corner Chloe was standing arm-in-arm with Mark in kinks of laughter at a joke Ollie was telling.

'It's turned out to be a successful evening, I'd say.'

She swung around to see Francis smiling at her. 'Oh, Francis, it's like a dream. I'm just afraid of waking up.'

'There's nothing to be afraid of, my dear. Just enjoy it.'

Ian was looking for a toilet when he came face to face with Chloe. 'Hi.'

'Hi.'

'Thanks again for inviting me. Can I ask, how did you know my number?'

Chloe blushed. 'Jade told me. She told me quite a lot of things. One of them was that I was lucky to have Toni.'

Ian grinned. 'I'm sure you knew that already.'

Chloe nodded. 'Yeah. She also told me that you were the one who found my dad.'

Ian shrugged uncomfortably. 'I was just helping Toni out.'

'And you didn't tell the police?'

Ian shook his head. 'Toni was sure that once he talked to you he would come back. She was right. He obviously loves you very much.'

Chloe smiled shyly at him. 'Well, I just wanted to say thanks.'

Ian grinned back happily. 'You're welcome.'

* * *

'Thanks for coming, Francis.' Toni kissed his cheek. Robert had offered to drop him home though Vicky looked none too pleased. 'Goodnight, Robert. Vicky.' Toni forced a smile.

Vicky smiled sweetly. 'Bye bye, Toni. I'll drop in and see you all sometime. We could do lunch.'

Over my dead body, thought Toni. 'Sounds great.'

'Goodnight my dear. Lovely evening.' Robert patted her arm.

And with a wink from Francis they were gone.

'Did you ever see anything like her?'

Toni looked around to see Sandra at her side. 'It was a bit of a shock all right. Where's Matthew?'

Sandra blushed. 'He's just gone to the loo. He's going to leave me home.'

'Really? So are you going to see each other again?'

'I don't know, Toni. Oh, I hope so. I feel like I've known him all of my life. He's so easy to talk to.'

'Oh I'm so happy for you!' Toni hugged her.

'Ready to go, Sandra? Thanks for a lovely evening, Toni.' Matthew smiled shyly at her.

'You're very welcome, Matthew. Safe home.'

Toni smiled as she watched them leave. Matthew looked like a giant beside the tiny receptionist. She looked around, stifling a yawn. Apart from Jade and Aidan, the only guests remaining were Mark, Daniel and Meg. Ian was nowhere in sight. Probably, still talking to her parents. They'd had him pinned in a corner all evening.

'We'll head off now, Toni.' Jade hugged her friend.

Toni smiled affectionately at her friend. 'I don't know what you said to Chloe, but thanks.'

'No problem.'

Toni watched happily as Aidan slipped an arm around

Jade's waist. 'Oh, it's so good to see you two together again!'

'We should try for a foursome,' Aidan said kissing her cheek.

Jade glared at him. 'Aidan. Don't interfere.'

Toni laughed. 'Yes, Aidan. You know your wife would never do such a thing!'

Jade made a face at her. 'Ha ha, very funny. Night, Toni. I'll see you on Monday.'

Daniel and Meg came over, leaving Mark and Chloe alone to say goodnight.

'Thanks for everything, Toni.' Meg kissed her. 'Such a lovely evening.'

'Lovely,' Daniel echoed. 'Mark? Come on, lad. The taxi is here.'

Chloe walked outside and stood gazing lovingly after her boyfriend.

'Goodnight,' Toni called as they piled into the cab and were driven away.

'Bye.' Chloe gave a final wave and walked back into the house, closing the door behind her.

Toni smiled at her stepdaughter. 'Thank you.'

Chloe hugged her. 'Thank you! It was a great party. How did you manage to organise it so quickly? Alice said you only decided to do it last week.'

Toni grinned. 'It wasn't easy. Come on. Let's go and have a last drink with my folks. If I don't sit down soon I'm going to fall over.'

They found Mary and Peter in the conservatory and Toni smiled to see Ian in her favourite chair.

'Is everyone gone, then?' her mother asked.

'Yep.'

'Except me.' Ian stood up. 'I'll head home and let you guys get some rest.'

'I was just about to make some tea,' Chloe said lightly. 'You're welcome to stay for a cup.'

After he'd finished his tea, Ian said his goodnights and Toni walked him to the door. 'This has been the strangest evening,' Toni said leaning her head on his shoulder and looking up at the stars. 'I can't believe Chloe called you.'

'I was a bit dumbstruck myself,' Ian chuckled.

'It's probably just the calm before the storm, you know,' Toni warned. 'Teenagers can be a bit unpredictable.'

'Oh?' Ian ran his fingers up and down her bare arm.

Toni nodded. 'When Theo gets back and the story hits the headlines, she'll probably hate us both again.'

'I see.'

'I'm just preparing you,' she said gravely. 'If she moves into the apartment with me, well, you're going to be seeing a lot more of each other. And she's bound to be upset when the trial is on. And then of course Theo will try to poison her against you.'

'You think?'

'Oh, yes! But you'll just have to keep your patience –'

'Toni?'

'Yes?'

'Shut up.'

And Toni had no choice as his lips came down on hers in a sweet and tender kiss.

'But I suppose we'll manage,' she breathed happily when they came up for air.

THE END

471